PRAISE F
SHE MURDERED ME

"In She Murdered Me with Science, *Dave Boop has created a wonderful, alternate-history thriller. Boop deftly weaves together influences like Phillip K. Dick and Raymond Chandler, marries them to the grand tradition of pulp adventure stories, to produce a story that is a joy to read. He's definitely an author to watch for in the future, and* She Murdered Me with Science *promises much for his career."*

—Mike Stackpole, *New York Times* bestselling author of *I, Jedi*

'She Murdered Me with Science *is fast-paced, stopping for the occasional breather as Glass tries to piece together clues, scientific-method style. If you're looking for a great combination of the private-eye novel, historical and science fiction, then you should find all those tastes satisfied here."*

—Josh Vogt, author of *Enter the Janitor, Forge of Ashes*

"I absolutely loved this book. It was great to be able to read something that was written like this. I have never read the "pulp science fiction of the Forties and Fifties" and this was a great experience for me. David's characters were very in-depth as was the plot. I hope David continues to write books like these."

—Melissa Cornwell, Romancingthebook.com

'She Murdered Me With Science *showcases David Boop's storytelling talent in a tale of intrigue when a disgraced scientist turned forensic analyst uncovers a conspiracy to take over the United States ... enthusiastically recommended for fantasy and science fiction* enthusiasts, and would make [an] enduringly popular addition to community library collections."

—Midwest Book Review

"Boop goes beyond the usual suspects when the conspiracy is uncovered for an interesting alternative history twist. There's nonstop action showing a love for private eyes, mad scientists and blues music."

—*The Denver Post*

"A delightful mix of hard-boiled detective story and good old fashioned pulp science story, with a dash of Jazz thrown in for flavor."

—Mark Urbin, *The Urbin Report*

"Classic deadpan noir … with a sci-fi twist. David Boop will keep you guessing—and laughing—to the end."

—Mario Acevedo, author *Rescue from the Pleasure Planet, Nymphos of the Rocky Flats*

'She Murdered Me With Science *takes the best parts of the pulp era and infuses them with witty dialog, intriguing characters, and real world 1950's events.… David Boop's novel is a fun, wild ride that you'll have trouble putting down once you start reading it."*

—Bobby Nash, author *Evil Ways, Domino Lady: Threesome*

SHE MURDERED ME WITH SCIENCE

SHE MURDERED ME WITH SCIENCE

DAVID BOOP

WordFire Press
Colorado Springs, Colorado

ISBN: 978-1-61475-562-3

Cover design by Rob Carlos

Cover artwork image by Rob Carlos

Edited by Peter J. Wacks

Kevin J. Anderson, Art Director

Published by
WordFire Press, an imprint of
WordFire, Inc.
PO Box 1840
Monument CO 80132

Kevin J. Anderson & Rebecca Moesta, Publishers

WordFire Press Trade Paperback Edition April 2017
Printed in the USA
wordfirepress.com

DEDICATION

Dedicated to Margaret "Peggy" Boop
June 21, 1936 – January 21, 2013

Prologue

Rain could wash the filth from Industry City, but it couldn't cleanse the smell born of manufacturing and human waste.

To the completely hairless man running down the alley, it smelled like death.

He didn't want his name, yet he was born with it. He didn't want the job life had given him, yet that job was going to get him killed.

He didn't want enemies, but they were there … hot on his trail. How could they find him, he thought, in the darkness, in the rain?

The man tried blending into a wall or hiding behind a garbage can, but nothing he did could shake his pursuers. He had been tagged and now was as good as dead.

The short time he had been running seemed like hours. Noise drew him down another alley. The unmistakable sounds of a party lit a fire under his feet. Fear found an untapped reserve of strength hidden inside his soul. He spent the last of his adrenalin sprinting the final leg. The splashes of his steps fell in unison with his erratically beating heart.

He stumbled from the alley's opening into sensory overload. There were lights and music and voices. Disorientated, he pushed his way through a throng of people only to be shoved and kicked in return. His peripheral vision caught an Atlantic Brewing Company banner announcing *1953 St. Patrick's Day Celebration Tonight!*

He cloaked himself in the revelry, shielding himself from his attackers. He pulled the collar of his soggy raincoat up, exposing as little of his smooth exterior as possible. Tilting his head to the sky, he let the deluge cleanse his soul. Despite the temperature, he felt warm. Maybe it was his blood, no longer running cold at the thought of capture and death. As the stress drained with the pouring rain, a chuckle erupted from the back of his throat. The scientist laughed louder as conviction grew inside of him. He would live for another night and seek help tomorrow. He'd find the man who could save his life … if he would.

A group of partygoers noticed the hairless man and patted him on the back. He reveled in their camaraderie, something he was not used to. They slapped a beer into his hand, and he drank it down heartily. He still had some cash on him, so he offered to return the favor. He moved through the crowd to the beer stand. The scientist thought that if he stayed with the crowd, stayed low and inconspicuous, he might be able to leave when they left and get back to his apartment unnoticed. He was happy Fortune had smiled upon him at last.

At least, until his head exploded from the inside.

The police would find no one else hurt. Psychological scars would be the only damage to those bystanders that had to pick pieces of flesh and brain from their hair and clothes. The explosion, whatever had caused it, had been meant for just the victim. Even in the coming days, the slightly charred remains would stump the city, state, and federal coroners. No fingerprints matched the body, and no traces of explosives were found. All examiners left their findings inconclusive.

On the top floor of the tallest building in the city, one man knew the answers. He knew the name of the hairless man, what had killed him, and why.

He also knew that knowledge would mean his death, as well.

SIX MONTHS LATER

Chapter One

The first thing I realized, as the synapses fired in the gray matter I called a brain, was that I couldn't feel the left side of my face. I was semi-sure this was due to the metal table I had fallen asleep on … again.

I was also pretty sure the feeling would return to my cheek if I'd just get up from my slumped position; however, one could never be too sure. I mean, this had happened almost every night for two years now and blood would flow freely through my cheek as soon as I moved, but what if …

What if this was one time too many? What if, by passing out at my lab table for the umpteenth time, I had permanently damaged the nerves in my face? I could have a drooping left side that would forever keep me from finding the future Mrs. Noel R. Glass.

Oh, well. There were always call girls.

I sat up and slowly rubbed life back into my stagnant cheek. I flexed my jaw, blinked my eyes at the morning sun streaming in, and stretched. When all my body parts were working to expectations, I concluded that this morning was already starting out much better than yesterday.

The day before had begun with Mrs. Lupton and a third scolding about late-night noises wafting from my apartment. It's unfortunate that no one has invented a quieter centrifuge machine, but try to tell her that. She also took the opportunity to remind me that I was two weeks overdue on my rent.

No, yesterday had not started out well.

Today, however, things were looking up. Last night I had solved a nasty problem on *The Atlantis*, my hydro-car. I know the idea of a car that runs on water must sound like something straight out of a *Flash Gordon* serial, but it was flights of fancy that led me to become a scientist in the first place. I wanted to make the unreal, um … real.

The Atlantis was one of a select few blueprints I had managed to abscond with when I had been removed from my position at the Theoretical Science Department of the New Mexico Institute of Technology. My job had been to take scientific discoveries and design practical uses for them. I was the bread and butter for the college. Both the government and the private sector paid well for anything I designed. Until … until I made the unforgivable error, the one all scientists fear, and it cost six people their lives. Guilt would forever be my mistress. I'd lost everything that mattered to me.

Even after the inquest cleared me of negligence, I was surprised I didn't do jail time. I'd been a golden boy for so long that without serious proof to convict, the government and the college just let me slip away once the hoopla died down. My reputation in ruins, I knew I might need a bargaining chip someday. Those blueprints were the chip, and today was the day.

As I looked around, I spotted the bottle of Old Johnny already empty in the trash. I guess I celebrated before passing out. That would account for the hangover I was feeling the first inklings of.

It was weird thinking of the libation as a celebratory device. I had been using it for so long as a sedative, something to settle down my rage, that it now seemed a part of the inventing process. If these designs brought me out of this mediocrity I called a life, I might have to give up the stuff.

Or, at least, buy better stuff.

You owe yourself this, Noel, I thought. *Today you can start showing your face in public again.*

Of course, I still needed money, lots of it. First I'd have to get a prototype car made. Nobody would take me seriously without proof. Then I'd need good clothes. I had hocked all my good clothes for food when my savings had previously run dry. Now all I owned was a trench coat, a hat, and some respectable street clothes.

The snoop jobs I took since becoming a private investigator were barely enough to keep a roof over my head, some food in my gut, and to supplement my personal research.

I stretched again, farther than before, and finally felt something pop in my back. I shook out my arms and legs, feeling the last vestiges of my poor sleep habits slide from my body. I needed to move around, so I walked through my three-room cell. I had converted both bedrooms into workspaces: one for the lab, the other as an office. When I did actually fall asleep like normal people did, it was on an old couch in the combined living room/kitchen. I left all the windows covered, save for the kitchen. That way I'd have a rough idea what time of day it was when I woke.

Despite being early morning, the Little Osaka district buzzed with the daily chaos. The barbecued-duck vendor bullied passersby on the sidewalk; carts rushed down side streets hauling herbs, roots, and rice to the restaurants before they opened; and kids pushed giant hoops down the middle of the road, much to the consternation of motorists.

It was 1953 and the view out this window didn't look much different than 1952 had, nor the eleven years prior to that. The world had changed, though. Communists had replaced Nazis as the "big bad." Police regularly raided Russians' homes on tips called in from little old ladies who swore their Chechen neighbors planned to kill the president because they never "talked proper American." The problem was more people had televisions, which fed the hysteria. The networks were all tuned in to Senator Joseph McCarthy's hearings and watched him proclaim that the "Red Menace" was around every corner. Meanwhile, the leathernecks had just finished ruining the landscape in Korea and were coming home. We hadn't dropped the bomb, but then the Russians and Chinese had stayed in the shadows, not forcing our hand. And to top everything off, the price of milk was up.

Good thing I drank hooch.

As I put stuff away, I scanned my rows of test tubes, beakers, and retorts. Each cent spent on them was worth it. Science was the tool for both my short and long-term goals. I used my genius to solve crimes, all the while designing the key to the prison of my own making.

One more snoop job—a big one—and that's it. I was out.

The phone rang as if destiny had a wiretap in my mind. The voice I heard didn't carry with it the dollar signs I needed, though, but it might be enough to get old lady Lupton off my ass.

"Glass? You conscious?"

"Yeah, Sweet. I've been up for close to thirty seconds."

Police Chief Charles Sweet was anything but. He was worse when he had to call me. That meant he was up shit creek and using his hands to row.

"I need that crap you fling around. What's it called? Foreplay?" The rhetorical question came accompanied by a small, sarcastic chuckle. He knew what it was called. Sweet loved yanking me around.

"Forensics."

"That's it. Be here in a half while the scene is still fresh."

He gave me the directions and rang off. I'd never make it in thirty minutes, so I didn't try. If Sweet was going to be moodier by the time I arrived, oh well. He hated science and loved instinct. He'd throw a guy in jail for murder just by smelling him. That is, if the courts would let him.

I checked to see if the communal bathroom was open. Unfortunately, it was. It must've been all-you-can-eat night at the Thai place down the street. I had wanted to get in and out, not spend ten minutes decontaminating it first.

After my shave, the smile that blessed my face held promise, like it might be there a while this time. I tightened my tie, slipped on my jacket and bundled my toiletries in a towel.

As I walked down the hall, the door next to mine opened. The nearly midget form of Mr. Wan Lee backed out slowly, not sensing my presence. Once the door was closed, Lee turned, startled.

"Ack, Glass! You frighten me. You lucky I not packing."

I always laughed internally at Lee's broken English interpretations of gangster slang. His regular English was not bad, but since he started watching Cagney, he tried too hard to incorporate that image into his lifestyle.

I firmly held on to the notion Lee was somehow involved with the Japanese mafia. He kept odd hours, had plenty of money, and brought home dozens of people at a time, and they all had the same last name: Lee.

Relatives? Possibly, but I'd spent enough time in Little Osaka to identify one family tree from another. "All Asians looking alike" is bullshit when you specialize in details.

The way he tells it, his grandfather's father came over to work on the railroad lines the same time as many of the Chinese did. Foremen, not wanting to deal with names like Zhéng, found Japanese surnames like Hisamatsu even more detestable. They'd go down the line of workers saying, "You're now Chan, Wang, Dong …" until fate landed Wan's Nipponese ancestor with "Lee."

Wan liked it, saying it gave him a secret identity, "like Superman," which is why I leaned towards the mob angle.

"Sorry about that, Wan. Off to work?"

He smirked. "No, I go see my moll. No let wife know where I go, okay?"

I raised an eyebrow. "Moll? You have a girl on the side?"

With a big smile, he said, "Yeah. Blonde bombshell with two big guns." He hovered his hands the appropriate distance to imply just how big the "guns" were.

This lent more credit to my theory. Lee was in his fifties and not attractive. He must be dealing in something big to be getting an easy ride. He could be pulling my leg, though; it wouldn't be the first time.

"Well, maybe you'll be lucky and die in the saddle, Lee. If the missus finds out what you've been doing, *she'll* kill you and it won't be fun."

Lee wiped a brow. "Nothing you can tell me I not already know."

He got to his tiptoes and sized me up. "First time you shave in months. You got hair all cleaned too. You have new dame?"

"Nah, finished my designs. Got to dredge up some work to get a prototype made."

"You spend long time on them. They really work?"

"I hope so. I need out of this place. Not that you haven't been a decent neighbor or anything. Well … you know."

The elder nodded. "I know." Then he got downright serious. "Always work, you. Need a hobby, like me. I collect loose women." Lee pointed an accusatory finger. "You spend too much time solving science mystery. Try solving mystery of love, once."

I waved him off. "Too expensive. I'll just read about it in the paper."

We both had a good chuckle before he bowed out and headed down the stairs. I dropped off my bathroom supplies, retrieved my hat and coat, and entered the unseasonably warm late September only minutes behind Lee.

The place where I kept my car wasn't far when I wasn't in a hurry, but the delay with the bathroom and Lee had now pushed me past the fashionably late mark. I jumped on a passing cable car to save time. These things were all the rage in San Francisco now, but they had started here, in Industry City.

Halfway between Denver and Colorado Springs, Industry City was a fulcrum of manufacturing and technology for most of the Southwest. Ore processing gave the metropolis a hazy sheen in the early morning light, but at night, when the companies burned off their waste and the flames shot out of smokestacks forty feet high, it was almost romantic. Ethnic neighborhoods framed the downtown commerce center while "good, white folk" moved to the 'burbs that were nestled in between the city and the mountains. I don't know that I ever truly fit in that crowd, even when I had money. I ate mostly in ethnic restaurants while working at the college and since leaving there, I haven't been in an upscale eatery once.

About ten blocks outside of Little Osaka, I got off in front of Hansen's Automobile Repair. Hansen himself came out to greet me as I entered the shop area. Always in overalls and covered head to toe in grease, I felt the briefest of sympathies for any wife that cleaned up after this man.

"Noel, you come for the '37?"

If you were blind and couldn't see the shoulder-length blond hair, Hansen's thick Nordic accent would have given away his Scandinavian heritage.

"Yeah, Inger. You check it out recently?"

"I just oiled and gassed her last week. I had a feeling in my gut you would be coming to visit soon. She has been a good girl, sitting and waiting for her master to return."

I didn't personify objects as Inger did. It was always "she this" or "she that" like the way his Viking ancestors always referred to their ships in the feminine. I liked to keep my machinery on a last-name basis.

We walked past the shop into the back lot where a dozen cars sat in various stages of disrepair. I recognized mine by its shape under a tarp. Hansen reached for the drape.

"What's it doing under that?" I inquired.

"Because of this …"

He yanked it off with a flamboyant gesture. There was my 1937 Hudson Custom 8 … in worse shape than I had left it. The rust spots had grown, and the passenger side mirror was gimped. The rag top was even more cracked, if that was possible. What once glistened with chrome and royal blue now was mottled gray and something the color of wiper fluid. To top my growing disgust, the antenna was so bent that the Z it formed would have made Zorro proud.

"Your car is an embarrassment. Why do you not let me fix it up?"

"Because I can barely afford to pay you to keep the engine tuned up." I lied, "I don't care about looks. It just needs to get me places."

The mechanic shook his head forlornly. "Ah, but you did once, did you not? When this car was new, it was a thing of beauty, was it not? It took a man of spectacular means and tastes to pick this expensive car from all the others available."

"I had—" I rethought my verbiage. "Someone had suggested it. I had just done something pretty special and earned a lot of money. This was supposed to be the best car out there. It turned out the advertising was a bit trumped up. More flash than substance. It's a decent ride, but nothing to get all steamed up about. As long as the engine works."

"That it does. My son, Sigarr? He take it on as a project. He is only twelve, but he knows his stuff."

I was twelve when I entered high school. I pulled out my last two aces and gave the singles to Hansen. "Slip these to the kid. Tell him to keep it up."

The keys were already in it. The eight cylinders started up like a cat getting a belly rub. The stick slid in easier than it had the last time. I eased out of the lot, tossing a thumbs-up to Inger, who beamed with pride.

The crime scene was jumping when I rolled in an hour later. My mug was familiar enough to be waved through without preamble. The mansion was everything you'd expect from the Cherry Knolls area, enough bread to burn a wet mule. Manicured hedges outlined a babied lawn. Grass shouldn't be this color in September, but it shown greener than a leprechaun's ass. My Hudson stuck out like a goose-stepper on Armistice Day.

When I reached Sweet, he went out of his way to make me feel welcome. "You'd think someone who is one step away from being ground up for dog food would jump when somebody offers him a job."

"I don't 'jump' for anybody." Cocky, I planned my reveal for after whatever Sweet'd brought me out for was done, but since he decided to press my hand right away, I pulled out my hole cards. "I'm finished with my Atlantis project, Sweet. This is the last cleanup I'm doing for you. Not to mention, I've made more money selling blood than what you pay."

Sweet seethed. "So I toss you work out of the goodness of my heart, and this is the thanks I get?"

Behind the contempt, did I sense something else? Maybe a touch of fear? In the eight years we'd worked together, we had built up some sort of rapport, almost a partnership for lack of a better word. I've known marriages that haven't lasted as long.

"No offense meant, Chief. I just want to it lay out. This is my last job, so I hope it's worth it."

"Oh, this should challenge that IQ of yours," he said, again with that special chuckle of his.

Forensics was a developing field. Chicago PD had the first full department, while most metropolitan crime units employed at least one person on staff now. Industry City's resistance to adopting a similar approach came from their blue-collar attitude toward crime, not my success rate, which was stellar. People weren't murdered here like they were in Chi-town or the Big Apple. ICPD ran every crime through two filters: acts of passion or mob hits. At least until I started freelancing as a consultant.

Within the first year, I had overturned three arrests, which gave them a black eye I still catch hell for. But I'd been right and proved it by handing them the real culprits. While this raised me only slightly above pond scum in their eyes, it was enough for them to call on me when the profile was high or the shit deep. Now, if it wasn't a bar fight, jealous husband, or concrete footmuffs, Sweet brought me in. You'd think with what they spent on me, they'd just hire someone full time.

I followed Sweet's blue-clad shoulders around back to a window. Five bulls milled around, bored out of their gourds. They, too, had been waiting for me. They jumped at our abrupt appearance and tried to look as if they had been doing something useful. Sweet sneered in their direction. He wasn't someone to mess with, a wrestler's physique compounded with a gunpowder burn on his left cheek—an unintentional tattoo from the war—made him intimidating to anyone in front of him.

I climbed the stepladder that had graciously been left for me. Sweet directed me to a bullet hole in a window. My eye tracked its trajectory to find the matching hole in the back of a chair. The chair was in front of a fireplace, and on the floor in front of the chair lay a tape outline. From the shape, it appeared the victim had gotten up then keeled over.

"Who was the stiff?"

"Montague Morrison. Newspaper magnate. Ran the *Industry City Post* until about midnight last night when he was capped."

"Bad editorial?"

"Worse, a squabble over his will. Looks like he was going to leave the bulk of his estate to a new wife half his age. There've been several threats on his life from his family, as reported by his staff."

The inside was as elegant as the outside. Mounted trophies adorned one wall, awards another. The rug looked expensive, one of those import jobs and not the type you'd find sold in Little Osaka.

I climbed down the ladder and examined the areas the police had marked off.

"Footprints?"

"Yeah. From the height of the bullet's entry and the depth of the footprints, we already have a suspect."

"Why am I here, then?"

A small flower garden rimmed the house. The soil held the perfect impression of a size thirteen footprint. The heavily watered lawn made the ground spongy and tracks led out from the dirt and across the lawn. I looked at the first of the prints. Something wasn't right, so I knelt down and took a closer peep.

"The only suspect tall enough to take the shot is the gardener. He's six-six."

"What's the problem?" I asked, knowing from his tone that Sweet wasn't happy with his suspect.

"The guy's a souse. He starts drinking when he's done working for the day and usually passes out by midnight. He was seen stumbling from the area, but there's no way he could've shot Morrison with any accuracy."

My fingers traced the imprint while my mind wandered. "Lucky shot?"

"Maybe, except the guy says he didn't do it, had no reason to do it, and wasn't hired by anyone to do it."

"How reliable is the witness?"

Sweet harrumphed. "Not great. It's the housekeeper and she's got glasses thicker than a bottle of cola. Something stinks about the whole thing, and I'm not ready to call this a done deal. We really need to make an arrest stick. The paper will massacre us if we screw this up." I could see his point. A quick resolution would paint the department as heroes. On the other hand, a long trial without a solid conviction would make them fools.

I opened my forensics kit. I already composed a working hypothesis, but Sweet would want facts. I started with the bullet hole in the window. I measured the distance from ground to hole. Then, with some assistance, I ran a string from the hole in the chair through the glass.

"Did the bullet go all the way through or embed?"

"It's still in Morrison."

"What caliber?"

"OT 30."

I paused. "Military rifle?"

"That's our guess." Sweet harrumphed again. "The old man kept a Springfield 1903 in the hunting shed. It was wiped clean of prints. Ballistics is checking the bullet to the bore."

"Ballistics and fingerprints, Sweet. You're halfway to your own forensics team."

The bull flared his nostrils, so I let it drop.

I paid out more string and stepped back another dozen feet. I had the ladder brought to me and retraced the bullet's path. It was going to be farther out in the yard than the footprint by the window indicated. For that powerful a bullet to not pass through, the shot had to be taken from at least a hundred feet back. I looked across the lawn; that would put it up against an opposing building. While it's possible the gardener needed the stability to take the shot, I doubt someone who was intoxicated could hit the mark unless he were a military-trained sniper. I asked for more string and got the detectives to line up to hold it.

I asked about weather conditions and was told that it had been a calm night, little breeze, which was unusual for fall but not unheard of. It made my job easier. Every twenty yards, an OT 30 bullet dropped 1.35 percent. I was eyeballing it, but by the time I reached the building, I measured the point of origin. I could put the gun being fired at six feet six inches. I showed Sweet.

"The gardener would have had to shoot Morrison while balancing the gun on his head."

"Boots?"

"With six-inch heels? Okay, it's a consideration. Let's go a step further. Why are there footprints by the window if he fired from back here?"

"He had to make sure the old man was in the room?"

"Doubtful, whoever shot from a hundred yards back would have the eyesight to see his target or, even better yet, had binoculars. Going to the window might alert the victim and cause him to move from the chair. I think the killer went afterwards, specifically to leave footprints and be seen leaving the scene."

"So, what? He wanted to frame the gardener?"

I pondered. "Or at least appear to be someone he or she wasn't."

I went back to the footprints with a ruler. I got down on my hands and knees and measured several of the impressions. I measured the front and back and did some quick mental calculations. I now had enough proof for my conjecture. I laughed inwardly because Sweet was going to have to chalk up another arrest to science, and that meant a serving of crow back at the station.

"Is one of his relatives short, say five feet or under? Maybe even a little stocky?"

Sweet smiled. "How'd you know? The nephew is a runt, I'd say five-one, if that."

I waved the chief in closer. "Look at the prints. I can see why you thought it was somebody big." I pointed at the heel. "See how deep the heel is, right? A good inch. That would lead anyone to believe that the killer was at least 250 pounds plus. Now look at this."

I moved his attention to the toe area. "Here the indentation is less, maybe a quarter inch tops. Means one of two things."

Standing up, I brushed the dirt from my knees. Sweet stood up as well. I gave him space to pad his skull about my supposition.

"He was putting more pressure on his heels than his toes, like he was walking on his heels, toes up?"

"Right, which makes no sense. When you tiptoe, you put more force on the toes, leaving a deeper impression in the front than the back. So why would there be such a difference in the heel depth than the toes?"

"He had no toes?"

I brushed a finger across my nose. "Right on the money." Sweet gritted his teeth. "Stilts."

"I bet Shorty's got a set stashed somewhere. I also wager you he checks out on that gun. He used the building over there to stabilize himself for the shot and then stilt-walked over to the window to check his work and to leave impressions much bigger than him. Knowing the staff, like I'm sure he does, he wore a trench coat to fool the housekeeper into thinking he was the gardener. I'd check the trash, his car. You know … the usual places.

"And I'll be by the precinct later for my check."

I closed my kit, proud of myself that this case hadn't taken weeks to solve. Sometimes things just fell into place. I was itching to search for a financier. Maybe I should demand more from Sweet, so I could pay rent *and* buy a new suit. I did solve his high profile murder quickly, and he should get a conviction. Saving the department's ass in the paper should pay extra.

I walked back to my car.

"Glass! Wait." Sweet moved quickly to catch up with me. His face twisted. It was hard to battle pleasure and anger at the same time. I had solved a case, but I was quitting.

"You're really shaking the investigator bit?"

I nodded.

"What? You going to try being a scientist again? You got screwed pretty badly last time."

"Not trying. I *am* a scientist. I did this"—I waved at the crime scene—"to live. I need more. I need to make a difference."

Sweet just shook his head. "You brainy types all think alike. Think you can save the world, you do. I think you just find new ways to screw it up. Bombs that destroy cities … ha! What good does that do? Especially now that the Ruskies have them too?"

It was an old argument. Sweet had lost a father in World War I, a brother in World War II, and a son in Korea. If the bomb wasn't going to stop wars, what was it good for?

"X-rays help doctors mend bones, diagnose disease, and aid healing. A scientist invented that too. Should we go back to leeches and acid?"

I'm sure he wanted to argue more, maybe to keep me there longer.

He needed me but couldn't admit it.

"Get out of here, Glass. Don't let me find you on the other side, okay?"

I shook my head. "Nah, nothing can go wrong with this one. I won't be breaking any laws."

I offered my hand, which he took. It would be the closest thing to a thank-you I'd ever get from him.

Chief Sweet was already barking orders to have the nephew brought in for questioning before I was out of earshot.

I collected my consulting fee from the station and slowly drove the Hudson back to my place. My head was filled with a dozen competing thoughts. Who should I take the plans to? Who could I trust? I needed money but how could I attract a high-paying client without resorting to some less-than-kosher tactics?

I parked as close to my block as possible, guessing I'd be going back out soon. There was nothing left to steal on the piece of junk, so I doubted it would ever be lifted. I always left it unlocked with the keys in the ignition. Should some kids want it for a joyride, they wouldn't have to break a window or hotwire it. There was a note in the glove box asking for it to be returned to the exact spot should that ever occur.

I ankled it along pavement, feeling empty enough to steal a dog's dinner. I looked up and the duck vendor was eyeing me. He had a sixth sense regarding hunger and was already reaching for a duckling to wave in my face as I crossed the street. For all the thugs I'd taken down, this old man intimidated me, and I would take the duck despite not really being hungry for fowl. Maybe it was the fact he always had a cleaver in one hand. I darted into the beef bowl place before I got near him, and I heard him curse. I knew enough Japanese to know what things he called my parents. After splurging on a double order with *gyoza*, I headed out the back door to avoid having a curse placed on my descendants by the still-stewing duck merchant.

By the time I got home, I had a list of former clients to call. From there, I'd hit my contact at the *Post* and see what the word was on the street.

As I reached my apartment door, I found it already unlocked and open a crack. While I might have still been suffering a little barrel fever from the night before, I remembered clearly closing and locking it. I listened and heard the subtle sounds of rustling inside.

I had no weapon to speak of, save for a pocketknife. I unfolded the blade and launched myself into the apartment.

The wall I ran into felt suspiciously like someone's back. I looked up until I found a neck. Sure enough, the mountain in front of me was a man. I jumped back into the hallway as the wall turned around. What best could be described as a shaved silverback gorilla smiled at me. His frame filled the doorway, keeping me from seeing who else was in the room.

"Sir?" the gorilla said, "I think he's here."

A weak voice came from somewhere behind it, err … him.

"Does the man have dark hair, intense eyes, and a hawk-like nose?"

I had never been sized up so quickly, but there it was.

"Yes, sir, that's him."

"Well? Let the man into his own place, Vincent. We have to talk." Vincent stared at my hand. "He's got a weapon. Should I take it?" The question left no doubt as to if he could, just whether he should.

"Heavens, no! A man can defend his castle, no matter what form that castle takes." He let out a hollow cough then, "Now move out of the way."

Like a boulder rolling aside to open a cave, Vincent slid over, allowing me access to the room.

"Open sesame," I whispered, but I'm sure the man-mountain heard.

I surmised from the angle of the second voice, the man running this show was in my lab. I moved cautiously past the gorilla-man, folding the blade back into its protective sheath.

As a child, you are taught opposites. The man looking over my blueprints was the best example of a contrast to his partner I could imagine. While Vincent was swarthy and bearlike, his master was anything but: tiny; frail; blotchy skin; and, as he ran a finger over the designs, seemingly intelligent. He used a cane to steady himself as he leaned over my drafting table. Dangling from his neck, a gold chain with a ring hung low. An indentation on his skeletal ring finger indicated that he had gotten too thin to keep it there anymore.

"This design is sound. You finally fixed the catalytic converter, I see."

I never like to look surprised. It has added to the legend that I'm some sort of genius. I had to come up with some quick deductions to keep the ball in play.

"Along with a few other changes, Mr. Reece, but then you haven't seen *The Atlantis* designs in quite a while. Not that you should have seen them at all, but I guess a man as affluent as you are has first dibs on everything coming out of NMIT, right?"

He kept running a finger around the prints. "First guess. I'm pleased your attention to detail hasn't weakened in your banishment. I was also glad to hear what you had chosen to do in the private sector. Keeps those skills sharp, doesn't it?"

Vincent, who had moved to fill in the doorjamb, grunted, "How'd he know it was you, Mr. Reece? You never have your picture taken, and you told me you'd never met him before."

Not wanting to be bothered, Reece waved the question over for me to explain.

"Well, you see, Vince, Mr. Reece's comment implied he had seen these designs before. I personally know everyone who had seen my designs during my days at the Tech. That means he had unofficially seen them.

"I also knew the government poked around our labs occasionally, so I ran down a mental list of 'sponsored' entrepreneurs, until I found one with the initials C.J.R."

I called his attention to the old man's pocket, while continuing to show off. "Those are the letters monogrammed on the handkerchief sticking out there. Cornelius Jacob Reece, third richest man in America; launched Little Technologies, which, to this day, holds more patents than any other company.

"Keep up with that, Vince?"

I watched Vincent as I laid out my theory and was amazed to see he had paid attention. I expected him to be one banana short of a bunch, yet as I had spelled everything out quickly, his thinking room was open for business.

"Okay, you know me and now I know you, Mr. Reece." With my sarcasm dial fully engaged, I asked, "How can I be of service?"

Old Money didn't want to let the designs go. I stepped in front of him. Vincent placed a hand on my shoulder as a warning. I stared up at him incredulously while I waved a finger at Reece. "Tsk, tsk. Just like the bearded lady at the circus, you get one look for free. You need to pay extra for a closer look."

He tittered at the comment. Maybe he liked bearded ladies and was remembering some long-lost encounter. I don't know; maybe he just found me amusing. He slid away and slowly moved into the area I call an office. Vincent heeled, helping him into the most comfortable seat.

I entered the room, took my usual chair behind the desk, and leaned forward expectantly.

"I'm being murdered, Mr. Glass, and it's your fault."

And here I was, thinking this day was looking up.

CHAPTER TWO

The one amazing thing about death is that no matter how hard you prepare for it, when it stares you in the face, it's always a surprise.

I had prepared myself many times for death to walk through my front door. I imagined some frail going off the deep end because I got her husband arrested, shot, or worse. Then there was the occasional fear of a jealous husband looking for blood; not all women carry cash when they come into my office, and their type of credit can't be handled by a bank. I even expected the Texas oil boys might try to steal *The Atlantis* designs once word had gotten out. I wasn't prepared for this fragile, old millionaire to accuse me of murder and bring muscle to do the dirty work.

Reflexively, my hand dropped toward the drawer where I kept my piece. Vincent tensed and exposed the gat he kept in his armpit. I slowly returned my hand to the desktop, laying my palms up in a gesture of submission.

"You're holding all the cards. It's your game."

Old Money tittered again. "Oh, don't fret, Mr. Glass. We're not here to kill you. In fact, we need your help."

If this conversation juked any more, I was going to need a program.

"Okay, you got my interest. You say I'm killing you, but I've never met you face-to-face before today. I don't, as a habit, off little, old millionaires, even if I would give my eyeteeth to be sitting where you do. With my brains and your money, I'd be dangerous."

I loved to fake power. You're expected to lay track, expected to be cocky, overplaying every hand. It kept my rivals guessing as to when I was being serious and when I was playing the fool. Not everyone played power. Reece's game seemed to be chess.

"Don't get ahead of yourself, Glass, and for God's sake, don't be such an arrogant ass." Reece's eyes darted around as if he was anxious someone would walk in any moment. "I would love to explain it all here, but if my enemies discovered I was away from my office, I might be dead before I finished."

Vincent chimed in. "Mr. Reece invites you back to his office. The limousine is downstairs, waiting."

What the hell? I shrugged. I'm cleaned, dressed, and in need of money. If my help is needed, then a paycheck couldn't be too far behind.

I stood to leave as the gorilla helped the Wizard of Odd to his feet. I stopped by my blueprints. Not wanting to leave them in the open, I rolled them up quickly and stuffed them into a tube I had ready. I turned back toward my office where I keep my safe, but Reece stopped me.

"Bring them along. You help me with my little problem, and maybe I can help you with yours."

There was little reason to trust him. He had said nothing that made sense, but there was that feeling again, like I didn't have a choice. Reece had the script, and Vincent had the gun. I shrugged and followed them out the door. Maybe there would be a trade of services; I scratch his back and he builds my prototype. This might be payday after all.

Christ! I just finished the designs last night, and I already have a buyer? That can't be right.

My guess was Reece had been spying on me, maybe for a long time. I wasn't too happy about that, but I couldn't do anything about it right then. Was I being played for the sap? As a scientist, I used my instincts tempered with theories, research, and facts. Doing the shamus bit called for some of that, but I also had to study human behavior, man's habits and patterns. The two skills, when combined, were powerful. I based my reputation on that.

However, Reece blindsided me. It felt as though he had always been watching over my shoulder and I never noticed.

We were blocks away from my place when Reece finally spoke again. "I like working in autonomy, Mr. Glass. The reason I don't have my picture taken is the same reason I have cars rotated every couple of weeks. I don't like to be spotted doing what I do."

I glanced out through smoked-glass windows, watching the intersections flow by. "And what do you do, Mr. Reece? Why is there a mark on you?"

"I acquire things, Glass. Or to be more specific, I acquire technology by any means necessary. I prefer the nicer routes: negotiation, buyouts, threats. Occasionally, though, I do have to break a few rules—or people—to get what I want."

He let the statement hang in the air as if it summed up the entire course of future conversations. Whatever else happened, he'd end up with my designs; he wanted that made perfectly clear. All I was left with was how much of my soul it would cost me when I let them go.

"You've been waiting, haven't you? For me to finish these." I tapped the tube.

"I've had a person watching you, if that's what you're suggesting, yes. You sleep too soundly, Glass, like a drunk. At the beginning, I put men on you casually, but as you got serious, I took an interest. When I found out I was dying, I stepped things up. Did you ever wake up and find notes you didn't remember writing?"

"Sure, all scientists do. Subconscious writing. Half-asleep resolutions to problems. There's nothing new about it."

Wait. What was Reece implying? What did I let him do to me?

My mind quickly took stock over the past few months. I'd made a lot of progress. I tried to remember any notes I'd found. Were they in my handwriting? Would I have even thought to question?

"I take it by your silence, you're already playing out this scenario in your head. Yes, I've been feeding you tidbits here and there. Nothing major, just things that kept your scientist juices flowing. How could you know that somebody had designed a fuel injector?

You couldn't because I have the patent and haven't revealed it to the public." He leaned forward a bit in a conspiratorial way, as if revealing some big secret. "So when my spies reported you were stuck in an area, I'd have a note dropped on your desk, in your own handwriting, that would give you a push forward. Again, nothing significant, but thanks to your own demons, you weren't making the progress I was hoping for. Each clue was like airplane fuel to you, Glass. You'd take off in a direction and make giant leaps forward. You needed guidance, motivation. You don't have the college, or your students"—Reece cleared his throat—"or *her* to push you forward. You would've taken a lifetime to design the smallest item, if left to your own *devices*." He chuckled at his joke. "Pardon the pun; I'm not usually so witty."

I felt used, but only on the surface. There was some truth in what he said.

Since … since the accident, I didn't rush things. I chalked it up to being cautious, not wanting to make a mistake again that might cost a life. That's why it had taken me ten years to finish designs that initially took me only a year to create. Like some Dickensesque story gone awry, I was Pip and Reece had been my Provis.

I changed the subject, trying to gain control of the conversation. "Cancer, right?"

Reece nodded. "Again, your skills recommend you. I was diagnosed last year and have been in treatment ever since."

He didn't yammer on like a man with a short lifeline. He acted like a cat with keys to a bird sanctuary.

"Have you heard of two scientists named Francis Crick and James Watson?" he asked me.

"I went to the same high school as Watson in Chicago, but many years earlier."

"Two geniuses out of one high school? Must be something in the water."

"Must be. I used to have a secret rivalry with him. He beat my SAT scores, but I graduated a year younger than him. I wrote him a congratulatory letter when he got accepted at Cambridge. He sent me a condolence card after …"

The accident.

The old man studied me as if he wanted to peel my brain apart.

It struck me, at that moment, that technology wasn't the only thing Reece acquired. A man couldn't live as long as he, doing the things he did, without an incredible information engine at work. The man liked stories.

I continued. "Watson's family kept a greenhouse, and he was always crossbreeding plants. Thought he might end up a florist. Glad it came for something."

"Strange little man," Reece agreed. "He, and this Crick, unveiled an interesting theory earlier this year."

"Deoxyribonucleic acid, right?" I kept well read, at least on things that had been revealed to the public at large. My connections to events behind the scenes in the academic world were severed long ago. Reece's connections were as solid as the day he snooped though my files.

"The press is calling it DNA for short," amended Reece. "Watson and Crick almost didn't have it, but I pulled their strings the same way I did yours. Of course, there's going to be fallout from it."

He leaned in closer. "But then you were never the type to leave classified materials laying around unmarked, were you? Kept a nice, tidy ship until you started drinking for sport."

I had no idea what he was talking about, but I'm sure I'd hear about it later.

"Doctors around the globe are running with this. They believe this is the big breakthrough that will make us all gods. We'll be able to cure everything from cancer to epilepsy, even the common cold. Death will be a thing of the past; birth defects can be fixed in the womb or sooner. They say in fifty years we will live in a Utopian society."

"Isn't that what Hitler promised?" I was being snippy, but Reece let it pass.

Old Money inclined his head a half an inch. "More or less, except the revolution will be led by science and not the military or politicians. Science doesn't have sides. The technology we derive from it has no morality of its own. It always comes down to the end user."

Reece's tone darkened. "While I am dying of cancer, it's a symptom, not the cause. I am dying from prolonged exposure to microwave radiation. Someone has been slowly poisoning me for a year using a MASER."

The words stopped my heart. He'd come to me because of my greatest failure, the black mark on my soul: my microwave radar.

So powerful.

Too powerful.

The experiment, the deaths, all my fault.

After fourteen years, my nightmare had returned and Reece was living proof of it.

Will pain ever go away?

I leaned forward to protest, to scream my ignorance, but felt the censoring hand of Vincent lay across my chest.

"We're here," said the man-mountain.

I scanned the street around the limo just as it slid into the underground garage. We had traded the dredge and depression of Little Osaka for clean sidewalks and the smart-dressed people who called the business district home.

Industry City's uptown worked like most modern metropolises did. Office buildings were the organs and flowing between them, the workers, and couriers and executive limos, acted like blood vessels keeping them alive. The heart, though, was plain to see to all.

The Liberty Tower, a monument to all the country had to offer and the tallest building in the free world.

We didn't say a word as the elevator ascended 101 floors to the Little Technologies offices. Still nothing was said as I was ushered past receptionists, worker bees, and their ilk. They rushed about, taking calls, passing papers, drawing on chalkboards in conference rooms. They took little or no notice of us. If the owner of a company walked into my business with Goliath in tow, I'd stop scribbling for the moment, but it was as though we were invisible. Could there be orders to not pay attention to anything Reece did? He said he resorted to less-than-honorable tactics. A blind eye may be a key skill for making it to the top floor of the Liberty.

We approached a huge vault door. I'd been in corporations before; none had their own bank vault to my knowledge. Maybe I was a bit naive, but it seemed whatever it held couldn't be worth all the trouble it took to build a vault on the top floor of a skyscraper. The floor under this monster must be reinforced. The metal of the door was different, not steel; it didn't shine. I ran a hand over the surface of the door and could almost feel the density through my fingertips—lead. I knew now what the vault was for. It was less vault and more prison cell.

Vincent punched in a code on a large keypad; each number responded with a loud click. This was state-of-the-art security. After we heard a final *clunk*, the bodyguard rotated the big locking wheel and pulled it open.

Reece proclaimed, "My office."

It took me a moment to register what I saw. The inside of the vault shone like an executive office, complete with windows looking out over the city. I could feel the heat from the afternoon sun. I leaned back into the hallway, double-checking that we had indeed entered what to all appearances was a vault. Yet here was a thirty-by-thirty room that looked like a president's office.

"Pretty convincing, isn't it? Only way I have survived this last year. Nothing like having the world at your fingertips, is there?" Reece pointed to the row of phones on one table, a row of newspapers on another.

There were also televisions, several to be exact. Each broadcast a different channel in all its black-and-white glory. He kept in the loop while being shielded from the world. I could see the outline of a Murphy bed set into the wall and a door that must lead to a bathroom.

"I have a room in my home shielded like this; nothing and no one gets in without my say-so. It serves as an office, bedroom, and prison."

I studied the windows. They couldn't be real; it would defeat the whole purpose of having the vault. A glass pane wouldn't block radiation of the magnitude he was getting radiated with. Yes, there was definitely something unnatural about them. The colors were slightly askew.

Finally, I caught the flicker.

"Color television?"

"Right on the money," Reece said with obvious pride. "They'll be everywhere by next Christmas, but I've held the patent for two years."

There was a spring to his step, despite his dependence on the cane. From his own confessions, nothing brought him more joy than technology. He took my elbow and guided me back the way we had come. "I should be safe enough for a quick tour."

We left the vault office and moved down a hallway to the side. Vincent aped my every move, casting his gargantuan shadow over me constantly. I was glad he kept the gat in its holster, but he still made me nervous.

When we had rounded the corner, where the fictional back wall was, I could see the building's real outside wall. Where windows would normally have been, two giant wooden boxes sat in their spots.

"I have two television cameras aimed out the actual windows, capturing the real world. I pay a small fortune to a guy who cleans the glass in front of them every Wednesday."

We reentered Reece's fortress with my guide pointing out little things as we moved farther in.

"Heaters strategically placed give the room a sense of the sun's warmth. The temperature is synchronized to reflect the time of day. Add ventilation and you have all the comforts of a real office …"

"With all the shielding of a lead-lined room," I finished.

"And I can tell you know why," Reece acknowledged.

Ignoring the prompt, I moved to the fake window and goggled at its quality. "You even get a sense of vertigo from this." I made swaying motions, which caused Vincent to take an involuntary step forward. He was just out of reach. I needed him closer.

"The detail is incredible. I can see this guy getting mugged in the alley next door."

Vincent stepped up to the window, not believing what I said. "You can't see that far. Nobody's eyes are that good!"

In a flash, I had my hand inside his coat. I drew his piece out and jumped way back, out of trajectory of his massive swing. I nearly dropped the gat, not expecting its weight. It had to be biggest pistol I had ever held in my hand.

"Jesus! What is this thing?"

"It's a .44 Magnum," said Reece while his bodyguard made attempts to grab at the gun.

"Bullshit! Nobody makes a ..." but I let the statement trail upon looking at Reece. He was gloating again. Another acquisition. He was enjoying this. The little runt was enjoying watching me dance with his bodyguard.

Vincent stopped moving when I managed to raise the gun at Reece. "Easy, Kong. Nobody has to get hurt. I just want to play the house this hand. I need the odds."

The man-mountain waited for his boss to acknowledge the change in management. Reece nodded. The bodyguard relaxed and took up a position next to the millionaire's desk after the old man sat down. I copped a squat on the other side of the desk, gat trained on them. I was indignant.

"So ... what? You played around with my magnetron design and got burned, huh? The prototype I built was too powerful and you knew that. Everyone saw that first hand. The eggheads out at NMIT got it right, so why did you go back to my flawed specs? If you're dying from working on my broken machine, then it's not my fault."

The fun had left Old Money's eyes. "Your first mistake, Glass. You aren't thinking big enough. And no, *I* did nothing with your original designs. I might place large bets, Mr. Glass, but only on potential winners. You were not a winner."

I waved the gun. "Play nice, Reece. It's still my game."

Reece was terse. "Oh, do get over yourself! Yeah, you had some success early on, but where are you now?"

I was offended and rightly so. "Some success? I was publishing papers by fourteen. I discovered positrons while still a student at Caltech, for crying out loud. Positrons!"

"True, but you lacked common sense. What good is discovering something if you don't make use of it? Anderson got the credit for your positrons, while it took you another five years before you did anything of note. Now, here you are again. It's taken you fourteen years to finish those designs."

"Yeah? Well, I don't have the resources I used to."

"*Resources?* Ha! You've been living in your own filth since you came to Industry City. The fact you didn't blow your brains out after the inquest surprised us all. You think you have cause to act righteous in front of me because you completed one design? Me, who made it happen? Go to hell, Glass. You were hot shit in your day; now you're just cold piss."

By the end of his tirade, he'd riled himself into a good coughing fit. Reece reached into his pocket and pulled out his handkerchief while Vincent patted him on the back. I suddenly felt very foolish pointing a gun at them. When Reece finished, he tucked the cloth back into his jacket but not before I could see the spots of scarlet.

I stood up and walked over to the desk. I dropped the gun on top, turned, and went back to my seat. Maybe I was a sucker and this was all a setup, but I really had nothing to lose at this point. This guy might be a lot of things, but I couldn't get him for being a liar.

Vincent made no move to get the piece, leaving it in the open as a sign of trust. His nod my way spoke volumes. He accepted the black eye to his ego as honorable.

"Talk," I said.

Moneybags appeared doubtful, as if he weren't sure what to say or how much. I think he never really took my feelings into consideration before now. I was always a means to an end. Now, here in the flesh, Reece played words carefully to avoid losing my support completely. "I had access to your designs, as you deduced. I knew what your microwave radar could accomplish. You manipulated frequencies in a way Marconi had never dreamed of. Hell, Tesla would have been proud of you.

"Noel, you are a singularly focused individual. This has served you well in the past, but it has also left you missing the big picture. You might say 'I discovered this thing, and it will do that,' but someone else looks at the same discovery and sees ideas you hadn't dreamed of—dark hallways you won't let yourself go down ... My people—those whose job it was to go down those hallways—looked at your magnetron and saw other uses. I wanted to approach you before you sold it to the government, but General Archdeacon made his intentions clearly known. I had to back off."

"Well, there was that nasty disagreement in Europe. What else could he do?" The chiseled image of General Duane Archdeacon returned undesired to the front of my memory.

If Vincent here was carved from stone, then the general was forged in titanium. Nothing about him was humorous. He made you feel like a scolded child while he was being nice to you. The consummate military man, you knew the general would sacrifice you in a heartbeat, especially if it meant victory.

"Exactly! He was the only person who could override me back then. I love my country, Glass, so I stepped back ... for a time. Archdeacon must have seen the same possibilities I had. When things went so horribly wrong at the test, I was sure you had been made the patsy of a bigger picture."

I could feel bile rising in my throat. I wanted to puke so bad, the hangover from last night seemed mild in comparison.

"What are you trying to say, Reece? I need to hear it. No bullshit."

"These people, Noel? Tangie and your staff? They didn't die because of any mistake you made. They were murdered, and you were framed."

* * *

In '40, I fled from NMIT to Chi-town, my home. The inquest had taken a year out of my life. While my lawyers showed that all the safeguards were intact and that the variances in the microwaves were nothing anyone could have predicted, I was still removed from my post and stripped of my credentials. I was no longer allowed to be a scientist ... officially.

After a year of dragging my family under the scrutinizing eyes of the press and accusatory glares of their neighbors, I left the city.

It was 1941. We had entered the war, and no one cared about a discredited scientist named Noel R. Glass anymore. Industry City was as good a place to vanish as any. I wanted to evaporate. The life I had knew had been greased, finished, dragged off in the meat wagon.

I found a fleabag in Little Osaka, the Asian district. No one recognized me there, or if they did, they didn't care. I was just another *gaijin* gone crazy, trying to lose himself in booze, drugs, and women.

I dissolved into the smoke of opium dens; my past life became vapor. Only Tangie's laugh wafted through the mist of my forgotten memories. Wan Lee gathered my remains and reconstituted me. Why, I may never know. When I press him on the subject, he just rolls his eyes and says that he couldn't allow no "round-eyes" to die on his watch.

Lee helped me find a better place to live and eventually got me work as a private eye. He seemed to know just what to say to get people to do what they least wanted to do.

Lee couldn't help me this time. My blindfold had slipped off, and I saw the world as it really was. Reece's explanation of the events behind my setup and subsequent removal from NMIT had dragged my mind, kicking and thrashing, through barbed memories. When he was finished spelling out the lies, I stumbled from his vault office. Reece called after me, telling me not to do anything stupid, but that's exactly what I intended to do. There had been so many clues, I would have tripped over them had I not been reeling from her loss. A new type of guilt walked beside me when I left the Liberty—the guilt of ignorance.

Tangie.

I could hear her scream in my mind as clearly as if I were there again.

I declined a ride back to Little Osaka from Vincent, instead directing a cab to take me right to my once favorite back-alley joint. I pulled out every bill I had in my pocket, dumped it on the counter, and proceeded to take in alcohol like water in the *Titanic*. The glue that had been used to piece me back together so long ago had dissolved, and I was becoming incorporeal again.

As I lay my head on the bar, my hair matted with dried booze and drool, I stared across the brass rail to the poorly lit hallway. I heard an echo calling to me from the rear of the bar. It came from that smoky room that made the world go away. I could almost see the hostess, hookah in hand, ornate fingernails curling toward me, beckoning.

My eyes refocused and instead of my olive-skinned queen, the figure motioning to me was Wan Lee.

"Glass, you every which way drunk. I need you out of here before last ten years of my life a waste."

His words sounded no more confusing than usual. I just didn't want to leave. The back room called; my slant-eyed goddess awaited. I hugged the bottle of Old Johnny in the crook of my arm.

"Beat it, Lee. I'm nothing. Let me find salvation alone."

But Lee wouldn't let my self-pity win. He grabbed the bottle from my intoxicated grip, walked to a garbage can, and waved it tauntingly over the top. I slid from my stool in desperation. Lunging like Frankenstein's monster, I moved too slowly to keep Lee from pouring out the whiskey and dropping the dead man into the can.

As I hovered over the lid, wondering how clean the plastic liner was, Lee slid himself under my arm and guided me away, once again, from the six-foot drop I was heading for.

"No more gongs for you."

In a half hour, I was drinking pitch disguised as coffee at the nearest Go parlor. I watched as Lee made arrangements to use their private space, a much safer room than where I was originally heading.

Lee crooked his neck toward me, and I got up to follow. A table was set up; *kifus* waiting by each of the two chairs. Lee took a seat, opened the lid of the wooden bowl, and then switched it with the other bowl.

"You play black in your condition. It hard enough to beat me when you sober."

I shook my head. "I don't want to play. I just want a corner to die in."

Of course, it was the booze speaking. I doubt I could drink enough to actually die, though I had certainly tried in the past. Lee knew that but his tone was serious, no joking, no remorse.

"Oh, but you will play. Your life depends on it. I tired of coddling you. You need to get your shit together tonight, or I kill you myself."

He didn't even look up from the board. Still not completely straight, I decided that if Lee was serious, then this was as good a way as any to cash in. I parked myself on a chair, opened my *kifu*, and placed my first piece of black shale on the board. I couldn't play by intelligence. I had to play by instinct.

"A-3, safe move. Maybe you not as drunk as I think you are."

He countered with his white stone, made of shell, also in a safe way. He didn't start aggressively and that might be my saving grace.

Go, for the uninitiated, is the oldest strategy game known to man, older than chess, older than even Egyptian Senet. Played on a wood board, nineteen lines cross from either direction to make a grid. Pieces, called stones, are played at the junctures. If your opponent surrounds your stones, he takes them and claims a territory. The object is for you to claim more territory than you lose stones.

Serious games have been known to take days. It has been said that there are as many different moves in Go as there are stars in the sky.

This game didn't become serious until about thirty-five moves in. I had made life—indestructible territories—in two places, but Lee was threatening to cut a swath through the middle of the board that would be nearly impossible to overcome.

I got more interested as the play increased in intensity. And as my interest increased, so did my worry that Lee had been telling the truth. Was he truly powerful enough to have me iced? What did he do, and for whom? I didn't have answers. It could be a bluff. It could be that I was a liability to him now. I decided to not give Lee the excuse and played with every ounce of skill I had. I might've waited too long.

I built territories, threatened to join them together. This would give me a quarter of the board and, maybe, stave off Lee's challenge. He never smiled, never took his eyes from the board. His strategy was sound, and I couldn't find a way to stop it, save to protect myself.

My cup was darkened so quietly, I never noticed it get empty. The hours wiled by until I spotted morning light through the front window of the parlor during a trip to the head. I sat back down at my chair and tried to focus on the board. If I continued at this pace, Lee would win. As the booze wore off, my moves became influenced by my past, and I played with all the emotion Reece had made me feel hours earlier.

When Reece had finished telling me I had been a fall guy, I went ballistic. I leaped from my chair and grabbed the front of his desk to keep my hands from going around his neck. "You knew? You fucking knew and didn't come clean?"

"Not didn't, *couldn't*," Reece said adamantly, holding up his hands in a gesture of defense. "I was put in a strict lockdown. Archdeacon threatened to pull all my patents, bankrupting me, if I didn't go along."

I was incredulous. "What about me? You left me to the jackals!"

I waited there, leaning against the edge of his desk, for a rebuttal that wouldn't be coming. Reece had made his point clear in the car. His obsession with technology would override any moral ambiguity. The rage slid from me as quickly as it came. I needed Reece and his connections. This dying old man was my key to freedom, not those damn plans sitting in the tube.

I dropped back to my seat, exhausted. Reece called Vincent to action. "I believe Mr. Glass will have a drink now. Single-malt whiskey, right?"

Vincent didn't wait for my acknowledgment. He went to a cabinet. I heard the telltale sounds of the clinking ice cubes dropping into glass: one, two. The bastard even knew how I took my medicine.

When I sipped from the expensive crystal, the booze was better than anything I had tasted in years, but it was like getting a

C-note from a guy who ran over your dog.

"Glass, I brought you here not only to save my life, but help you take yours back as well." He glanced down at the tube. "A trade. I give you names while you let me build your prototype."

Reece was right to wait for the plans to be finished. I was tapped out in this game and the only thing left of value for me to bet was *The Atlantis*. He wanted me to win but wouldn't let me take the whole pot.

I'd get the ones who set me up, while Reece would get to live longer. I'd get *The Atlantis* built, but Reece got all the profits. In the end, all I'd truly win is my reputation back and a good night's sleep. Would selling my soul and my car to Reece be a good bet in the end?

I drained the scotch.

Hell, yeah.

I was all ears while Vincent refilled my glass. The millionaire launched into known facts and unknown theories. He told me many things I didn't want to hear, the conversations that went on behind my back, secret nods and winks and money exchanging hands. By the time he had finished, I had a place to start but the reality that I'd been betrayed by such a close friend was a hard pill to swallow.

"Jorge Mendelssohn? My assistant? Sure, he had access to the magnetron before the demonstration, but why would he do it? Money? Blackmail? He was a good kid and a hard worker. What did he have to gain?"

Reece spoke as if the words left a bad taste in his mouth. "Because Archdeacon knew Mendelssohn had a thirst for power. Mendelssohn was on a fast trip to the top, and he'd take any route to get there. They promised him unrestricted access to everything the government had, and would get, if—and only *if*—he'd sell you out."

"The government was getting the radar. Why screw it up?"

"Spies, Glass. They wanted your test to seem like a failure while they developed their device in complete secrecy. Like when they split the atom, it wouldn't take anyone long to figure out what our government had on their hands, if they saw the readings."

I ignored his comment. I wanted to poke holes in Reece's theory, prove it was all a lie … The ice readjusted itself in the almost forgotten glass of booze. It had melted too much and watered down the premium hooch.

"So why now? What happened a year ago to make them want to kill you?"

Reece shook his head. "I don't know. Near as I can figure, they're cleaning house. Could be why Mendelssohn has gone to ground as well."

"He's gone? The only link I have to Archdeacon is gone?" I made no apologies for being livid, I had the right to be.

Reece cast an accusatory look at Vincent, who checked the shine on his shoes. "We lost him in March. Archdeacon had been keeping him underground lest he be captured by enemy forces."

"Enemy forces? I'm pretty sure the war is over."

"We're still at war, Glass. Use your imagination. Formerly friendly countries are now in a race for technology, especially weapons. Oppenheimer's bomb was too indiscriminate. Archdeacon, and the people he answers to, didn't want your magnetron for tracking purposes. They converted it to something different."

I wanted to stay naive. I didn't want to get on the train of thought Reece had leaving the station. He saw my reluctance to buy in, so instead he spelled it out, crushing my self-righteous beliefs.

"They wanted an assassination device."

Replaying those words in my mind, their unbelieved truth, shocked me back to the Go game in front of me. Wan was staring at me, obviously wondering why I hadn't moved yet and where my mind had gone. I shook the memory off and continued.

I played a stone, forcing a *ko* fight in the heart of Lee's territory. He would have to battle for that spot, buying me time to build a greater defense. While he schemed, I thought about the first time I had met Albert Einstein.

The man had been my idol. His theories had opened so many doors that, as a young scientist, I couldn't contain my enthusiasm. I leapfrogged much of my earliest work off of his.

I had a chance to see him when he spoke at Caltech. It was 1931 and he had been touring the country talking of physics, of peace, and of our responsibility as scientists to protect both.

I recalled something he said: "It is not enough that you should understand about applied science in order that your work may increase man's blessing. Concern for the man himself and his safety must form the chief interest of all technical endeavors."

Safe. Something I'm not right now.

Lee ignored my challenge in his territory, instead choosing to branch out from the left side into the middle spot. He would be firmly embedded there. I was left to grab as much territory as I could in the closing moves of the game and hope Lady Luck had actually played instead of me. Lee stopped me from taking my next move.

"We are through," he said with finality and clapped his hands twice. I expected thugs to come through the door but instead was burned to see a little old Asian woman, in her late eighties if she was a day, shuffle in.

She was certainly not the hitman I expected. I could probably take her even in my hung-over state.

Lee slid off his chair, offering it to her. Seeing his reverence, I stood up. She declined either seat, instead choosing to angle her head over the board and gaze down at the patterns created there. Lee motioned me to a corner. His manner had changed from deathly serious to friendly serious.

"You know there are three-hundred sixty-one intersecting points on the board?" I nodded.

"Well, that how many days there are on Chinese calendar. In ancient times, seers would look at board after match and be able to tell future of players. The way you lay stones is way you live life."

He left the comment hanging.

"How'd you find me, Wan? How'd you know I'd be there?"

He snickered. "I figured that if you *never* got designs to work, you end up back there someday. I not expect it to happen if they work! When you no show up at dinnertime, I go looking."

"I had a rough morning."

Lee's voice was pensive. "This have to do with Big Bucks and Mount Fuji who break into your place?"

He didn't miss a beat. Lee must have people watching the building. That meant he knew Reece had people sneaking into my apartment as I slept or while I was out and chose not to tell me about it. Did he think it wasn't his business, or did he already know who they were?

Lee could see I was reluctant to answer. "No say nothing now. You know, if you need a place to hide, I can arrange safe house."

"Thanks," I said, swallowing my other thoughts. "I hope I won't need it."

The old woman said something, and Lee took my elbow and moved us back to the table. Lee made the introduction.

"Noel, you call her *Obasaan;* it means grandma. She will be talking to you, and you can ask questions; I will translate. Do not look at me. Always look directly at her."

I wasn't sure what I was getting into, but Lee made it sound serious enough that I took his instructions as law.

She made a gesture for me to sit back in my seat. Like watching a poorly dubbed foreign film, her lips moved and Lee's translation followed, slightly out of sync.

"You are a dangerous man," she started. I wanted to retort but she continued. "You play this game with little regard to what your opponent is doing. You think you strong, but only build a wall around yourself that can be easily overwhelmed."

She waved a gnarled hand over spots on the board. "You start out sloppy, but sonny give you chance 'cause you drunk."

I imagined Lee, his face wrinkled in disgust at being called "sonny," even if it was by an elder. I suppressed a chuckle.

"You spend most of game building a fortress to defend yourself, but enemy get stronger. When you finally notice how strong, you attack, but it too late.

"However, you had chance to redeem yourself here," she said, pointing to an area I had left unexplored. "Had you attacked from least protected place, you could have brought enemy down. You will have this chance in the future."

I started to ask a question, and by reflex, turned toward Lee. Obasaan's hand shot out and grabbed my chin, forcing my face forward.

"Obasaan, when will this happen?"

She let go and scanned the board again. "Not sure ... but soon. Black pieces eclipse day of full moon. If something special happen, then you act."

The full moon was twelve days away.

"Thank you, Obasaan." I bowed forward, a sign of respect. She bowed slightly in return then shuffled back to the door.

Just before exiting, she stopped and said in perfect English, "Do not play Go drunk again. Reading that mess gave me a headache."

Lee slapped me on the back. "Sound like good advice. Breakfast?"

CHAPTER THREE

Lee didn't talk about business as we scarfed down our grub. He chose innocent subjects such as movie-star gossip and the construction on Industry City's new motorway. The beanery we sat in, Hank's Diner, was nearly identical to the hundreds of other Hank's Diners across the country, as if God himself had dropped big silver mobile homes from heaven everywhere he thought someone might need a stack of griddlecakes and bad coffee.

Lee always ate like a man with no regard to the people around him. He cut his bites too big and shoved them into his pie-hole like a little kid. When his mouth got too full from the chewing, he'd drink something to wash it all down. I'm surprised the man didn't choke.

As our waitress produced the check, Lee snatched it with lightning-quick reflexes that unnerved me, considering the man's age. He waved an empty coffee cup for a refill as she started to leave. In a moment, our cups reloaded, Lee exhaled the question he'd been holding in since we sat down.

"What you get mixed up in, Glass, and how much it cost to get you out?"

I sprayed my mouthful of joe, sputtering, "I-it's not like that. This has to do with what happened before we met."

"Ack! You pitiful then, even more so than last night. Last night you ... how you say ... fell off wagon. When we first meet, you under wagon and run over few times."

Lee's analogy made me smile. He had been my first friend in a new town, and despite my incessant teasing, he was still my only one. While I occasionally had drinks with guys on the police force, when Lee and I fellowshipped, there was a camaraderie I didn't feel with others. He had seen me at my worst and still wanted to know me. Not many friends can say that.

I perceived him with an investigator's eye. His irises were jet black, like 90 percent of his hair. Lee had gray expanding from his temples, but not so much so that he looked old from the back. His nose was flat and lumpy, like a prizefighter's, indicating that it had been broken many times and not properly set. His shoulders slumped away from his body, as if they were subtly trying to escape.

Yet despite his outsides always being a mess, internally, Lee was all right. His eating habits, his women, and whatever he did for a living, they were bound by commonality; Lee lived life without fear.

I had trusted him for this long, no sense stopping now. I couldn't go this road alone, and I didn't trust Reece. Lee had connections; I knew that for sure now. I'd give him everything and see if he still wanted in.

I wondered, since English wasn't Lee's first language, whether he'd understand the technical jargon. I decided to dumb it down for him as best I could, as I had for many an administrator at the college.

"While I still held the title of Theoretical Physicist, NMIT put on a project to improve radar accuracy. This was '39, before we got in the war. There was a race going on with two other science colleges, one in London and one in Amsterdam. Radar was still just being developed, so experimentation was wide open. Whoever got radar to work more effectively over a wider area would be known for changing modern combat forever. It would be the feather in NMIT's cap, not to mention a nice fat bonus for me at the end of the year.

"We played with different carrier wave frequencies, exciter elements, and power levels. That's when I hit upon it: the magnetron. The Germans had designed a multi-cavity oscillator but couldn't keep it working, so they discarded it. We took their principle and added a liquid coolant. We could produce high-powered microwaves strong enough to hit the moon and back. It was an incredible breakthrough!"

"How so?"

"Well, as the microwave signals bounced off an object, it would return back to home with the shape of that object, allowing for command to see if an object was a bomber, and what direction it was moving."

I paused to see if Lee translated all the jargon, and by his urging me on, I gathered he had.

"With such a powerful output, we could—theoretically—track every plane on the planet. It was all a matter of angle and power."

"But what if moon not out?"

I had to give him credit. It was a well thought out question. "Well, daytime wasn't such a big problem: if you can see the planes, you can shoot them down. Night is where the problems came in. Plus, once we got nighttime working, Mendelssohn was proposing the idea of floating big mirrors in space to bounce the microwaves off of. This would reduce the power output and allow for tracking of aircraft during the day."

He seemed satisfied by the answer, but not as excited as I was back then, and I guess still was.

"Think about it, Lee. We could have tracked all aircraft. Not just for military purposes, but like Amelia Earhart. We'd have known exactly where she went down. Better yet, ships broadcasting the signals could know about icebergs well ahead of time. No more *Titanic*s."

He smiled and nodded. I guessed he'd never truly understand the scientist's heart.

"Our preliminary tests worked fine. Using a small magnetron, we tracked a plane from Albuquerque to Phoenix, but the Brits already had that level of success. What would make our names and change the world would be a full-power run."

Lee interrupted. "How small was this small magna-whatits?"

"About the size of a bus."

He whistled. "Then how big was big?"

I chuckled. "We had to build two new buildings for the test."

I remembered the operation clearly: one building was where the magnetron was housed and the other was the radar room. We wanted no signal interference, so we kept them separated. If the test was successful, we'd be able to move them closer together.

Everyone was in attendance. We had set up an observation platform in the broadcast room. General Archdeacon was there, along with the mayor, the press, and Department Dean Amanda Orchid. Amanda was especially nervous as NMIT's current dean was retiring, and if this project went off without a hitch, she'd be in line to become the college's first woman head dean.

"We set up a test broadcast, from New Mexico to London. Everything had been checked a thousand times. The source was contained in what I called a *traveling wave tube*. Despite its size, the radiation it projected was well within limits, much less than an X-ray.

"That day, something went wrong with the tube. I missed some random element, or misread a reading. Despite checking and double checking. For fourteen years, I've never doubted that I was the one who blew it … Me."

To replay the horror of their deaths over and over in my mind with the gut-wrenching guilt that rode shotgun next to it, could wake me up at high in physical pain. Even awake, if I went too far into the memory, I'd spasm.

Tangie. Oh god, no. NOOO!

Lee kept me in the now, which was what I needed. He placed his hand on my twitching wrist. He wanted to comfort, but he also wanted to hear the rest. It seemed like I was suddenly everyone's Hans Christian Andersen. Reece, Vincent, Lee—they all wanted to know what I knew.

"Their bodies had exploded from the inside. The radiation pulse that pumped through the lab was a higher frequency than we expected. The wave excited the molecules in their bodies as it passed through, heated them up, and caused internal combustion. The last thing on the tape recorder was someone saying how hot it was in the room. The thermostat never moved from room temp. Most of the pieces weren't identifiable."

Tangie. My colleague. My lover.

A woman of her intelligence and dedication was rare. She'd moved through the college system quicker than anyone else and worked twice as hard to do it. She never used her looks to her advantage, downplaying them behind thick glasses she really didn't need. Papers billed her as the next Marie Curie. But to me, I just wanted to make her my wife.

In my most private moments, I imagined reaching out to brush a strand of auburn hair from her face, drawing it to my lips. Her skin was like silk, almost translucent save for the 247 freckles I once took the time to count. She squirmed as I touched each one in turn.

"I know most of that from paper." Lee took another sip of coffee. "Scientist who kill six people make even Japanese papers. They say 'dumb round-eye playing with stuff he shouldn't killed other dumb round-eyes who let him.'"

"Really?"

"Basically." He smirked. "Well, maybe not word for word."

I laughed, the first laugh in twenty-four hours. How'd he always manage that? Lee continued, undaunted. "Next year some eggheads in Cambridge do it, right?"

I nodded. "It's impossible to keep secrets in science. They'll find their way out. Even powers of the universe we couldn't dream of harnessing today, we'll own all their secrets eventually."

"Sound like you want the power of a god."

"I want …" I shook my head. "No, I *need* truth. Science is truth."

"It is? You sure you got that right, smart boy?"

"Can you drop that into reverse and go by once more?"

Lee put his hand to his chin, trying to look the philosopher. "I thought science fact. Truth more personal. 'To thy own self be true.'"

"Shakespeare, Lee?"

Beaming with pride, Lee confessed, "*Hamlet* come on after Cagney marathon other night. But am I not right?"

I conceded. "Yeah, science is about facts. Truth is how you interpret them."

He pointed a fork at me. "Then what is your truth, Glass?"

"The man who came to visit me yesterday, Reece, he had wanted to buy the magnetron for use in the private sector, but the army overruled him. He says he's been holding on to proof that I didn't make a mistake that day."

Lee hemmed and nodded thoughtfully.

"Hmm, what?"

"I never think you type that would miss something that big. You always notice smallest details. I never pull wool over your eyes."

"Even more than that, Reece said I was deliberately set up. The last fourteen years of *this*"—I waved my arms around—"was for nothing."

Lee was unsure. "You believe him?"

I shrugged. "I was a wreck after the accident. I didn't retrace my steps to see where the mistake had been made. It was like the saboteurs knew an accident of that nature would devastate me."

My neighbor raised an observant eyebrow. "Especially when it kill one you love, eh?"

I blinked at Lee, who just smiled. "Oh, I pretty smart for dumb old man. I see you with occasional B-girl, but you no let anyone get close. Pain inside you too deep. Remind me of guys who seen their loved ones iced."

It was no use hiding it anymore. I slammed fists down on the table, spilling the salt and pepper shakers. "The bastards killed her, Lee, knowing I'd crumple like a cheap suit! They swept it under the table and me with it. Her killer has been free for fourteen years and I've done nothing!"

I followed this tirade with a few choice, off-color words. My rant had drawn attention, but like well-trained Hank's Diner customers, no one spoke up or complained. It was an unwritten rule: never butt in at Hank's.

I simmered, clenching and unclenching my fists. I could see Jorge Mendelssohn in front of me. Snide little man, always so helpful, always watching my back. I trusted him, let him into my deepest thoughts. Those thoughts were probably the basis for everything he's done since. I had to find him. I had to see my meat hooks around his larynx. Maybe that protruding Adam's apple of his would wiggle beneath my fingers as his lungs convulsed for air. Then, just before he died, I'd let him go and drag him back here to Sweet and make him confess everything. Sweet will bring in trustworthy men, men who Archdeacon can't touch.

"So why moneybags show up now?"

"They're trying to kill Reece because he knows the truth. Him and my former assistant, Jorge Mendelssohn. He's the guy who set me up and now he's vanished. Reece is being radiated. Looks like my former benefactor, General Archdeacon, is tying up loose ends, and Reece is one of them.

"Then there's my designs. Reece wants *The Atlantis*. He wants to leave a legacy before he dies. He gave me no choice but to trade. I catch the ones trying to kill him, clearing myself in the process, and he'll build *The Atlantis*."

I was still deciding whether or not to let Lee in on the other bomb Reece dropped. This was military secret stuff. It would include Lee in a quest that could ultimately get him rubbed out just for knowing this thing existed. If Lee had really been all talk all these years, if he didn't have women on the side and secret deals and was really just a guy who watched too many Cagney films, then I was putting a black mark on him he would be unable to escape.

Some friend I am, huh?

But I wanted someone else to know. I needed to hear the words spoken and have someone tell me that what I was going to do was the right thing. I stared into my coffee and continued.

"The whole setup was so the military could make a weapon. They're calling it a MASER, microwave amplification by standard emission of radiation. It can kill from far away and leaves no trace. They target someone, use the weapon, and the victim explodes from within, just like the people in the lab."

I stared directly at Lee, removing any doubt as to the veracity of my words.

"That means we're on the short list of people who know the truth, Lee."

He let this sink in a moment before asking, "Only this Reece know you know, right?"

"And his right-hand man, the big guy, Vincent."

Lee slapped a hand down on the table. "Then no problem. He not talk anytime soon. You safe for now."

He made it sound so simple. He smiled as if I hadn't just told him the government had a way to kill him—or anyone, for that matter—in an anonymous way. It spooked the willies out of me, and it was based on *my* discovery.

"What about you?" I said, perplexed.

"Aw, who I going to tell? Anyways, who believe some old Asian guy anyway? Let us go home. We find this Mendletree tomorrow."

"Thanks. And it's Mendelssohn."

I had made the right choice to involve Lee, but didn't realize how right until we turned a corner near our apartment complex. A young Asian boy, no more than ten, ran up to us and started pushing us the other way. He looked as if he had been in a fight. Blood and snot ran from his nose, and scuff marks covered his hands and face.

"Uncle Lee! It happened just like you said it would! A truckload of men pulled up to the building. Only they weren't the guys you thought would come."

"What they look like?"

The kid wiped his nose on his sleeve. "These guys were all in suits and carried badges we never seen before. They said CIA."

"Did Uncle Yu do everything I asked him to?"

"Yes, he put up a good fight, but they beat him pretty hard. I tried to help, make it look good too. See? I lost a tooth."

The boy grinned big, showing bloody gums where the tooth must have been. He was proud to have a scar. I understood a little of the honor code. Defending a family member ranked pretty high with the gods.

"What's going on?" I asked. "Why is the CIA after you?"

Lee scanned the area and allowed the boy to guide us away. Lee talked as we ran. He said a few more things in Japanese to the boy, who nodded and darted off a different direction. Lee turned.

"Not me ... you. You think this general guy have Reece watched 'round the clock?"

"I'm sure he wou—" I didn't have to finish the thought. Reece was paranoid for a good reason. If Archdeacon was watching Reece and had figured out his car-switching thing, the tail would have followed him to my place. That meant the general knew Reece and I had talked and now assumed I knew everything that Reece did. I was Archdeacon's new threat.

I wasn't beyond thinking that Reece knew this would happen; otherwise he wouldn't have made such an open play. The government seizing my apartment would light a fire under my ass. The Central Intelligence Agency didn't answer to the army, but I was sure Archdeacon had some pull.

Black cars drove past the entrance to the alley, heading in the direction of the apartments. Lee pressed me against the wall.

"How'd they make it happen? You just don't roll into town and take over a building without a reason. What was the charge?"

"Nephew say they come to arrest you for selling military secrets to the Koreans. They don't care this is Little Osaka, not Little Seoul." I stopped dead. It wasn't enough that I was branded a failure; I would be a traitor too. If this got to the press, I'd have nowhere to run, nowhere to hide. It would be horrible on my family, my friends, once again. Chief Sweet would shit kittens.

Lee turned, saw me standing there stunned, and grabbed my arm, propelling me forward.

"We go to safe house now. Your stuff already there."

"What? How?"

Lee breathed heavily. Trying to run and talk at the same time was daunting for the old man.

"Had Uncle Yu start fight in front of building while my family get your safe, gun, and things out back."

"My safe?"

"Yeah, pull it out from other side of wall. Nothing ever safe about wall safe."

I was having trouble getting my words out. It didn't seem that long ago I was down with the fishes. "You saw this coming, didn't you?"

"I know people spy on you. They cause no trouble, so I let them. Your stuff no work anyway. When you get something to work, I know people would want it. I expected Texans, not military. Texans we make go away easy. Not so with Feds. We lucky we not there to see mess."

"Will your family be okay?"

We darted down a different alley and took a staircase down. "Oh, I not worried about family. I worried about G-men. They mess with my wife, she will chop them up and make pot stickers of them."

* * *

Lee's safe house turned out to be a laundry in the heart of the Little Osaka. We pushed our way through starched-shirt hell until we reached the back. The smell of detergent permeated the air so thickly, I could swear the shirt I was wearing was clean by the time we had reached our destination.

A row of empty canvas laundry baskets was lined up on a conveyor belt. Lee flipped a switch, pulled a lever, and got into the first cart. Like a carnival fun house, the cart moved forward. He waved at me before the track took him down an incline and out of my sight. I climbed into another cart before it, too, disappeared below.

The ride was short, and nothing jumped out to scare me. I banged into the back of Lee's cart, which had stopped. Lee pulled another lever.

"Only way down here is to pull lever. Carts circle through steam room if lever not thrown. This only way in or out."

I doubted that. There had to be a back way out. Always was.

Lee led me to a fairly large apartment. Its open architecture housed a kitchen, living room, and bedroom. There was a television and a radio. Lee showed me a chute where the morning paper would be dropped down. I thought of Reece and his vault. This wasn't that much different. I examined the walls—concrete. Would it be enough to stop a focused radiation beam?

"Why is this here? Who do you hide?"

Lee ignored my question, instead reaching into the fridge and pulling out two beers. "They send down lunch later."

I took one of the beers and glanced at the label. "This brand won the best of show at last year's Oktoberfest, right? I saw it show up in all the ads." I stared at the squiggly logo. It was a stylized *A,* for the Atlantic Brewing Company. It reminded me of Sanskrit. In fact, the whole label was drawn like an old tablet. I read it out loud.

"Ancient Stout. Brewed today just like they did in ancient times, with our special recipe handed down from generation to generation."

"It is historic brew," said Lee, mimicking the beer's radio tagline.

"I'm going to need some things, Wan. Some things that will be hard to get."

He waved it off. "Nothing hard to get if you know where to look."

"One item is of a medical nature. I might be able to protect myself with it if I become Archdeacon's new target. It'll only be available at a hospital."

"This place," he indicated the laundry above, "does bed sheets for Saint Luke's. My cousin will get what you need."

Lee claimed to run errands for a produce distributor, but never talked honestly about his work. I had played the guessing game because it was fun, but if my life was going to be totally in his hands, I really wanted to get more out of him. I needed to know where he stood.

"Who are you, Wan? Really. No bullshit. You rescued me ten years ago and now twice in twenty-four hours. Why me? What do I have that you want?"

He answered quickly and decisively. "I cannot tell you. Too many people could die if I do. You might be one of them. It better if you know little about me as possible."

I thought he was through, but he added, "Just know I am your friend and that you staying alive make me very happy. Now, what about this stuff?"

Good to his word, by nightfall, Lee had the first couple of items on my shopping list.

We ate dinner, duckling with brown rice, while we watched the news. I nearly choked on my fowl when I saw the six o'clock lead story. Lee had to thump my back.

"Tragedy in downtown Industry City tonight as a four-alarm fire broke out at Liberty Tower today. The damage was contained to the penthouse offices of Little Technologies. The tower was being evacuated as rescue personnel arrived on the scene."

They showed a picture of the tower; smoke billowed from the very same floor I had been on the day before. I wondered what the fire marshal would think when he saw the vault. How was Reece going to explain that?

"Little Technologies' long-ailing president, C.J. Reece, perished in the ensuing chaos, apparently from smoke inhalation. This brings to a close a forty-year …"

The anchor droned on, but Lee and I turned to look at each other. A duckling leg bone hung limply from his mouth. It dropped and splattered on the table.

"Oh, boy. As they say in Korea, 'You in deep *kimchi* now.'"

CHAPTER FOUR

I never got the bodyguard Vincent's last name even though we spent most of the day in each other's company. It wasn't that I didn't want to be on a first-name basis with the guy, but when you've suddenly inherited a bodyguard, you like to know the background of the man guarding your life.

"Richmond, like the city." A non-revealing name for a guy keeping cards hidden. I casually studied his features, trying to determine his makeup. He was six feet nine inches and about 350 bricks worth of muscle. His features, especially his jaw, cut at hard angles to his short, straw-colored hair. Somewhere between thirty and thirty-five, his size bespoke a mountainous region, anywhere from Yugoslavia to the Ozarks. However, with no accent, I wasn't getting a lead. In fact, his voice was so clear, I started to think he'd had voice coaching to remove an accent, like many actors do.

He was clearly no actor, though. He wore his job on his face, along with his emotions. As his form absorbed a majority of the railcar we sat in, his somber mood was starting to bug me.

When he appeared at Lee's safe house, it created a whirlwind of problems. He couldn't be dissuaded from the idea that I was there. When Lee's "family" started getting rough, he produced a piece of paper that was then brought to me. According to Vincent, Reece had written the note in the hours before we met.

Glass,

If you are reading this after we have had the chance to meet, I am dead and you'll know why. If we haven't met yet, my bodyguard Vincent will fill you in. He will tell you things that won't make you happy. Don't shoot the messenger.

I always believed death would be my only release from the obsessions I held fast to on Earth. Now that I'm dead, I guess I'll know whether or not I was able to take any of it with me.

You have a lot stacked against you so I am giving you Vincent. He is being paid through a fund I set up, so you won't have any worries there. His job is to protect you as if you were me. Of course, me being dead, that probably doesn't mean as much to you now. I can only say he'll protect you with everything he's got.

Last tip, you know that old saying about keeping friends close and enemies closer? It goes double when they're both.

—*CJR*

Lee and I left the safe house and met Vincent upstairs, seeing as he wouldn't fit in one of the laundry carts anyway. I had expected a tail when I left Reece's office the day before, so I darted down alleys, made quick, unpredictable moves, until I was sure I had lost any possible snoops before heading to the bar. I'd been right to worry. Vincent had me tailed, but I lost the amateur. So, he himself staked out my place until the early-morning hours. When the CIA raided the place, he didn't want to get caught in a sweep of the area.

Vincent caught a glimpse of Lee's nephew slinking off nervously from the siege, so he hedged a bet and followed the boy to us.

Lee was miffed that his tail-losing skills were not as good as mine. I promised him I'd teach him some tricks.

Once Vincent had established where we were, he headed back to the office to report in, only to find the place in flames and Reece reported dead.

"Reece left very specific instructions for me, upon his death, to guard you, Mr. Glass, with all the resources I have available to me, including my life."

"But, Vinny, what if I don't want you to?"

He grimaced at the name and made it clear with a look that this was non-negotiable. The death of the old man had clearly shaken him. I was not in the habit of taking in strays but decided to let him stick around anyway and keep him busy. That way he'd be out of my business.

Vincent made all the safety arrangements for our travel. He thought it best we leave by rail instead of plane. It was easier to get on and off incognito. We decided that the extra time would be not a hindrance, but a boon. Our prey might surface by the time we arrived. After Vincent left to get things moving, Lee and I returned to the safe room and talked.

"You trust Mount Fuji?"

"Nope, but the energy spent trying to lose him will be better spent in finding Mendelssohn. Plus, Reece had a point. Vincent was close to Reece, and we can use that. He can open doors we can't."

Lee shrugged. "Doors, nothing. That man open gates to hell without breaking sweat."

When my new bodyguard returned, he hustled us to the train station. Cops and Feds were scattered around inconspicuously, looking for someone of my description. I had to give Vincent credit; he managed to move us only when the law was distracted elsewhere. I never noticed a break in our stride, and every time I thought we were going to be spotted, we just weren't there anymore.

So there we sat, on the nonstop to Nevada, not saying much until Lee finally broke the silence.

"Why we go to Nevada? Why not New Mexico?"

I waited for Vincent, who seemed content to let me explain. Reece obviously had done most of the talking.

"I got a tip from these guys," I said, casting a thumb toward Vincent, "that Mendelssohn had a girl in Chance City. For the last few years, until March, he was holed up at some government think tank near there. Every time they'd let him out for R & R, he'd head right to her. It's a sure bet she helped him disappear. She's our link."

Lee perked up at the reference to a skirt.

"She 'good time' girl?"

"Nah, a lounge singer."

"Down, tiger," I said, knowing she was our prey. "Word has it they were pretty tight. If anyone knows where to find Mendelssohn, it'll be her."

"So what this Mendelsonny look like?"

"I'm not sure anymore. Vincent? Care to give us the skinny?"

Vincent rattled off his facts like a police officer reading from a rap sheet. I glimpsed a possible previous life for our man mountain. He must have been on the force before heading to the private sector.

"Five foot, nine inches. Weight, about one fifty. Blue eyes. Scandinavian heritage, light skin."

Lee whistled. "Only buck fifty? People call him Slim?"

"Not altogether, no," I said. "Mendelssohn had a thing about weight. His goal in life was to have zero body fat. He was constantly weighing himself."

"It got worse," Vincent interjected. "He started shaving himself completely, like some bodybuilders do. He eventually had all his hair removed when the obsession got worse. He refused to eat anything that wasn't pure protein."

Shaking his head, Lee said to me, "What it about you geniuses? You all kinda screwy."

This drew out a smile from my new bodyguard. Vincent had worked for Reece, a brilliant man with more than a few eccentricities. It must have been therapeutic to hear someone say what he could never voice.

"You gamble?" Lee directed the question at me, still not sold on the idea of Vincent along for the ride. I bounced a questioning look over to the bodyguard, trying to keep him included in the conversation. The more I knew about him, the safer I'd feel. Vincent gave a non-descriptive shake of the head, so I turned back to Lee.

"You mean besides this endeavor? Nope. Can't."

"What you mean?"

"Unethical. I studied probability. Not only could I beat every game they offer, my face is known."

"We have fake IDs."

"No, Lee."

"But, but you could play little at a time. Don't win big, just steady."

I shook my head. "No, Lee! I've done enough things to knock me from the pillars of heaven. I don't need another. Call it karma or keeping the odds in my favor. I enjoy my occasional poker game with the guys. There is the chaos of people decisions. No math can completely cover for it. Will they take a card or stay? I won't play blackjack, either. I'd win and what's the fun in that?"

Lee smiled. "The fun come after with all that dough."

"No."

"They have poker ro—"

"No."

He screwed up his face in disgust and waved me away. He wasn't content, though. I could tell gears still turned in his head. Why was he so concerned about making money?

"Speaking of IDs …" Vincent reached into a briefcase and pulled out three driver's licenses that had descriptions close to ours.

"How'd you get these?" I inquired.

"When I saw the mess at your apartment, I figured we might need to travel light. I had busted this guy a while back who knew this other guy who could forge quickly. I had him whip these up."

"So you were ICPD?" I had been right about Vincent being a former cop.

Vincent seemed unconcerned. "For a while. I did a stint as an MP in the army. Then moved around from state to state, but police work didn't sit well with me. I needed something less constricting, so I went into the private sector."

I wanted to ask him more about Reece—how Vincent came to work for him and more about the MASER—but his posture was closed off. He'd given as much as he would give tonight, maybe even more than he wanted.

Lee yawned. We'd been going on adrenalin and coffee long enough. It was time to rest. We retired to our sleepers as the train started its journey through the Rockies.

* * *

I was looking forward to my first solid night's sleep in the bunk. Having fallen asleep so many times at my desk, the thought of a night spent horizontal was nirvana. Later, Lee would tell me it had been no heavenly rest for him. I tossed and turned as I dreamt and woke him up several times. He didn't know which was worse, the sounds of the train or my thumping.

While dreamers rarely realize they are in a dream, I have, on occasion, been cognizant of my dream state, though powerless to change the dream to my advantage. I'm told this is called *lucid dreaming*. I guess my brain is wired differently. I also have total recall when it comes to my dreams. *The Atlantis* came to me in one, the solution to its problems in another. Now, of course, I wasn't so sure if those solutions weren't ideas Reece had whispered into my ear as I slept.

The first night on the train, I dreamt of Tangie.

It's not as though I hadn't dreamt of her before. I've dreamt about the day we met, key moments in our relationship, the first time we made love … the day she died. Something about this dream was different, as if the events of the past two days had woken something inside of me.

Everything in the dream was fish-eyed, like I looked through the bottom of a bottle. She was there, as beautiful as the day I met her. Her long, molten lava locks pulled into a ponytail, showcasing her cute ears and librarian glasses. She hated the cheaters, but I loved them on her. It made me feel like she was revealing her true identity when she took them off, like some superheroine from the funny pages.

And oh, when she took them off …

In the dream, however, she was the *überscientist*. She could be cold when she was like this, distant, a theoretical engineer to the core. She ran around, checking and rechecking the link between her power station and my lab next door where I had the radar equipment. I gazed with pride at my partner, my love.

The power needed to bounce the magnetron signal off the moon would be tremendous the first time out. Tangie had designed the transformer to run quieter than conventional power stations, thus cutting down interference. That was her gift. She could take one look at a design and see a way to make it stronger.

Tangie had done that with me as well.

In the dream, Tangie strode up to me, her green eyes locked on to mine. I couldn't see anything else but those eyes, piercing my mind. But then the dream deviated from the memory.

"Behind you."

I originally left after the double-checks. In this version, Tangie took a hold of my arm and kept me from leaving. She wanted me to see something.

Again she said, *"Behind you."*

I turned to look. Behind me was the power station.

Mendelssohn stood in front of it, looking as I remembered him, Mozart-like hair and perfectly balanced body.

From his lab coat, he withdrew two almost identical oscillators, the heart of the magnetron, and held them both out for me to see.

"Which one, Glass?"

I tried to remember which one had been the original but found it hard to focus. They both started oscillating. The one in his right hand glowed soft blue. The left hand started pulsing flashes of red light. Mendelssohn's laugh reverberated as I spun back to Tangie.

"Get out!" I pleaded.

Her face was boiling. Despite her bubbling flesh, she showed more concern for me than for herself.

"Wake up, Noel. You're in danger."

Her head popped like a bloody kernel of corn and I cried out.

I woke to a start, my heart racing, only to find something hideous leaning over me with a gun.

I kicked up, causing the bunk above me to tilt. Lee rolled off it and landed on the back of my assailant. I heard a noise, like that of a capacitor blowing. Feathers plumed up from the pillow scant inches from my head. Lee let loose a string of Asian curses, still not sure what had happened. I grabbed the thug's arms and pushed my way out of my sack.

I could see now the horrific visage was a mask. It was stone-like in appearance, some sort of South American-looking statue frozen in a hideous scream. The top part of the mask was a cat-creature, maybe a panther or jaguar. The rest of him was garbed in black, military-style fatigues.

My opponent was strong, but the bruised back had sapped some of his will power. I pushed him backward until we toppled over an escaping Lee. Lee crawled into the space between the two bunks, exuding even more curses, while I managed to get the intruder down on the floor. We wrestled but I kept the upper hand.

Lee shouted, "Hold him while I get gun!"

All three of us turned our heads when a loud thump hit our sleeper compartment's door. That's when I noticed Vincent's empty bunk.

The door blasted open and a second masked man was propelled into the fray. He collided with us, twisting me loose from my captive. Vincent stood in the doorway, sandy blond hair askew, blue eyes wild and searching. His quarry wore a similar, but slightly different mask.

Thugly One took advantage of his newfound freedom to leapfrog over me, grab something from my pillow, and fling open the window sash. Unfiltered noise and wind roared into the compartment. He pulled himself up and out before Vincent could cross the sleeper to snag him. Thuglier Two untangled himself from our yoga pile and bolted for the now unguarded door. I jumped to my feet and started after him.

"Wait!" Lee yelled and tossed me my piece.

Other travelers were poking their heads out of their compartments to see what the ruckus was about. Some slammed doors quickly as they saw my prey running down the hallway. We darted from sleeper to passenger car. I couldn't get a clean shot with people still milling around late-night poker games and snack service. The masked assassin headed toward the caboose, as opposed to the engine. He would bail out the back, I was sure.

I got an opportunity to slow him down as we crossed into the empty dining car. He paused long enough to open the door. I squeezed off a shot, which caught him in the leg. Knocked off balance, he reached into the car for something to grab onto, finding only a coffee trolley. The last thing I saw as he dragged the metal cart over the edge with him was his mask, the top half in the shape of a skull. I heard a sickening crunch I hoped wasn't just the coffee service.

I moved slowly into the opening and scanned up and down: no one. I spun at the sound of a door opening behind me. Vincent displayed open palms in a friendly gesture. He called to me, but I couldn't hear him above the roar of the wind. He came forward and gave me a questioning look.

I answered his unspoken question. "I tagged him. Might've finished him. No way to know for sure right now."

"I think the other one is on the roof."

Reflex had me look up just as I felt a sting at the back of my neck like a mosquito bite. I slapped at it and pulled away a dart, like the type fired from a tranquilizer gun. A chill ran down my spine. I looked up again to find the twisted animal mask standing on top of the next car, gun pointed down at me. The hideous mask laughed, though no sound came from it. I started up a ladder between cars, but Vincent dragged me back. The masked gunman jumped from the roof into the darkness that engulfed the side of the train.

Vincent sounded panicky. "You've been injected, Mr. Glass. I need to get you to your room!"

"Injected? Injected with what?" I sputtered.

"A targeting fluid. It's what the MASER excites to make someone explode."

"What?"

Vincent was taking me back to our room as fast as I would go. He checked windows and ushered me across each car by using his body as a shield. I doubted whatever he was protecting me from would be stopped by even his bulk. My heart was racing. Sweat poured from my forehead.

Our compartment was empty. "Where's Lee?"

"He went to talk to the conductor."

After we were inside, Vincent alternated between apologizing and cursing. "Damn! I fell into their trap. I'm so sorry, Mr. Glass. This is all my fault."

He wasn't making sense. "What just happened, Vincent?"

"I heard a noise at our door. I got up and saw one of them leaving. I chased him, thinking I could take him out quickly and get back in time to stop the second one I knew would be coming. I'm sorry. I'm such an idiot! Damn! Damn! Damn!"

Vincent pounded his fist against the wall with each curse. He left a dent in the wall and elicited echoed curses from the neighboring cabin. His carefully manicured professionalism was unraveling, and I could swear he picked up an accent that was definitely not English in origin.

"Who were those guys? Did I see right? What were those masks they had on?" I was on edge. I paced the cabin back and forth.

"They're the Hero Twins. Guatemalan killers. They modeled themselves after the Mayan myth of two brothers who killed the lords of the underworld and won humanity's freedom. The one you shot is the hunter; the other is the jaguar."

"Why would Archdeacon hire assassins? If he knew where I was, wouldn't he just stop the train?"

Vincent incessantly repeated, "I don't know! I don't know!"

I swear the lug was sulking. Lee came back into the room and told Vincent, "They say they move us to new room." He noticed me. "Hey, Glass? You know your neck bleeding? And you don't look so good."

"Vincent was just about to explain all that. Seems like I've been doped with something, right?"

Vincent finally stopped pacing and plopped down on his bunk. I don't know how it supported him. He took two controlled breaths. All signs of the accent were gone when he spoke. "I don't know much about technology. Reece would just start talking, and I'd try to keep up."

I'd seen Vincent keep up. He was selling himself short, or maybe he was downplaying his intelligence for effect. Either way, he wasn't going to tell me everything. That much I knew.

"The MASER takes too long to kill a living being because of the amount of water in our bodies. So the group that developed the weapon invented a drug that makes the MASER work faster."

I hated to admit it, but despite the junk floating through my veins, the scientist in me was curious and excited. "How does it work?"

"I'm not sure. Something about priming the molecules."

"What?" Lee blinked confusion.

"The MASER," I took over, "causes molecules to speed up, creating heat and eventually resulting in a cohesion breakdown." I apparently hadn't done any better explaining. Lee looked at me like a dog trying to understand why the Yanks keep making the World Series.

"So drug make things blow up faster?"

Vincent and I nodded.

I continued, "However, since the microwaves are pushed forward on a radioactive carrier, prolonged exposure at smaller amounts can create the effect we saw in Reece: cancer or radiation sickness or even blood disease. That's why it was taking them so long to kill Reece. They probably didn't have this drug a year ago."

The bodyguard nodded. "Reece only recently discovered its existence. That's when he really started getting paranoid. While the damage was done and he was marked for death, I think he was afraid they planned to take him out sooner, before he could spill what he knew to anyone."

"Not anyone, the only one person in the world who would believe him is me. They didn't want him to get to me."

Lee was unconvinced. "He big, important man, this Reece. Why could he not go to papers?"

Vincent was embarrassed. "The boss has … had done some questionable things in the past. It wouldn't take much to discredit him."

"So," I said, getting the topic back on me, "I have this drug in me, which means they can kill me anytime?"

Vincent shook his head. "Depends. There are two MASER designs. One is a personal weapon, though it requires a backpack. It's line of sight and has little range. The other is mounted on a tripod and has greater range and power. The Hero Twins are most likely using the personal one since hauling the other around is time prohibitive. It helps that we're moving, so we're safe on the train. I imagine they'll try something when we get off, though."

"Try what?" asked Lee.

Vincent wasn't sure. "Anything from grabbing Mr. Glass and finishing him in some undisclosed location to waiting in an alcove and irradiating him without us ever seeing it coming."

"This drug, does it concentrate in one part of the body, or does it spread out?" I asked.

Again, Vincent wasn't a huge help. "It's been known to settle in the motor cortex of the brain."

"But that …" I was aghast. Vincent nodded.

"What that mean?"

I put my mitts on either side of my head and showed Lee. "*Pop!*"

"Or," Vincent added, "if you're really unlucky, you might just end up a vegetable."

Now Lee was just as worried as the rest of us. "Yuck."

"Yeah." For a guy such as me, whose whole life had been built around his intellect, it was the worst type of life or death.

"Can you help me get my trunk from the back?" I asked.

My omniscient smile worried Vincent. "Why? What do you have in there?"

"Insurance."

CHAPTER FIVE

Chance City will never catch up to Las Vegas. Vegas had five brand-new, multi-story casinos. Chance City, on the other hand, was more intimate—each casino catering to a certain crowd such as the Italians, the old farts, or the high rollers. Chance's casinos looked more like back-alley dice-joints, if you asked me, but since no one did, I still called them casinos. Of course, from where I was currently boxed in, I couldn't see even a single slot machine.

When I was eight, my brother once dared me to climb down a well by our house, assuring me there was treasure below. I slipped halfway down and broke my leg. The entire neighborhood had to be mobilized, and eventually I was lifted out to cheers of a score of people. My brother was properly chastised, but his punishment didn't keep me from being mortified that I couldn't even climb down a well without injury.

Where I had chosen to hide was much more embarrassing than that.

If anyone *were* looking for me, he'd have to seek out the back of the train first; then he might have spotted me: the satin blue steamer trunk being offloaded by baggage handlers. Not one of my prouder moments.

And I had to piss like a racehorse on a flat rock.

According to Vincent, once the targeting solution hit my bloodstream, it took forty-eight hours to completely pass through the system, twenty-four if I peed a lot. So I had drunk the

Colorado River's worth of water, which didn't seem like such a great idea at the moment.

I was left completely to my imagination in the darkness of the trunk. A noise could be anything from Vincent coming to get me to one of the Hero Twins aiming for the kill.

It's in moments such as this you get to reflect on the mistakes of your life. I thought when death came for me, I'd be glad. I hoped to see Tangie waiting on the other side of the bright light with welcoming arms. I feared seeing Satan waiting with open arms to punish me for my sins. I thought of the people I had done wrong—women I had lied to, clients I had cheated.

Ultimately, I convinced myself that I had done every wrong thing for a right reason. Had I forgotten what it was to be the good guy? Maybe working for the police was a subconscious attempt at balancing the scales. What if my insincere actions are what brought me to this end; splattered all over the inside of this trunk?

Did I deserve this?

I got warmer. Beads of sweat rolled unbidden from my temples. Sure, Nevada was a desert, but that didn't stop my paranoia level from escalating. I was being irradiated, and those would be my last thoughts. I swore to myself, to God, and to anyone who would listen that I'd be the good guy again. I wouldn't lose track of Einstein's words. I would put mankind first.

Right after I bashed in the head of the son of a bitch who murdered Tangie.

Three raps came in quick succession—the code. Lee and Vincent had me.

Vibrations told me I'd been lifted and deposited into the trunk of a rental car. Anyone with a brain watching Lee and Vincent would put two and two together and realize I was in the steamer. The trunk had some protection but not enough.

Whoever was driving took off like the start of the Indianapolis 500. There were screams but not of adoring race fans. It also sounded like he rebounded off of something hard. Good thing this was a rental. Of course, it must be Wan Lee behind the wheel.

After five minutes, give or take, when I was sure we were clear, I pounded on the trunk and yelled. Lee found a Hank's Diner with a public restroom. When they let me out, I bolted for the men's. Two minutes of relief later, I was sitting in the backseat of the Mercury, scowling at the back of my partner's head as he snickered. Then Lee realized it had been a while since he'd hit the head himself and stepped out.

At times, Wan Lee was so childlike, but then Mafia Lee came out. Maybe he had a split personality. Maybe he needed both elements to balance the two sides of his life. Could his goofiness be a coping mechanism?

Vincent, on the other hand, seemed pleased for the first time that his plan had worked, and for my part, I was too.

"How do you feel, Mr. Glass?"

"Like I just pissed a barrel of Ancient. This exciter fluid, what's it composed of?"

"No idea," Vincent admitted.

"How does it work with the microwaves?"

"Not a clue."

"Are you only this obstinate for my sake, or are you always this oblivious?"

He smiled. "Oh, this is just to keep you guessing. Mr. Reece said to not make things too easy on you."

"Well, you certainly followed that instruction to the letter."

His laugh was low and deep. He had taken the ribbing well. The success of our escape had made him pliable, but if he was going to talk, I wasn't going to him stop now.

"How long were you with Reece?"

We got out and stretched. Vincent's bones clicked like the sound of a gun being cocked, while my cracking sounded sick, like the breaking of a branch.

I got a look at our car for the first time; I had rushed back from the bathroom so quickly that I hadn't had a chance to examine it before jumping inside. It was a '52 Mercury, blue. It was a little road worn, being a rental, and Lee's additional dings added to the overall mystique, but it was still a hell of a lot better car than mine.

"He hired me about eight months ago when they tried to MASER him full on but failed."

This was new.

"Reece was attending an opening for a new science wing of the State College of Colorado. Little Technologies had donated a huge chunk to SCC to see it happen, so he was invited to speak. It was pure coincidence that saved him."

"How's that?"

Vincent chuckled. "Reece wasn't feeling well as he sat waiting for his turn to speak, but felt completely better when he got up. He happen to glance out and witnessed the Hero Twins off in the distance, trying to get around a lead statue Reece had unknowingly lined himself up with."

"Holy shit!" It was just crazy enough of a story to be true.

Vincent leaned against the trunk, took out a cigarette and lit it. I hadn't seen him smoke before now. Was he slipping off when I wasn't paying attention, or was talking about Reece stressing him to the point he needed a crutch?

"I was brought in to design safety protocols; he made them all work. He was very agreeable to my suggestions, and I believe they kept him alive longer. I wanted him to stay at the house, but he pushed for the office version of the vault. It's hard to imagine every eventuality. I didn't take fire into consideration. I should have designed a quick escape route."

"I doubt a hundred-and-one-story fireman's pole would have passed inspection."

He dropped the half-finished stick to the dirt, ground it in, and looked at me with a grin. "No, I doubt it would have."

Lee returned with a rolled-up paper. He splayed it out on the hood of the car so we all could see. The morning blab sheet wasn't good. My picture, about twelve years out of date, was on the front page with the headline *American Traitor!*

Not since the arrest of Alger Hiss has America been so shocked to find the enemy in our midst. The Central Intelligence Agency has issued an arrest warrant for once-noted scientist Noel Robert Glass for suspicion of selling military secrets to a foreign power.

Glass, who was cleared of negligence charges in the failed New Mexico Institute of Technology experiment that cost the lives of six colleagues, has been working as a private detective in Industry City for the past twelve years. Industry City Chief of Police Charles Sweet has agreed to fully support the CIA in the apprehension of Glass. At the joint press conference, Sweet remarked:

"You just can't trust those brainy types [...] always think they're smarter than you."

General Duane Archdeacon is coordinating Army Intelligence efforts with the CIA to close down travel to and from Industry City, where Glass was last seen. Roadblocks and checkpoints will be in place until Glass is apprehended, according to Archdeacon. Glass's apartment laboratory was discovered and searched, and investigators found much that disturbed them.

One army official, who wished to remain anonymous, said, "He could've been making anything in there, from a milkshake to an atomic bomb for all we know."

According to unnamed sources, Glass was in possession of several military-level documents and blueprints that were property of NMIT. The army has called upon NMIT in the past to develop military-grade technologies, including those recently used in Korea. It is their fear that Glass has been selling secrets to the Communists in North Korea and may have compromised our brave men and women serving overseas, thus prolonging the police action.

It is of note that Glass was last seen in the company of two men. One, Wan Li of Industry City, is believed to be Glass's North Korean military contact. The other, Vincent Richmond, is the former bodyguard of C.J. Reece of Little Technologies, a frequent contractor to the U.S. government. Richmond is wanted for questioning in the fire that killed Reece yesterday. The ICPD are now classifying the fire as arson and Reece's death a murder.

The picture they had for Vincent looked even older than mine, and the character sketch for Lee looked as if Kim Il Sung himself had sat for the artist.

"I'm not Korean! Lee! L-E-E! Not L-I! What it take to make these yahoos get it straight? I not bust my ass to protect my family from internment camp only to get thrown in jail for being wrong slant-eye devil!"

Lee had told me how hard it was on him during WWII and immediately afterward. Luckily, one of his immediate family had been a member of the 442nd, the all-volunteer Japanese-American fighting division. When the war was over, the 442s were treated like the true American heroes they were. Japanese across the country had found a smooth integration back into society, more so than the blacks had after the Civil War, or even the Germans. However, if this mess wasn't cleared up, Lee might bring shame down upon his family. Even worse, he risked the wrath of Obasaan. That was someone I'd be afraid of making mad, too.

I placed a hand on Lee's shoulder. "It's going to be okay. We'll find Mendelssohn and clear all our names."

He kept staring at the article, as if willing it to rewrite itself. He finally nodded.

Vincent took the paper, crumpled it into a ball, and tossed it in the nearby trash. "We have to take different precautions now. Luckily, they used old images of us, but seen together, we'll stand out. We'll need to take that into account."

Vincent had picked a fleabag hotel away from the main drag, knowing full well the place wouldn't examine our identification too closely. We checked in under our aliases one at a time, being careful not to look anyone in the eye. Vincent had gone first then sat at a slot machine and kept the lobby under surveillance as I checked in. Lee was fortunate to arrive at the same time as about seven other Japanese gamblers. He blended into the crowd. We got to our rooms without incident.

I didn't bother to unpack. I just threw my suitcase on the dresser and plopped down on my bed. I was feeling out of sorts. Since this affair began, I felt more like a spy than a gumshoe. I was not accustomed to all this subterfuge. Sure, I had gone undercover once or twice, but normally my investigations revolved around a logical set of facts and clues.

I treated every case as if it were a science problem: cause and effect. If the lips were purple instead of blue on a stiff, then what caused that? Okay, poison. Take a blood sample. Analyze what poison and how long it took to kill and how it should be administered. Next, how could the victim have come in contact with the poison? And so on. Sweet and I weren't that much different. He looked for the same clues I did. I just used a different set of formulas, and I kept digging until I had the solution that fit all the facts.

Here I was being driven by other people instead of taking the lead myself. I wasn't in control. Reece set me on a trail and I went, but he gave me a watchdog in Vincent. Lee was there to watch my back, but because of General Archdeacon and the CIA, now I'd be watching his too. I had no clues, just Mendelssohn's name. I had no facts, just conjecture.

I kept a little, leather-bound journal in my jacket pocket for taking notes during a case. I retrieved it and wrote the following:

In the case of the murder of six people and subsequent framing of Noel Glass for that murder.

Who rigged the microwave experiment?

The obvious answer was Jorge Mendelssohn, but did I know that as a fact? No, I had no confession, just Reece's word. But for the sake of kick-starting the brain box, I wrote his name.

Why?

Reece again said this was due to greed, power, and control. As I thought about it, I really had nothing that didn't come from Reece. Certainly his death would seem to confirm all that he had said, but Reece wasn't an investigator. Mendelssohn could have been railroaded as easily as I had.

Yet there was the dream. Whether brought on by subconscious desires or fears, seeing Mendelssohn there felt right. My gut, as Sweet would put it, was telling me Reece had been right. Yet the reasoning was off. I knew Jorge. I knew how power hungry he was, but I also knew he was patient. He wasn't that far off from running his own projects. Hell, if the experiment *had* worked, he would have been in a great position and been able to ask for almost any job he wanted. I wrote instead:

Someone forced him.

It fit better. Wrong as the deed was, I was guessing Jorge was coerced into it. Maybe I was still feeling sentimental, but it fit with my hypothesis.

Who?

Archdeacon? It also didn't seem likely. While our government lambasted assassinations and formally outlawed them from as far back as the Lieber Code to the currently accepted Geneva Convention, they were no more above under-the-counter dealings than any third-world country. Yet, a weapon that could be used openly in combat such as a gun wouldn't cross that morality line. There had been write-ups in the war journals about snipers and how they had made a difference on the Russian front. The MASER didn't fall into the same category. It was tool for evil, built for deception and not the weapon our government could ever admit to using.

I left the answer as *Mr. X* since I still wasn't sure if our government was that devious. Corrupt, yes. Murderous, well, despite Senator McCarthy's regular ranting, I couldn't believe a conspiracy around every corner.

Instead I wrote, *Why hide this weapon?* Then added, *Why did Mendelssohn go into hiding six months ago? Why did they want to kill Reece a year ago? What did they both discover last year that caused Mr. X to act? Why do they want to kill me?*

As I thought of more questions with no answers, there were three sharp raps on my door. Through the peephole, I saw nothing. Vincent must be standing in front of it. I drew my gun anyway. I placed the chain on and cautiously opened the door a crack.

A shrimp cocktail was shoved in my face. "Look! They give this away free!"

Lee's overwhelming excitement had me wanting to close the door and throw the deadbolt.

They had brought lunch. Vincent went directly to the window, took a peek, and settled down on the second of my two beds. Lee set a tray covered with cold cuts on the table. I slapped a couple of slivers of ham and Swiss cheese on a slice of rye and folded it over. It reminded me of staff luncheons at NMIT. I think the cheese was reused from one of them.

Lee talked from behind a mouthful a food. "Whabout-dissungburd?"

Vincent and I gave each other a questioning look. He said, "Sorry. I only speak drunk."

Lee swallowed hard and asked again, "What about this songbird? What we know about her?"

"She goes by Merlot Sterling," Vincent relayed as he opened a bottle of beer for himself and one for me. "She does a blues review over at the Money Tree Casino. Broke free from the Chicago scene a few years ago. It seemed like she was going to go somewhere with it, but then she settled in to the club thing right after meeting Mendelssohn. They got along like a house on fire. Success didn't seem to matter to her anymore. That's what my contacts came up with, anyway."

I took the offered Ancient. "So tell me, why is she still alive, Vincent? I'm surprised Archdeacon didn't make her tops on his list. She was intimate with Mendelssohn, so he had to have told her things, things Archdeacon wouldn't want revealed."

"Maybe Mendlebaum not only guy she cozy with? Maybe she got big-time benefactor that even Archdeacon afraid of."

Lee's suggestion made sense, especially since he had his own moll.

Vincent liked the way it sounded too. "What? Like the Chicago mob?" Vincent stroked his chin. "That's a thought. There could be a hornet's nest where she's concerned. Yeah, it fits together nicely."

"That means we take it easy with her. Spook her and she'll go running to Mendelssohn. Hurt her, and she'll run to the mob. Last thing we need is another enemy. I recommend we grab some Zs after lunch. It's going to be a long night if we plan to tail her."

Vincent disagreed. "We can't tail her if we're watching our backs. We need to take care of the guys after you, Mr. Glass. I did a little looking around, and I have an idea. I think we can catch them and maybe get one of those guns for you to examine. You know, so you can present it as proof."

"But what about Merlot? She's our link to Mendelssohn."

"I think we'll have time for both. Let me explain …"

* * *

After the guys left, I noshed a few more pieces of pig flesh before hitting the hay. By the time I awoke, it was dark. Lee had left a note at the desk for me to find him by the craps tables. When I got there, the stack of chips in front of him represented twice my income for the past two years, before taxes.

Let's go! I indicated with a gesture.

One more!

He took the dice he was handed. He warmed them in his palm, letting them tumble one over another. I reviewed his bet on the next roll. He was betting four to place. He had already rolled his point, so the odds would have been in his favor if he bet single on the pass line, but he chose to go for the big payout. If he won, he'd make enough to fund my prototype himself. If he lost, the casino would breathe easier tonight.

After the dice flew and the dealer took everyone's chips, Lee shrugged as if the loss hadn't been any worse than tossing two bits in a bum's tin at Christmas. I would have cursed a blue streak, yet for Lee, it was just cop and blow.

I envied Wan Lee at that moment, yet I couldn't decide if it was for the ability to control his emotions or the size of his imagined bank account. Crime must pay, and well.

"So, Lee …"

"Don't want to talk about it. We have show to catch."

The Money Tree Casino was nicer than our hotel, but that didn't take a whole lot. You'd think it was the most popular place in town, if you counted its size as a factor. We walked between row after row of slot machines, all occupied by aged tourists, foreigners, and clydes.

We staggered our entrance to the Gaslight Lounge as we had at the lobby. Lee had made acquaintances of the Japanese tourists earlier and invited them to Merlot's show. Some were in attendance; they waved to him as he entered.

I thought it was too convenient. The timing was too perfect on Lee's end and they had all gotten chummy really quickly. I know casinos are colorblind when it comes to money; they can see only green. But Chance City wasn't particularly known as a great place for Asian tourists. Lee had taken his time back at the Hank's when we arrived. Was it enough time for a phone call? Did he send for backup?

I chose to lean against the bar along the right side of the room. I made no visible recognition as Vincent entered and took up a position toward the back. Vincent's size would be our only tell. He couldn't blend in anywhere.

The bartender brought me an Old Johnny and cola. When I discovered in Reece's office that my patterns were so predictable, I decided to switch embalming fluids every chance I could. My first foray into uncharted territory was simple, safe.

I turned and took in the lounge. Crushed red velvet hung loosely from the walls. The wall sconces were made to look like Victorian-style gas lamps, the fake flickering flames cast moving shadows in every nook and cranny. Faces, even comely ones, appeared dark and evil in that light. Anybody could be out to kill me; my observational instincts were useless here.

To the left of stage, an easel displayed a sign:

Merlot Sterling in "A History of the Blues."

At five after, the lights dimmed and someone started tapping on the eighty-eights. Having grown up on the outskirts of Chi-town, I was an alligator when it came to the blues. I had no musical talent, but most Friday nights you'd find me in a club, enjoying the music. I recognized the tune within the first few notes, a Bessie Smith classic called "T'ain't Nobody's Bizness If I Do."

The music abruptly stopped as a spotlight illuminated the center of the stage. Bathed in blue, the ebon skin of Miss Sterling appeared gunmetal gray. She stood motionless, a steel statue wrapped in the finest silks. The audience held its collective breath as we waited for the artwork to come to life. Even the bottle tippers were quiet.

We didn't have to wait long as her eyes slowly opened and she took in the room. Her eyes pierced the darkness, as if she were looking at each one of us. That was talent. I knew full well the spotlight would blind her from seeing anything but the first row.

Merlot reached out and pulled the microphone closer to her full, red lips, as though she wanted to honor it with a kiss. Many men in the audience, Lee included, wanted to be that mic.

The piano man started blowing on the box again as she sang:

> *There ain't nothing I can do, or nothing I can say*
> *That folks don't criticize me.*
> *But I'm goin' to, do just as I want to anyways,*
> *And don't care if they despise me.*
> *If I should take a notion*
> *To jump into the ocean*
> *T'ain't nobody's bizness if I do, do, do.*

Her pipes were clean. She sang with Bessie's passion but wanted to step out from Miss Smith's shadow. Her rendition was clearly her own. She wasn't beautiful in the conventional sense; she was a bit too Rubenesque for me, yet she implied a level of grace that one didn't see in your average canary. Merlot was classic and everyone wants to own a classic.

I could see why Mendelssohn locked on to her. She was everything he wasn't, a yang to his yin. She was his taboo, and as she sang, she showed signs of knowing that she would forever be every man's taboo.

Dare to know me, Merlot implied, *and risk your soul.*

After the first number, the stage lit up and the rest of the band blew up a storm. She got friendly, talking to the front row about where they were from and taking requests. When she spoke, it came with a slow, Memphis drawl that didn't reflect her big-city upbringing—another indication that she knew exactly what she was doing up there. The fact she played small venues like this meant something held her back.

Merlot stayed focused on Lee longer than the rest. Through

the next songs, she flirted with him almost to the exclusion of the other patrons. This raised the hairs on the back of my neck. I checked Vincent's reaction and saw him cock an eyebrow. For his part, either Lee was a good actor or he was falling for her attentions, hook, line, and sinker.

How had Lee become the Alvin? Maybe she's still alive because she's in on the whole scheme. Archdeacon enlisted her help from the beginning to keep Mendelssohn in line. Could she still be here on Archdeacon's orders? The Hero Twins knew where we were going, so that meant Archdeacon did too, right? Had we walked into another trap? How did everyone stay one step ahead of our plans when we went to such pains to conceal them?

The thing I've learned about traps is everyone expects you to know it's a trap, but necessity forces you to enter it anyway. Our course was laid and all we could do was follow it.

Merlot walked back to her bandleader, and they had a little chat. He dug through a pile, pulled out some sheets, and distributed them to the others as she walked back up.

"I'd like to finish with a special number for you tonight. It was written by the great Sidney Bechet and originally sung by Margaret Johnson."

Her eyes got catty as she leaned over the top of the microphone; she talked the intro in a singsong style:

> Honey baby, there's one more thing I'd like to know
> Before it's my time to go.
> You know and I know too
> You've been running around ... all over town
> And now that your mama is Chicago bound ...

Merlot left the stage and walked up behind Lee. She twirled his hair for a moment then subtly cued the band. They broke out like measles as she sang:

> Who'll chop your suey when I'm gone?
> Who'll corn your fritters Sunday morn?

She moved to the front and leaned across Lee's table.

When you're feeling chilly ... And heat's your
    desire,
Who'll go down to your cellar and put coal on your
    fire?

The crowd whooped at Merlot's innuendo. The blues were as naughty as one could get without taking off clothes, and Miss Sterling sung them with raw sexuality. She made men think bad thoughts and women feel restless. All the audience members not made of stone would be heading back to their hotel rooms after this show.

She pulled Lee's chair back and sat on his lap. I wondered if she had room.

Tell me while I'm putting chili
On your con carne,
Who'll chop your suey when I'm gone?

Merlot returned to the stage, leaving a sweating Lee to his voyeurism. She finished up the number and thanked the crowd for coming. She blew Lee a kiss before heading behind the curtain. By all accounts, that was an invitation to her dressing room and Lee was ready to take her up on it.

In the hallway behind the lounge, he exclaimed, "What a woman! Two big smokestacks and a fully loaded caboose. I think I am in love. I go call wife and tell her I leaving her."

I grabbed Lee by the collar and pulled him away from the phone booth in his mind.

We found Merlot's dressing room door and knocked.

"Who is it?" she inquired from behind the closed door.

I gave her my best impersonation of Wan Lee. "I got an order of chop suey to go for Miss Sterling?"

I heard a giggle as she opened the door. Her eyes low, her voice sultry. "Now, kind sir. What type of lady do you take me—"

Merlot stopped dead when she saw my face. There was no hesitation. She knew me immediately. That must be why she landed the left hook to my jaw.

CHAPTER SIX

I t is a common belief that a woman's right hand could never be as strong as a man's. Take from that the left hand is on average weaker than the right, a wallop from a lady's south side shouldn't be more than a nuisance.

Not so with Merlot.

To my credit, I went neither out nor down. However, I did see spots when I shook my head clear of the blow.

"What the hell did you hit me with?"

"My fist! And you set one foot in this room, you're going to get another!"

Merlot pushed up to her full height, like a wild animal trying to scare off a predator. Lee came in from under Merlot's radar and grabbed both her wrists. At half her height, he had a struggle on his hands. She flung him around like a rag doll.

"Glass! Help!"

Merlot bared her teeth and tried to pull free from Lee's grip. Every time she pulled up, he held on with vice-like strength. To his delight, this would pull him off the ground and into her massive bosom. I'm not sure if he was even trying to subdue her anymore.

I shouldered both her and Lee into her dressing room and locked the door. I walked over to a phone on her armoire and yanked the cord free. Together, Lee and I managed to tie her wrists. Merlot continued to growl and kick at us. When I was content that she wasn't going to get her hands free, I pushed her back onto her bed. She tried to jump up, but I pushed her back again.

"I can do this all night, toots."

"Yeah, and if Charlie finds out you've touched me, he'll have you screaming all night!"

Concerned, Lee said, "If she mean Charlie the Spic, then he no one to mess around with, Glass. We need to find out what going on and leave fast!"

Everyone who had ever had to deal on the wrong side of the law knew the name Charlie the Spic. He was the only Hispanic to make it up the ranks to Big Barracuda status in the Chicago mob. His brutality was legendary, but so were his tastes.

"So that's how you stayed alive? Became one of Charlie's chippies, eh?"

Merlot spit venom at me. "I ain't nobody's whore. I'm under his protection, but I ain't never boiled the man's cabbage. And you'd have to kill me before I would."

She dropped the southern act and reverted to Chi-town street. It took some of the glitz away from her and I liked that. I could get down to brass tacks without feeling guilty.

I could tell my chin was red. I rubbed at it.

"Where'd you learn to throw a punch like that?"

"My brother, Tyrone Sterling. You may have heard of him?"

A chuckle from Lee had me curious. "Boxer, Glass. Current welterweight. He good."

"Yeah, and if Charlie doesn't get you, Ty will. So whatever you're gonna do, enjoy it, 'cause it'll be yer last wish."

"We no want your body, toots." Lee paused. "Well, maybe I do, but Glass here want your boyfriend, Mendleville."

"Mendelssohn," I corrected. "Jorge? Where is he?"

She faced away from me, not letting me lock eyes with her. "I know who you are. I seen your picture in the paper, and Jorge talked about you. Noel Glass, the inventor who done in all those people in pursuit of science. He wanted to vomit at just the mention of your name."

Merlot settled down some. She shook her locks around to get them clear of her face. She batted her eyes at Lee. "What's a handsome guy like you mixed up with riffraff like him?"

Her ploy didn't work, despite Lee's desire to find some way to make it work. He instead stayed true to form. "Listen, muffin, you work that magic on somebody else. We have business and we mean to get the skinny."

Close up, she was even better looking than on stage. I'd place her in her late twenties, though I'd guess things hadn't been so easy on her. She had the beginnings of crow's feet around her haunting eyes.

"Why'd you mark Lee here if you didn't know he was with me?"

She acted all haughty. "Mark? Mark nothing! He just caught my eye, classy gentleman that he is."

"Ha!" Lee scoffed. "Even my wife know I never 'classy.' She call me *buta no hana* , mean 'pig nose.' She don't say it as pet name either, toots. No, you smell my money."

Lee had her. Merlot resigned herself to the inevitable. With a sigh, she said, "Charlie calls me when there's a butter and egg man at one of the casinos. We usually give him a free ticket to my show. My spotter just thought it chance you were coming to see me already.

"My job is to make sure the mark stays at our casino. I give him a reason to stick around for the second show. There's an hour in between. Plenty of time for an out-of-towner with deep pockets to lose his shirt."

Lee had dropped that wad on purpose. That's why the nonchalant act. He must have picked out the spotter quickly and put on a show for him. It hadn't been Merlot or Charlie or Archdeacon who was one step ahead, but Lee.

"I'm going to ask again nicely. I need to find Mendelssohn. His life is in danger."

She guffawed. "Yeah, pull this finger, I sing 'Lady of Spain.'"

Originally, I wasn't going to give her anything I didn't need to, but she was getting on my nerves. I wanted to take her lofty ideas down a notch.

"Listen, sister. You think I'm some evil son of a bitch, but I'm going to tell you something you aren't going to like. I'm not the one who killed those people; your boyfriend did!"

"The hell you say!" She tossed her head violently. "That's bunk! Jorge ain't that type of man."

"The hell he do say, toots. General Archdeacon set Glass up. That is why we look for your squeeze, to get proof to clear his good name."

She shook her head violently again. "No, it's not true. I ain't going to believe it. It's a dirty lie! You're a filthy, dirty liar!" She lunged off the bed again before I could push her back down. She rammed into me and knocked me to the floor.

Merlot ran to the door and started screaming, "Help! Charlie! Somebody get Charlie!"

Lee was on her in a flash. He had his hand over her mouth, though he had to leap on her back to do so. They twisted around—he trying to stay on, she trying to shake him free.

I got back into action. I pulled out a handkerchief just as she clamped down on Lee's hand. He let go with a yelp and dropped to the floor. As she took in air to scream again, I stuffed the cloth in her mouth. I deposited her back on the bed, my hands locked around her wrists, my body to the side to avoid her shapely but powerful sticks.

"Why do you think Archdeacon set Jorge up here? Why do you think he has all those clearances? Did Jorge ever tell you about Tangie? You think I would have done anything that put her in danger? I thought I had checked everything and I *did*! And if I ever see that backstabbing sideshow freak again, I'm going to wring a confession out of him! You hear me? I'll kill him!"

I was breathing heavily; red tinted the edges of my vision. Merlot was truly scared; she recoiled in horror from me. Even Lee was taken aback. I wanted to break something, anything.

Three sharp raps sounded on the door. Lee went to open it, and I could hear him talking in hushed tones to Vincent. I had forgotten that we had left him outside as the button.

Lee closed and locked the door again. "Everything out there is jake. Are you?"

I controlled my breathing, let go of Merlot, and wiped my brow of sweat. "Yeah, I'm good. You ready to talk, Merlot, or should I just leave you bound and gagged until your next show?"

She nodded.

Lee asked, "She mean she want to talk or she want to be bound and gagged more?"

I could see in her eyes she would fess up. Fear had driven bravado away. "Take out the handkerchief, Lee."

The songbird blanched and cleared her mouth of the cloth taste. "I don't know where he is. That's the truth."

"Why? You two call it splits?"

She shook her head. "No, everything was good. It really was. He said he had something to do and disappeared. I looked for him, waited for him. I even had Charlie look into it. Jorge just took a powder. He must have been scared of something real bad. I never figured it would be you."

"Not me, sweetheart. I haven't made a blip on the radar in ten years. I only got dragged into this two days ago."

"But that other thing you said, about it being his fault, it don't make sense. He wasn't working for the military here. It was all privately funded."

Finally, she gave me something to lock on to. "What company?"

"I never knew the name. He called it *T.I.* Like, he'd come in and say, 'The guys down at T.I. need me to work tomorrow,' and that. Never the whole name."

I could find a company with those initials located in Nevada. Did Archdeacon have something going on the side? Or was this a totally new player, a piece of the puzzle I didn't have before?

"And the name Archdeacon never came up?"

She laughed. "Yeah, in the same breath, he'd curse you then Archdeacon. He hated the son of a bitch. That's why he went private. Said the military would never actually help anyone with what he was building. They'd just use it to make war." She was wistful. "He hated war, you know that. You worked with him for two years. You know his story. He lost his parents in the first war. He would have done anything to stop one."

Her romanticism had me all choked up. "Yeah, right. Even kill a room full of people, eh?"

She returned from her dream state hard. Her eyes destroyed me, tore me apart down to the molecular structure. She'd kill me given the chance. But I knew I planted a seed of doubt. She wouldn't be defending Jorge so adamantly if she weren't trying to convince herself. Her eyes told me that as well.

I couldn't fault what she was saying, though. I did know my assistant—long hours spent over blueprints, beers at the local pub. His parents' death carried an echo into the young man's life. When I left him, the world was gearing up for yet another war, and he was fervently against it. Yeah, he hated Hitler. We all did. He just believed there was a better way to solve the problem. Maybe assassination was the "better way" in his mind?

"How long he work for them, toots?"

She answered Lee's questions without the sneer she gave me. She was still trying to worm her way into his good graces. Her body language changed. When she talked to me, she balled her fists. When she talked to Lee, her hands were open, submissive on her lap. She wanted Lee to see her as a victim. She wanted to divide us, which told me she still wasn't won over to our side. Merlot was one smart cookie, I had to give her that. She was keeping stuff back, maybe important stuff. But what she gave me, if true, was a good start.

"Ever since his contract ended with the college. Maybe eight years ... or nine." She snarled at me again. "Plus, he said something about you ignoring a warning he had given you about the test."

"He never warned me about the test," I said.

"Not to your face. He said he had left you a note that you had to have read. I'm telling you the truth!"

She tried to keep up the tough act, but it was cracking. Under it, I saw eyes that pleaded for belief. Unshed tears hung on her lashes. Maybe she was trying to throw me off the trail. If I chased some fictional note, then it would give her time to contact Mendelssohn and have him bury himself even deeper. Again, there was what I knew about Jorge. If he was forced to gremlin the project, he might have tried to warn me. It was as good as a confession, so I went for it.

"Okay, where did he leave it?"

Merlot paused as she tried to remember their conversation. "He was stomping around, angry about something. This was about a year ago. He said it was all your fault. If you hadn't ignored the note he left in your ... book. Yeah, book. I asked him and he said your favorite book. You read it every night before a big test."

My brow furrowed as I thought back. She was right that I used to read from the same book before an experiment. It calmed my nerves so I could get to sleep.

Lee walked over to me. "Glass?"

"She's right, Lee. I did have a favorite book. If Jorge wanted to get a note to me unnoticed before the experiment that would be a good place to leave one. Over beers, we'd talk about things like pre-experiment habits. For him, it had been exercise. That's where his weight obsession started. He'd know that I'd pick up that book the night before. Only I hadn't that night."

Puzzled, Lee asked, "Why?"

My cheeks felt hot, and I looked at the carpet. I was cavalier when I talked to the guys about the women I rolled, but never about Tangie, never her.

"Oh." Lee put the pieces together in his head. He let the subject drop.

"So?" asked our hostage. "What about the book? You still have it?"

"I returned it to the college library. I wasn't going to be a scientist anymore, so it belonged back on the shelves. It might still be there."

"But will note still be there?"

"Yeah, maybe. It's not a popular book. Heck, I was the only one to check it out for three years before that. That's why I still had it; nobody else wanted it."

"Where does that leave me?" Merlot wanted to know.

Lee took the handkerchief and stuffed it back in her mouth. "Tied up until we out of here."

Merlot's eyes went wide with fury. We could still hear her muffled protests as we closed the door behind us.

"She'll be out of that in thirty seconds," I said.

"Then we outta town in twenty-five."

I thought about Merlot. She knew more than she said, I was certain of it, but there comes a point where you can't reason with a frail. They have to come to the decision to help you on their own. I doubted she'd roll over on Mendelssohn, even if she believed our story. She had given me a clue, though, and pointed me in a direction.

I was going back to NMIT.

Vincent was outside the dressing room when we stepped into the hallway. "I saw one of the Heroes."

"You sure? Where?"

"I caught the Jaguar's reflection in a window. It was quick." He checked for our buy-in. "You ready for this?"

If our preparations worked, I was ready. Otherwise, I was dead.

I got the item Lee had procured for me before we left Industry City. We stepped into the shadows and Lee helped me get ready.

The Hero Twins' appearance was opportune. While we didn't have much leeway, an organization as big as Charlie's requires some time to mobilize. Even if Merlot blabbed right away, which I doubted she would, they'd have to search for us. With the tip she gave us, we no longer had to follow her back to Mendelssohn. We had time to spring our own trap on the Mayans, then head straight for New Mexico.

Vincent took the car, leaving Lee and me to walk back to our hotel. We ducked down alleys; we didn't want to be caught in the open. This would force our stalkers to pursue us in the narrow confines of the side streets. Before lunch, Vincent had mapped out the alley he wanted us in.

At the pre-determined intersection, Lee peeled off down a different alley, leaving me solo.

We knew our plumbers wanted to act fast before the fluid left my pipes. I ticked off the seconds until I was confident Lee and Vincent were in place.

I ran. It didn't take long before I heard the crunching of gravel behind me. A single set of footfalls, his backup must've gone to the rooftops.

I went down the chosen street and spun at the dead end. My would-be killer entered the alley's opening. His jumpsuit was dark as midnight and blending into the alley. All I could clearly see was his jaguar mask with its ancient, frozen laugh as he raised the MASER at me.

The weapon was like something I expected to see on the cover of a Buck Rogers pulp, a large rifle-thing with a disc around the muzzle. A cord ran from below the stock to a backpack. I could hear the hum as it charged up.

I made for the gat in my shoulder holster, but jaguar boy pulled his trigger first. The electromagnetic wave wasn't visible to the naked eye, but I could imagine its trajectory as it struck me. Instinct and speed had caused him to aim for my chest, not my head. Had I donned a helmet, our ruse wouldn't have worked.

Sparks flew as I fell backward.

From the corner of my eye, I watched the hit man cock his head to one side. He was obviously puzzled at why I hadn't exploded. He moved closer but kept the device trained on me. Maybe he hoped my heart had exploded … or my brain.

There was a cough behind him, and the Hero Twin turned around and discovered Lee with a gun drawn. As I stood, the Jaguar sidestepped to keep us both in his field of vision.

I hated to be indebted to Mendelssohn, who I presumed had designed the weapon. He had chosen a narrow beam deployment, as opposed to a field burst. I opened my trench coat and showed the X-ray technician vest I wore. The flexible, lead-lined smock was great against the targeted beam but would have been useless against an area effect. The thing was hell to run in, though.

The Hero Twin dropped his useless weapon and drew two blades in its place. Lee gave him the heat before he could take three steps toward me.

"What? He think I fight fair? Honor no good in real world."

I paid no attention to Lee. Not only was I happy to still be sucking air, I was just as excited to examine the MASER. I knelt down by it. I could still hear the hum of its power source. Everything was years ahead of its time.

So focused was I on the weapon, I never heard the grenade hit the ground near me.

Luckily, Lee did.

He yanked me to my feet and threw me around the corner so quickly, everything blurred. He was on top of me when the concussion hit us. After a moment, Lee got up and I opened my eyes. Vincent stared down at me, his lips moving but no words reached my brain. The two pulled me to my Buster Browns. I got the gist of what Vincent was saying.

We have to go!

People were coming down the alleyway, and I could see the telltale red and blue of police lights reflecting off buildings in the distance. We supported each other, Lee and I hobbling slower than Vincent would have liked. The ringing quieted and I started to hear sirens and commotion. Vincent directed us to the rental, our meager belongings already packed in.

"How long before we ID'd?" Lee said much too loudly.

"Depends on Miss Sterling and whether she'll talk," Vincent suggested from behind the wheel.

I intentionally kept my voice lower, trying not to overcompensate for the lack of hearing.

"Where'd the grenade come from?"

"The other Hero Twin." Vincent gunned the engine, not looking directly at me.

"How'd you miss him?"

Vincent kept his eyes forward as if the road needed all his attention. "I-I don't know. I got topside and waited. When I found him, he already hovered over you two. I managed to get a shot off, but not until after I saw him drop the grenade."

For a bodyguard, he was a disappointment, and I decided to express my displeasure.

"Damn it, Vincent! You need to get with the program. Since you've been my bodyguard, my life has been in jeopardy twice. I don't think I can survive a third time."

The hulking form said nothing, so it surprised me when Lee came to his defense.

"Ack, Glass. Give man a break. We did get one of them."

Yeah, I thought, *and now there'll be a brother looking for revenge. This won't be just a job to him anymore. It'll be personal.*

CHAPTER SEVEN

We drove in silence through the night, each of us taking a shift behind the wheel and stopping only for roadside bathroom breaks and cups of coffee. We heard no APBs over the radio, but that didn't help me sleep any. Too much information danced upstairs for me to drift off.

There was a new player, someone powerful enough to manipulate events. They'd be the ones behind the sabotage, Mendelssohn's disappearance and the Hero Twins.

Well, make that twin.

I knew nothing about this person or persons, nothing about the company they worked for, nothing about their motives. They could be anywhere. Mr. X could be one of the guys in the car with me. All I really knew was that they wanted me dead.

I ruled out Lee. He'd had plenty of opportunities to kill me. Whatever his motives were, they depended on my being alive. Vincent, on the other hand, had flubbed at least one attempt to protect my life, most likely two. He could be intentionally putting me in jeopardy, but that was counterintuitive to our situation as well. Why even pretend to be on my side? There were easier ways to kill me.

This was ridiculous. I needed more cards. I needed someone's tell.

I needed a drink.

At one of the pit stops, Vincent excused himself to make a phone call, saying that he still had contacts he could trust in

Industry City and he'd see what static was on the line. He came back moments later, saying his contact hadn't heard anything yet, but Chance City was a remote location. It might take a day.

We headed south to Arizona then veered north from Flagstaff, having had to skirt around the little hole in the ground called the Grand Canyon. From there, we turned east before the Four Corners area. By sunup, I saw the sign for T'laquepaque, New Mexico.

The town was named after an Indian god, and you could see his hieroglyph along with the dancing *Kokopellis* all over town. The mines that once supported the area had long since been tapped out. There were no oil deposits, and the scenery was better in Taos. There was no other industry in town save for the New Mexico Institute of Technology.

NMIT was founded in the early twenties, shortly after World War I. A new breed of engineers had come back from the war, tougher and worn by combat conditions. Their idea was to put design and technology in place before the need arose. Unlike their apprentice-trained predecessors, these guys wanted future generations prepared for all contingencies, though none could have predicted the world being back at war in just two decades. The knowledge imbued on a generation of engineers became a dagger in the Nazis heart. By building and blowing up bridges in quick order, the Allies moved forward while the Nazis were held back.

The founders of NMIT wanted their school to train only the best of the best. They wanted to compete with Massachusetts, California, and London. The recruiters grabbed geniuses before they had even hit puberty. I was one of those, set to graduate at sixteen. They taught me the wonders of science, and in return I sold my soul to the school, coming back to be a professor after spending very little time in the real world.

The college sat in an area free of distractions, the school believing students and faculty would put education above all else.

We tried, but there was always room for … distractions.

Throttle jockeys found flat roads for quarter-mile strips.

Flagstaff had skiing and Albuquerque had nightlife, after a fashion.

Plus, bored students and staff would forever find great pleasure in upsetting the locals.

The people of T'laquepaque were a mix of Mexicans and Indians. They were regularly looked down upon by many intellectual "gods" of NMIT. The locals, who regularly worked their asses off in servitude, would then spit in the food of said gods. It was a balanced existence.

I checked my watch. It was 6:30 a.m., and I told Lee to pull into a Hank's Diner. I could see four of my former colleagues through the glass of the diner's window. We always took the same table toward the back because of our heated discussions. Will this experiment work or fail? Will they split the atom or not? Did Franklin really fly a kite, or was it a metaphor?

Yeah, it pales in comparison to whether the Yankees will take the pennant this year, but for the learned, we were every bit as passionate as sport fans.

I remembered the first time I brought Tangie to the otherwise all-male group. They were nervous having a female invade their sanctum of knowledge. That was until she challenged the head of the chemistry department, Fred Ligerman, on his theory that there were no more naturally occurring elements left to be discovered, with astatine having been produced in a lab that year. Tangie argued that we could never be sure since there were still so many periodic equations left unaccounted for.

The two were hopping mad by the time we left; me physically dragging Tangie away before she could gouge Fred's eyes out. It was his fault for insinuating her intelligence could be biologically or hormonally adjusted. One week later, she came back with an article written by McMillan and Abelson on their discovery of neptunium, and while it was a by-product of nuclear research, it could be found in trace quantities within the natural decay of uranium. From then on, Fred, the cynic, always placed himself at odds with Tangie, the pragmatist, right up until the day she died.

Fred sat there. He never drank coffee, only tea. He squeezed a lemon wedge into his cup. I could see steam rising from it.

I got out of the car and breathed in the crisp, dry New Mexico morning air.

Vincent asked, "Are you sure this is a good idea? You are wanted by the military as a spy. They could turn you in."

"It's your job to make sure they don't succeed."

Lee stayed. "Bring me bagel with lots of cream cheese, okay?"

I walked up to the door, opened it, and stepped back in time.

"Good morning, gents!"

Besides the cook, the waitress, and my four former compatriots, the place was empty. This made Vincent's job easier. He turned the diner's sign to *CLOSED* and locked the door.

"We don't have much time. Cops come here for coffee, right?" he whispered to me.

I nodded and moved down to the booth. I could hear Vincent talking with the waitress about a big tip if they behaved.

The foursome froze in midbite. I took a seat next to Tangie's favorite sparring partner, Fred. His bald head and handlebar mustache shined like a car with a new coat of wax.

"Fred! How are things going in chemical engineering these days?" I knew Fred's instinct would be to brag. That's why I chose him first, to break the ice, but he was too scared to open up. A "fine" was all I got.

I turned to Dr. Horatio Chastain, the head of biology with so many letters after his name, you could play Scrabble with them. Perfectly groomed, as always, Horatio showed the telltale signs of age. Strands of gray poking through his dyed-black hair. Still in a state of shock from my sudden appearance, his fork hovered above his plate. Yolk from his standard fare, Adam and Eve on a raft, dripped onto the plate.

"I've been keeping up on the news, Doctor. You're going to work with Salk on the polio vaccine?"

"Well, yes. That is a true thing you are saying. It should be a rewarding experience."

"Cut the crap, Glass. The small talk isn't going to cut it here."

This came from my arch nemesis, Rockford Stone, Esq. Yeah, I know the name Rocky Stone seems redundant, but I have heard worse. Rocky thought he was a king bee despite his rotund size. He threw his power around, what little he had, until he'd gotten himself the illustrious Assistant Dean position.

"You're right, Rocky. Must be all that time you spend down in Theoretical Math. You have my motives plotted out to the tenth decimal. I'm not here for small talk. I came here to tell you something."

Rocky set his hefty jowls to launch a tirade of insults at me when we all turned to a small voice from next to him.

"W-w-we don't want to hear it, y-y-you traitor."

Gray-haired and meek Yousev Studanko hardly ever spoke up at our group meetings, patient to wait for lulls in the conversation. Sometimes he didn't speak at all. We had gotten used to asking him if he had any thoughts by the end of breakfast. His speaking out of turn was new.

"Whoa, Yousev. I know I've been gone a while, but this? You've changed more than these three combined if you're now taking the bull by the horns these days."

But Rocky, Fred, and Horatio all shook their heads, as flabbergasted as I was.

"Y-y-you have no right to involve us in your c-c-crimes."

I was proud that the head of electronics engineering had challenged me, but I was concerned of what would cause him to do so. He was meek, the "inheritor of the Earth" type. His forthrightness threw me off my game to the point I almost forgot what I came there to say.

"*The Atlantis* designs are done. I finally got them to work."

In many ways, the car had been a pet project for all of us since I relied heavily on their knowledge to solve problems during the initial design stage. I knew only what I knew, so I pumped them for as much of their input as I could get away with and not have to put all our names on it. Some car enthusiasts I know buy a fixer-upper and have the guys come over on weekends to work on it. When we got together, we dreamt the car. The same love was there, regardless. Three out of the four scientists launched into a myriad of questions, thoughts of treachery long forgotten. Yousev sat in his stew.

I answered as many of the questions as I could in rapid succession: "Yes, it was the catalytic converter ... No, the oxygen-hydrogen mix didn't need to be adjusted past where we had set it … I don't know how many miles to the gallon it will get. It's not built yet."

They stopped at this last statement and stared.

"Yet?" said Rocky. "Who'd invest in it? Given your suspicious history and the fact you've been accused of being a traitor, no one will touch you."

I hung on the word *accused*. It wasn't like Rocky to give me the benefit of the doubt, which led me to believe he knew something. What could he have heard?

He had brought up a point I had pushed to the back of my mind. What did Reece's death do to *The Atlantis*'s prototype? The deal had been to track down the people trying to kill Reece and stop them; then he'd build my car. And while I still wanted to get Mendelssohn for my own reasons, would I be back at square one when that was done?

Sheepishly I said, "Well, I had a backer, but he sort of … died."

Vincent had eavesdropped on the conversation. He interjected, "He still does. Little Technologies still plans to finance him, once he clears his name."

"What is this you say about clearing your name?" Chastain inquired.

"I was framed, gentlemen. I didn't screw up the experiment; I was screwed by Mendelssohn. And someone pulled his strings."

This brought me a round of contemplative looks from the house. They tested the theory like any scientific proposal. No one leaped up with a conclusion, though. Yousev got up, saying he was going to be sick, and headed for the bathroom.

"Archdeacon was down here yesterday looking for you," voiced Fred. "We're supposed to report you if you showed up here."

"That's fine. I don't want to drag you guys in as accomplices. I just need to get something from the school and I'll be gone. Just give me a couple of hours' head start, if you would?"

Horatio chimed in. "This is true, what you say about Mendelssohn?"

"Yeah, he built a weapon out of the magnetron. I've heard what it can do, and it's not pretty. I barely survived an encounter with it. This is top-secret stuff, guys. I don't want you being the next victims. Keep out of Archdeacon's or Mendelssohn's way."

Fred offered, "We haven't seen Mendelssohn in a year."

"Yeah," added Rocky. "Last I heard he was going to see you."

"What?" I was livid.

Rocky looked down at his half-eaten Danish, hating that he had opened his mouth at all.

"Yes, Rocky. Do elaborate. This is the first we have heard such a thing."

Rocky coughed it up. "Okay, fine! I wasn't supposed to tell anyone. I was in good with Mendelssohn, since we both sort of hated you. I mean, I never really hated you, but didn't … err, don't like you, that is for sure." This was no screaming headline. Not everyone liked me, which was fine. It made me work harder and made the victories sweeter. "So Mendelssohn would stop by when he was in town," he admitted. "The last time, about a year ago, he came in all agitated, asked if I had an address for you. I got it from Amanda's office and then he left."

Amanda Orchid, as former dean of Research and Development Technologies, had my current address because she had to hold my last check for a year, due to nondisclosure agreements. Once I was settled in, I sent her a note with the location. I hoped for some sort of letter with it, something to say how sorry she felt for Tangie, for me, but she had grown cold, bitter after the experiment. The shock of its happening on her campus, while she was in charge, had altered her deep inside, maybe even in that stuff they were calling DNA. I'd read she had finally made dean after being passed up twice.

"How is the head dean doing?" I inquired.

"Still mad at you for making her wait another six years for the title. She would have had it back then, well, you know. She travels a lot now. We don't see her much. I fill in for her while she's gone," Rocky answered.

"I knew it'd come to her in time, but she didn't need to take it so personally. It was never her fault. Accepting that truth is freeing."

"Speaking of time, Boss." Vincent indicated the door. Someone was looking in, saw Vincent, saw the gun, and ran away.

"Looks like my time is up. You may not have to wait an hour after all."

I made to leave, but Fred grabbed my sleeve. "They won't hear about you from me. For Tangie's sake."

Horatio echoed him, "For Tangie." Even Rocky gave a quick nod.

"Thank you. I really mean that. Thank you."

I experienced something right then. The closest description I can come up with is a sense of brotherhood. I had been judged by my peers, and they were willing to trust me.

All save for Yousev.

"Where *is* Yousev?" I turned to look. "Still in the can?" Vincent dragged me away. "We don't have time."

"We will talk to him, for sure," called Horatio as we left.

Vincent dropped a century on the counter for the waitress, and we sprinted to our waiting car.

"We need to get to the school before they open. There'll be less people."

We burned rubber.

"Too bad place not a drive-in, like burger place. Hey! Where my bagel?"

* * *

Lee told us he had seen Yousev bolt from the back of the diner just before we came out. It was be a safe bet he'd tell the cops where we were heading.

The campus only had one story, done in the standard adobe fashion of the region. The offices, student union, cafeteria, and library formed the central hub. Classrooms and labs branched off the center like an Anasazi drawing of the sun. Each wing was a different department of study, such as my former playground, theoretical sciences.

The library itself was situated along an outer wall, so getting in unobserved wouldn't be difficult this time of day. If the overworked and underpaid campus security did get a whiff of us, dollars to doughnuts they'd call for backup before taking any action.

"So what we after in here again?"

"A book."

"What type of book?" Vincent asked.

"It's a biography. Nothing special. Unassuming. We may have to search for it if they've changed the place around."

"Great! What it called?"

"*Passages from the Life of a Philosopher* by Charles Babbage."

We pulled right up on the sidewalk by the library's main doors. I took a deep breath and got out.

"There could be library staff getting ready to open."

Vincent and Lee both drew guns. I didn't like the way this was going down. Things were happening too fast. I wanted stealth when I planned this, a classic B&E. What I got resembled a snatch and grab. Reluctantly, I drew my gun. Vincent had no trouble opening the locked door.

There were no lights on, just the morning sun filtering in through the windows. I called out, "Vincent, keep an eye on the door. Lee, there will be a file with checkout cards. The titles are arranged by author. See if the book has been checked out."

"Spell *Babbage*."

I did. Lee kept talking as I went to see if it was on the shelf. "Who this Babbage?"

"He was many things, but foremost he was an inventor like me. I liked reading his journals because he was the nineteenth century's greatest success and failure."

"How could he be both?" Vincent inquired.

"Despite a lot of small successes and being a great scholar and teacher, his big thing, the one to make or break him, was the world's first computer."

"What that?" asked Lee.

I bent down to where the book would be if it had been filed correctly. No luck.

"It's a machine that can do math really fast. Thousands of calculations in a second. He invented it a century ago. Only, it didn't work, or so everyone thought."

I moved to the front where Lee was going through a stack of cards. "It seems that he was only off by a couple of calculations, but there was such an uproar made about its failure that Babbage never tried it again. I did an essay in high school on what science would be like today if it had worked."

Lee peered up from his task. "He sound not that much different than you."

It was a familiar thought.

"Got it. No one check it out since you, except for one guy: Yousev Stu … Stud …"

"Studanko?"

Of course! The head of electronics meant working in the realm of computers. He would be one of the few people who might pick up that book. He's probably seen the note.

"He knew. The little shit knew. That's why he was exceptionally nervous at the diner."

"Wasn't he a friend of yours, Mr. Glass?"

"Friend or not, he's too much of a wallflower to get involved. He's probably had ulcers since he read it, not knowing what to do."

"Where you think he is now?"

I calculated. "He wouldn't go to his office knowing that I was on the way here. Since I mentioned coming to the campus, he must have figured I'm after that note. Something like that he would have hid … or destroyed. My guess is he's at home in a tizzy about what to do with it."

Vincent piloted the boat off campus, just in case we were spotted.

I trusted his ability to lose a tail over Lee's.

Yousev's house was a small, one-bedroom affair not far from the campus. The front door was wide open.

"This doesn't bode well." My bodyguard took the lead, gun drawn.

"Either he flew the coop very quickly or he not alone." The detective in me knew there was another possibility.

I didn't bother to draw a gun. Between Sydney Greenstreet and Peter Lorre, we had enough firepower. We cautiously entered a living room-turned-study area. He, like I, had converted areas of his place into a workshop. There were benches arrayed with all manner of electronic testing equipment.

In a corner was a floor-to-ceiling metal box loaded with hundreds of lights, switches, and two tape reels. When Yousev brought his work home with him, he really brought it home. I'd seen pictures of computers, but never one up close. I wished I'd had all day to play with it.

It didn't seem that much time had passed since the encounter at the diner, but whoever had ransacked the place had done a thorough job. There wasn't a drawer that wasn't turned over or a couch cushion not shredded.

Vincent moved quickly through the place, checking to see if the intruders were still there. It didn't take long for an "all clear" sign.

"The rest of the house is not nearly as messed up as this. Whoever it was didn't get a chance to do a thorough job."

"Maybe something spook them?"

We spotted Yousev's diminutive body sticking out from an overturned bookshelf. Vincent flipped the wooden rack off him. A quick check of his pulse confirmed my instincts.

Just one more death to avenge.

"Don't touch anything else," I told them, "not until we have some gloves."

I found a couple of pairs under the sink. I tossed one set to Lee. They wouldn't have fit Vincent anyway. He took up a position by the door after carefully closing it with his elbow. Lee got a towel and wiped our prints off of anything we had already touched.

Once we removed the scattered books, I saw that Yousev had taken two shots in the back. It was a rotten way for the shy, little man to go. They had not passed through, so it had been a small-caliber gun. Why had they pushed the bookcase down on top of him if he was already dead?

I looked at his position in relation to the shelving unit. He was pointing toward it. I moved more books and found a smear of blood along the carpet. Yousev had been shot closer to the door. I did some quick calculations.

"Stand here," I told Lee. He was close to Yousev's size. I drew imaginary lines from the impacts points and gauged the originating point by estimating the velocity of a small handgun bullet. If I was right, then the killer had been standing in the doorway to the kitchen. He had dragged himself across the floor to the bookshelf. He must have wanted something on it. I looked at the bottom shelf. There were scratches, like fingers had gripped the board and slid off. I found a similar set on the next shelf.

"Yousev was pulling himself up, trying to reach something."

"Found the book," Vincent called out. "It was between the mattresses. No note."

I followed the curve of Yousev's arm to find a decidedly different book within his reach, *Shape of Things to Come* by H.G. Wells.

I retrieved it and flipped through the pages. While Yousev had highlighted many passages and there were many jotted notes, nothing jumped off the pages at me.

Vincent was suddenly alert and moved to the window. "Damn!"

Lee joined him and also cursed. He cocked his head to me. "Company."

I still leaned over the body when I heard the voice. It was rife with the local accent, and it sent a chill down my spine.

"Noel Glass, we know you are in there. The boys and I would like to have a little talk with you. If you could please join us outside, with your hands up?"

I went to a window and peaked out from behind the drapes covering it. Three squad cars sat perpendicular to the house. Eight officers crouched behind them, guns drawn.

"It would be Vasquez."

Vincent gave me the eyebrow. "History?"

"Yeah, Armando Vasquez. I subbed at the high school as a science teacher. I had to give his son an *F*. Next thing I know, I'm getting speeding tickets, parking tickets, and my car towed. When I slipped away from town, he was the one waiting on the outskirts to make sure I was gone for good."

"Guy sure hold a grudge, eh?"

Vincent turned to Lee. "Give me your gun."

Lee handed over the weapon without consternation. He took

Babbage's autobiography in exchange.

Vincent scanned the arrayed officers. "Okay, if this doesn't work, you crawl out on your bellies, hands in the air, got it?"

"What—?" I started to ask, but he was already through the door.

I can honestly say that I have never seen its like before and most likely never will again.

Vincent stood sideways, making the smallest target possible. He held his monster .357 in his right hand and Lee's .45 in his left. He pivoted each arm, making the smallest corrections to his aim as he fired. He took great care not to hit any of the officers, instead making their vehicles the brunt of his fury. The .357 sounded like cannon fire as he squeezed off shots. The bullets punched through the metal of the cruisers to embed in the engine blocks. The previously idling cars sputtered to a stop, and the hiss of escaping coolant could be heard between blasts. With the gun in his left hand, Vincent shattered glass and blew out tires. When he was done, none of the cars would be running, but not one lawman was injured. He'd let them all flee the barrage. It was the type of mechanical precision you saw in a factory that used automation.

An officer had managed to sneak around the side of Yousev's house. Vincent saw him just in time to take the blast of the man's shotgun in the gut. My bodyguard flew across the porch, spread-eagled, and lay nearly motionless. I could see the heaving of his chest. Blood began to pool under him, but at least he continued breathing.

The officer kicked the guns away from Vincent's hands and yelled for us to come out. We crawled on our bellies as Vincent suggested, our hands clearly not brandishing firearms. We didn't get as many kicks and beatings as I had expected. I guess they were still too shook up.

Cops ran in and out of the house while others watched over Vincent's prone form. One had a towel and was pressing it down on the bodyguard's stomach, staunching the flow of blood.

Another officer reported to Vasquez, "It's just like the guy on the phone said, Chief. They killed that teacher."

Vasquez was happy … not about the report of Yousev's death, but at having caught me at the scene of a crime. It was a crime he could implicate me for and collect not only a healthy reward, but also keep his "no unsolved murders in T'laquepaque" reputation intact.

I'm not saying this guy delights in his job or in doing it well, he just hates to lose. That it was me he'd beaten was all icing for him. I couldn't even begin to defend myself. I had nothing to offer, no facts, not even names worth a crap. He had me dead to rights.

I heard an ambulance coming down the road as we were driven off in the only cruiser fixable. I wondered if that same meat wagon would be the one to claim our bodies from the desert after we were hanged.

CHAPTER EIGHT

Lee and I sat in a musty cell. Its disuse hadn't surprised me. As the TPD drove us through town, I didn't see anything that could be called change. Occasionally, locals got embalmed and started a fight, but since the locals were thicker than thieves, the arresting officer usually just dropped the offender off at home.

But then there were the occasional college students needing to let off a little steam. Since it was a college of geniuses, however, the pranks were more of an intellectual nature. The traditional target of NMIT boredom was the mayor's pool.

In the past, the water in the pool has been turned into a solid, a gas, and a gelatin-like substance. It has changed colors, temperatures, and chlorine levels, sometimes while the mayor was swimming in it.

When the guilty party was caught, they might have spent a couple of hours in jail, but normally they were let go with a warning. I say normally because this wasn't the first time I had spent a night in this cell.

When I first came to the school as a student, my reputation had preceded me. My right of passage was expected to top everything done before. As it is, I'm sure it is still talked of in the halls of the school.

But then how was I to know it would be the mayor, not his beautiful twenty-one-year-old daughter, who would have his bathing suit dissolved? Or that there would be a party … with the governor in attendance?

I look back at times like that, when I had the world by the short hairs. I was respected by the staff, the students, and the woman I loved. Today I had crapped out. I would probably be dead in twenty-four hours, branded a traitor and a failure.

It seemed like the world had conspired against me. What could I have done differently?

You could have read your damn book that night, that's what!

The note was gone, and whoever had killed Yousev and Reece wasn't just going to confess his crimes, regardless of if I asked him nicely or not.

Lee was sleeping off the rough treatment. I should have done this alone. Wan may have come into this voluntarily, but loyalty like that is hard to keep. Friends who stick out their necks one too many times eventually get their heads lopped off. I thought about bargaining for his release but figured the prosecutors would probably need a "Korean" spy to go along with my guilt. Lee would get what I got, and that made me angry.

I heard someone opening the outer door to the jail. Vasquez strutted in, the cock of the walk.

"You ladies up for some company? You have a visitor."

Smiling, he stepped aside. Vasquez liked being the one in control. He enjoyed saying who could or could not come in. That didn't surprise me. Who he let in did.

Fred Ligerman looked more out of place here than he would at a sorority party. He sized up the surroundings as he shuffled in nervously. Our jailer didn't bother to let him into our cell. That was reserved for mouthpieces and hymn-hustlers. Nor did he completely leave. He propped a chair in the doorway and swung his overly large set of keys in an annoying fashion.

"Fred? What are you doing here?"

Fred leaned close enough to the bars that his mustache touched. His voice was unsure, nervous. "You didn't kill him, right? The three of us decided that you knew Yousev well enough to make him cave in under pressure. You could get whatever you needed without having to kill him, so that meant someone else did, right?"

"Right, Fred. He was dead when we got there."

The scientist was relieved. "Good! Then I can give you this."

He offered his hand. It was a strange gesture. Did he want to thank me for not killing Yousev?

When I took the hand, I realized there was something in it. He had palmed me a note. He glanced down at my hand to make sure I had gotten it. Fred smiled nervously.

"Things were never the same after Tangie and you ..." He reexamined his thoughts. "Well, after you left. We still do the same things, but there isn't really any heart in them anymore. If you get yourself out of this mess, come back, okay? We all agreed, even Rocky. We'd love to have you back, even after what happened to Yousev."

I was surprised that these men of science, who rarely talked about anything but facts and equations, were ... what? Sentimental? There was always an unspoken respect for each other, but no one would dare verbalize it. Fred had been chosen to speak their first honest words of affection. I needed to repay the compliment with the same honesty.

"I doubt I'll be back. I'm pretty sure I'm a short-timer, but even if I'm not, I can't go back to the way things were."

Fred was disappointed, so I continued. "But that doesn't mean you have to go on trying to live like nothing happened. If you're not enjoying life the way it is, then do something different. Throw a party in my honor. Make it a 'Noel Glass Is Dead' party."

He must have thought me deranged; he wouldn't meet my eyes.

"You know, Fred? I've never told anyone the formula for the bathing suit-dissolving chemical."

Fred slowly raised his eyes to mine and gave me a mischievous grin.

After explaining the components and their mix, Fred shook my hand earnestly.

"Good luck, Glass. Be safe, okay?"

"As safe as I can be."

After Fred left, I read the note. It had two pieces of information.

The first was that my big friend had disappeared from the hospital despite a gunshot wound and armed guard.

The second was Mendelssohn's address in Industry City, probably from Rocky.

It was a while later, as I was contemplating using the toilet in the corner, I heard the telltale rattling of keys again. Vasquez entered, sans the shit-eating grin he had last time. In fact, he was pissed. A second man, dressed in a business suit and carrying a briefcase, followed him in.

"Your lawyer is here."

I kicked Lee, who woke with a start.

Vasquez addressed the newcomer. "You have five minutes, but I get to hold them without bail, seeing they're wanted on federal charges. A representative of the United States government is expected within the hour, so you'll have to continue your business with them."

He spoke with the arrogance of someone who had seen the end of a movie. Vasquez opened the cell door, let in our mouthpiece, relocked the door, and walked out of the area.

I sized up this new guy. He was nearly as big as Vincent; however, be it youth or training, he seemed slicker, more like a Kodiak bear than an ape. Finding nowhere comfortable to sit, he crouched down by us instead.

"I know not if they listen to us."

His accent was thick. I recognized it from having worked with so many foreign scientists over the years: Russian, probably the Leningrad region.

"Do you speak Russian?"

I shook my head no, but Lee nodded.

"You do?" I asked. He could barely speak English.

"I have dealings with Russians." He tried to look convincing. "As produce distributor."

"Uh-huh," I commented noncommittally.

The lawyer said a couple of things to Lee, who then glanced at his watch. Lee nodded and responded in what sounded like the affirmative. The man then opened his briefcase and pulled aside some papers to reveal a false bottom.

I asked Lee what was up as the man handed him a small, yellow package.

Lee spoke barely above a whisper. "One minute after he leaves, we are to stand against the bars and pull this string."

I didn't like the way this looked. I had flown before and had a fair assessment of what the small package was.

Our lawyer nodded, got up, and called for the jailer to let him out.

He turned as he left and winked. Lee acknowledged the signal.

I was paranoid. "What's going on, Lee? Who was that? Why is he helping us? What's going to happen in one minute?"

"Actually, in about thirty seconds now."

Lee was being coy. Whether it was to tease me or pay me back for the beating he got, I'll never know. He causally got up from the cot and made his way to the bars of the cell.

"Okay, I'll play. What is going to happen in thirty seconds?"

"Ten."

I was losing my patience. "Tell me now!"

Lee smiled. "We going to hit wall, Glass. Big time!"

Lee pulled the ring on the portable flotation device. It sprang to life just as the back of the cell exploded in a shower of sound and dust. My ears were still ringing when a second explosion rocked the front of the police station.

A voice carried through the ensuing chaos, "You come! Now!"

I peeked behind our raft, and there was our lawyer, now holding a machine gun and dressed in a flak vest. He was motioning to us with his hand.

"You come! Now!" he said again.

What the hell? What's one frying pan compared to another? I wouldn't be any less dead for leaving now.

A jeep idled on the other side of the blast point. A second man, who was dressed like the first but with small wire rims in front of his eyes, sat behind the wheel, and in the back seat …

"Vincent?"

My bodyguard looked like death warmed over. He tried to smile, but there was so little life in him, the best I got was a smirk.

The jail door opened. The bear laid down suppressing fire that kept Vasquez and his men pinned. We got into the jeep and made for the hills.

"How? Why? What was that stunt you pulled back at Yousev's?" was all I could ask as we bumped over back roads. I didn't want to task Vincent, but I wanted to know what was going on. Forces were moving us forward, and I had no clue where.

"I decided it would be easier to break out of the hospital than jail."

I stared at his swollen gut. I could see it was wrapped with thick layers of bloody gauze.

Our lawyer—though I had trouble still thinking of him as such—leaned over and said something in Russian to Vincent, who answered in the same tongue.

I could see it now, once Vincent started talking in Russian. I could see his roots, his Cossack heritage. I chastised myself for not having placed it earlier, but sometimes X doesn't equal Z without Y.

Lee filled in the blanks. "We heading for mountains. They have safe house there. He expects that once Archdeacon hears of breakout, he send air support.

"Oh," Lee added, "and he called Vincent 'Comrade Rezvoi.'"

Great! I thought. *Now I really am cavorting with spies!*

*   *   *

The desert brush gave way to evergreen trees then snow-laden woods. Once we entered the Sangre de Cristo Mountains, the driver took us up rugged trails that tossed us about. Lee and I did our best to stabilize Vincent, but he frequently winced in pain.

The path became increasingly covered in snow and we lost traction twice. Our trek eventually brought us to a remote cabin. I would've missed it were we not beside it. A white tarp draped over the roof blended it in to the surroundings.

We got out and hauled the pain-racked Comrade Rezvoi into the building.

The driver barked orders once we got him on the bed, pointing to each of us in turn. "Sacha, tend to Vadim's wounds. You, Jap man, start canned fire and get water boiling. Sacha will need it. You, scientist, write up list of supplies we will need for long stay and then make up three cots."

I stood my ground firmly. It wasn't that I couldn't take orders; I just didn't like the guy's attitude. "You know, I'm grateful and all for the rescue, but I didn't come here to be your housewife. So if you don't mind, I'm not going to do a goddamn thing until I get some answers."

Our host growled, "I do not have time to make scared little scientist happy. I go to cover our track so your CIA friends do not find us. When I get back, I think about telling you some things, or maybe I just kill you for fun. It depend on whether you have done things I ask by time I return."

I watched him go. He got on a snowmobile with a small cannon mounted on the back. I'd seen something similar in a *Popular Science* magazine a few years back. It looked like a snow cannon. Larger ones were just starting to be used at ski resorts. Had Vincent stolen a trade secret of Reece's? The man had technologies way ahead of everyone else. It would make sense.

Sacha came out for a bowl filled with boiling water. He stopped by a medicine chest and grabbed fresh gauze and some instruments. I got my first real look at him. He was smoother than either Vincent or the bear. His hair, though mussed, was blond and feathery. He had small, round glasses and a slightly offset nose. Overall, he seemed much safer to be around than his cohorts.

After a few minutes, I heard Vincent yell out once then silence. When Sacha came out again, his hands were covered in blood. He disposed of the old bandages and washed up before joining us in the living room. We sat huddled around the Sterno fire.

"He will live. He may be able to eat in the morning but broth only. It will take time for the wounds to heal."

"How did he survive a gut shot like that?"

Sacha laughed. "He is truly amazing man. Since he was little boy, he trained to endure all sorts of pain. He can tense up his … um?" He indicated the muscles around the lower stomach region.

"The abdomen?" I suggested, filling in the blank.

"The breadbasket," Lee colorfully added.

"Yes, tense up muscles in the abdomen, the breadbasket, as you say. He could deflect knife point at certain angle, if so desired."

Who wouldn't desire it?

"Who are you? Why are you in America?"

"That will be up to Vadi—Vincent or Ilya"—he indicated outside toward his partner—"to tell you why we here. All I can tell, we are MVD, Secret Police."

Everyone had their secrets while my life was an open book for people to run their fingers down. I was uncomplicated, trusting. Until the accident, I'd never had one truly bad event happen to me. Tangie said once that I couldn't be "deep" as it used brainpower I was delegating elsewhere. My life as a PI had forced me to keep other people's secrets, but I had none of my own. I did some bad things but few things that would destroy me or others around me.

Now here was another dark past come to light. I still didn't know Lee's, but Vincent's was coming together. For years I didn't allow people to get close, but I had let both Lee and Vincent into my immediate circle. I trusted them with my life, but what were they doing with that trust? They were playing their hands close. I had been a fool. Lee, Vincent—they were bottom dealers. While I played by the rules, they rewrote them. I wasn't going to survive to see another day if I didn't start doing the same thing.

I needed a plan, one that didn't rely on other people's contacts or help. I had survived to this point on luck. Now … now, I would work with my skills, my contacts, my goals. The company, TI, and the shadowy Mr. X behind it, needed to be brought into the light. I would do it. I would do it alone.

"I don't know what you need for medical supplies. Can you add it to the list?"

"*Da.* I mean, yes, I can."

As he wrote, I could see his hands weren't as rugged as Vincent's. His attitude wasn't hard like his partner's either. Sacha wasn't a spy or a triggerman. He struck me more as a doctor or scientist, like me. He glanced over his shoulder to the room where his patient lay, and the concern on his face was evident. I looked at his handwriting when he was done. He'd written in English, not Russian. This would make it easier to forge.

Ilya returned before nightfall. We could hear the snowmobile machine approach, so Lee and I watched it from the window. As I had predicted, the tank unloaded its snow-like contents onto the trail as he retraced his path. By the time he had parked, there was no sign that the machine or the jeep had come his way.

Comrade Ilya threw a tarp like the one on the roof over the Jeep and snowmobile. His precautions paid off later in the night as we saw a helicopter with a search light pass over.

Lee made dinner from the meager supplies we had. The Russians hadn't been there long before procuring us. I gathered, through the course of conversation, that Vincent had called them from the pit stop we made on the way to New Mexico. The safe house was previously stocked with only rudimentary gear, medical supplies, and canned food. The two agents had only just gotten here when Vincent dropped another dime down the street from the hospital.

How did he know how to reach them? They were within hours of this safe house. Had he set them up before we left Industry City? And how did he contact them here? I looked around and saw a phone. I went to the window and found a phone line running through the trees. They probably tapped into a party line down near the highway.

Ilya made plans to go to the nearest store for supplies the next day, his face only seen briefly by the police. They hoped Vincent would be up and around so they could plan the next step. For me, my next several steps were already planned.

"So? Made the decision yet? Is my death going to be tonight's entertainment?"

Ilya placed his spoon down with a loud clink. He folded his hands in front of him. "This how we are to spend next few days? Barking like dogs, seeing who leads the pack?"

His English was precise, despite the heavily accented words. He kept his hair cut short, a speckled conglomeration of blond and gray. His companion's was long in comparison.

Sacha and Lee tried to make themselves invisible as I squared off with the other alpha male. "I just want to know where I stand and with who. All I know is you're Russian agents. Beyond that? I could be eating with Khrushchev."

"Honored Leader Khrushchev does not eat beans and franks for dinner. Nor would he like what we do here in America."

"And just what are you doing in America? Can we be let in on this little plan since you have made us a part of it?"

Ilya pushed away from the table, his dander rising with each of my snipes. "I would not have chosen to make you part of the plan at all if not for Vadim. You should be grateful you not being tortured by your C-I-A." He said each letter with obvious spite. "The only reason you are alive to make your wise cracks because Comrade Rezvoi assured me of your importance to plan."

"And I will ask you for the last time," my voice rising, "What is your plan?"

"They are here ..." came a weak voice from behind us. We turned to find a heavily bandaged Vincent Vadim Rezvoi Richmond—whatever—leaning against the doorjamb to his room. "... to find the murderer of Joseph Stalin."

CHAPTER NINE

"Comrade! You should not be up!" Sacha implored.

Vincent shook off the concern. "I have endured worse than this. Your ministrations were fine. I'll rest in a bit. There is much to discuss with our guests."

His relaxed accent was thick with guttural words and sharp, demanding tones. He had emphasized *guests* while looking at Ilya. A reminder of his station perhaps?

Sacha helped Vincent to a chair. Lee got up and brought him a cup of coffee. My former bodyguard, for I didn't know what he was now, thanked him, took a sip, and winced.

"I think this coffee has been here since the last time I was. That was five years ago. Maybe you can get some fresh beans tomorrow?"

Ilya nodded.

"So what do we call you now?" I asked. "Vincent? Vadim? Comrade Rezvoi?"

Vincent settled back as if getting ready for a long story. "My Russian name is Vadim Rezvoi, but I have not gone by it since my family moved to America when I was ten. I had already passed most of my sleeper training and had perfected my accent before leaving the fatherland. However, it is good to let the tongue return to its roots every so often."

"I'm sorry? Sleeper?"

Ilya cast Vincent a stern look, but he ignored it as if the man weren't there.

"After World War I, it was obvious to our military that Americans were bred for fighting. It was no small feat to turn the tide of the war, nor was it due to sheer numbers. No, the United States' military knew how to wage war. They perfected it. Conventional strategies were tossed out and burned. It was time to plan for the next Great War."

"With Germany?"

Vincent leaned forward and rested his forearms on the table. He locked his fingers as if in prayer. "No, you are looking at the past through the eyes of today. No, if you remember, the world war immediately led into a period of civil war. Mother Russia was weak, and territories we once controlled reverted back to independent countries. While the Bolsheviks gained control, our immediate fear would be an invasion by outside forces."

"America?"

"Yes, the new Communist regime was led to believe that America, feeling the strength of their victory, would expand its holdings into Russia. You all but owned the Alaskan territory, which would make an excellent place to launch an invasion. So we prepared for war with you. One of those steps was to plant agents in America, some of them young children, with the hopes that their indoctrination would hold as they became adults and worked their way into the highest ranks of society."

"Wait!" I couldn't adjust to this new reality. "You mean McCarthy is right? There really are Communist spies in America?"

Sacha corrected me. "Well, not all are Communists. Many have become accustomed to capitalist ways of America. These sleepers are people with best interest of *Otechestvo,* the fatherland, at heart."

"But America not do what Russia thought they do, right?" asked Lee.

Sacha continued the narrative to give Vincent a rest. "Right. America went into period of isolationism, refusing to get involved with other countries' problems, let alone start world conquest."

"Which put many sleeper agents into frenzy," Ilya spoke softly, his eyes still downcast. "Where was war they were bred for? When Germany turned out to be enemy, they were happy to sign up for service. They then served both our countries against greater evil. But now, the original vision of future is finally coming true."

I didn't understand his comment and asked Vincent to explain.

"The war took much out of our homeland. Unlike America, we had a battlefront throughout the war. Supplies and men were drained to the point of ruining our country. Now, barely eight years after the war, we are slowly rising up to our full height again. Yet there is still that terrible fear, the fear of your country and what it can do. Not invasion, so much, but instead fear of your controlling the most fearsome weapon ever created."

"The atom bomb."

"Yes, and now that Russia has it too, we believed that you would take advantage of our weaker position to attack before our armaments rival yours."

I waved my arm in a big, sweeping motion. "You live here, Vincent. Do we look like we are preparing for war with Russia?"

Ilya rebutted. "It took only one act of aggression to get your country to break isolation and enter war. Your military was prepared for combat. Too prepared. They wanted to be part of conflict. Your fight was with Japan, yet you commit to whole war. How convenient."

The Russian forced me into a defensive position. He couldn't be implying that Pearl Harbor was a setup, could he? "Listen, it was the right thing to do. Hitler was a madman. He slaughtered how many Jews? What would he have done to Europe if we had left him alone?"

"Don't preach to me, little scientist. We were first to find out about that slaughter and denounce it, one full year before your country even acknowledged it. Why is that?"

"Oh, and Stalin wasn't setting himself up as the next Hitler? What are all these things in the wind about Russian death camps? Rumors?"

Ilya got up. "*Da!* Just that!"

My dander was up. "I doubt it. Maybe instead of finding Stalin's killer, you should be pinning a medal to him?"

Vincent raised a hand before Ilya could counter. "Enough!"

Ilya's face was redder than his country's flag. He turned his back to the table in a huff and paced around the kitchen area, making motions that he was actually cleaning something. Vincent again ignored him. What type of rank did Vincent have that stopped Ilya so quickly in his tracks?

"Comrade Ilya implies that Americans gather around a cause very quickly if it is a righteous one. If we are painted as the next great evil, it would take no time to get your country ready for war. You could even strike with your nuclear missiles and say it was a first strike to keep us from using ours against you.

"Stalin wanted to attack America first. He was going to commit us to a war we had no chance of winning in our current state. He'd started building anti-Semitic concentration camps to drive your country to action. Stalin said, 'A single death is a tragedy. A million deaths are a statistic.' And that is why he was murdered."

"That second time you say that. Rags all say he had a stroke."

"Sorry, Mr. Lee," Sacha apologized. "Newspapers were fed lies. It had to be covered up, or no government would trust Khrushchev. They would all think he did it."

"Did he?" I was beyond belligerent at this point.

Ilya stepped back to the table and pointed a finger in my face. His knuckles were as hard and calloused as his tone. "Premier Khrushchev is honorable man, decent man. That more than one can say for your president!"

I wanted to lay the Moe down, knock some sense into that vodka-soaked brain of his. I started to get up, but it was Vincent who beat me to the punch. His chair shot back from the table, and with adrenalin-laced speed, he was up and had a meat hook around Ilya's neck.

"I shall not remind you again who the ranking officer here is. If you provoke a fight with either of these gentlemen, we will give General Archdeacon a body to find in the snow."

We held our breaths, waiting for the next move. Ilya's posture finally relaxed as he acquiesced to Vincent. Vincent released him and they returned to their seats, Sacha righting Vincent's chair. The damage had been done; Ilya didn't speak again that evening.

Vincent picked up the conversation from my last question. "No, he did not. While it was in the best interest for our country not to go to war, at that moment, we still believed calmer heads would prevail. His death, unfortunate as it was, was well timed on someone's part. We have a man in custody we believe is tied in with this assassination, but we do not know who he worked for or with. After intensive questioning, he revealed a contact who, upon discovery of his death, had in his possession a note with 'Jorge Mendelssohn, America' written on it. I was 'awakened' to find out who that was and if he was attached to Lavrentiy Beria in any way."

"Chief of Russian secret police?" Lee asked.

How did Lee know all this stuff?

"Yes. These two were sent to assist me because of their connections with the case. Ilya was a subordinate of Beria. Sacha was one of the scientists to examine Premier Stalin's body during postmortem and determined cause of death.

"Part of his brain had exploded as a result of microwave radiation."

I now had no doubt why I was being kept alive by these guys. I had just been recruited to solve yet another murder I wouldn't be getting paid for.

* * *

I didn't sleep well that night. Wind rattled trees against the old, rarely used cabin, which smelled worse than the New Mexico jail. I had traded one cell for another. In the distance, a train whistled as it crossed a road. It didn't sound too far away. I lay on my cot, staring up at the wood slats that made up our roof, and my mind wandered recklessly through theories, denying me quality sleep.

In times like that, I normally drank myself to unconsciousness.

There had been so much new information at dinner. They gave me details on Stalin's death, starting with his guards having been sent away, an uncommon occurrence. No one was ever allowed to enter his room uninvited, but after a half day passed without sight of the premier, one brave soul entered and found him sitting in a chair, staring out the window, and mumbling.

He was incoherent and untreatable. After a couple of days, he passed on to the great Stalingrad in the sky.

I hypothesized that the targeting drug had been used. However, for whatever reason, the assassin didn't have a clear shot or only trace amounts entered his system, and it had not done a complete job.

Vincent had his own theory. "I believe it was deliberate. If Stalin had been recognizably murdered, then that would have sent ripples of revolution through the entire country. We have had enough of that with the Romanov family." He pounded a fist on the table for emphasis, causing us to grab our coffee mugs before they tipped over. "No! The premier was killed in such a way as to leave enough of a doubt as to the nature of his death."

That took me back to point A, so I got up and sat by the canned heat. The cabin was stocked with them. One would think we were hunting in Wisconsin.

Sacha was on guard duty. I told him I'd start my shift early and he could go to bed. He thanked me and offered me a shot of vodka from a flask he kept. I gratefully took a swig, feeling the harsh liquor burn the length of my esophagus.

My notebook was back in the car, which I'm sure Archdeacon's men or the CIA were going through inch by inch. Maybe when the general read my notebook, he'd get a glimmer of my innocence. Lacking the notebook, I found a piece of paper and started organizing my thoughts afresh. The flicker of light from the tiny flame only brought more questions.

Who rigged the experiment? Mendelssohn.

But why the change of heart? Merlot said he'd do anything to build a better society, but what did that mean? Did someone convince him that sabotaging the test would lead to that? Did he have doubts? Is that why he tried to warn me? How specific was the note? Did he come out and say the experiment was rigged? Without it I couldn't tell. He had liked Tangie, and they had worked well together. Maybe he had had second thoughts about killing *her* specifically.

On whose orders?

Mr. X and the company he controls, T.I., whatever they did.

I could deduce some things about him. Mr. X was as connected as Reece back then. He knew about the magnetron experiment, reviewed my designs, saw the potential weaponization of it. He was intelligent or had a team of very intelligent people under him. He spent money—lots of money. Hiring hit men wasn't cheap. Nor were building weapons, trips to Russia, and killing premiers.

Why kill people during the test? Why not just make it not work?

Like Reece suggested, Mr. X wanted it to look like a complete failure so the military wouldn't pursue it and T.I. could build the weapon quietly.

Why hide this weapon?

Because it was going to be used to kill Joseph Stalin.

Why kill Stalin?

To stop another war? Possibly. It seemed too obvious on the surface, though. If that were the case, this would be over and done with. They wouldn't have needed to kill Reece and certainly wouldn't be pursuing me. Not unless … I wrote more.

Why did Mendelssohn go into hiding six months ago?

Because he found out that Mr. X was doing something that was counterintuitive to his own ideals. Mendelssohn wouldn't have a problem with Stalin's murder if it meant stopping a war. He showed that by allowing the test to go through. Mr. X must be planning something else, something that could *start* a war.

I rolled this around. Mendelssohn, the pacifist, who'd let some die that the majority would live. But if the majority was in danger, he might be prompted to action. He went into hiding, risking all to come find me. At least, according to Rocky. But Jorge never made it. Something spooked him, or someone got to him.

For the first time, I thought I might not find Jorge alive.

* * *

The day passed uneventfully. After I gave Ilya the list I had altered, he went into town for supplies. I watched him easily take the snow cannon off the back of the snowmobile and noted its fairly simple design.

I made small talk with Vincent over lunch. He had given everyone but me busy work to do. He wanted some time for us to plan. I felt more at ease to ask personal questions. The temperature dropped throughout the morning, so Vincent decided to risk a small fire for an hour or two.

"Did Reece know your secret?"

"I don't know. He must have done a background check, but I have done the same thing on myself and it always comes up clean. I can only assume, if he did know, it never interrupted his plans."

"Reece said that it was General Archdeacon wanted the experiment sabotaged, not some shadow corporate figurehead. Did he really believe that, or was Archdeacon a convenient scapegoat?"

The big man didn't answer immediately. He pondered on it, then said, "I can't say for certain. I was his bodyguard, not his personal confidant. He told me the things I needed to do my job better. Things like what I was up against. He wanted protection from a military-like assault, but from Archdeacon, from Russia, from this unknown company? I can't tell you."

"Mendelssohn fled about the time Stalin was killed, right?"

He nodded. "This didn't escape my notice either. All these things—the obvious attempt on Reece's life, Mendelssohn disappearing, Stalin's murder—they all are connected."

I kicked myself mentally for being so out of the loop for so long. "I was blindsided by all of this. A war was going on around my invention, and no one thought to include me."

"Reece did." Vincent gave me a look that was part apology, part "buck up, little camper!"

"And why was that? Really? Not just because I had finished *The Atlantis*."

"No, not because of that. The timing was too good, and Reece took advantage of it. He would have approached you, regardless. Forces were in motion he couldn't control."

I got up and stoked the fire. "Then why?"

An ember popped from the dried pine and landed on the rock surrounding the fireplace. I watched its glow fade as it burned out all the available combustible material and turned to ash. I squished it with my shoe to be sure it was dead.

"He liked you. As a security protocol, I made Reece write down all his known associates. As he listed all his scientist contacts, his face wrinkled with disdain. I asked him, 'You don't like scientists much, do you, boss?' and he laughed and said, 'There isn't a scientist on this planet that can match the creative genius of Noel R. Glass.'"

I turned around. Vincent was lost in the remembrance. "He said you had more potential than all those 'jokers' combined. So I asked him why you weren't on the list. He told me that he'd never met you, but before he died, he hoped to."

For a man mountain, Vincent grew soft, warm. His posture suggested grief at Reece's untimely death. "You really liked the old man, huh?"

Then that giant Russian sleeper agent, a man who took a shotgun blast to the gut and lived, looked up. Grief softened his edges and a tear hung in the corner of his eye. "My parents loved me like their favorite hammer. I was a tool to create a better Russia one day. And maybe Reece used me too, but it wasn't the same. He was funny, an odd duck. He laughed at the world and his place in it. It was different than my parents or my experience in the military or the police. When they used humor, it was just to cover up their fears. Reece really had no fears. Not even of death. He knew he'd die before the end of this; you saw that in the letter."

I nodded. "Yeah. He was ready to be taken out at any moment. Did he have family?"

"None to speak of. He did want to see your success over all others, though, Mr. Glass. If you'd been friends all along, I'm sure you would have been like a son to him."

I walked over to Vincent and put a hand on his shoulder. "Yeah, maybe. I know he thought fondly of you. He said that in the letter as well."

He reached up and grasped my forearm in a sign of respect.

"Look at us," I said, "bastard children to a crazy, old coot."

I thought Vincent would tear his stitches, he laughed so hard.

* * *

I offered to make dinner to everyone's surprise.

"Hey, I didn't just live on booze for the last ten years. I did have to eat, and a guy on my salary can't eat out every night."

They laughed, even Ilya. I made my Texas chili. I stole the recipe from Rocky's mom. He had made it for a potluck once. I liked it so much, I asked her for the recipe. Rocky hated that she gave it to me. It was meant for only family. She said her son never cooked for himself anyway. Always made women do the work. Another mark against me in Rocky's book.

They ate heartily and found places to stretch out. The yawning came shortly after.

"Who knew doing nothing make you tired?" voiced Lee. The rest echoed him, between yawns.

We all agreed to turn in early. I volunteered for the first watch.

When everyone was down, I pulled out the sleeping powder made from the innocuous materials I'd had Ilya pick up. I hoped I hadn't doped the chili with too much, but with Vincent's and Ilya's sizes to consider, I dropped in a lot. Grabbing one of the pistols, I made sure everyone still breathed before letting myself out into the frozen night.

I sucked hard on the cold air and shivered, not being dressed for this. I'd packed for Nevada, and I still had on my clothes from there. I stepped back in and found Ilya's coat. That left the arrogant Commie to deal with the cold.

Yeah, I can be a right asshole sometimes.

I hated forcing Lee and Vincent to make their own way back home. I wondered if they would keep moving forward or wait for the eventual fall-out I would naturally create. Vincent had a job to do, so I figured little would keep him from finishing it.

Lee would take my vanishing act personally, especially since I hadn't included him in my plan. I shook away thoughts of that. I needed to move fast and imagined I'd be walking on the other side of the law for some time.

I removed the snow making contraption from the snowmobile with ease. On our way up, we had crossed railroad tracks, and last night I had heard the distant sounds of a train whistle. If my luck held true, I'd be on the train to Industry City soon.

CHAPTER TEN

I knew the movies lied to me as a kid, particularly the westerns; mainstay of Saturday morning cinema. It is not, for instance, as easy to jump onto a moving train as they show—especially cargo trains traveling through the night.

The level stretch of track I had chosen for my attempt proved to be a place engineers used to make up time. The speed at which the train passed blew me away from the track and into the snow. Dusting myself off, I got back on the snowmobile and pursued it. The train eventually reached a mountain pass where it slowed down considerably. I got a little bit ahead of the engine, dumped the snowmobile and prepared to run alongside the cars. A loading door was slightly ajar, so after winding myself considerably, I managed to launch myself up and into a freight car.

The comforts of this train were Spartan in comparison to the one I had taken to Chance City. I moved crates around until I'd made myself a nook to sleep in. Finding sleep was difficult—the noise, the motion—however, exhaustion did get the better of me, and I finally dropped into another dream.

I was in the control room, the sound board in front of me. This would be the first ever attempt at breaking through the ionosphere and reflect a signal off the moon. We adjusted for the sun's radiation, return trajectory, even temperature variations in London. A big dish sat out in the middle of the New Mexico desert and its pitch, rotation, and maw were at my left hand. Signal strength was at my right. I had monitor gauges that oversaw Tangie's board at the power station.

A separate room sat off to the side, a glass partition kept General Archdeacon, Dean Orchid, and a dozen spectators from the scientific community and press from getting in the way. I made final preparations with Tangie on the intercom. Mendelssohn, who had been beside me, said he wanted to check one more thing and left.

Tangie paused for a moment and said, *"Hold on, Noel. Jorge needs me for something."*

I waited. A minute went by. Jorge Mendelssohn returned to the room, and Tangie gave the all clear signal.

I looked around. Jorge took his station and nodded. I flipped the switch to on.

There was a hum. I waited for my team to make adjustments and check readings. When no one spoke up, I turned the power dial up.

Twenty-five percent. Fifty percent.

A voice from the intercom said, *"Is it getting hot in here?"*

Tangie said, *"I think we're all a little nervous."*

Her voice sounded odd. Was her confidence gone?

I said, *"I think we should stop."*

Tangie replied, *"The temperature gauge reads normal. We're okay."*

Dean Orchid placed a lithe hand on the call button of the intercom in their area. Her voice was as shaky as Tangie's. *"Is this going to work?"*

I smiled reassuringly and she tilted her head at me, trying to see through my bullshit. She was in her thirties back then, yet dressed like a schoolmarm. That combination made lying to her convincingly difficult, as young and inexperienced as I was. She kept chestnut hair pulled back tightly into a bun, which I believed kept her perpetually in bitch mode.

I nodded and turned the switch up to 75 percent.

"Jorge? Is the tracer plane in the air?"

"Yes, they left Davis-Monthan fifteen minutes ago."

I finished turning the dial. I flipped the switch to scan, and with it came screams. A tech's voice cried, *"Oh my G—!"* but then was cut off by a burst of static. They hadn't all died at once. At least one man, that last voice, had seen the others die and knew he was next.

His name was Rupert and I could still hear his voice when I woke in a sweat.

Light sneaked its way in through the wooden planks of the rail car. I opened the door a crack and looked out over the snow-encrusted Rockies. It was a magnificent sight, but I couldn't enjoy it. Wind battered me as something from the dream lingered, but it wouldn't come forward to make itself known. I tried remembering every minute detail, but time had weakened the memory; the moment was lost.

I had time to think. I took out a can of the baked beans, opened them with a knife I had taken from the cabin, and continued the investigative process I had started the night before.

All scientific analysis starts with an idea, a theory. Even if the theory is proved wrong through the analysis, it can lead to, or remove doubt from, other ideas. As I sat in the cold, shaking boxcar, I got an idea. I looked at all the facts again: Reece, Mendelssohn, the MASER, the Hero Twins, the mysterious T.I. and its elusive Mr. X, Yousev, and now Stalin. It took me a while to see it, but when I placed them in a mental flow process chart and drew connections from one to the other. There was a piece of the puzzle missing—one piece to make the whole picture come clear.

When I proposed a theory, back in the day, and my intent to investigate it, I needed to convince several people, money people or other scientists of its worth. This time I needed to convince only one person to start. If I could get Chief Charles Sweet on my side, I'd have the means to find the puzzle piece to make everything fall together.

It became evident that going all the way into Industry City by train would be a mistake. I spotted military roadblocks on the highway the few times it was visible. I couldn't take the chance there were cinder dicks checking the boxcars as they arrived.

I caught a break just outside of town. The track took a bend around the foothills, obscuring my exit from either end of the train. I jumped off, tucked into a roll, and found a place to hide from the rear conductor.

Maybe my luck had changed. It wasn't more than a short hike to the Industry City Downs. I dusted myself off and went to place a bet on a man.

*　*　*

The Downs was Industry City's premier horse-racing establishment. While I had been known to drop a fiver on the ponies before, more often than not, I was there getting the skinny or chasing a chalk-eater.

And … that's where Sean Burke worked.

Burke could put clothes on a fish and could hear a mouse fart in Brooklyn. He knew everyone and everything that happened in the underworld. His job as horse trainer didn't bring in nearly the cash that being a stoolie did. Whatever was for sale, whoever was for sale, Burke knew about it first.

And he owed me a favor.

I got there just before the fifth. I became smoke, flowing with the air currents of excited bettors as they gawked at the frothing, four-legged warriors in pursuit of glory on a circular field of battle. Picking up a discarded program, I scanned down the page, looking at horses', jockeys', and trainers' names. Burke didn't have any runners again until the seventh and last race.

I knew how to get to the stables unnoticed. I slipped under the stands and made my way around to the back of the horseboxes.

Burke trained for Martin Sully, the local barracuda, who was on par with Charlie the Spic. Sully was the artesian well Burke tapped for information. He was careful not to sell too much or risk the big sleep. Burke erred on the side of caution, this gig being the best he'd ever had.

The Irishman brushed down a chestnut. I opened the stall door and pushed Burke into the back corner quickly, my hand over his mouth. I leaned in hard, my body pinning his scrawny form. His face turned red as the bangs that hung over his noggin.

"Hi there, Burky. I came for the favor you owe me."

"Gwash!"

"Yes, Glass. Seems everyone's got a bull's-eye on me, Burke. If you open your trap to say anything other than 'Hi, Glass,' I'll gut you where you stand, got it? Nod if you got it."

He nodded. I let my hand off for a moment. "Hi, Glass."

I covered his mouth again. "Good, we're still on speaking terms. Now I'll ask some questions and you'll answer them yes or no. Got it? Nod if you got it?"

Burke was nervous. I'm sure bladder control was secondary on his mind. He nodded.

"Good. Is Charlie the Spic after me?"

He shook his head, confirming something I suspected. Merlot hadn't given up anything yet. She, too, needed aces in the hole.

"Is General Archdeacon in town?" He gave me a nod.

"Good. See how easy this is. Keep this up and we're even, okay?" He nodded.

"I want the word on the street about me. Is my face everywhere? What are they saying? How much is being offered for me? I'm going to take my hand off. If you so much as say something that begins with an *H* for help, I'll gut you, but I made that clear, didn't I?"

He nodded. I slowly took my hand off his face. He spit on the ground to get the taste of my meat hook out of his mouth. He reached into a pocket and pulled out a small flask. I could smell the burn from where I stood.

"Jesus, Glass! We didna have to go through all the threats and such. Yer hot property now. I can make more off of lyin' about ya den tellin' the truth."

That was Burke.

"So what's the pitch, Glass? Ya really gone mad?"

"I'm clean, Burke. Who's whispering about me?"

"They say yer the biggest threat to national security since Yamamoto. They say yer workin' for the Japanese, the Koreans, *and* the Russians. They say that you torched Chance City to the ground and are on a three-state killin' spree, takin' out everyone who has ever gotten in yer way. They say—"

"Okay, enough. Who are they?"

"Mostly the papers, lookin' for headlines. The grapevine is different. Charlie the Spic was screamin', wantin' to know what ya were doin' in Chance City, but he was told to clam up by Chicago. CIA's gotta hundred gees on you. The state of New Mexico doesn't have that cash, so they're only askin' fer five."

If Burke were a cartoon, he'd have dollar signs shooting from his peepers. I kept him in sight at all times, but I didn't feel like standing anymore. I motioned for him to grab a straw bale and sit.

"There is someone else looking for me, isn't there?"

He chuckled and gave me that Irish grin that meant he had something good, something worth the money he normally asked. "We're inna clear after this, correct?"

"Yeah, we're clear."

"Oh, there's someone all right. But that's the weird thing. The first hit came down before ya even disappeared. They had the Hero Twins on retainer. No one else was supposed to be touchin' ya. If Archdeacon or the Feds got to ya first, the Twins were to break ya out then kill ya before ya blabbed somethin'."

I shook my head. "I have no idea what that could be. Do you?"

"Nobody this side of the dirt knows what it is, but I'll tell ya straight. Chicago sent word that if anyone inna family had dealins' with you, they were to pull out. They didna want any heat comin' down on them." Burke gave me a rueful smile. "Plus they're very patriotic, ya know."

"So who put out the hit on me?"

"If anyone knew, I'd know, and I don't know. Ya couldna beat it outta me if ya wanted. I only knows that the Twins were set on yer trail. Nothin' else." He lolled his head to one side. "Did ya really ice one of them in Chance City?"

"Someone did, not me."

"Damn, if that gets out, I'll have to refund some money. Can ya take credit fer it, fer my sake?"

I ignored him. "You know any big dealers working for a company with the initials T.I.?"

He thought a moment. "Nah. Should I?"

Noise made us jump up from our bales. Someone was walking through the stables. I covered Burke's mouth again and dragged him down to the floor. When the noise abated, I said, "I'm going now. Say, 'Good-bye, Glass.'"

"Good-bye, Glass."

Then I turned out his lights. He'd be sore when he got up, but he'd have a story to sell. I figured we were still even.

Charlie the Spic's non-reaction meant Merlot kept quiet about our visit to her. Her keeping quiet meant she knew more than she had let on. I wish I'd had more time to pump her for information, but what was done …

Also, Burke confirmed that there was someone else pulling my strings even before I found Reece in my apartment. The Russians wanted Mendelssohn, and he had wanted me. The U.S. military wanted me. The heat wanted me. And as far as I knew, Lee was Yakuza and they wanted me. Now there was this mysterious third party putting hits on me, chasing me across the country. What did I know that they were so afraid of?

I mingled into the crowd and waited. Burke must have woken up and found security. I could see flashing lights off in the distance before I heard their clarion call. I was out of the Downs with the crowd of the last race before the police got organized enough to lock the place tight. Burke's horse had placed last. God, the man was a piss-poor trainer.

It wasn't long before Sweet's beat-up cruiser arrived. He never liked to park too close to the action, in case he got a lead and had to follow up on it quickly. I slid into his backseat and lay down on the floor while he ran around barking orders. Sweet must use his backseat as a trash can; empty coffee cups, old newspapers, and toothpicks covered everything. I lay there for a half hour, trying not to gag before Sweet climbed back in.

"You're going to want to stay down until we get clear of the parking lot."

"How long did it take you to figure out I'd be in here?"

"Not long. That thing with Burke was too blatant. No one with your profile announces he's back in town unless he needs a ride."

I had to ask. "Are we going right to the station, or do I get to talk to you first?"

"I have my orders; they knew I was tight with you. They expect you to make contact with me."

He didn't say more. I held my breath, waiting for the follow-up. We were a couple of miles from the Downs before he said, "Okay, you can sit up now."

We were entering the beginnings of a subdivision. The ground was turned up, and the foundations were laid on a half dozen buildings. If anyone but Sweet were driving the car, I'd have said this was a good place to get rid of a body.

Sweet pulled in to the markings of a driveway and turned off the motor. He wordlessly got out of the car and opened my door.

I followed him to the shell of a house, the framework and floor already in place. It would be a nice size—two stories and a basement, three hay parlors, two and a half baths. Respectable. I could see other shells like it dotted along the neighborhood. Industry City was growing toward the mountains. This place was nestled between the city proper and the foothills. Suburban living with a view. Hard to beat.

He entered the front door and walked into the living room. "This is my house."

I stepped through the eventual wall. "You might need a throw rug, Sweet. It's sort of bare."

"I've been working all these years to get my family a house like this. It's going to be a good neighborhood. There's a school planned across the way, a park to take my dog to, a YMCA, and a shopping plaza with an ice cream parlor."

"Sound like a nice place, Sweet," I said, afraid of where this was going.

"And the only thing keeping me from it is … you." He turned, gun drawn.

"You have one minute to tell me why I shouldn't haul your ass in. I told you not to let me find you on the other side. It took you less than half a day to turn the whole damn country against you."

"You still love me, right?"

But Sweet was in no mood for wisecracks. "Glass, I swear to God almighty, I can shoot you right now and collect half a mil. This isn't the time for glibness. Now talk!"

"It's going to take longer than one minute."

"You start breaking it down, and I'll tell you when to stop."

So I did. I talked. I laid out what had happened up until then, from the moment I left him at the murder scene, which seemed so long ago now, until the moment I crawled into his car. I left nothing out, including Vincent's Russian ties. Having worked with the man, Sweet was most appalled by that revelation. His arm got tired, so he eventually holstered the piece. I'd made it outlining my theories before he couldn't take anymore.

"Jesus Christ on a crutch, Glass. How am I supposed to believe that? Freakin' H.G. Wells wouldn't believe that load of crap!"

"Some of this you can get from Burke. The letter Reece gave me might still be back at the safe house. If you follow my trail, you'll see that everything I've told you fits."

Sweet paced nervously back and forth, mentally poking holes in my story. There was too much for a simple cop to grasp. I could tell he regretted even letting me talk. I made his life more complicated. "It'd be easier to just arrest you as a Commie than convince anyone there is some secret conspiracy to overthrow the government."

"Careful, Sweet. Your red, white, and blues are showing."

"Damn right! I lost a lot protecting this country. I'd gone over fully expecting not to come back. I'd do it all over again."

"Even losing Chuck?"

"Chuck died a hero. They all did. Hell yeah, I'd want my son back, but not at the cost of losing the country I love to those godless bastards."

"Dulce et Decorum est pro patria mori."

Sweet put a finger in his ear, as if trying to unclog it. "What was that crap?"

"Latin. Means 'Know it is a wonderful and great honor to fight and die for your country.' It was something said to excite Roman soldiers before a battle."

"Yeah, so?"

"Rome fell."

His face turned a shade of blue. I knew this meant he was trying to calm himself down by holding his breath and counting to ten. It would have been funny had the situation not been so dire. When he exhaled, the color returned to his face. "Taking you in might just be the favor I need. I get to serve, protect, and retire early."

"I'm telling the truth, Sweet. Mendelssohn created a weapon against his principles. Why? Because he believed it would help the greater good. Not just here in America. He was sold on the idea that it could help the whole world."

"By who, Glass? Convinced by who? Give me a name I can arrest."

I continued, overriding the question. "Originally, it might have been designed to kill Hitler. Only we got into the war and Hitler did himself in. Plus, with the bomb, the MASER wasn't necessary anymore. Countries were staying in line."

"A name, Glass."

"Stalin was the first to step out of line. He wanted another world war, so Mendelssohn built the device after all and helped to kill Stalin, stalling a military conflict, but instead creating a cold war, one of words and military buildup. Mendelssohn hadn't expected that, but the people behind him did. They have people in high places on both sides, intent on stalling open hostilities until America and Russia are at equal strength and armaments. All it will take is a match to light the fire."

"Glass!"

I steamrolled on. I had to get these points through to him. I sounded frantic and must have looked maniacal. "The next assassination will be one of ours, maybe the president, and it will be the match. It will be obvious, and the Russians will be the fall guys. Whoever is behind this T.I. company wants the war. They want to wipe the slate clean and start over with their own agenda. Mendelssohn found that out and rabbited."

"Enough! I can't hear this anymore!"

Sweet was shouting, so I shouted louder.

"If we find Mendelssohn, I'll give you *your fucking name!*"

I was breathing hard, panting. I placed my hands on my knees and drew in deep breaths. Sweet stood there, watching me. He didn't say anything for a few moments. He just took me in.

"Why should I believe any of this? Give me one good reason!"

"Because it's right. You've never put the wrong man in jail intentionally, and I've never been wrong identifying the right one."

Sweet turned from me and walked through his house, pausing at each room. I assumed he imagined what they would look like when finished. He stopped by the kitchen and eyeballed the backyard through an imaginary window. I joined him. It was as bare as hell's backyard, but the view was fabulous.

"Bay window?"

"The missus wouldn't have anything else. It was how I convinced her to move."

"Nice view."

"The best."

And he was right. The house was located at the end of the lot. Behind the property was nothing but fields and foothills.

I smiled. "You know, they'll probably build more houses back there in ten years."

"Shut up, Glass. What do you need me to do?"

* * *

Sweet came out from the address Mendelssohn had left with Rocky, a run-down apartment complex. He sat behind the wheel, talking over his shoulder to me there on the floorboards, again.

"The landlord says the rent was paid for six months, up front, cash. Just about the time the lease was up, he found an envelope in his box for another month's rent. He says he hasn't seen anyone come in or out in that time."

"Did the original tenant match the description I gave you?" I asked.

"To a tee."

Pay dirt!

"I'll be squatting here, Sweet. If you change your mind and want to arrest me, you'll know where I'm shacked up."

He made a harrumphing sound. "I'm going to follow up on some scuttlebutt I heard a while back. Might not be anything, but all this stuff you told me reminded me of a case we caught around St. Paddy's. I'll be back tomorrow to pick you up. Don't let anyone see you!"

"I'll sit tight."

"So you really think you can save the world, huh?" Sweet was back to sarcasm. I guess the planets realigned for him.

"As soon as I know who's behind this … Yeah, seems like the job I inherited."

"There are many reasons to hate you, Glass. You're cocky, you're a drunk, and you never served in the military. Oh, and you think too much." He paused, gauging his words. "Yet you keep trying to do the right thing. You've never let me down on a case, and that says 'balls' to all that other crap."

"Thanks, Sweet. Don't go all misty on me, though. You already have a wife and I'm the jealous type."

I slid from the car. I instantly stepped in something unidentifiable and squishy that stank to high heaven. The garbage can in front of me had been tipped over by a cat, who continued to scrounge despite my abrupt appearance. Sweet must've parked the car there deliberately, knowing what I'd step into. I could see his grin in the side view mirror as the unmarked cruiser pulled away.

Condemning these apartments wouldn't be justice enough. Once the high life of lower east side, the area now represented everything that was wrong with Industry City. The new was in; the old was left to rot, forgotten. When it got bad enough, the city would till it under and grow a new area over it. The moochers, mud kickers, and mashers would move to a different area, spreading their waste until it became the new slums, and the process would start over.

The lock was nothing to pick. I opened the door expecting stale air and an inch of dust on everything. Astonishingly, the place had been tidied up and the air smelled fresh, like windows had been opened. Maybe the apartment manager had kept up the place with the idea of subletting or having less work to do when the lease was up.

Mendelssohn rented it furnished. As with most rentals, the accoutrements were not of high quality. There was a kitchen table, sleeper couch, and a radio on top of a small dresser. The nicest thing was a recliner chair that looked almost new. One unusual addition to the place was a small piano tucked neatly in the corner. Mendelssohn must have had it brought in, expecting Merlot to join him. This is part of what she was keeping secret. She was going to join him here, and not just for a weekend. They'd planned to be here a while.

I moved to the refrigerator hoping for a beer and not year-old bologna. I found an Ancient Stout and a smattering of foodstuffs, all fresh. Someone used this apartment, and from the labels on the meat, it had been recently. Whoever had paid the extra month was in residence. I went through the trash. This morning's paper was rolled up and stuffed in. I also found wrappers for various women's sundries. My soon-to-be roommate was female, and it wasn't hard to guess her identity.

I sat on the couch, gun on my lap. Whatever errand she had run might bring her back in a minute or in a day. I unrolled the paper and glanced through the last couple of days' news. My mug still graced the front page, but now smaller and in the corner. The story, moved to page two, rattled my soul. Reporters must have bothered my parents, relatives, old acquaintances. Quotes of how "bright a lad" I had been got old quickly. I moved on through the paper until I found something of note in the business section.

Little Technologies' board of directors had chosen a successor for Reece promptly. Cecelia LaMent, a distant relative of founder C.J. Reece, was approved by unanimous vote of the six-person board of directors. Miss LaMent oversaw Little Technologies' Jakarta branch for the past 14 years. While estranged from Reece during most of that time, the two recently resolved their dispute, forging the way for LaMent to be the first woman chief executive officer of a large technologies firm, especially one with close ties to the military. Little Technologies has been the primary electronics contractor to the U.S. armed forces for more than 40 years. As much a recluse as her infamous predecessor, Miss LaMent has never been photographed at large and no pictures were made available by the company.

What was it with that family? They weren't hideous to look at; at least, Reece was no Elephant Man. Why all the subterfuge?

I showered. While I wasn't even close to Mendelssohn's size, I did find some usable clothes. I rinsed out my two-day-old, fifteen-hundred-mile shirt and threw it over the window sill. It was two hours before I heard the key in the lock. She had grocery bags in front of her, so she didn't see me. She moved into the kitchen, depositing her parcels on the table. She had kicked the door closed, but I moved in behind her to lock it. Once I threw on the chain, all was ready.

"Hello, Merlot."

She spun, anger flashed across those haunting eyes once again. I seemed to bring out the worst in this woman. She didn't notice the gun as she moved toward me, so I flashed it.

"We're not going through this scene again, sweetheart, and you're not in Charlie's territory anymore. We're both here for the duration, and we both want the same thing: Mendelssohn. So why not play nice, kitten?"

"Ain't you in enough trouble without adding kidnapping to your sheet?" Merlot recovered quicker than she had at the club. She knew the score.

"You know this whole thing is trumped up. That's why you didn't turn me into Charlie the Spic. When he wasn't hot after our asses, I figured you couldn't implicate us without implicating yourself. 'Why were they here, Merlot?' he would've asked. Maybe you couldn't lie quick enough. Or worse, he might force you to give something away about your boyfriend."

She waved it off. "Maybe I just didn't want to embarrass myself. You know how those mob types are. He might not let me perform after a scene like that. Or worse, put bodyguards on me."

"Yeah, that'd be a shame. Then you couldn't move freely about the country, like now. Charlie know you've left Chance City?"

She shook her head and returned to the groceries. "You think you got it all figured out, don't you? You and that big brain of yours."

Merlot put away items as I rebutted her. "Not everything. I still have a few pieces to fill in, so why don't you show me how smart you are? Start spilling the beans, and I won't get word to Charlie where you are."

I flipped a chair around and saddled up to the table. I didn't have the gun directly on her anymore. It wasn't needed.

"I don't know where Jorge is, Glass. Really and truly. I haven't seen him in six months. Haven't heard anything about him either."

After the supplies were put away, she took out a pot and filled it with water from the tap. She placed it on the stove and lit the burner underneath. She took stew meat from the fridge, unwrapped it, and tossed it in the pot. Next, she grabbed carrots, celery, and potatoes and rinsed them off.

"So how'd you know about this little nest, songbird?"

"He told me he was coming here to see you." Her chopping rhythm was erratic as she focused on her memories of Jorge. "He knew that you'd be the only one to get him out from what he was in."

"And what was that?"

She cut down hard on the board, her anger flaring up for a second. "How many times do I have to tell you, *'I don't know'*? I was his lover, not his priest!"

I could see a tear as it stopped its descent from her eye and hovered on her cheek. She didn't strike me as the leaky type, so I had hit a nerve. She wanted to know more about him, but he'd kept things from her, important things. She hated it and imagined that they fought over it. Could she have been a part of Mendelssohn's change of heart?

How a woman, especially the one you love, looks at you can mean all the difference in life. I knew that one well enough. Tangie knew I'd never intentionally make a weapon of war. She said it was part of the magic that was me. Her respect of science reflected my own, and I'd never do anything to lose face in her eyes. Jorge may have decided that causing a world war would lose him Merlot's respect, regardless of the outcome, and he risked everything to get to me in hopes of stopping the impending catastrophe.

I watched Merlot continue her prep work. There was nothing similar about Tangie and her, save for an inner strength. Was that all it took to change a man?

"Do something useful, Glass. Peel these."

She plopped a couple of the potatoes in front of me with a peeler. I shrugged and returned the gun to its holster. I peeled the spuds and chopped them into cubes. She took my finished pile and dumped it into the pot with her own. She reached for an onion and began its dismantling. Her mind distracted, she cut through the onion and into her thumb. She cursed and brought the digit into her mouth. Tears rolled freely, and I went to her.

"Let me look."

She shook her head. Drops flew from her cheeks and landed on my shirt.

"If it needs stitches, I can do that."

From around her thumb she said, "You ain't no medical doctor."

"No, but I've had enough experience to know how to stitch a cut. Done several of my own. Now let me look before it gets infected; then you will have to see a real doctor."

She took the finger out and let me examine it. I moved us over to the sink and washed the seeping blood away. "Keep this under the faucet," I instructed.

Unlike my own place, this unit had its own bathroom. I checked the medicine cabinet and found some gauze and tape. Returning to Merlot's side, I turned off the water and dried her thumb on a towel. Quickly I wrapped the extremity in bandages and looked at my handiwork. Merlot had followed my progress with helplessness, but as I worked, she grew attentive, even interested.

"Not bad. It's been a while since I've done that, but I think you'll live to hold a microphone again."

"Well, ain't you the cutup?"

She looked at me a second, her expression one of gratitude, but shook it off and looked away. Her voice was distant. "Thank you. I'm not normally this clumsy in a kitchen."

"You do the cooking for your family?"

The mention of her family awoke something in her, and she started back on her dinner project. "Yeah. Daddy worked at the train yards; Momma was a cabaret singer; and Tyrone, well, you know what he was doing."

"Fighting?"

"Ever since he was a kid. If it wasn't fighting to protect me, it was fighting to protect Mom's honor. Finally, Daddy figured Tyrone should put all that energy to some good."

She pulled out another onion after dumping the bloodied one in the trash. This time she minced the veggie without incident. It joined its brethren into the stew. She wove spices into the creation.

"So that's where you got the voice, huh? Your mother?"

"Yeah. She was good." Merlot smiled. "A voice that set the world on fire. She worked mostly speakeasies, so she could never get famous. She wanted that for me. Had me singin' my first words."

Merlot got distant again. I had a hunch, but I didn't want her to pull away, so I asked, "What happened to her?"

"Mob war. What else? You can't play in that world without getting burned. She got caught in the crossfire. That's how I ended up under Charlie's protection. I inherited it. They don't even ask Ty to throw matches out of respect for her. Everybody loved to hear her sing."

The waterworks started again. I moved in next to her, close. I brushed a tear away.

She stepped back. "It's just the onions."

I stepped up to her again. "They're already in the pot."

"Don't," she said in a whisper.

"Don't what?"

"Don't be nice. I can't handle you being nice."

"Okay, I won't be."

And I kissed her.

She wanted to resist. She put her hands to my shoulders to push me away, but then they slid around my neck and drew me to her. It became an urgent kiss, one of loss and desire. She went to unbutton Mendelssohn's shirt, but gave up and ripped it open, buttons flying everywhere.

"I always hated that shirt," she said through gritted teeth.

Everything on the outside of her was soft—her clothes, her underwear, her dark skin—but her soul was hard. That came through in her passion; fierce, unforgiving. She bit my shoulder as I reached around to undo her bra. She pushed me down to the couch and straddled me, taking control. It didn't stop there. We danced on the floor, standing up and sitting down. It wasn't the sex of two lovers, but of necessity, like reaching for a hand while drowning. More often than not, the person drowning drags their rescuer down, too.

I didn't know which one of us was drowning, but we never said a word the entire time we sank.

After our much delayed dinner, I gave Merlot the bed, while I slept sprawled out on a chair. She didn't complain nor did she ask me to be a bed warmer.

The night before the magnetron experiment played on my subconscious theater as I tried to find peace.

I'd just finished showering and had slid between the sheets of my bed. I reached over to the side table drawer and pulled out the Babbage book. Tangie didn't knock. She wore a green silk robe, one I had brought back from a lecture tour of Asia Minor and given her for Christmas. It slid from her body the way milk slides from a bottle. I dropped the book back toward the drawer and missed it completely. It hit the floor with a thump and Tangie laughed. She knew she had me; she had always known. Our lovemaking held a promise. She also liked being the aggressor, her gams strong. Often bruises ran up and down my legs and deep scratches lined my back.

I was going to ask her to marry me after the test. I never wanted to taste another's lips, feel another's body next to me.

Of course, Freud would attest this dream to guilty feelings about my body-scissors time with Merlot. Maybe he'd be right, but there was something in the dream I had forgotten. After we fell asleep, I'd gotten up to relieve myself in the middle of the night, careful not to wake Tangie. I had reached for the Babbage book to put it away …

But it was gone.

CHAPTER ELEVEN

I looked over to see Merlot's form under the sheet. The steady rise and fall of the blanket revealed a peacefully slumbering thrush. I knew I wouldn't be sleeping again tonight.

The book had been moved. When I noticed its absence from the floor, I opened the drawer and saw it was back in its place. Tangie had put it away while I slept. I opened the book by habit. She had taped a lock of her hair to the front cover. She had written,

You won't need this to relax anymore.

She had to have intercepted Mendelssohn's note and read it herself. It made sense because she was different that next morning over breakfast in bed.

"I think Jorge is worried," Tangie said.

"Why is that?"

"I don't know. He acted a bit strange when I saw him yesterday afternoon."

"He's always acting strange. Smart kid, but he's a queer duck. Did he say anything specific?"

"No, just wanted you to know he was going to go over the diagrams again last night before turning in."

"I'd be amazed if he found something we didn't. We make a formidable team, don't you agree, Miss Taylor?"

"I believe we've crossed all the I's and dotted all the T's, if that's what you mean."

"No, I mean something else entirely."

She drew in to herself. She set down her fork on the tray and stared at the half-eaten eggs.

"What?" I asked.

I placed a hand on her bare arm, and in a moment, she turned her lamps on me.

"What would you do for me?"

"Huh?"

"What lengths would you go to for me? Would you cross a burning desert? Climb a snow-capped mountain? If I was missing, would you ever stop searching for me?"

This took me by surprise. Tangie was the realist. She wasn't taken in by poetry, chocolate, or acts of romance, which was ultimately how we got together. I wasn't any good at those things. I wooed her mind long before I tried for her heart.

"What's come over you?"

"I know where you're going with this, Noel. And before I answer you, I have to know: What lengths would you go to for me? Where is the line? If I fell off a boat in the ocean, would you dive in after me?"

"Yes, and tread water as long as I could to keep you alive."

"If my plane crashed in the mountains, how long would you search for me?"

"Until I found you, no matter how long it took. I'd never give up. I love you, Tangie. It is as real to me as the matter that makes us. I would do anything to protect you and find you."

"Would you kill?" She had a weird smirk on her lips.

"To protect you? Yes."

"Would you die to protect me?"

"Without regret."

She smiled—the last real smile I'd ever bring out in her.

"Then yes, we make a damn fine team, Mr. Glass. Shall we get married tomorrow after we change the world?"

"Yes."

Then we made love one last time.

Six hours later she was dead.

I leaned forward, palms pressed against my eyes. I hadn't protected her. I hadn't saved her. I hadn't found her killer. I didn't even know who that was. I had made a lot of promises to her I hadn't kept, all because I had given in to emotion instead of logic.

A hand touched mine. Embarrassed, I shook away the demons and looked up into Merlot's face. She smiled, took my hand, and guided me to her bed. She spooned me from behind, holding me close. I could feel her breasts against my back, full and soft, like warm pillows. She slid one arm under my head; the other lay across my chest. Her legs intertwined with mine and we melded there. Thoughts of Watson and his strands of DNA gave me a chuckle before falling back asleep.

*　*　*

Sweet had brought me a change of clothes and waited while I rubbed myself down with water.

"Think the CIA is watching you?" I asked Sweet once we were on our way.

"Maybe. That might change after what I have to tell you."

The outfit he'd brought came with fedora, trench, and dark shades. Downstairs, I had progressed to the front seat of his car. He reached between us and grabbed a file sitting there. He tossed it hard onto my lap, then took the main stem out of town.

"That right there could end my career."

"As if having me in your car wouldn't?"

"Oh, I already have a plan for that. I would say I was playing you until you took me to the rest of your posse."

"Not bad. Are you?"

"Ha! Not after reading that. Your story and the facts have a match, but you aren't going to like the results."

I looked at the folder, a case file dated March 17, 1953, with John Doe 091652-1 listed as the victim. It took only five seconds of reading the stiff's description before I let out a string of curses that guaranteed I would never see the pearly gates.

Hair: *None. Anywhere.*

"I take it that's Mendelssohn?"

I was cursing again.

"So it turns out that if you don't take your earned vacation, the department's policy is to charge you for it anyway. So in March, my doll and I took our first trip since the honeymoon. Let me tell you, Glass, it was like a honeymoon all over again."

I opened the file again, not at all interested in Sweet and wife's marital bliss.

"We went to a hot spring. Ever been to one, Glass? Well, if you haven't, you should. It was great. Very relaxing."

"And the point being?"

"That's where I was when the freak got capped. Fuse box exploded over half a dozen people. I heard about it when I got back, but out of the blue, it gets yanked upstairs. And get this, I checked with the state, and it got yanked upstairs from them. The case is supposedly being investigated by the FBI, only when I called them, they never heard of it. My guess, it got yanked from them by the CIA."

I thought back to March. I had been hired to solve a series of robberies on the western slope, on Sweet's recommendation. It had been good pay and the per diem covered a month in Grand Junction. This would have been old news by the time I returned.

How could Mendelssohn have been stupid enough to get himself tagged and scratched by the very thing he invented? Was I back to square one?

"We're here."

I peeked over the edge of the window. We were parked in front of what could best be described as a cottage in an older Industry City neighborhood. The place, once meticulously cared for, now sat in disrepair. Bavarian-style edging that used to lace the cottage hung loosely by a nail or two. A little wooden Dutch boy and girl lay flat against the unkempt grass.

"Where are we?"

"The Beckenbauers'."

I knew the name. I flipped open the file and saw it again.

Autopsy performed by Fritz Beckenbauer, Industry City Coroner.

"Didn't he die last July in a car accident?"

"Hit and run," Sweet answered as he climbed out. "His wife hasn't quite recovered. Come on."

Confused, I got out.

Sweet offered me a badge. "She hasn't left the house much since then. The Fallen Officers' Wives Association brings her food and supplies a couple times a month. She doesn't read the papers and doesn't own a television. She won't know who you are, but just in case, flash the badge when I do."

I took the proffered cookie cutter and shadowed Sweet to the door. "Why are we here?"

"Did you see anything missing in the file?"

"Beckenbauer was listed as having done the autopsy, but I didn't actually see it. Just the death certificate listing cerebral trauma as the cause."

"There was an autopsy when I looked at it, after my vacation."

It took quite a while after we had knocked before the shattered remains of Mariel Beckenbauer answered. She had a shawl over stringy hair that may not have been washed in months. I could see through to the purgatory inside. Nothing living should exist in that mess.

"Mariel," Sweet said with a level of affection I'd never heard him use before. What do you know? Sweet could be sweet after all.

"Oh! Hello, Charles. I wasn't expecting visitors today. Is it the fourth, already? Where is Katrina?"

"She's not here today, Mariel. It's not the fourth yet. I'm here with one of my detectives about Fritz."

Her pupils widened in surprise. I could see fear, but also anticipation.

"Have you caught him? The man that murdered my Fritz?"

I stepped up. "No, ma'am. But we have a lead now."

Sweet nodded. He was following the same track I was.

"Mariel? We need to take a look at Fritz's notes. The duplicates he kept."

"I don't know. He didn't want anyone to look at them, not even me."

"Ma'am," I cajoled, "why did he keep a second set of notes if not for this very thing? He must have been very dedicated to the truth and didn't want it covered up, even by his death."

She looked away from us, still thinking, still unsure.

"Mariel, please?"

The old lady acted as if she had been stuck in time. There was the promise she'd made to her husband that kept her trapped in the past, but the need to know the truth pulled her unbidden toward the present. A storm waged inside of her and we didn't have time for it to pass.

"Mrs. Beckenbauer, I spent fourteen years mourning the death of my wife." I went for broke. "Her death and his might be connected. Would he want her murder to go unsolved? What if there are other murders yet to happen and you could have stopped them?"

A look of horror came over her.

Sweet leaned into me. "You're going too far, too fast. Give her time."

I stared him down. "I don't have time, Chief. There is a murderer on the loose, and I want him caught!"

A sudden boom came from the doorway. It was Mariel's voice, as if she had just found it. "You're right! My Fritz loved his job, almost as much as he loved me. He made the copies for you, and so you should have them, Charles. How foolish am I to hold on to something that was never mine."

I patted the hands that were held out to me. "I'll be right back," she said, a twinkle in her eye that hadn't been there when she opened the door.

After she handed us what we came for, Mariel looked me right in the eye and said, "Get the son of a bitch!"

I'll remember those words until my dying day.

*   *   *

It didn't take long to search through Beckenbauer's notes. Mendelssohn was one of the last cases he worked on before his untimely death. While I read the handwritten documentation, Sweet made calls.

He came back after close to half an hour. "You were right."

"Dead too, huh?"

"Yep. Every coroner that looked at this file all died under mysterious circumstances. What did they see?"

"From the looks of it, nothing. Certainly Fritz didn't find anything. Everything looked normal to him. I'm no sawbones, but I do know human anatomy, and I can't find anything out of the ordinary here either."

I sat cross-legged in Sweet's unfinished house. He'd brought a folding chair from the car and used it. Then he reached down to a lunch box and grabbed a wrapped sandwich. I had notes splayed out in front of me like a game of gin rummy. His side-armed toss of my share of the lunch fell short and nearly splattered on the autopsy report.

Toxicology came up zilch, but then without knowing the makeup of the exciter drug, Beckenbauer wouldn't have known what to test for. I had no clue yet either. Fritz had run residue tests and found no evidence of explosives. The absence of fingerprints baffled him, as it did me. They weren't just filed off, as some second-story men are known to do. It was like they had been surgically removed. There was no scarring, no sign of incisions.

I checked the contents of his stomach. Mendelssohn had found time for a beer in the hours before his death, but there was very little food left inside the stomach or intestines, leading Fritz to believe he hadn't eaten in days.

How long had you been on the run, Jorge? And from whom?

Sweet chowed down while I worked. "Science failing you for once, Glass?"

"Try not to sound so happy about it. It's not just my neck on the block ... not even yours. I get the feeling whoever is behind Jorge's murder knew these coroners would see something they shouldn't have."

I heard the clinking of a bottle then a pop and release of gas. I looked up to see an Ancient waved before my mug. I had been over these enough to justify a break. The suds went down easy. It had been only a couple of days since I shared a brew with Lee in his hideout, but so much had happened. I unwrapped the grub and dived in.

"Let me take a crack at these. Maybe they need something you don't have."

I took his bait. "And that would be?"

"Finesse."

"Yeah, right."

Sweet flipped pages around and started scanning them. He pushed aside report after medical report until he found the notes he was looking for.

"Here we go. Contents of one John Doe, now know as Jorge Mendelssohn's pockets:

"One set of keys; one book, *A Brave New World* by Aldous Huxley." Sweet paused. "The guy read science fiction?"

I cocked my head as if to say, *Don't all scientists?*

Sweet shook his head and whispered, "Freaks," before continuing.

"One receipt from Hank's Diner, T'laquepaque, New Mexico; one train ticket, one way to Chance City, Nevada, unchecked, dated for the day after victim's death; one receipt for—" He stopped and stared at a piece of paper. "I've got something."

I was all ears. "What?"

Sweet smiled. "Chalk one up for instinct over science." He handed me the list.

The receipt was for two people. Mendelssohn hadn't traveled alone.

* * *

I nearly knocked the door off its hinges when I busted in to the apartment. Merlot gave a startled scream until she saw it was me. "Noel, you scared me. What's wrong?"

I'd caught her in the middle of writing a note at the kitchen table.

A red tinge at the corner of my eyes appeared, just as it had in Merlot's dressing room. She recoiled in panic. Deep down I hoped I was wrong, but I knew I wasn't.

"You were here, weren't you? You came with Jorge to Industry City last September. You were here, with him, in this apartment."

Her orbs grabbed floor. A nearly inaudible, "Yes," came from her lips.

"You sent him to his death, didn't you?"

I took a step closer.

"*What?*" she yelled, standing up, facing me full on. "No, he's not dead! He's hiding from you! Or from them, whoever. He's not dead; he couldn't be."

"Can it, doll face. You damn well know he came here to see me. Why? What did he want to tell me?"

I took another step.

"I don't know! I really don't." She backed away from me.

I took yet another measured step forward.

"He wouldn't tell me. He kept saying it was better if I didn't know. He said only you could save him now. He left to talk to you, but he didn't come back. I figured you killed him, so I'd run back to the casino and tried to forget."

"You could have told me this!"

"When you showed up, I thought you'd figured out I was with him and come to finish the job. But then you was looking for him, so I started thinking he was still alive."

She quickly ran out of space between us. I knew how tough she was, so I wasn't going to be crazy and lunge after her.

"I thought maybe you scared him into hiding, but then you said all those things about him, and I had to know, so I came back here to try and find him."

"He's dead, sweetheart! Someone popped his lid all over Main Street."

"No! You're lying! He's alive! He's got to be alive!" She had backed up against the kitchen counter. She started throwing things at me: spoons, a peppermill, a dish rag. I let them bounce off me like bullets off of Superman. "Yourelyingyourelyingyourelying!"

Her voice was fading into sobs. She slid down the cabinet to pool into a heap on the floor.

I went over to the note.

Noel,

I'm going back to Chicago. Don't follow me. I need time to sort things ou—

"Like I have time to follow you? I'm trying to stop a madman. All you've done is kept secrets. Secrets that could have saved time and lives." I looked down at the weeping mess. "There are three widows who wouldn't be if you'd come clean when Jorge disappeared. Every coroner that came in contact with Jorge's file is dead."

I wasn't sure she listened anymore, but I continued anyway. I wanted to slap her around, make her see how badly she'd screwed things up. She was taboo, all right. She had said people die around me, but she'd have enough blood on her hands before I left.

"There's the body of a harmless man cooling in a morgue down in New Mexico. Hired killers have tried to kill me twice, and all you've done is play the frill. Is that why you gave me an easy ride? Did you think I could protect you? Well, I see what happens to men who try to protect you. They get their brains splattered over half of Industry City. I thought you were made of tougher stuff, Merlot."

I turned and spoke with my back to her, but loud enough to reach her over her sobs. "Maybe having the whole world protect you has made you weak. Go back to Chi-town. They'll take care of you there."

I closed the door behind me on her renewed wails of despair.

* * *

I had nowhere to go. I had no leads left. All I could do was track down Archdeacon and turn myself over to him with what I had. Maybe it was enough. Maybe I could cop a plea for Wan and Vincent, try to get them deported as opposed to a stint in cold storage. I hoped they'd send Lee to Japan, not Korea.

I headed toward familiar territory. Little Osaka was on the other side of downtown from where I was. I grabbed a streetcar and watched as businesses went by. We passed the Trinity Methodist Church. Its gothic structure appealed to me in the way certain art appealed to me. No other church in the Front Range carried such mathematical improbabilities. Its giant stone spire was once the largest in the United States, yet no one knew how it held up against the harsh Colorado winters and Chinook winds. The rhyolite exterior gave the church a crystalline appearance and beckoned all, as if to say, "My house is built on rock, not sand."

I'd never set foot inside the church. What I wanted—no, needed—was a scientific method church. I wanted answers here, not in the next life. I thought, for the briefest of moments, of stopping off at the church and seeing if there was any power to prayer.

I went to the library instead. I knew every inch of the place from my eleven years as a detective. I no longer had access to college libraries, but the main branch of the Industry City Library District was stocked well enough to keep me busy. I rarely had to special order a book.

There was a string dangling from memory, like a loose thread on a good shirt. You didn't want to pull it in case it ruined the shirt, but leaving it alone annoyed you.

I kept my head down and grabbed several scream sheets as I went. I found an area on the fourth floor years ago where I could sit and never see another soul. At times, I had fallen asleep there, and no one noticed me when they closed up shop. I had to be let out by the night watchman.

I combed the newspaper pages, looking for my thread until my legs went numb. Something in these pages would jog my memory. Stories about me and my escapades had already moved farther back in the order. Mostly it was wild speculation of what I'd do next—flee the country, turn myself in, commit suicide.

Other articles made it clear that it was becoming a good time to be a scientist. New uses for nuclear energy were being unveiled every day. One such article talked about the first nuclear power plant, set to open next year. Our new president, Dwight D. Eisenhower, was a proponent of nuclear technology. He'd be a great guy to chew the fat with.

I thought about *The Atlantis*. Next year would be a perfect time to get it on the market. The country was shifting away from oil and the power it had over us. Clean energy was the future, and a society run on nuclear energy would be perfect, a utopia.

Utopias.

Who else wanted utopia? Not Russia. They wanted war. And not Archdeacon. Mr. X used technology whereas Archdeacon would just use a gun.

Somebody. Somebody else in the recent past pushed the idea of a world free of pain, money, war. A brave new world … A shape of things to come.

The thread came loose.

I had it!

Damn it to hell! I had it!

I knew who was behind T.I. and what the initials stood for now. I had been thinking too linear, looking at immediate causes and effects, but beneath it lay a much bigger picture when you looked at the goal of a perfect society.

All the killings made sense now—Tangie, Mendelssohn, Stalin. I wasn't sure why they had killed Yousev since he didn't have Mendelssohn's note, but once I got one of the sons of bitches responsible, I'd wring it out of him.

I ran down two flights to the fiction wing. I was in luck. Both books were in. I grabbed them and ran down to periodicals again. The newspapers I wanted were twenty years old. I doubted they'd have copies, but I was fortunate to find they kept old newspapers in an airtight room in the basement. I avoided the research librarian's gaze as I jotted down the dates I needed. She sighed; I had interrupted her reading.

I tapped my leg nervously. It had been years since I'd thought about the events of 1932. The Great Depression hadn't affected me the way it had the rest of the country, with me already safely ensconced in college.

For many, it had seemed like the end of the world.

For others, that was exactly what they wanted, the end of the old world and the chance to build a new utopia.

The librarian returned with a stack of papers sealed in plastic sleeves.

"Please return these the way you found them, sir. Try to avoid any tears. You will be responsible for any repairs we have to do. May I have your library card?"

On reflex, I went for my wallet but thought better of it. "Um, I left it on the table upstairs. I'll bring it back when I'm finished with these."

She stared at me skeptically. That's when I discovered that the hardest thing in the world to do was to look sincere while trying not to look directly at someone. I pulled a ten spot from my pocket. "Here. This should cover my responsibility for the moment. You keep it even if I come back and they're perfect." Hamilton's face was more sincere, so she gave me the stack after she tucked the bill into her brassiere.

Back in my hidey-hole, I opened the papers one by one and carefully reread all the articles. I found what I needed in December of 1932. I closed my eyes, sat back in the chair, and let the facts cascade down the waterfall of my brain. I looked at each one in turn and knew what lay at the bottom.

I opened my eyes, and the unblinking eyes of a Mayan hunter stared back. I had time for an "Oh, sh—" before things went black.

.

Chapter Twelve

The first thing I realized, as the synapses fired in the gray matter I called a brain, was that I couldn't feel the left side of my body. I was semi-sure that was due to the concrete floor I had woken up on. There was no light, but I could hear the *plink-plink* of droplets forming a small puddle. I sat up and rubbed feeling into my numb extremities.

There was no light, so I felt my way to a metal wall. I rapped on it and heard an echo. Three walls connected to open space, the back against concrete. I was in some sort of storage locker. The door was predictably locked from the outside.

Sweet had gotten my clothes from Goodwill. On the offbeat chance, I checked the pockets and came up with a lighter. It looked as if it had gone through a wash, so I tested it to see if the torch would light. The gasper lit on the twelfth try. I extinguished it because I saw nothing I hadn't already guessed before.

The dripping came from one of three pipes that ran perpendicular to my room. I touched one; it was hot. The second was cold, but the third was just right. The hot line was the one dripping a slow drip. There was rust around the joint, and it gave me an idea.

I was counting on the third line being the gas line. I'd have a chance to escape if the joint would give. I gathered water from the puddle and poured it on the junction. There wasn't enough water to do the job I needed, but any extra help would be appreciated. I started pushing against the joint. The pipe was old, and I worried I would break it in two, which wouldn't do me any good. I needed just a little crack.

I was still alive, which meant things had changed for the mysterious Mr. X. The fact that the Hero Twin hadn't immediately avenged his brother led me to believe Mr. X had him on a tight leash, and if that was the case, Mr. X was someone to be afraid of.

Lights came on outside my container. There were the sounds of people filing into the area. I pressed my ear against the front wall. I could hear the buzz of a crowd. Then things quieted down. Footsteps approached. Whatever was going to happen to me was happening now. I worked the pipe quickly, applying all my strength to the joint. I felt it give some and placed my hawk-like nose near it. I smelled the telltale trickle of gas leaking out. However, it was too little, and it needed to pool more for my plan to work. I needed to stall. I scrunched down in the corner just as the door swung open.

The Twin that ankled in was different than the one I remembered from the train and from the library. He was smaller. His stance was off, less rigid. The angle of his body was smoother, and the outfit seemed a size too big on it. The mask was different too. It looked more feminine. This was no Hero brother, but a Hero sister.

Hero Triplets?

She cocked her head at me, taking in my disheveled appearance, my cowering act. Satisfied she saw whatever it was she needed to see, she turned on her stems and walked out. There were words directly outside my cell, my name was definitely mentioned, but everything else was muffled, indistinct.

In a moment, the Hunter visage I remembered so vividly stepped into the light. He held the exciter injector in his hand. The mask still had its evil grin, but now I was sure the man underneath wore the smile too.

"Don't hurt me!" I curled up in a ball. I needed him closer, under the pipe. "It wasn't me. I didn't kill your brother!"

He'd have to come get me, and I hoped he'd do it with gusto, not paying attention to the smell that must be accumulating at the ceiling. He moved in, and I could hear the growl from under the mask. When he reached the spot, I ignited the lighter and tossed it above his head. I rolled back into a ball as the flames filled the small room. The Twin had taken the brunt of the blast, while I was sure I'd lost hair on the back of my head. His mask, a melted goo, adhered to his face. He stumbled out of the locker while trying to pull the burning material from his head. I ran past him, picking up the discarded exciter gun as I went out.

I launched onto a loading dock. A cargo hauler was parked at a downward angle in front of a huge overhead door. What was more surprising were the nearly two hundred armed personnel clad in pseudo-military tactical gear who had turned to stare at me as I emerged from the storage container.

"Oops, wrong room. I was looking for the Salvation Army."

The Hero sister was standing on the back of the semi, as if to address the men. She made a silent motion, and the men sprang to action, raising guns and moving *en masse* toward me.

Before any of them could open fire, I hoofed it past a row of identical storage containers until I found a door marked *Stairs*. It opened to a hallway, and I had to try more doors until I found the one up. As I entered it, the men poured into the hallway. The first report rang out, and I stayed low as I made my way up the first flight. As I rounded corners, the stairs looked as if they would continue up to heaven. It was ages before I saw the lobby door. I slammed against them and immediately saw Liberty Tower's logo.

I spun around in amazement. I'd been in this lobby not three days before on my way to Reece's vault. Why was I here? Why was there a secret army below the Little Technologies offices?

I didn't have time to think. I made my way to the front as two black-clad men exited the stairwell. They shouted something to a guard behind a desk in the lobby. I heard a buzz, and the revolving door I was making for stopped dead, trapping a patron inside. I was cornered. I looked for another route. My bulk was insufficient to break through the glass, so I moved quickly away from my pursuers. Fortune was with me as a ding sounded and an elevator opened. I ran across the tile floor. Two additional soldiers joined the chase. I slid between closing doors, narrowly escaping their grasps. I punched the top floor and headed for the only place I knew there.

If Little Technologies was in on this, then there'd be men waiting for me. I popped the escape door on the roof of my car and hoisted myself out. I could see a second car ascending next to mine. I waited.

When my car stopped, there would be a rush to grab me. It wouldn't take long for them to figure out where I went. I looked around frantically. I blocked the trapdoor with a wrench I found lying there. It would take the soldiers a moment to clear it. That moment was all I needed.

My car stopped. I heard the door below me open and the sounds of men entering the car. The second car arrived and their door opened. I moved over to that car as the bangs against the trapdoor started. I opened the second roof hatch and dropped into a now empty car.

I ran full throttle from the open elevator and down past Reece's vault. Police warning tape still hung loosely in front of his open office. The black army was on my heels. I didn't have a lot of time. I remember it was Wednesday. If my luck held out, I'd have my escape route.

As I rounded the corner, I grabbed the back of the big box that housed one of Reece's color television cameras. The whole contraption rolled back, probably on wheels. I pushed it with everything I had toward the men as they came into sight. They slammed into it full on as it toppled over.

I about gave the window washer a heart attack as he cleaned the pane of glass from the outside.

I waved him to the side and kicked at the window. It took two kicks, but broke free. Wind whipped at me hard, which made the jump to scaffolding difficult. I nearly continued past it into freefall, but the window man grabbed me and pulled me back. I thanked him and indicated I wanted to go down, my words barely audible in the howl of the wind. He nodded and slowly loosened our counterweight.

We descended. As we passed other offices, I held my fingers to the side of my face, showing the universal sign for *call the police.* One of the black-clad men had crawled to the window opening; I could see another holding fast onto him. He extended his gun over the side and tried to take a shot at me. I moved over to avoid the bullet and nearly tipped our lift. The cleaner pushed me back the other way to rebalance us. I leaned as close to the building's front as I could, trying to make a smaller target. My assailant leaned out farther to get a better angle, and his partner lost grip on his waist. The man went by too fast to catch, but not so fast that I couldn't see the terror etched on his face.

When I die, I hope it's not like that.

As we got closer to the ground, I could see black shapes mingled into the crowd surrounding the red splotch. However, by the time we touched down, the yodel of police sirens had drawn close. The black army men had vanished.

The police cars pulled into classic barricade formation, squawking on loudspeakers for the crowd to move away. They got behind their cars, guns drawn and beaded on me. I was told to remain where I was.

Shortly thereafter, military vehicles arrived. They, too, set up a perimeter. Their guns were much bigger than the police's. I could see down the barrels of theirs.

Next came black cars and men in suits. This must be the CIA. They didn't draw any guns, seeing that there were enough already on me. Instead, they moved within the ranks of the police and army, taking positions near those in charge.

Sweet pulled up, an exasperated look on his face. I shrugged when he caught my eye. The motion made everyone with a gun uptight, but they relaxed when I didn't explode. I don't know why someone didn't just arrest me. I wasn't armed, save for the exciter gun and a lighter. Everyone was afraid.

And from what I knew, they had a right to be.

An army command car pulled up. General Archdeacon stepped out, his presence making ripples in the crowd. His first words were, "No one shoot! I am under direct orders from the president to take this man alive."

The president knew my name? *The* president? I wondered if I could get his autograph.

Archdeacon walked past the assembly, past the barricade, and up to within five feet of me. A good six inches taller than I, even without the army boots, he leaned his blond and gray buzz-cut toward me a good half an inch as a greeting.

"Glass," he said civilly.

"General," I returned his greeting the same way. "You're looking good. Lost some weight?"

"You're a funny man, Glass." There was no sign of his finding the joke funny. "Well, you got my attention. I hope you have something of value."

I motioned to the stain on the sidewalk. "There were two hundred more like him in the basement of this building twenty minutes ago, but I wouldn't be surprised if they were all gone now. They were getting ready to move out. Loaded into the back of a semi truck. I'm sorry I didn't get the license plate."

"Two hundred?"

"Yes."

"Like him?"

"Similar."

Archdeacon chewed his lip for a moment. He shouted orders over his shoulder, never taking his eyes completely off me. "Sergeant! Secure this building. No one goes in or out. Start a ground minus sweep. Highest level precautions."

"Sir! Yes, sir!"

The general, focused on me fully again, nicely asked, "May I arrest you *now?*"

"By all means."

*   *   *

"You know, Glass," Archdeacon began, once we were safely situated in the army recruiting office he was using as a temporary command center, "if you had just let the CIA take you into custody, this whole 'traitor' thing would have been cleared up quickly. We've been watching you for some time, ever since the CIA got word of Mendelssohn's death."

The office displayed much of the same propaganda it had before WWII, only the Nazis had been traded out for Commies. Slogans like "The Mark of a Man" and "A Man Among Men" sold the idea that only through service could you obtain the right to adulthood. There were certainly more posters aimed at women than the last time I saw the inside of this type of place. Women's Army Corps took up nearly as much space as the men's advertisements. Rosie the Riveter was no longer content to stay at home. They were leading whole divisions of the armed services. Hell, there had been a mystery woman in charge of a whole squad of black army soldiers.

It *was* a new world order.

"And how long have they known, General? I just traipsed halfway across the southwest chasing a dead man."

"Again, Glass. You wouldn't have had to do that if—"

"If I had just let myself be arrested for crimes I didn't commit. Yeah, that's an easy sell, General."

He didn't like the sarcasm, but since I was a guest, I didn't get a browbeating. "They, like me, just wanted to know what you know."

I got up from the table and moved around the room. "I had nothing anybody would have wanted before this started, but I'm assured by attempts on my life that I did. General, everything I've learned about this mess came after Reece's visit."

We'd spent the first hour catching up. The general sat quietly while I outlined everything I had done. I gave him descriptions of Vincent and his two stooges but made sure he knew to capture them alive as they were not an immediate threat. I took special care to reiterate the innocence of Lee and Sweet in the whole process so there would be no blowback on them.

The general took a loud sip from his coffee. He hated to wait for it to cool and usually burned his lip. This time was no different. He patted his upper lip with his tongue, cooling it off. He set down the mug and crossed his hands. "Glass, since the CIA came into existence, they have monitored communiqués from all corners of the globe, especially those that are generated domestically." He reached down to a satchel, the type with folding compartments, and pulled out a thick binder. It landed on the table with a *thump*, and I was reminded of the case file Sweet had procured. I discovered it contained much of the same information, including the missing pages from the autopsy.

"Where did you get these?"

"I didn't. This is a CIA file. When the autopsy of Jorge Mendelssohn reached the national level, it sent red flags all over the place. Remember, we had done the official inquest on the microwave incident."

Oh, so it's an "incident" now?

"To the trained eye, the state of the bodies recovered from your lab were too similar to Mendelssohn's cause of death. It had not even crossed my mind your discovery could be used as a weapon."

Reece's story, that the general was orchestrating everything from behind the scenes, shouldn't have held any merit. Archdeacon, in all the meetings we had during my military research, was bored when it came to technology. I swore he slept with his eyes open. He would've looked at the designs and seen gobbledygook, not a weapon. Give him a gun, and he would fire it. Ask him to build a gun, and he was lost. He was the least technologically savvy person I knew. He could never have been the one behind a conspiracy laced with science.

"Well, it seems you and I are the only ones. I wanted military technology with my name on it. The Glass Radar or something. I wanted to make a difference and make my mark doing it." It was a hard pill, but it was the truth. "I was blinded by my pride."

"Are you still blind, Glass?"

It was a pointed question, so I parked myself again and gave him an honest answer. "I don't know. I've been chased across three states in the same number of days. I've been told many things I didn't want to hear. I've been responsible for at least three deaths, one just by association. If you're asking me if I'm still clueless, then no; I have an insight into the big picture. If you are asking if I have delusions of grandeur, those died with Tangie."

"So what do you have?"

I motioned to the exciter gun. "For starters, I have that. It will need to be analyzed."

The general nodded. "We're bringing in some people for that. We understand the MASER weapon and its methodology, why do you need to go further with it?"

"Mendelssohn built the thing. There was no way he would have let them drug him with the exciter fluid. So it had to get into him some other way."

That confused Archdeacon. He reached for his cup, thought better of it, and sat it back down. "How do you know he had the fluid in him and, for that matter, that he didn't know?"

I smiled. I would get to showcase the skills I'd developed as a detective since I'd seen him last.

"Witnesses say that Mendelssohn ran from an alleyway out into the middle of a St. Patrick's Day party. He tried to lose himself in the crowd, believing that the MASER wouldn't be useful picking one guy out of hundreds. He knew the effects of the gun and the exciter drug by then, especially after helping take out Stalin."

"And you're sure what the Ruskies told you was on the up-and-up?"

I shrugged. "As best as I can guess, them being spies and all. So the killer had to know Mendelssohn had the fluid in him, or they wouldn't have targeted the crowd."

"Why?"

I was exasperated. It should have made perfect sense, but here I was, dumbing technology down for him, as I had so many years ago. "When you use the magnetron without something to reflect the microwaves back, the MASER takes much longer to excite the molecules. The fluid acts as a reflector or speeds up the molecules in some way that cuts the time down. Think of it as a blender with two speeds. Without the drug, it's on low, with the drug, it's on high."

"And?"

"*And*, well, they could zap the area. Mendelssohn would blow up first before anyone else did."

"And so when he goes pop, they just stop the gun before anyone else does. Okay, I'll grant you that. But you still haven't told me anything about this organization and why they have an army."

I got back up and went to a chalkboard. "Let's look at this like a murder case. For a murder conviction to stick, you need three things: means, motive, and opportunity, correct?" I took up a piece of chalk and wrote the three words across the top. "But we have three murders." I wrote *Tangie*, *Stalin*, and *Mendelssohn* down along the side. I filled in *MASER* for all the spots under means.

"Rigging my experiment was a way for Mr. X to test a theory, to see if my microwaves could kill. But not only that, it discredited the project. In doing so, the microwaves were branded too dangerous, and they could go about making the MASER. It'd be years before microwave radar would be 'fixed' and by then, they were well ahead of the curve."

I wrote *The Test* under Tangie's opportunity.

"So why did Mr. X want the weapon? And why hasn't it been used before Stalin?"

"Ah, two questions for the price of one. And the $100,000 answer is …" I let him hang for the moment to build suspense. I might have let him hang a moment too long as his brows furrowed and he started looking annoyed. "Hitler."

The general sat up. "What?"

"Yes, the organization behind the MASER wanted it to stop the war. They couldn't afford to let Hitler win Europe. He would set his sights on America or Russia next. That wouldn't help them reach their goal."

"Which is?" He was clearly annoyed at my roundabout explanation. I knew this, but I was still perfecting this theory as I went along. I didn't have all the answers, just enough to get his attention and the attention of those above him. I needed to sound like I knew more than I did, which is, of course, what got me into this to begin with.

"Not yet, General. I'll get you there. I have to convince you if I'm going to convince anyone else."

I swear the man growled at me. I wrote *Stop WWII* under Tangie's motive. I liked it. I knew why Tangie died now. But I still needed to prove it.

"Only, we beat them to the punch. We won the war without Hitler's assassination. Confound it if the Yanks didn't mess up their whole plan. But since it was what they wanted anyway, they waited."

"Twelve years?"

"Yes."

"For what? Another war?"

He was catching on. He reached for his cup again, put his hooks on it, but then as he tried to follow my logic to its conclusion, he pulled his fingers away. He needed all his faculties for thought, and I'm sure the coffee would be cold before he would actually have the concentration to drink it.

"Yes, only Korea wasn't big enough for their plans. They needed another world war. Things are ripe for a conflict with Russia. The Communist Block, the Iron Curtain. Stalin itching for a fight. The time was almost here."

"But killing Stalin stopped the war. If he'd lived another six months, we'd be at war with them now."

"True, but it wasn't quite time. Stalin was pushing a war too soon. Russia wasn't ready. Their people, resources, and military weren't ready for another prolonged war, plus they were missing one key element."

That one he got without prodding.

"The bomb."

I nodded. "While they successfully created a nuclear explosion in '49, they didn't have the control of a hydrogen bomb. Now they do."

I wrote *Political Struggle* under Stalin's opportunity and *Delay WWIII* under his motive.

Archdeacon shook his head, reached for the coffee, committed to it, and brought it up to his lips.

"Glass, this doesn't make sense. That would mean that Mr. X has people in the Russian government, even KGB. You've already implied Mr. X has people in our government. Are you saying they're playing us against each other? For what means?"

"The total destruction of modern society."

When the general spilled his coffee, I believed I had finally made my point.

CHAPTER THIRTEEN

General Archdeacon's hincty nature got to me. In the hours since I laid out my theory, he hadn't stopped to take a piss. If he wasn't barking orders at some hapless grunt, he was on the phone talking to superiors. The worst part was his belief that there would be another attempt on my life soon. He had a troop mover modified with lead-lined walls. We took it to Fort Palmer.

"The exciter fluid should be clear of my system. They can't just zap me anymore."

"Doesn't matter. I got orders to protect you from anything short of a nuclear strike. This might even survive that."

It wouldn't, but I didn't want to take that hope away from the man.

Fort Palmer was the army's barracks and hospital just outside of the town limits. A state-of-the-art facility, it could house several hundred men and was as safe a place as any in Colorado. The decision to move base camp there made sense, but I also felt a little like I was being placed under lock and key. I wouldn't be able to make a move without Archdeacon knowing. Our convoy included a CIA tail, which the general was less than happy about.

Everyone would get a piece of me all at once.

Shortly after arriving through the heavily patrolled security gate, I was ushered into a large room filled with chalkboards, charts, and maps. On a table in the center, nameplates were set in front of several seats: Allen Dulles, head of the CIA; J. Edgar

Hoover, director of the FBI; Arthur William Radford, chairman of the Joint Chiefs of Staff; and at the head of the table was the jaw-dropper, President Dwight D. Eisenhower. Each setting had a microphone and speaker in place of the person. I was struck by the irony that their communication with this room came in through microwaves.

I found my place at the opposite end from Ike. Hey, I voted for him and he knows my name, so I figured I could call him Ike. Maybe just not to his face.

I had been given my own file similar to the one Archdeacon had when we met. I flipped it open and found dozens of reports, each written in military language I was woefully ignorant on.

Archdeacon sat to my right. He whispered, "Don't embarrass me."

Radford's voice got things started before I could respond.

"Okay, let's call this meeting to order. Let's start with the FBI's findings since yours was the first report of trouble on my stack. What do you have, Ed?"

The voice of J. Edgar came through loud and clear. I had no idea where all these men were. For all I knew, they could be all in the same room back in Washington or in the Bahamas.

"Mr. President, Chairman, as you all know, it is the Bureau's job to investigate suspicious activities within the boundaries of the United States of America. This can include monitoring the activities of suspicious groups to unusual deaths. We take great steps to ensure the safety of our citizens domestically."

I leaned over to Archdeacon. "He sounds like an advertisement for FBI recruiting."

The general shushed me.

"Our first indication that there was a threat came from a coroner's report regarding the suspicious death of one Jorge Mendelssohn, scientist by trade and a person of interest to the FBI. Mendelssohn became so when he left the New Mexico Institute of Technology and disappeared shortly after the events of 1939, case file 1F5678-AG29."

I could hear the pages flipping, so I flipped my own folder and found my name. It was a report on the microwave radar failure.

Hoover continued. "While reports had him still in the country, specifically Chance City, Nevada, we could not ascertain the nature of his current employ. He was seen in the presence of a woman with known mob ties, a Margaret Sterling a.k.a. Merlot Sterling, lounge singer. Attempts to recruit her were met with failure, as were attempts to trace Mendelssohn back to his employer.

"The report became red flagged when three coroners, each who had investigated Mendelssohn's death, turned up dead themselves. This includes an FBI coroner, thus making this a top priority with us. Despite efforts on the Bureau's part, no connection was made between the agent's death and Mendelssohn's. Movement in Chance City has been typical mob activities within normal range.

"However, since an event three days ago, there has been a buzz of traceable activity. That event was the death of Rafael Itzamna who, with his brother Loren, worked as hit men under the alias the Hero Twins. We traced Loren to a compound seventy miles into the desert, but by the time forces were mobilized to raid the target, it was vacant. This compound hosted both a research laboratory and military training ground."

It was apparent J. Edgar had big lungs. I don't know that he took a breath during his whole dissertation. I turned to look at the pictures of the compound. It was impressive. Most of the buildings were covered in sand the way Ilya had covered the cabin in snow. It was definitely a military-designed place. Add to that the platoon I'd discovered under Liberty Tower, and this group had someone seriously backing them.

Dulles's voice shot out. "Ed? How'd this get by your guys?"

Ed's tone of voice didn't change an iota. Myself, I'd be fuming. "I'll have you know that we have not had the funding we did before the war, Al. Men and resources been stretched thin. Also, a good deal of our budget now goes to your branch to—"

Radford cut in. "Ed, now is not the time for money squabbling. Let's stick to the task at hand. What else did you find at the compound? Any clue as to their identity? Their goals?"

"I have a team of investigators going over the place inch by inch. However, for such a quick move, they left the place bone dry. One obvious finding was the initials T.I. and a logo, which was evident on many walls."

The logo was a pyramid built inside an engineering compass. The *T* and *I* were inscribed within the blocks of the temple. It gave credence to what I was about to propose.

"Sir? If I might add," interrupted Archdeacon. "This logo was also on the uniform of the body we examined from the Liberty Tower incident."

"The one Mr. Glass was responsible for?"

I didn't like the tone coming from Radford's speaker.

"Yes, sir. That one."

Dulles asked me, "You have a habit of leaving little to interrogate, don't you, Mr. Glass? We have Mendelssohn, a hit man, and a soldier, all working for the same people, yet all we get is the pieces when you're done. Is that your M.O., Detective?"

I knew he was trying to push a button, referring to the experiment gone wrong. He had the same reports I had in front of me and knew Tangie Taylor was listed as an "intimate acquaintance" of mine. He goaded me, and I took his bait.

I started. "With no due respect, *sir* ... " Archdeacon grabbed my arm, cautioning me, but I didn't have to continue. The president spoke up for me.

"Al, that was in poor taste and unnecessary. I want you to apologize to that American citizen who has done nothing but cooperate with us since his capture."

My what?

"He has brought us valuable intelligence, and I'd ask that you please remember this man was and still is one of America's prize scientists, regardless of his tarnished past, unjust as it was."

It was a moment before Dulles said, "I apologize, Mr. Glass. Please retract my statement." That was a lawyer for you.

Radford took the reins back. "Since you're anxious to speak, why don't you go next, Al?"

Dulles cleared his throat. "The valuable intelligence you spoke of, sir, apparently points to the assassination of Josef Stalin, once considered a death by natural causes. The Stalin angle is not completely new to us. Word of Beria's arrest and subsequent interrogation came to us from an overseas operative."

"What about this sleeper agent Mr. Glass reported? How'd this happen?" Ike asked.

"I would let it be known, Mr. President, that this information has yet to be confirmed, mostly due to the lack of the agent in question. We found the safe house Mr. Glass's Russian spies were using."

I held my breath. I was expecting to hear one of two things. Either it was vacant or everyone was "accidentally" killed in the line of fire.

"The cabin was empty, having been vacated two days prior."

I exhaled and it may have been just a stray burst of static, but I swear I heard J. Edgar Hoover chuckle. "It is alarming to discover that the Soviets have placed these sleeper agents in our midst, isn't it, Al? That is, if what Mr. Glass is telling us is true."

"Cross my heart and hope to die, Mr. Hoover. Stick a needle—" Again Archdeacon stopped me.

"Ed, if he's telling the truth, then that would have been before the agency's time. We were created just for such a thing because the Bureau wasn't equipped—"

Radford stepped in again. "Archdeacon? You ready to present your findings?"

"Yes, sir."

Archdeacon nodded to me. There was a cameraman in the corner to capture anything I wrote on the board, so I signaled him to follow me. I hadn't given symposium in years, let alone to such an audience. I hoped I wasn't rusty. I hoped I wasn't wrong either.

I looked directly into the camera. "Mr. President, gentlemen, there is a plot to assassinate President Eisenhower and send the world into World War III." There were sounds from the speakers like a frat party, so I raised my voice over theirs. "A war our enemies hope will dismantle the infrastructure of society so they may rebuild it in their own image."

There were simultaneous questions from all the speakers, save for the president's. He knew not to interrupt a man on a mission.

"Hey!" I shouted over them. "Let me finish, then you can ask questions."

Dulles was the last to shut up, but he did.

"Okay, then. Most of this you got with the general's report. But let me break it down."

I moved to the board where my notes from the recruiting office had already been transposed.

"We now know that my experiment was rigged to test a weapon. We also know that that weapon was used to kill Stalin. Why? Because Stalin was ready to go to war even knowing we had the bomb. Politically, we were impotent. If we were the type of country to strike first, we could have nuked North Korea. Yet, Stalin wasn't willing to wait for his scientists to finish their own bomb."

"But they have now," said Radford.

"Yes, they have. But at the time, they had no idea if it would work. Stalin was ready to risk everything on a fool's errand. So Beria took him out with help. That help came from the same group we're pursuing here."

Hoover couldn't wait. "How? How do you know this?"

I hated being interrupted, but if I could prove this point, then that would go a long way toward my not having to prove everything else. I nodded to Archdeacon, who got on a phone and gave an order. After he hung up, he addressed the group.

"Gentlemen, a folder is being brought in to you by my men. In it are clippings from newspapers dated over twenty years ago. Mr. Glass has stumbled upon a global conspiracy that started before World War II."

He motioned for me to continue, so I opened my own copy and flipped along.

"In the article dated July 23, 1923, you'll see that author and engineer Alexander Bogdanov was arrested by the OGPU for suspicion of being tied to an organization called The Worker's Truth. He was let go after seven days of interrogation."

Dulles asked, "The Worker's Truth? Wasn't that a splinter Communist party? They wanted to remove all government control and place it into the hands of the engineers, correct?"

I nodded, and then remembered the camera was focused on the board, not me. "Yes. They felt, even back then, that while Communism had points, it focused much too much on singular power."

If I was playing Go with Wan Lee, this would be my first star point. Though, like recalling a match before a crowd of people, I had to show how each side played their moves.

"Like on Lenin? Or Stalin?" Radford questioned.

"Or any one central figure. The People's Republic wasn't for the people. It was for the power-mongers."

"I'm sorry, Mr. Glass," the voice of the president broke in, "but as interesting as this all is, what does it have to do with Stalin's assassination, or an attempt on my life?"

"I can shed some light on that," said Dulles. "Beria was chief interrogator for the OGPU. Glass, you think Bogdanov coerced him?"

"Bogdanov planted the seed in Beria that Communism would fail. That thought became germinated with the next article in your folder."

Again, I heard flipping as they came to the 1929 article, "Walter Polakov Goes to Russia."

"Polakov? No, not Polakov," Hoover said, his voice filled with denial. "We had him thoroughly checked out before we let him travel."

"Ed, as you seem familiar with the individual, why don't you fill us in?" Ike suggested.

"Well, Mr. President, he *is* a Russian immigrant. Over the years he proved to be a successful engineer. The only hiccup came from some of Polakov's ideas. Crazy ones, but ultimately harmless."

"Harmless?" I laughed.

"What ideas?" The President asked.

"He was a devoted follower of the New Machine philosophy created by Henry Gantt. It was all about engineering a radical new society without a central government. It would be controlled by scientists and engineers."

"Like the Worker's Truth?"

"Well, yes, sort of. Gantt's philosophy spawned two radically different sects—one believing change must be gradual, the other believing change must be forced. The principal voice for the calmer of the two groups came from Thorstein Veblen. Polakov promoted the latter, a group led by—"

Hoover stopped dead. His contemporaries grew silent. I figured that if they all followed the flow, they reached the same conclusion.

When you look at a finished GO board, after one player has surrendered, all you see is a mass of black and white stones. Dissecting the game from start, though, you can see the flow of the game, where mistakes were made. Letting Polakov go to Russia was the political equivalent of connecting one area of life on the board to another and would ultimately create the series of events that led to me talking to these heads of state. That I was able to put it together in three days while they, with all their resources, let it slip under their communal radars baffled me.

"Who?" Archdeacon asked. "Glass has been keeping me in the dark on some of these players. Whose vision of a new world order did Polakov sell to Beria in order to get him to kill Stalin?"

"Frederick Taylor." Ed practically spat the name. Of course, Hoover's influence in political events started long before the New Deal. Dulles, Radford, and Ike, as well. If they knew nothing else, they knew of Taylor's efficiency movement, often called Taylorism. It's still taught in colleges, I hear.

"Yes, Taylor, who believed no government would turn over power willingly." I hoped even Archdeacon would recognize that name. He instead sat there blank-faced, still trying to catch up. I had so much to teach him. The other's, especially Dulles, were right there with me.

"Are you meaning to tell us this is *their* work? They killed Stalin? I thought their movement died with the New Deal. They became a punch line economists told each other in men's rooms."

"Like you said, there were two groups. One who tried to play by the rules and lost, Veblen's group. The other group, Gantt's, hasn't been heard of since. What have they been doing these past twenty years, I ask you?"

The general's impatience manifested as sweat coming off his brow. He took out a handkerchief and dabbed at his forehead. All this sociology was going over his head.

"Who are we talking about, Glass? Marxists? Socialists? Communists? Give me someone to target."

I walked over to him and flipped the page on his folder where the last headline, dated December 1932, read, *Technocracy to Take Over America!*

"Yes, gentlemen. The Technocrats are back and they want to start World War III."

* * *

The meeting broke shortly after I laid out what I thought the Technocrats next steps would be. Archdeacon made appropriate commitments to action, but asked me for more details as we walked back toward the laboratory he'd set up for me. I explained the Technocrats were a group of engineers who believed society could be designed to run on machines with very little supervision, allowing people to live a life of leisure, contributing only to the betterment of mankind. This would involve removing governments and the current price-wage system. Money would be replaced with an energy contribution system, where everyone's needs would be met based on how much they gave back.

"Isn't that the basis of Communism?"

I shook my head. "They have similar philosophies, but Communism still holds on to many of our current ideals—politics, power, money. Technocracy is a complete reset. Everything we currently use to determine worth, from hourly wages to the price of the *Mona Lisa*, would be erased and started from scratch."

The general's strides were twice mine, so I was hustling to keep pace. He stopped and I walked three steps further before I realized it.

"So they wanted the Soviets to have the bomb so we could blow each other up. That's what this is all about. If we destroy each other, then there is no winner. Society has to start over."

I faced him. "You're not all muscle, after all, are you?"

He laughed. "I understand strategy, Glass. It's just the scale I couldn't see. What would benefit a group if America and Russia destroyed each other? I see now. It's like a chalkboard. If you erase everything, you can write whatever you want on it." He started walking again. "That article, the last one, it implied that America was going to go the way of this ... Technocracy once upon a time?"

He slowed down his pace so I could keep up with him. "After the depression, people were grasping at anything to save the country. The Technocrats had actually predicted the collapse of the American economy decades before. They saw the crash of '29 as a chance to rebuild America in such a way that money would never be an issue."

"What happened?"

I was puzzled. "General, I mean no disrespect, but you're a little bit older than me. Weren't you there when all this happened?"

"Son, I am a military man, through and through. I really don't need to know politics and agendas. All I have ever needed to know are two things: who I report to and who I'm up against. I leave all that philosophy stuff to the brainiacs."

As an ally, Archdeacon was exactly the man you wanted leading your troops. A never retreat, never surrender sort of warrior. Wouldn't ever be president, though. Eisenhower, the strategist, fit the role of world leader better.

"Well, the Technocrats fell apart because they weren't willing to stage a coup when they didn't know who to answer to."

We approached an elevator. He pressed the up button. "What do you mean?"

"They had two leaders, and the group splintered. It's been their problem from the beginning. Fredrick Taylor's ideas became the cornerstone. The concept begat two completely different think tanks, Veblen and Gantt. Veblen influenced Howard Scott, an engineer, while Gantt produced Walter Rautenstrauch, a professor."

We stepped into the elevator, and the general stuck a key into a lock. The elevator seemed to know where to go after that.

"Scott. Who's that?"

All this was in the notes I'd given Archdeacon, and I'm sure he'd read them in bed at night, stocking cap on and four-star teddy bear on the pillow next to him, but I knew then that what the general really wanted to know was who to shoot when the time came.

"No one knows much about him, and he likes to keep it that way. From what I've gathered, the Big One really messed with his mind and he came out of it with this idea of changing society so it'd never have to go to war again. It came down to energy resources for him. He liked doing surveys of America's energy consumption. Difficult work, but he swore he could show how the whole world could move away from money to energy production.

"Scott hooks up with Rautenstrauch and forms the Technocracy Alliance, but each person brought ideals that were as completely different as their mentors. Scott wanted the people to take up the cry for Technocracy, while Rautenstrauch tried to effect change within the leadership of the country, get them to step down voluntarily. He had President Hoover's ear for a while even. The Technocrats called Hoover 'the Great Engineer.' It's their highest rank, like president."

Archdeacon shook his head as if he had water in his ear. I think I drowned his poor brain in facts. "How do you know all this? None of this was in any of your reports."

"I attended some seminars run by Rautenstrauch while he was still at Columbia. Remember, I was in college by sixteen. I was one of the minds he wanted to influence. He made great points about greed influencing business and government and ultimately, who knows? An engineered society might have been better for us, even for the world. There'd be no wars because everyone would have whatever they desired and the freedom to do what they needed to do. A perfect utopia."

The general scowled. "Do I have to worry about you, Glass?"

I laughed. "No, sir. For all its dreams, Technocracy has too many faults. Things like how do you assign an energy value to the arts or what to do with mentally or physically handicapped who can't contribute to society. No, my father held to the idea, 'If it ain't broke, don't fix it.' That's good enough for me. I like money. In fact, I've missed it. Done some things I'm less than proud of to get some of it. I'm okay with the system we have."

"Good to know. What then is TI? The new Technocracy Alliance?"

"Technocracy Incorporated. There's a legitimate business side to their scheme, does a lot of energy research. The public side seems to know nothing of the secret world-overthrowing side."

The elevator dinged and I walked into the incredible laboratory the government set up for me. It had everything I'd ever used at NMIT, plus fourteen years worth of brand-new equipment. Even the Bunsen burners had that never-turned-on shine to them. The beakers and cylinders had to be new; I could never get anything that clean after I used it. There was even a computer, a giant slab of a thing in the corner with tape reel eyes that glared across the room. I grinned. Babbage would be proud. I hoped the army threw in a cute assistant that knew how to make punch cards for that beast.

I took in my new staff and found two faces I hadn't expected. "Fred? Horatio?"

"Glass! About time you got your hands dirty. I always thought you spent too much time in meetings. We've already started working." Fred's smile extended past the handlebars. Behind him a flurry of lab coats tried to look busy.

I rushed to him and shook his hand heartily. "Well, what can I say? I have a face that looks good telling people bad news."

Horatio patted me on the back. "I think it is a good thing to say at this point how glad we are to be working with you again. It is a shame that Rocky could not be here, but Dr. Orchid is away, and as assistant dean, his detainment was unavoidable."

That suited me fine. I wasn't quite up for the hugs and handshakes with Rocky anyway.

Archdeacon stepped back to the elevator. "I'll leave you eggheads to your work. I have to plan for war."

I caught up with him. "I've been thinking about that, General. I don't think, however radical this splinter group of Technocracy Incorporated is, that they are still planning a coup."

"Then what?"

"I think," I said, putting words to my theory, "that they are training an army for reestablishing order after the fall of America. I imagine there is a similar army on the Russians' side. Call them the cleanup crew. It would be suicide to attack while we're still strong. But any group that looks official could potentially rally survivors after the bombs finish dropping."

The general thought about this and nodded. "So they're not going to mobilize until after. That's good. That means somewhere in this country *and* in Russia, there are men being housed and fed on someone's dime. Maybe the FBI or CIA can work with the MVD to find a money trail. They haven't found them any other way."

"Didn't someone once say something about an army moving on its stomach?"

"That they did, Glass. That they did." The general smiled. He liked to have targets he could aim a gun at. Secret armies fought secret wars, and he wasn't comfortable with that. But he wouldn't give up either.

Archdeacon grinned. "Now, get to work. I think your cohorts have something for you."

I returned to the lab and found both Fred and Horatio huddled conspiratorially. They were giddy, which didn't suit either of them well. "Okay, guys. What's up?"

The two scientists, my peers, turned around and held out a frame. In it was a decree from NMIT reinstating my credentials. On the frame was a note from Rocky that read, *Welcome back, Glass.*

"Turns out you really couldn't step in here without this," Fred revealed. "So Archdeacon pulled some strings."

I wanted to cry. To laugh. To hug them and jump up and down. I hadn't felt so childlike since I'd earned those letters the first time. I'd done it. I'd returned to the science community that once shunned me. I'd been redeemed in their eyes …

But redemption lay at the end of the Technocrats' plans. I swallowed everything save for my gratitude.

"Thank you, gentlemen."

"Dr. Glass." Horatio offering a respectful tilt of his head. "Shall we proceed?"

"Doctors," I said, returning the bow and then leading the way forward.

CHAPTER FOURTEEN

The army let Fred and Horatio bring with them some of the brightest talent the country had seen from NMIT. The army's science core was no slouch, but they lacked the vision of the country's youngest geniuses. So my newly formed research team had four students of varying ages. Our first task? Find out what was in the MASER's exciter fluid. Once we'd accomplished that, we'd work up an antidote.

"I've got the first chemical," trilled a senior, her excitement palatable. "Radioactive iodine."

She looked more like a cheerleader than a scientist, blonde with more "bounce" than others in her field. Her name was Shirley, and like Tangie, she'd have a hard time in the overly male-saturated world of science. But then, if Marie Curie could do it …

I wrote *Iodine* on the chalkboard under *Components*.

"Horatio?" I wanted his opinion.

He didn't bother to come over. Instead he called out from across the room, "It would seem that it is an attempt to stimulate the thyroid gland at the base of the cerebellum, seeing that that is what currently exudes iodine, as part of the thyroid hormone, in trace amounts anyway. Increasing the hormone increases the metabolism of the individual."

I remembered the train. "Yeah, when I was injected, I felt my heart rate go up. I thought it was just fear, but it could have been the drug."

"Or both," Shirley suggested. She brushed back a piece of hair, giving me eyes that offered sympathy. Dangerous lady, I deduced. Real dangerous.

Under *Effects* I wrote *Increased metabolism*.

Fred mumbled, "Well, this is weird."

His team and I gathered around the electron microscope Mr. Chemistry was bent over. He adjusted the lenses then switched slides while we waited. When he looked up and saw us there, he snipped, "I'll let you know when I'm ready. I talk to myself sometimes. Go back to work."

An anxious junior went to the board and started writing a chemical equation. I glared him down until he stopped. "Sorry, Professor Glass. I didn't mean to—"

I laughed. "It's okay. Go ahead. And I haven't been 'Professor Glass' in quite some time. Dr. Glass will do just fine."

Relieved, he finished his addition to the list. I looked it over. "Methyl Xanthine? Why does that sound familiar? That's an alkaloid, right?"

"Yes, Prof—I mean, Dr. Glass. We've been ingesting it all day." He snickered and motioned to my coffee cup.

"Caffeine?"

"Yes, but I've never seen it in such a potent form. It's like the power of ten cups of coffee in a single gram."

"Then combined with the increased thyroid activity, the metabolic rate of a person injected with this would be off the chart."

In addition to the heart rate, I remembered sweating. In someone older, this fluid could induce a heart attack or stroke.

"How are your tests coming, Horatio?"

Horatio finally joined us on our side of the room. "These things are agreeable with the experiments that I am running. A human cell becomes like the egg on a hot skillet when introduced to this chemical. However, these two chemicals act only on their individual targets and, in either case, would cause the brain or the heart to seize up long before exploding. Another agent must be acting upon the body's natural water."

"Magnesium sulfate?" Shirley again.

"Ah yes, that would be a true thing you suggest. A compound of magnesium sulfate, stimulated at this level, would get the kettle boiling." He laughed at his own joke, but all I could think of was how close I'd been to dying. "Please check for it," he asked the girl, and she returned to the test tubes.

"Horatio? I need you to look at this."

Horatio joined Fred at his station. After switching slides and microscopes a few times, they huddled, whispering excitedly. They didn't keep me out of the loop for long.

They approached me, Horatio moving in front of me, Fred to the back. I wondered if they had something else to give me. Fred was hiding something behind his leg. Horatio's bright white teeth offset his dark olive skin as he gave me a broad smile, as though waiting for something.

I hadn't even gotten to "What?" when I felt the scissors clamp down on my hair and a lock fall away.

I spun around but Fred was already moving back to the microscope.

I wheeled on Horatio. "And what were you? The distraction?"

"No, I said I just wanted to see the expression on your face."

"I was right!" cried Fred.

He moved the second microscope closer to the first and called us over.

"Glass, you've heard about James Watson's discovery, right?"

"Yes, DNA. I know all about it."

Why do people keep asking me about that?

"But have you heard of selective chemistry yet?"

Apparently, I had been out of school too long. The students got all excited and began chattering. I hushed them, only to have to do the same to the army's scientific observers who also seemed excited by the term. I cast them a look and they quieted down, as well.

"No, I haven't. What are you going on like schoolgirls about?"

"You would know it to be true that every person has a specific DNA, no two are alike. What if you could design a chemical that would respond to only your genetic makeup?"

"You could repair hereditary damage, like mental retardation," A senior suggested.

"Or poison an entire dinner and kill only one person."

"Or wipe out a race with chemical warfare, better yet, call it selective genocide," Fred added. "It's an offshoot of the DNA research called eugenics."

"And this chemical has that ability?"

"Watch."

Fred dragged me over to the scopes. "In the first scope, we have a sample of Horatio's hair since, of course, I have none to cut."

I was glad my hair wasn't the only one being donated to science.

"Now watch it as I run the wave generator."

Apparently Fred and Horatio had stayed up most of the night building a device to act as the MASER, or at least how they figured it worked. They used the description I had placed in the report, plus what pieces of the destroyed device that had been recovered by the FBI in Chance City.

I put my eye to the lens and heard the click of the switch on the wave box. Slowly, the hair began to twitch and eventually curl. At about a minute thirty, the hair sizzled and charred.

"Okay, now come over here to the other station. This one has Shirley's hair laced with the exciter drug."

I looked over to the senior. "You volunteer or get conscripted, too?"

She made no false allusions with her answer. "I have no problem donating my body to science."

I swallowed hard and turned back to the microscope.

This time it took less than a minute to char. Shorter time than Horatio's, but that was to be expected.

"Finally, here, we have your hair."

I barely had time to focus the lens before the hair curled, smoked, and charred.

"The drug reacts stronger to your DNA than it did Shirley's. I've concluded that this fluid was designed with you in mind."

The ramifications were astounding. "So with a sample of DNA, they could target a single person out in a crowd of hundreds."

"Yes, they wouldn't need to inject the person. Just get him or her to eat or drink the same thing everyone was. When the MASER was activated, only that person would explode, leaving the others feeling only slightly warm."

One of the students asked, "Couldn't they do just the opposite, as well? Kill everyone in a room that didn't have the right DNA sequence?"

"Yes, yes. What you say is most definitely true. A dictator could wipe out all his opponents at once and keep only a specific strain of DNA."

"This is what Mendelssohn was afraid of!" I slammed my fist on the table. "Not just the idea of war, but what he had invented. Something that was worse than the atomic bomb. The Technocrats had a weapon to specifically wipe out any group of people they wanted."

"Yes, but who would they target? They've never shown a racial basis previously, have they?" asked Fred.

I sat down. One of the problems the Technocrats had the first go-round was the question of what to do with the imperfect people—those with birth defects, those without the intelligence to handle technology. They would be a drain on the energy system because they couldn't give back what they took. It made sense to think they'd want to wipe out the gimps and the idiots. The possibility was too horrible to imagine.

I leaned forward, put my elbows on my knees, and held my head in my hands. I could see towers all over the world, broadcasting the MASER wave, and everyone whose DNA didn't contain the right sequence would die. One gigantic scream heard around the world, and then nothing but a deafening silence.

This wasn't the dream of Taylor. Not even Veblen, Gantt, Scott, or Rautenstrauch. Someone had bastardized it, mutated it. It was like looking at pictures of the survivors of Hiroshima. You could almost find the real person under the burns, but so much of the flesh had been melted away, you couldn't look at it long enough to see.

"You've been at this a while," Fred said, trying to comfort. "Why don't you go down to the PX for dinner? I'll report what we have to Archdeacon. He'll need to pass this on to all involved. This is too big for just us."

Horatio offered to get a hold of Watson and Frick and see if they had any insights.

I jotted down some notes for Fred to take to Archdeacon. Before getting in the elevator, I looked out the window.

The sun slowly descended between the worn-down peaks of the Rockies. It was best if you didn't miss sunsets in Colorado. All the science in the universe couldn't sum up why the sky burned so magnificently. Earth orbiting the sun. The sun orbiting Earth. It didn't matter. What mattered—people were alive to see it.

I got off on the first floor.

"Glass? Glass! Just man I look for!"

I turned and watched the squat form of Wan Lee walking toward me, escorted by two armed guards, a six-pack of Ancient Stout in each hand.

* * *

"You ditch me. The Ruskie I understand, but me? How many time I got to save your ass before I get a little respect?"

If Wan weren't grinning like the Cheshire Cat through the whole tirade, I might have taken him seriously.

"I had things to do that I couldn't do with two or more people hanging around."

"What? Like get arrested? Oh, that great plan!"

"It was and it worked. I've made more progress in three days than the four previous."

"I would have come with you, watch your back."

I placed a hand on his shoulder. "I know, Wan. I just needed time to think."

I arranged security clearance for Wan. They took him to a room and asked him a whole bunch of questions. They handed him a temporary pass on the condition he not leave the base. Lee seemed sure the background check would come back clean … too sure.

In the lab, the team had departed for dinner. Lee appraised the place with a whistle.

"You not do so bad, I guess. In four days you do what you could not in twelve years."

I nodded. "I know why Tangie died, Lee. I know who and why."

"Good. They go arrest him now?"

"Can't. Not yet. And I don't think it's a him."

He raised an eyebrow. "A dame? What? Bam we met in Chance City?"

I cast Merlot in the role but couldn't make it stick. She was in many of the right places and had the right connections, but she didn't have the background to pull off something this big. Plus, the Hero sister I met was the wrong shape, too tall and thin.

"Nah, she's clean." Lee smiled and I decided not to tell him about me making my own chop suey with Merlot. He still acted as if he had the hots for her. "Wan? Your wife?"

"Yeah, yeah. Tell it to my priest." He waved me off and took another draw from the beer. He set it down and gazed across to the downtown area. The city lights looked like stars reflected on black water with Liberty Tower a lighthouse beacon.

"What?"

He didn't say anything.

"Wan, what? Are you really upset that I bailed on you?"

"Nah, not really. I take care of myself pretty good for old man. It's just …"

He trailed off. I wanted to prod, but I've learned people will tell you what they want to when they want to. It was almost a full minute before he spoke again.

"Those men, the Russians, they say some things when they think I asleep. Things not good over there. They really planning for a war. This not good, not good at all."

"Not to put too fine a point on it, Wan, but we've done war before. I think we'll be okay."

He shook his head. "No, this not going to be like other wars. They will come here. They will destroy our homes. Kill our families. And if they use bombs, there will be places you can never go again."

It struck me then that Wan, being Japanese, knew intimately the horrors of an atomic bomb.

"Did you have family in Hiroshima?"

He shook his head. "Nagasaki. A whole bunch of relatives. Great aunts, uncles, cousins. Cannot even go lay flowers for them; area still off limits. I build shrine at safe house so family can burn incense. I still remember traveling up to the mountains as a child to my uncle's place."

Then Lee did the incredible. In almost perfect English he recited the following:

The maids were singing in kitchen, and I heard the shampooers in street.
Then I turned over on my mat, and say, "I think it is time I arose."

I was flabbergasted. "Wan, that's beautiful. What is it?"

"Was my uncle's favorite poem. He born tired, that one. He never do any work when we come visit. He say it because we there. His wife say he like that all time."

We briefly laughed at his recollection, but Lee grew somber again. "Do not want to lose another town, another family here."

"I won't let that happen, Wan. If there is any chance to stop it, I will."

"You promise? With your life?"

"I do. With my life. But I had made that same sort of promise to Tangie."

* * *

We stayed up late catching up. He clued me in on the events after I had hit the bricks.

Comrade Ilya was so mad that Vincent had to smack him. They went out to track my path, despite Vincent's wounded condition. That made me feel guilty.

Once they found the snowmobile, they came back, gathered up their belongings, and headed north, toward Colorado. They stuck mostly to back roads, avoiding the roadblocks. Once they made Colorado Springs, Lee split from them and found his way home. He awoke this morning to papers stating I had been arrested. The police called off the search for Wan, but kept an

APB for Vincent. Wan reasoned where I was being kept and decided to pop in.

I told him I was glad. We said our "good nights" and headed off to our assigned rooms.

But I didn't sleep; too many thoughts circled my head. For all the progress, we still knew so little. I rolled over, flipped on the light, and started writing again.

Under the orders of Mr. X, now Miss X the current Great Engineer of the new Technocracy Inc., Jorge had rigged my experiment to test how deadly the enhanced microwaves could be. At some point, he saw the long-term potential for the technology and had second thoughts, thus the note he tried to leave me. Only, I didn't get it. Tangie did.

What would she have tried to do with that knowledge? Tried to fix what Jorge had done? Yes, that made sense. She would take it upon herself to undo Mendelssohn's work, only she failed. Why didn't she stop the experiment all together? Especially if she wasn't sure?

Unless she went to someone else. Like Jorge. Maybe she convinced him to fix things and he convinced her he had. Tangie trusted him. We all did. She would forgive him his brief wavering from the cause and instead give him a chance to make things right.

That meant she knew what was going on just before she'd died. Tangie died knowing Jorge had betrayed us all.

So Jorge left NMIT with the data he'd gotten and built the MASER to kill Hitler. And then WWII ended, so his Technocrat sponsors sat on it. Maybe Jorge developed other things for them. Maybe they kept him to advise them on only scientific things, things that would be needed when they were in charge of the country.

Somehow, word got back to them about Stalin's domination plans, probably from their Worker's Truth contacts, and TI set the goal to stop him. It was too soon. They weren't ready for WWIII. Yet in their storehouse, they had the unused assassination weapon. The MASER got dusted off and put to use. Only, it failed. Stalin's death didn't look to be from natural causes as they hoped. Beria became the sacrificial lamb. The USSR sent Ilya and Sacha to activate the sleeper agent Vincent. Together, they were supposed to uncover who was involved on our side in the assassination.

Meanwhile, Mendelssohn split from his keepers with Merlot's help. He had a crisis of conscience and came to me, only he didn't make it. What did I know that would make him think I could help? And how did C.J. Reece figure into all this?

I doodled on my paper. I drew names and lines, trying to connect Reece to someone. All I had at the end was a lot of circles and lines with no one connecting Reece and Mendelssohn. How'd Reece know so much about what Mendelssohn had done? Where had his data come from?

I had access to your designs, as you deduced.

I remembered his words. He had access. Someone let him in. Reece had told me it, but I was too full of myself to hear it. He led me in a certain direction. Why? Why spin the tale about Archdeacon? He deliberately misled me, all the while giving me clues.

I stood up and walked around. We weren't the only two in the room. Vincent. He didn't want Vincent to understand. Reece must have known Vincent was a Russian spy. He knew or guessed it. Reece told me information was his tool. He had to know. Stalin. He had to know about the Technocrats. He told me he had seen in my designs what others had seen.

Reece *was* a Technocrat. His love of technology, how perfect he thought it was. The black army was working out of the basement of his building. Reece was not just any Technocrat, mind you, but one high up the ladder, but not the leader. Not the Great Engineer, though. But someone high enough to be trusted with some, not all, of the plans.

It hit me. With his money, he must've been a bankroller. He financed TI's plans! When the war was over and society needed rebuilding, who would be around to rebuild technology? The person who was already controlling it—Little Technologies, the largest holder of patents. Reece held back advanced technology for his own use until he was ready to put it on the market. Reece had to have been a major player in their plan, but he turned on them.

If my enemies find me.

He must have split off from them, had a falling out, as Jorge had. Did Mendelssohn take what he knew to Reece? Did my former assistant trust the weird eccentric? Two peas in a pod.

Reece may have started to have doubts even back in '39.

I don't back losers.

My head spun. Thoughts coalesced. How did TI know Reece was a threat?

Mendelssohn again.

Finding that I was out of town, Jorge goes to Reece, but he's followed by the Hero Twins who were sent to kill him. After doing in the traitor, they report to Miss X that Jorge visited Reece, which now makes her not trust him. Reece, knowing what the MASER can do, sets up guards, but they still get enough juice into him to give him cancer. Knowing the writing was on the wall, he comes to me, costing him his life. I was the last person TI wanted on the scene. I would recognize the MASER's effect instantly and though I'd been asleep for fourteen years, I could be a wrench in their plans.

Little Technologies held an interesting place in their organization, though. The place where they kept an army. Where? How did it go unnoticed? How would they stay unnoticed and have access to all that high tech goodies they'd need when they rebuilt the world?

They must have another insider, one who could be trusted. They'd put someone loyal in charge, someone who would support the world plan, someone nobody knew anything about, another enigma like Reece.

"Cecelia LaMent!"

As much a recluse as her infamous predecessor, Miss LaMent has never been photographed at large and no pictures were made available by the company.

She had to be the Hero sister, the one who has been manipulating two different branches of the Technocrats, the Russians and Americans, for fourteen years.

Right after the experiment!

I got up and ran to Archdeacon's room. I pounded on his door until the general said to come in. He was still dressed in his blues but had fallen asleep at a card table piled high with paperwork.

"Sorry, Glass. I must have dozed off. So many reports."

"Damn the reports, General. I have someone for you to aim at!"

CHAPTER FIFTEEN

In the hours after my escape from Liberty Tower, the CIA combed the offices of Little Technologies and found nothing to link them to the T.I. army. They went floor by floor with an armed escort and searched every room, every closet, save for one.

The area below Reece's vault office had been cordoned off by the fire marshal.

Fred, Archdeacon, and I looked over the marshal's report. Lee looked out the window; reports meant nothing to him. When I'd visited Little Technologies, I'd assumed that the area under the safe was reinforced, and by the rough drawings laid out before us, I'd been correct. The vault's supports separated the west side of the floor into three areas. Area one had been labeled *Storeroom C*. Within the largest one, labeled *Main Floor*, there sat another area *Electrical Room*. Comparing it to the drawing of the floor above, it appeared that the fire started in the electrical room, directly under the vault.

Passcode doors secured one area from the next. Few knew both those codes, which ultimately hampered the firemen's effort when they first arrived. When they did get the door open, the backdraft was instant and several men had to be pulled out with burns. The rest managed to get the fire contained, but the damage had been done.

The arsonist had cut the power to the offices above and sealed Reece in his vault. The fire hadn't been created to burn Reece.

The old man had died of smoke inhalation, funneled directly from the fire through the ventilation into the vault. The fire marshal brought in the best locksmith in Industry City to open the vault, and it still took him more than two hours to do it. By then, the old man was cold.

The police went the direction of inside job, but none of the employees questioned by the police or fire investigators added anything relevant to the investigation. Little Technologies workers had been trained to ignore anything dealing with Reece and his office unless specifically addressed. They could have been working for a different company altogether, so little did they know about the inner workings of Little Technologies.

Whoever the torpedo was, I'm guessing he or she walked right in as if belonging there. Vincent was their primary suspect, seeing as how he disappeared right after the fire. I could fill in that blank, as he was following me at the time of Reece's murder.

Cecilia LaMent would have access to those pass codes and one of her Hero Twins could have waltzed in and out without notice—maybe even in his mask. She controlled the whole hit remotely.

What I found so puzzling from the report is the way our firebug set the fire. First was location. While the ventilation did run through the electrical room, there were other places that would have been a far more effective area to create the fire. The arsonist removed a lot of asbestos from around the ducts first. Then they removed insulation that was packed into the walls. Why?

Fred found yet another irregularity. He said the type of accelerant used resulted in a high-intensity burn, meant to create the fire, burn hot briefly, then burn itself out, leaving no trace. According to their calculations, had the firefighters not created the backdraft by opening the electrical room door, the fire would have been out shortly. They estimated the total burn time as about fifteen minutes. That would have just been enough smoke to kill a man but not enough to burn down a building. They wanted the offices intact. Specifically, they wanted the rest of the floor intact.

We arrived at Liberty Tower and ascended to the floor in question. I stood surveying the store room with Archdeacon, Lee, and Fred—them, and about a dozen armed soldiers. Archdeacon had insisted on their accompanying us. The CIA had all but ignored this room in their search due to the fire damage. My gut told me this room was made to be ignored.

"Okay, guys. Spread out and look for anything … I don't know—wrong."

The general didn't spread. He stayed with me. He wanted to pass on intelligence he'd gathered that morning.

"So this is what we have on Cecelia LaMent. Little Technologies lists her as a distant relative of C.J. Reece, but his actual family has no record of her. We subpoenaed the company's employment records, and they show her coming into their employ in 1939, hired directly by Reece himself, and then she was immediately sent to Jakarta."

"Let me guess. Right after the experiment, correct?"

"Almost to the day. The CIA sent operatives to roust Little Technologies employees over there and found out that few people have ever met her. She has an almost empty office. Her personal secretary says she travels a lot and rarely spends more than a week there a year."

I walked around smoke and water-damaged boxes. I motioned for them to be popped open and a couple G.I.s went to work with a crowbar. They found nothing but packing materials. Desk drawer were empty of everything but office supplies and empty folders. It all seemed very kosher.

"She must have a passport, then?"

"Not that we can find in her name."

"An alias?"

"That's the idea. We have only a cursory description, as she usually wears dark glasses and a hat with a sun veil around it."

I looked at him. "For fourteen years?"

"What do you want, Glass? It's only been six hours since you put this together. We're not miracle workers."

He was right. I was angry for no reason. I felt itchy and I don't think it was the asbestos.

"I want answers. If she was the one, the one that put this into play fourteen years ago, then she's the one responsible for Tangie, for Mendelssohn, for Reece, for Yousev. She's the murderess and I want to be the one to bring her down."

Fred beckoned us, having overheard our discussion, "Don't forget she'd also be responsible for the other deaths. NMIT lost five students, as well."

I wasn't discounting them. Fred nodded and continued his work in the electrical closet.

"She is a vile creature with nine known kills, Glass. We know that," said Archdeacon. "I hope she doesn't go quietly. I've never fought against a woman opponent before. History shows they are fiercer then men. They think much farther ahead and actually derive pleasure from seeing men suffer."

"Oh? You've met my wife?" asked Lee.

"Glass, come here!"

I moved quickly to where Fred was. He had put on a mask and pried open an asbestos-lined box. I could see sophisticated electronics inside, some which had melted in the heat.

"Something bothered me about the fire report," he began. "How did the firemen know there was a fire when it was behind two locked doors and the power had been cut to C.J.'s office so he couldn't call for help?"

I hadn't considered that. "Smoke?" asked Lee.

The engineer shook his head. "No, the smoke was all trapped in the vault. There was no sign of the fire until they opened this door."

I added, "The report said the fire would have been out if it hadn't been reported so quickly. How did they find out so soon?"

Fred pointed. "I think this. It's some sort of warning system."

I knelt in close by him. I could see a battery inside, smaller than any I had come across.

"What do you think, Fred?"

"I think this thing powers up when the power to this room gets cut. See the phone line here? I believe this device somehow calls for help."

I stepped out of the room and went back to the file. I reread the initial report. It listed an older man's voice as making the call. The voice said, "There is an emergency at the Little Technologies offices, forty-third floor of Liberty Tower, electrical room." The operator tried to ask questions, but the voice repeated the message again and disconnected.

"Reece prepared for this too."

"Glass?" Fred sounded nervous.

"Yeah, Fred?"

He stood up and handed me a thin piece of metal. The label on it was burned, but I could still read the name, Noel R. Glass, written on it.

"I found it behind the wiring."

It was a calling card case. I opened it and found a single note. It read, *Go to Storeroom D.*

"That's strange. I didn't see a Storeroom D on the blueprints. We're next to Storeroom C, with A and B on the opposite side of the hallway."

Lee was over by another set of doors leading into the second half of the room. "Maybe they mean here?"

The room had been sectioned off. It didn't take up the whole floor, so maybe Storeroom D meant the other side of Storeroom C. I looked in. The door had been opened during the fire investigation, but since it was clean, they didn't need to go in. I stared at the empty room. It went back as far as the south wall and was completely empty.

I kept staring. Something wasn't right. I remembered staring at Reece's "windows" in the vault until I figured out the trick. That time the illusion was broken by a flicker in the image. This time it was a dust particle. It floated down and froze in midair, as if it landed on something. "General? Your gun."

"Huh?"

I asked for the gun again, and he begrudgingly acquiesced. I picked a spot in the ceiling just beyond where the dust had settled and fired.

The mirror shattered into a quadrillion pieces, and with it, the illusion. Hollywood and magicians employed the same trick to make sets look bigger, only the technique had been enhanced to make a near perfect representation of an empty space that was anything but.

On the other side of the magic, a medical bay sat empty. There were beds by the dozens, each with electronic equipment around it. Wires led to lit boxes situated on adjoining shelves. These boxes had screens labeled with numbered gradients. A pole with two hooks sat between each bed, and empty tubes lay limp across every pillow.

"This tech," Fred said, "It's like nothing I've seen. I don't think there's a University with a lab this advanced."

Fred and I moved in closer while Lee and Archdeacon went through the desks. The guards set up a perimeter, but it was clear that no one had been back since they were evacuated.

"This is a transfusion setup."

"Fred?"

"Seriously, Glass, this is the most technologically advanced apparatus I've ever seen. See here and here? This drains blood, this replaces it."

"And these electrodes?" I showed him the vine I found dangling at the side.

"For monitoring heart rate and brain waves, I guess. The readings show up on this screen." He indicated the box. "These empty tubes look like they're to deliver plasma."

I took one of the boxes and tried to get inside. I finally had to smash it, which elicited a panicked yelp from Fred.

"Don't break it!"

"What? There're others."

The insides were even more complicated and wondrous than the stuff we saw on the outside. The way the circuits were laid out was just short of miraculous. Like one of my half-remembered dreams, there was a sense of *déjà vu* when trying to understand it all. It looked like something out of Babbage's designs, only moved forward a hundred years.

I had an idea of who'd done the evolving too. I opened my mouth to speak, but Lee opened a cooler door and gasped. "Ai-yah!"

We gathered behind him and agreed. It was filled with bags and bags of blood and plasma, labeled by type.

I turned to Archdeacon. "What did you find?"

He shook his head. "Nothing. Anything important left with them."

"I have something," said Fred from inside the cooler. "A name." He held up a bag; on the label were the words *Project Bogdanov.*

* * *

Finding the medical lab made finding Vincent and his two comrades imperative. The topic of Alexander Bogdanov's questioning by the Soviet secret police came up during the meeting with Ike and team, but what was discussed and revealed was still unknown to the CIA, FBI and military.

I knew, personally, two Soviet agents who might have that information.

According to Lee, before they'd parted company, the three Russians had talked about going underground. They hoped to connect up with operatives of the Russian mafia and find a safe house. If they succeeded after Lee left, then I would have to go underground too.

Tracking them was near impossible, starting with an escape from the military base lockdown. Archdeacon didn't want me out from under his thumb. He would nix any plan involving me leaving the base. Sending his people after Vincent had proved futile. Hell, they hadn't caught me, and I wasn't all that sneaky. We'd have to escape from our temporary holding pen. Lee was the one to come up with the idea.

We ordered pizza.

A new service had started in Denver called pizza delivery. A local pizzeria would actually drive a pizza to you if you called them. There was an extra fee, but they'd come out in all weathers and drive however far. The base had started using the service regularly, so it was not out of the ordinary for us to place a call for dinner. I had Fred pay for the pizzas when they arrived, while Lee and I picked the lock on the trunk of the delivery car and slid in. If we were lucky, Archdeacon wouldn't notice we were missing until noon the next day.

Once again, I was hiding in a cramped space, but I wasn't alone this time.

"Lee!" I said in a serious whisper. "Move your hoof. It's in my groin."

"Glass, I should tell you. I have *kimchi* for lunch."

"Damn it, Lee! It's been you stinking up our bathroom! When we get out of this mess, I swear I'll cement that ass of yours closed!"

* * *

Sean Burke had quarters next to Sully's stables. I guess being on a Mafioso's property gave you a false sense of security because he hadn't bothered to lock his door.

Quietly, we hovered over the tight-eyed trainer. Lee drew his gun, and I placed a hand over Burke's mouth. He woke with a start.

"The only thing I want to hear you say is—*ow!*" I pulled my hand away.

"Not that shite again, okay, Glass? And thanks fer the lump, you basterd. I woulda kept mum until you were gone. Oh, hiya, Wan. I've got a great bet in the third tomorrow. You interested?"

I shook my hand and rubbed the bite marks out of my palm while they chatted about "sure things."

After Burke got dressed, he'd poured us three fingers each of some fairly decent sauce. We sat around a table in what passed for his kitchen; a lazy Susan, sink, and a hot plate.

"I knew you'd be back."

"How so?"

"Well, I don't be meanin' to brag, but I've been gettin' some hot juice about you. Seems like since you've been in custody, the price on yer head tripled. I heard the survivin' Twin won't even take the money anymore. He's got somethin' wicked personal with you now. It wasn't what you did to his brother; that's a hazard of the business. Hell, I'm not even sure they're really related."

"Then what?"

"It was what you gone and done to his face. He had to get a new mask made, and I hear tell there's nuthin' but bandages under it now with two mean-looking eye holes." He mimicked a mummy, making angry eyes between fingers. With Sean, it wasn't just the information you got, but the show that came with it. "I thought you only made women that mad, Glass."

"So then he's probably not at his best?"

"I wouldn't be sayin' that. Word is he put three guys in the hospital that tried to calm him down."

This was going to be harder than I thought. Sean offered a shot and I threw it back. "What do you know of the Russian mafia in Industry City?"

I thought the runt would choke on his medicine. "There's no Russian mob here, Glass. Sully wouldn't be allowin' it. Hell, Chicago would have kittens."

"Don't shit me, Burke. They're here. They put people in every major city, looking for holes within the current underbelly to exploit. They may be quiet and they may be avoiding the same trades as the Italians, but they are here."

Sean's eyes darted around in their sockets quickly, nervously. It was his tell. The only time he did that was when he had information he couldn't sell.

"What, Sean?"

"Nuthin', Glass. I got nuthin' to give you."

"What if I had something to give you? Something worth an even exchange?"

"You'd have nuthin' that was worth me—" But it was too late. Burke has slipped and he said a few curses. I smiled at him. "Okay, Glass. You caught me. But I really can't be tellin' you anythin'. These Ruskies are brutal. Not in the Italian way. Fer the wops, it's enough to see you dead. The Reds, well, they like to see you suffer even after you've given them everythin' you know. Then they kill you … if yer lucky."

"I just need a place to start. We'll climb the tree and shake the monkeys loose."

"Do you really have anythin' worth that?" Always the bargainer, that Burke. We both knew he'd gladly trade his life for a hot bit of information.

"Yeah, I know who's after me and I'm coming for her."

Sean gave me the Irish grin again. "I knew 'twas a woman, Glass. What's her name?"

"Cecelia LaMent."

He cocked an eyebrow. "Little Technologies' new head honcho? You don't piss them off small, do you, Glass."

I leaned in closer. "No, and I'm going to take her and her whole damn organization down with me. You got that, Burky? You get that out to as many people as you want. She wants a war? I'm going to give her one."

* * *

The Russian immigrant area of Industry City didn't go by some fancy name, like Little Osaka or Greektown. In fact, if you didn't have a bit of Russian blood in you, you wouldn't even know where to look. Having worked the streets, I knew the place existed within a several block radius, but with anti-Communism in full swing, they did their best to stay low key.

Eleven at night and the streets from downtown to the suburbs were bare. People stayed at home, watching Ed Sullivan. Lee and I could see them through the windows of the cab—flickering glow on laughing faces; Mom, Dad, sometimes the kids. In too many homes, we just saw Mom and the kids. Whether that was because Dad worked a night shift to make ends meet or he hadn't come home from Korea, I didn't know.

The little corner grocery store where the nighthawk dropped us still had its open sign lit. Bells rang as we entered. I hurried forward past rows of Quaker oatmeal and various sundries, checking for other shoppers. I nodded to Lee that we were alone. He pulled the chain on the open sign and locked the door behind us. The owner, who looked to have been doing paperwork in the back office, stepped forward at the bell ring. When he saw what Lee was doing, his face drained of color and he reached under the counter for something heavy. I drew a gun I'd borrowed from Burke and put one round in the neon Atlantic Brewery sign above the registers. Sparks rained down on the man, which distracted him long enough for me to slide over the counter. I batted the shotgun from his hands before he could aim it. He was a beer barrel of a man, but small enough for me to push against the wall.

"You know who I am?"

He shook his head violently. "Wrong answer. Try again."

"*Da*—I mean, yes. I know who you are. Your picture—"

"No, not in the paper. You were told to watch out for me, weren't you? By Ilya, correct? Comrade Ilya. Or maybe Vincent. One of them must have warned you I would be coming."

He tried to deny it again, but Lee reached the counter and added conviction to our cause. The owner admitted that Vincent/Vadim had predicted my arrival. The shop owner was supposed to stall me long enough to make a call.

I told him to call.

Two thugs showed up within five minutes. Lee and I were ready for them. We jumped and bagged them in record time. I didn't know why I'd rarely used Lee on cases before. He was fast and efficient, wasting no energy. I thought back to Merlot's dressing room and how helpless he looked. I'm sure that was an act for my benefit, or maybe he just didn't hit the dames.

I peeked out the window and saw a wheelman in the mob's coupe. Taking the hat off one of the thugs, I kept my face low. The plan entailed me getting into the car before the driver noticed his mistake. There were few lights outside, so I planned to reach the car before being recognized. I moved quickly toward the car while Lee made his way toward the driver's door. When I popped into the backseat, the driver turned and said something in Russian. By the time he discovered the switch, Lee had opened his door and pressed against his ribs.

"*Da*," I said. "Slide over." He moved and I pressed my gun to the back of his head. "Now give us directions to where Vadim, Ilya, and Sacha are."

"I know nothing of—"

The click as I drew back the hammer was enough to change his mind.

He directed us back into the city, which worried me, but then he veered us out toward the airport. There were hangars there, storehouses and a hundred other places to hide someone. Plus, if my three Ruskies were sent home because they'd blown their cover...

Vincent would have no trouble arranging more fake passports for them all.

Once our Russian guide identified the warehouse where the spies waited, we drove around the back and made him get in the trunk. Next, Lee scaled a ladder while I picked the backdoor lock. I slid in as quietly as I could, the exit sign as my only light. The hallway was lined with offices on both sides. I moved down the hallway, gun out, checking each room as I went. I reached the door into the main loading dock and paused. Lee needed enough time to make it to the top, jimmy his own lock, and get into position on the scaffolding above. We both assumed there would be scaffolding. There always was.

When an appropriate amount of time had passed, I opened the door slowly and slid past it. The warehouse was empty, save for a single light that hung over three men tied to chairs, back to back to back. One slumped motionless over his bonds, so I couldn't see his face. A second sat upright, fresh blood glistening in the illumination from the bulb. He moaned just a little, and I recognized Sacha. The third was shirtless with three times as many ropes as the other two. He was facing me.

Vincent looked at me through swollen eyes, the black and blue clearly decorating his face and body. Recognition swam into his battered consciousness and he mouthed the word—*Trap*.

Chapter Sixteen

Lights came on and a dozen men dressed in black fatigues of the Technocracy, Inc. Army drew on me. I looked up to see Lee standing on the scaffolding, disarmed and held at gunpoint.

Two more chairs were brought to bind us to the Russian spies. It wasn't making any sense until Burke stepped out of an alcove. "Wow, Glass. Yer really gonna take down Cecelia LaMent, are ye now?"

"Burke, you son of a bitch! You ratted us out?"

He walked over to where I was being tied down. "Come on, Glass. You said you owed me one. Well, we're square, you and me now, aren't we? She was payin' good, and well, you know the horses; I'm a shitarse trainer. Now I can break free from Sully fer good. Sorry."

And then he gave me some chin music. "That was fer the lump in the stalls, you bloody basterd."

He packed an Irish wallop. I blinked water from my eyes and tried to see past the blur.

"She'll be wantin' the big brute," Burke said to the soldiers.

They cut Vincent loose from the rest of us, but he was in no shape to fight, especially a losing battle. One got under each of his armpits and hoisted him up. They showed no outward signs of exertion. That took strength considering his size. Burke walked back over and addressed a twist in the alcove. Probably LaMent.

I could just make out her silhouette. She was lean, but that was all I could tell with her hair pulled up tight under a hat and scarf. She wore sunglasses even in the dark, but then a soldier stood on either side of her, so she didn't have to worry about running into anything. She handed Burke a package, which he quickly opened and checked. He tipped the rim of his hat then vamoosed with the guards hauling Vincent away.

LaMent looked my way, and I saw again that strange sort of puzzlement she had shown in Liberty Tower when she wore the Mayan mask. I sensed … what? Some sort of recognition. I knew this woman, but I couldn't tell from where. Her manner, bearing … it was familiar. She turned on her gams and was gone.

Our armed guards didn't hover over us, so I felt safe to lean toward Lee. "How's Sacha?" I whispered to Lee.

"He loopy, but better than Ilya."

"Sacha? Sacha?" I whispered as loud as I could without attracting the guards. I got a slight moan as a reply. Lee, who was closer to Sacha, kicked him as best he could until he got a coherent reply.

"Wha—?"

"What happened? How'd you end up here?"

"Vadim … knew guy … named Burke."

I thought back to what Vincent had said outside Chance City, that he knew a guy who knew a guy. I should have figured it was Burke. Everyone knew Burke.

"Vincent wanted in touch with the local Russian mob, only, as Burke said, there is no Russian mob. He sold you to LaMent instead." Sacha nodded against my back. I kicked myself for not checking to see if there was a price on Vincent's head. He'd been with Reece to the end. There was no telling what secrets the old man had passed on to him before his death. LaMent would want him dead, too.

"Sacha. What can you tell me about Alexander Bogdanov?"

"Wha—? Ilya. Ilya would—"

"Ilya's dead. I'm pretty sure about it. He smells dead, at least. His chest wasn't moving when we came in."

"No," Sacha whispered. "Ilya."

Lee managed to get a reassuring hand on Sacha's leg. "We mourn him later. For now, answer Glass."

"Bogdanov?" Sacha went away from us mentally for a while, and I thought he might have passed out again. "Scientist. Specialized in blood."

"Like vampire?" asked Lee.

Sacha laughed, but it cost him. He coughed and had to spit blood when he regained control. "Yes, like vampire, only for science. Believed he could extend life through blood transfusions. Even bring back dead."

Lee and I gave a collective, "What?"

"His institute specialized in such research. He was given Lenin's brain in hopes of restoring Communist party at roots. He failed."

Lee, stunned, said, "Yes, if he succeeded, we hear about it by now."

"However," came the shattered voice of the physician, "he did prove he could extend life, make men more powerful through transfusions. Men in their fifties looked like they were thirty and were just as strong."

I looked at our black army captors. These men had been strapped to those beds. Hundreds of beds, hundreds of soldiers. No—super soldiers, if what Sacha said was true.

He continued as a bit of his strength returned. "Bogdanov felt he could keep a man alive indefinitely in what he called stasis tubes. Constant supply of fresh blood, alpha waves to stimulate brain while inducing coma. Electrodes stimulated muscles to prevent—how you say? Atrophy? Government gave him all best technology. Even had those counting machines, what do you call?"

"Computers."

"Da!"

It didn't make sense. "When did Bogdanov die?"

"In 1928."

I couldn't believe that. Bogdanov had computers twenty years before anyone else? That meant …

"Ah, shit!"

"What?" asked Lee, but I had slipped up. A guard had heard my curse and came quickly over to me.

"No, wait!" Too late. I saw the butt of the rifle come down, and I went back into the dark.

* * *

It hadn't seemed a big thing at the time, but as I recalled the scene in a dream, the planets aligned and it all made sense.

I was back at NMIT.

Tangie and I were on our way to the lab. We swung by Dean Amanda Orchid's office to ask her if she wanted to walk with us to the lab. Orchid had Yousev in the office with her, but he waited nervously, as he often did, while she talked on the phone.

"I'm sorry, C.J. I can't help you.… No, I won't take it higher up.… We have everything in place.… Good—" She paused as a male voice spoke loudly through the earpiece. "Good-bye, C.J.!" She slammed down the phone. She was about to say something to Yousev but caught sight of us. "Oh. Tangie, Noel. How are things progressing this morning?"

"Fine," I said. "How are things with you?"

Tangie echoed, "Yes, Dean Orchid, that sounded concerning."

She looked down, away from us for the moment. When she straightened up, it was like the phone call had never happened. "No, no problems. Nothing the board can't handle."

I wrote the whole conversation off. I instead asked Yousev, "Are you coming to the test today?"

"No. I have to, to—"

"He has to get ready for a trip. We're sending Professor Studanko to a conference in Russia."

"The USSR? I didn't think we even recognized them as a country yet. Didn't the Bolsheviks steal power?"

"Ah, but Noel," Amanda said with the air of her station, "science knows no political boundaries, nor nations."

Tangie elbowed me. "Yes, Noel. Don't you remember Goethe?" I remembered, but I let her refresh me.

"'God could cause us considerable embarrassment by revealing all the secrets of nature to us; we should not know what to do for sheer apathy and boredom.'"

"And what does that have to do with Russia?"

"It means," Amanda said as she joined us in the hall, "that God has chosen to reveal something to a research organization in Russia and we should see it as a sign to go investigate."

I laughed. I was stuck between two women who loved science more than anything in the world. "Fine, you win! Does this organization have a name?"

"The Bogdanov Institute for Hematology and Blood Transfusions."

Focused on radars, I could've cared less.

* * *

I woke at the sound of yelling. Men were running around and there was gunfire. I don't know how long I'd been out, but I could feel the throbbing of a stock-shaped bruise on the side of my head.

"What's going on?"

But before Lee or Sacha could answer, one of the side doors blew open and armed men stormed the warehouse to the shouts of "FBI! Drop your weapons!" One agent got to the big hangar door and rolled it up on its tracks. There must have been two dozen agents waiting to get in. The black army soldiers dropped their guns quickly. As I had suspected, these operatives were better suited for relief efforts than combat.

The lead agent strode over to us after making arrangements to hold the prisoners. He took out a knife from a belt holster and made quick work of our ropes. G-men must shop at the same department store; gray three-piece, fedora, holster under his armpit. I'd seen pictures of Eliot Ness in the papers, and this guy could be a ringer.

"Dr. Glass? I'm Agent Cartwright. Are you okay?"

I rubbed the side of my head. "Yeah, but these guys need attention." I indicated the two Russian hostages. As I deduced, when they cut Ilya free, he fell forward into a lump. An agent bent down for a quick check of his pulse and shook his head. They flipped him over and I had to turn away. No man endures that sort of torture and lives. My guess is he never broke, even at the end.

Cartwright asked, "These are our two MVD agents?"

I nodded.

"Where's the other one? The sleeper?"

"They took him. I have no idea where." I watched federal agents as they performed their mop-up operation. I asked Cartwright, "How'd you find us? Wait!" I thought about their history and Al Capone. "You watch all racketeering in the United States."

"Bingo! We have a wiretap on the grocery store owner's phone. Got a tip from an outside source that the Russian mafia was taking an interest in Industry City."

"I don't suppose this tipster had an Irish brogue, did he?"

He smiled wider. "Now, Dr. Glass, I'm not at liberty to reveal our sources, but needless to say, this source has been useful in several operations. In fact, we're also taking down Sully, the local Italian Mafioso tonight, based on the same source."

Burke.

He sold me out because he knew I'd be rescued. He gets to start a new life with LaMent's money and, by turning state's evidence on Sully, there would be no one to come after him.

That little, red-headed ba—

My thoughts were interrupted by a field agent rushing forward.

"Sir?"

"Yeah?" Cartwright answered.

"We got a black army member to talk."

That was quick!

"They loaded the sleeper agent on a private plane that just took off."

That meant we were not that far behind the Technocrats, for once.

"Where to?"

"The soldier said Chicago."

Chi-town. Home. I'd find LaMent where it all began for me. Only I had a pretty good guess who I'd find under those glasses, hat, and scarf.

*　*　*

"Amanda Orchid is Cecelia LaMent?"

I broke the news to my former NMIT peers first thing in the morning, after a shower and a fruitless attempt at sleep. Fred couldn't believe it. He rubbed the top of his head while he tried to make sense of it all. No wonder he didn't have hair—probably rubbed it all off.

Horatio found it easier to adjust. "Yes, yes. I can see it being so. This LaMent woman, as described, travels a lot and how many times has Rocky filled in for Amanda? Plus, from conversations we have had, I can now see she was trying to recruit me as well. Can you not also remember such conversations?"

"I suppose." Fred gave in. "But to have done all this?" He waved his arm around the lab were they had been working on a counteragent for the exciter drug. "Does that mean she …?"

"Killed Yousev?" I nodded. "Yes, most likely. He knew too much, and if I got to him first, he wouldn't have held up under interrogation. I'm guessing he helped design all the equipment the Technocrats are using to make their super army. His visit to Bogdanov's institute and those computers above the stasis beds must have been his work."

They ruminated on this. I hated to add insult to injury. I knew they had just found out their boss was the leader of an evil organization bent on world domination and all, but …

"Guys? I'm sorry, but the FBI is going to question you again. Your security clearances are revoked until then."

"But—but …" Fred stuttered, again casting a glance around the room. "We have work to do!"

Horatio walked up to me and handed me his pass. "The sooner we get on with this, Fred, the sooner we will be getting back to the task. I know I am clean. How is your conscience?"

Fred was outraged. He marched behind Horatio, who winked at me as he passed by. We both knew the only way to get Fred to do something unwillingly was to challenge his ego. Fred's ID card in my hand, I motioned them forward to the waiting guards. I tossed their clearances onto a bench. I had no doubt they would be cleared. Neither was any good at poker.

Archdeacon came in shortly after they left. I'd already been reamed for my escape, but since I'd given him two Russian agents and a hand full of T.I. soldiers, he stopped yelling after only twenty minutes. A record, I was sure.

"Wheels up in an hour, Glass. We're going to Chicago."

* * *

"He's coming with me!" I shouted over the whirling of helicopter blades to the soldier blocking our path aboard. Lee and I were bent low, each with duffel bags.

"I'm sorry, Dr. Glass! But Mr. Lee has not been cleared for this operation! The background check came back inconclusive! There is still too much we don't know!"

We had been allowed to stop by our tenement to pack a grip; our other bags were still somewhere in a T'laquepaque evidence room. For Lee, the homecoming had been hard. His wife hugged him then proceeded to chew him out. He cringed at every other word. Someone had retrieved Obasaan, Lee's granny, and she kicked one of the guards in the shin to get by. She stared at me so intently, I had to avert my eyes. She asked for my hand and placed a black Go stone in it.

"Don't forget."

I told her I wouldn't.

We were driven straight away to the airfield. A soldier had directed me on to a waiting helicopter but had stopped Lee. I stepped back to address the obvious SNAFU. "He's coming with me or I'm not coming! Have I made myself clear?"

Archdeacon approached from behind, put a hand on each of our shoulders, and shouted, "What's the holdup?"

"Sir! This man has not been—"

"Soldier, get these men on board. Time is of the essence. Orchid's plane went off military radar over Iowa. There's no telling where they landed."

"Sir, yes, sir!"

"You're not coming?" I asked the general.

"I'll be coming with the president! Didn't anyone tell you?"

"No! Why is the president going to Chicago?"

"Oktoberfest! Geez, Glass! Don't you read the papers?"

From his back pocket he pulled a folded, crumpled section of the day's newspaper and stuffed it in my duffel. He pushed Lee and me onboard then moved quickly away to allow the Piasecki H-25 mule to lift off. As the noise increased with the rotor's spin, I strapped myself in and unfolded the fish wrapper, the *Chicago Tribune*.

Trumble Park Riots Continue, President Urges Tolerance

Ike to Attend Chicago's First Un-segregated Oktoberfest

Local Blues Singer Merlot Sterling to Sing National Anthem.

Oh, man. That wasn't good.

CHAPTER SEVENTEEN

I couldn't get Archdeacon on the phone. The army's Fort Sheridan stayed in strict lockdown as it prepared for the president's arrival. The CIA and FBI had set up command posts, and despite my having clearance just shy of knowing Mamie's shoe size, they ignored me.

"What part of *global annihilation* do you not understand, Cartwright?"

The agent was my liaison to Hoover, but he, too, had his hands tied.

"I'm sorry, Dr. Glass, but until the plane touches down, we're staying on radio silence. No one groundside knows their flight plan, nor will they be able to track them via radio signals. When they land, there will be an emergency briefing that will give you a chance to state your case."

"But the president won't land … not alive anyway."

"The army has this base well protected. Nothing is going to shoot the president down. Plus, they have a fighter escort."

Cartwright had been transferred up to Chicago after the Sully takedown was foiled by yet another tip-off, this time to the mob. Burke worked overtime trying to stay one step ahead of everyone.

The agent placated me, but I didn't have the time.

"They don't have to shoot him down. The Hero Twin can sit in a boat in the middle of Lake Michigan and zap the plane when it goes by. With the exciter fluid in him, especially if it's been keyed to his DNA, they won't even have time to say, 'What's a matter, Mr. President?' before matter is all that's left of him."

Cartwright seemed genuine in his apology. He promised to send a patrol out to check the bay for suspicious boats, at least, but the problem with being near the harbor was there were lots of boats to check.

I had similar bad luck with the CIA. Agent Chauncey Ream showed no concern for my continued existence on this planet. The man was a walking German shepherd; a gaunt face capped with prematurely white hair and ears that shot back like antennae. "I understand I am supposed to take what you say seriously, Glass, but I've read the briefings you've given, all the evidence and materials presented, and I'm sorry, but I don't believe a word of it."

"You don't?"

"No. Mindless wanderings, flights of fancy. Unless I see this MASER in action, I discount most of what you've said as being Saturday matinee garbage you've concocted to keep yourself from going to the chair as a spy."

I looked him in the eye, which was hard behind the sunglasses. "And is that what your boss thinks?"

"Commander Dulles does what the president tells him to do, and I do what the commander tells me to do. I am told to listen to you. What Commander Dulles thinks is none of my business."

"Well, the commander thinks what I'm saying is the truth."

"Again, unless I see the—"

I finished for him. "Thing in action. Hopefully, you won't see it used on the president."

He leaned across his makeshift desk to within a finger's breadth of my face. "That is close enough to a threat against the president that I can have you arrested, held someplace no lawyer will ever find you, and never think twice about it."

I returned his sneer. "You have a problem with me, Agent?"

He straightened some but not enough that I couldn't picture him snapping my nose off with one bite. "Yes, I have a problem with all you scientists. It's because of people like you the Commies have nuclear technology."

I remembered a similar conversation with a certain Police Chief. "If you ever get to Industry City, you should have a beer with Charles Sweet. You two will have a lot to talk about."

He ignored the suggestion. "Anyway, doesn't the president need to be injected with this special fluid to put him in immediate danger?"

"Yes, but—"

"Well, then you can cool your jets. He's been under twenty-four-hour surveillance. No one has gotten anything in the president."

"What about food?"

"We have had all his chefs' backgrounds checked thoroughly. They are all trustworthy people who have been with the White House for years. He's eating on the plane, anyway, today, and that's all strictly military-cleared food."

"Yeah, so was Stalin's," I said under my breath.

"What was that?" He looked down at me from over the top of his glasses.

"Nothing."

I left.

Lee and I sat in the commissary. Soldier and civilian contractors milled around, filling trays with food. In this arena, it wasn't hard to spot the table where the feds sat or the operatives or the grunts. They did their best to look serious, even while trying to relax. None would address the other branches, each doing their level best to ignore the mixed company. It bugged me.

Lee and I hadn't figured a way off base as of yet. I doubted the pizza trick would work under these conditions, though I'd kill to get a slice of Chi-town deep dish. The stuff in Colorado couldn't compare, something about the altitude and the way the crust rose. If I ever wanted to go into the private sector, I'd put all my scientific resources into creating a pizza dough that rose properly at any altitude.

"We can't just sit here. I need to track Orchid."

"Maybe this where you need to be right now," Lee suggested, swallowing down bits of Salisbury steak. "Maybe you need time. You been running toward something, day in and day out. You take the day and be you."

I guffawed and pushed around my hardly touched shepherd's pie. "I don't even know who that is anymore, Wan. Ten days ago, I was a former scientist working as a peeper. Ten days ago, I thought I had found a way back to the life I once had. The car, *The Atlantis*, was my redemption. But all that did was open a door to pain and heartache. Now Reece is gone, Vincent nowhere to be found, and even if we knew where he was, he's a fucking Russian spy!"

"But you scientist again, no?"

His optimism was annoying at times like this. I wanted to wallow in self-abuse or worse, to scream, but he made it seem childish. "Yeah, sort of. But things have changed. I didn't want it to come like this. Not at the cost of Yousev's life. Not finding out that a person I once respected is an evil mastermind and most likely ordered the death of my fiancée."

I dropped the fork, crossed my arms, and exhaled loudly. It was not quite a sigh, but it was close enough to elicit another pep talk from Wan.

"Glass, how many people get killed in experiment?"

"Six." Did I even remember all their names? Their parent's names? I thought I'd never forget.

"And since then, how many get killed since we start this?"

I thought about it. "That I personally know of?"

He nodded.

"Yousev, one of the Hero Twins, a few black army soldiers, Ilya—"

"Don't forget Big Red!"

"Yeah, Stalin. So maybe six more."

"And how many responsible?"

"Well, I'm pretty sure I know who orchestrated the whole thing, right? It all can be funneled back to Orchid."

"And you find that out, what? In ten day time? You solve bunch of murders, some fourteen year old! That make you a pretty good dick in my book, in anybody's book."

Again, he was making it hard to stay despondent. "I suppose you are making a point?"

He took a swig of beer and tilted the bottle at me. "You say you don't know who you are. I say you good at solving murders.

You figure out everything. Well, except for one thing."

"One thing?"

Lee set down the bottle and shoveled in another bite, swallowing quickly. He nearly choked, so he pounded on his chest a couple of times until the mouthful went down. He took another swig of the Ancient before speaking. "Why now? Why wait until now?"

"I thought we had covered that. The bomb."

"Ruskies had bomb since '49."

"True, but it wasn't very good or effective as a weapon. They created the reaction. They needed something on par with our hydrogen bomb."

"But still, they want to kill old money year ago, right? No bomb then, huh? Or Stalin, no bomb then either."

"I guess. What are you getting at, Lee?"

"I thinking something else happen. Something sooo big this flower lady—"

"Orchid."

"Right, flower lady need to clean house. Little guy at college, old money, even Mendelbum. She no want loose ends. That mean you loose end 'cause she want you dead too."

"I still don't know why I'm a loose end. I'm the one that figured out her secret identity. I suppose that's something." I took a bite of my food, not really tasting it. Lee had my gears turning.

"What good knowing that after end of world?"

He had made good points. Any decent scientist could break down the exciter fluid and come up with an antidote. I started a chain reaction when Reece dragged me into the game.

The hit on Reece was sloppy. Were they hesitant? They had no idea what his death would do. He was high up in their chain of command, so they didn't kill him way back when he first objected to the course the Technocrats were taking. But right after he talked with me, the Technocrats laid all the cards on the table, even at the cost of their Industry City lab.

Then my presence precipitated the murder of Yousev because he'd crack too easily if I got to him. Not to mention Mendelssohn's attempt to reach me had cost him his life.

Lee was right. I still didn't have the whole motive. I had the big *Brave New World*-style picture, but why was Noel R. Glass in the way of that?

Mine was the last murder I needed to solve.

I started eating with more gusto. It hit me that the food here was better than I had expected. I hadn't grabbed more than a doughnut or piece of fruit at Fort Palmer, so this was a surprise. "This isn't half bad. It's just like the stuff I get at Hank's."

He belched. "Good grub, that place. This almost identical to lunch I had three weeks ago."

I let the food sit in my mouth, savoring it. I let the spices ruminate, the taste tickle around my tongue. This wasn't just like Hank's …

It *was* Hank's.

I pushed back my chair hard and ran past the serving counter into the kitchen. I heard the cries of alarm from the staff and more chairs being pushed over. I made it to the cooler before the first armed men showed up. I looked at the boxes of food stored there. From floor to ceiling were stacks of boxes marked *Hank's Food Service.*

An army travels on its stomach.

How do you feed a secret army? You start by feeding other armies. How do you get the exciter fluid into the president of the United States of America? You don't put it in just his food, but everyone's. Hank's Diner. There was a receipt in Mendelssohn's effects. That's how they had gotten to him.

Two MPs grabbed my shoulders and pulled me away from the cooler. I ignored them and looked for the lead cook. A woman in a tall white hat stood nearby.

"How long has Hank's been servicing the armed forces?"

She was startled I had addressed her directly but answered, "About six months."

"Do they do all the armed forces or just the army?"

She thought about it. "I think they service them all."

Bile rose in my throat. "Even the air force?"

By this time, someone had alerted Cartwright and Ream, and they came in just as the cook nodded.

"The president can't land here," I said.

"Why not?"

Ream continued to be annoyed with me, but panic wouldn't let me take it.

"Because, idiot, he's already been poisoned with the exciter fluid. If he shows his face, they can hit him with the MASER from anywhere, and pop goes his top."

There was enough conviction in my voice for the man in the shades to say, "Okay, tell me what we're dealing with."

* * *

Air Force One opened communications to the base after Ream contacted their escort. I explained how the food was laced, maybe with the president's specific DNA. We wouldn't know until it was tested back at Fort Palmer. Dulles quickly established a backup plan and had the eagle touch down in Cleveland. I tried to convince the president to go to the first game of the World Series and skip Oktoberfest altogether, but he assured me the situation in Chicago was worsening, and if he didn't step in soon, there might not be a country to save.

"Dr. Glass, civil rights was a big part of my campaign. It is something I feel strongly about. If I turn away now, it will make my administration look weak in the eyes of those who would intimidate and beat others down. I need to take a stand in Chicago, sir. It will be up to you, and the resources I have given you, to make sure I come to no harm and this republic is here to stand for eternity.

"I'll do my job, Noel, if you do yours."

All I could say was, "Yes, Mr. President."

* * *

The plan was simple yet completely unbelievable. Agent Ream planned an assault on the Hank's Food Services' processing plant to get the evidence we needed for a court order to raid their corporate offices. There he hoped to find ties from Hank's to the

Technocrats. Cartwright and the FBI would enter their main offices downtown.

Meanwhile, Fred and Horatio were close to a breakthrough on the anti-exciter fluid.

So the choice I had was to accompany Ream or Cartwright. I was likely to find technical data at the processing plant, but I was more likely to find a lead on Orchid at the offices. I chose to go with the Feds. After communicating with the exciter antidote team, I gave Ream a list of things to look for. If any or all were found, they'd have enough to get the warrant. Apparently, the CIA didn't need a warrant for their end of the operation. It made me wonder how much power they wielded.

If we timed it right, the three of us would be in Hank's offices when the word came down from Ream. I had done undercover work before but not often enough for my tastes. I didn't consider myself an actor, but when one spends years as a pariah, it's nice to be someone else every once and a while.

Lee took a crack at changing my appearance, as my face would clearly be known at a Technocrat funded operation. He'd made me up to look somewhere between Groucho and Harpo. Cartwright had people who did a better job, though my hair was still a bit wild for my tastes. The base commander's own tailor fitted suits for us in record time. I wondered why he was here and not on Park Avenue. I looked sharp as a tack.

A limo took us off the base.

As we exited a convoy of army haulers pulled up to the gate. Their canvas-covered cargo lay strapped down to the bed.

"Preparations for the president?"

Cartwright looked away as if they didn't exist. "No, nothing to do with that."

His reluctance piqued my interest. "Then what?"

"Army business, Glass. I have nothing to do with it." But behind his disinterest, the delivery bothered him. He clearly didn't like whatever those trucks contained.

We worked on our cover story during the thirty-minute drive down Sheridan. I could catch glimpses of the lake through the trees and houses. I thought back to summers down by the pier, my family and me. My older brother used to race me to the boardwalk as our mom called out for us to be careful. I remembered spitting from the Ferris wheel and calculating rate of descent, trajectory, and velocity. My brother, who was not like me in so many ways, would give me noogies every time I hit my target.

"How'd you do that, pea-brain?"

I'd wrestle out of his headlock and try to noogie him back, my small arms never long enough to reach. *"My brain's not a pea! It's not! It's not!"*

He'd laugh and keep me at arm's length.

I wished he'd return my calls.

We turned west due to road construction. Cartwright fretted about our timing. We had to be in the diner's offices before Ream entered the factory with his men. I assured him, barring something unforeseen, we'd get there with plenty of time to spare. Unfortunately, we had to go through the worst part of downtown.

The Westside was every bad thing that could happen to a city. There were buildings built on top of each other, covered with signs advertising everything from miracle healings to sex—and sometimes both. I saw a man with no legs, pushing himself forward on a board with wheels. He stopped at a newsstand for the afternoon edition. He was handed a bundle by the owner and wheeled himself away to deliver them, hand over hand, papers on his nonexistent lap.

Everyone had a cigarette. If they didn't, they were bumming one off someone who did. The only people to smile were overly made-up women who looked into each car that passed and hoped for a stooge to date them for the night. Cartwright made a sound in the back of his throat. "Whores. It's unfortunate that, in this era of prosperity, we still resort to this."

Lee took offense. "Let me ask you, buddy. You not married. You go on dates?"

"With them?" The Fed looked appalled.

"No, with normal floozies. I bet tough guy like you no have trouble with ladies, right?"

Cartwright turned a little red. "Sure, I date."

Lee smiled. "Okay, how many dates before she kiss you?"

The agent boasted, "Usually the third or fourth."

"How much dough you spend each date?"

He doped it out. "Twenty or thirty. Maybe more."

"And how many before you get lucky?"

Now Cartwright did take offense. "Now see here! That is none of your business."

Lee sat back triumphantly. "I mean no trouble, but think about it. For what you spend on dates before you get slow ride, have you not spent same amount other man spend on hooker? All women chippies. Some like the cash in one big lump."

I didn't know if I agreed with Lee, but Cartwright certainly didn't.

I thought about Merlot. She was in this city. In a day she'd meet the president of the United States and sing for him. I wondered how that came about, especially so fast. Charlie the Spic? Or some other mob head still looking to ease his guilt over Merlot's mom? If she returned to Chi-town to get serious about her career, she found a big way to do it.

We pulled into the parking ramp of the Hank's Tower. Five stories lower than Industry City's Liberty Tower, it was number three on the tallest buildings list. Our car descended into the darkened depths of the parking garage, and I became overwhelmed with a sense of foreboding.

As I got out of the car, I caught a glimpse of a black woman getting into a different limo across the garage. It could have been Merlot. The tower hosted several radio programs, and certainly, as the singer performing for Ike, she was sure to be interviewed.

I thought about rushing over.

To do what?

Tell her what else I'd found out? To say I was sorry? Nah, she was moving on, and I wasn't going to get in the way of that. She was better left out of it all.

We presented our motley crew to the front desk receptionist of Hank's Food Incorporated. She took a look at us and blinked. Three distinctively different men stood in front of her in tweed suits, horn-rimmed glasses, and matching briefcases. Cartwright took the lead.

"Yes, ma'am. We are the Wheat, Oat, and Rice Co-operative and we have just flown in from Washington, D.C., to talk to your president, Mr. Arliss Vaughn."

His nasally voice added to the overall effect. She blinked again before asking, "You're with who?"

I stepped forward and gave her a smooth, dulcet voice to sooth her consternation. "We're with WOR …" I looked at her name tag. " … Stephanie. We represent the majority of grain growers in the United States."

She wasn't swayed. "Do you have an appointment with Mr. Vaughn?"

"We just spend three days at House in meetings about impending threat to agriculture in America. We no have time to make appointment. We come right here."

She looked down at Lee, who smiled widely. "And this threat?"

Cartwright answered instead of Lee. "Communism, ma'am. Communism."

"But that," I cut him off as if he had said too much, "is for us to discuss with Mr. Vaughn. *Is* he available?"

She picked up a headset and punched some buttons. She took us in again as she spoke. "Mr. Vaughn? There are some gentlemen from the Oat, Wheat, and—"

"I'm Wheat. He's Oats."

"Sorry, the Wheat, Oat, and Rice Co-operative to see you."

Lee whispered, "How come they never mix me up?"

I kicked his foot.

"Yes, sir." Addressing us, she said, "If you'll go down to the first door on your left, you'll find a conference room. Mr. Vaughn will join you shortly."

We thanked her, but before leaving, Cartwright asked, "I'm having a call forwarded here. Would it be too much trouble to let me know when it comes in?"

"I'll have it transferred to the conference room, sir."

He thanked her again. She picked up a buzzing line and said into it, "No, Sheila. I haven't been able to reach the processing plant either. Not for the last half hour."

As we walked, I noticed two particular things. The first was all the two-way mirrors. They were everywhere: in the lobby, down the hallways. I'd been in enough interrogation rooms to recognize the special reflective material they used. Hank's security probably watched our every move. There may even be security cameras recording us.

The other thing I took note of was the PR; posters touting company propaganda such as, *Hank's Foods: Efficient Foods for Efficient People!* and *If It Tastes Good, They'll Waste Less!* and *Hank's! Lower Cost and Higher Quality Go Hand in Hand!* With the words came pictures from the heartland of America, good salt-of-the-earth people in front of harvesters and tractors.

We found the room without seeing another soul. We seated ourselves and put our briefcases on the table in front of us. There were no cameras visible in this room, but I'm sure they were just hidden within the trappings of the place. I tested the lock on the false bottom of the briefcase but didn't open it to check if my gun still waited there.

"Sorry, y'all," came a voice from a hidden doorway that opened to reveal a stocky gentleman who looked as if he'd just flown in from Texas. His gray suit was topped with a cowboy hat the size I previously imagined came on only Yosemite Sam. "We've been having some phone problems today. Can't seem to get any calls in or out. It's creating a bit of a wildfire."

His Southern drawl would be better on an oil magnate than a former Department of Agriculture head, but Arliss Vaughn was known worldwide as the shrewdest businessman on the planet. He'd been responsible for keeping food production going during the Second World War before stepping out of politics and into the private sector to create Hank's Diners. He fully believed in the affordable quality his company marketed, and he himself refused to eat anywhere else when on the road.

"Oh, my," Cartwright squeaked, "I do hope you get it fixed. I'm expecting a call."

"Stephanie told me about that, son. I do hope it clears up soon. Now, getting down to brass tacks here, how can I be of assistance? It's been a while since I've been in the know on

Capitol Hill, and I can't say that I'm familiar with your group."

I spoke up. "We have recently formed as a request of grain farmers who are concerned about the supply and demand of their product. With each war, the demand goes up, but there is always a sudden drop when hostilities end."

He furrowed his brow. "Are you saying that you want America to stay at war?"

"No such thing," said Cartwright. "Due to the recent end of hostilities in Korea, the military will be requiring a step-down in food production, and as the new food supplier to the armed forces, we were concerned about how to keep production steady and create a slower descent."

Vaughn looked at us suspiciously. "You do know that I produce all my own food for my restaurants and food services, correct?"

"Yes. You see, that's the problem," I said. "We'd like you to outsource a certain amount of your grain production to other smaller farmers, so they don't risk foreclosure."

"Out of the question. Quality control is paramount with our organization."

I could see where he was going and decided to head him off. "But not only quality, but efficiency, correct? The least amount of energy that produces the maximum effect?"

He was startled by my correct assessment of his philosophies. "W-why, yes, Mister …" He fumbled around, realizing we'd never given our names. "Wheat, was it?"

"I'm Oats. He's Wheat."

"I'm Rice, but you guess that already."

"Wait, something is wrong here. What are your names? Not who you represent."

The phone on the conference table rang and, still flustered, Vaughn picked it up. "Yes? A call for Mr. Wheat?" He offered the handset to Cartwright, who got up to take it.

"Looks like the phones are working again."

Vaughn nodded suspiciously. "It would appear they are."

"Hello? Yes?" He flapped his ears a bit. "Well, that's great news! Give my best to the little missus!"

He set the phone back on the cradle and returned to his seat.

"My wife just went into labor," he told us, which was our password to go.

Vaughn, still not completely sure what was going on, said, "That's wonderful news!"

"For us, yes. You, no."

He drew from his briefcase his ID. "Mr. Arliss Vaughn? I'm Agent Cartwright of the Federal Bureau of Investigation, and you are under arrest for conspiracy to assassinate the president of the United States of America. Will you please stand up?"

"I don't think he will."

We all turned to look at the owner of the new voice. Amanda Orchid walked in through the same hidden door in the wall Arliss had originally entered from. Crow's feet edged what were once matronly eyes. Now they bore down on me with hatred and scorn. Behind her filed in four black army soldiers, pistols out. Cartwright went for his gun. "No!" I yelled, but it was too late. They drilled him before he had his equalizer all the way out. Lee grabbed me and pulled me down to the floor as more bullets passed over us.

"Stop!" commanded Orchid. "She wants him alive!"

She?

Lee sprang up, using the momentary distraction. I saw him fling something from his sleeves and heard cries of pain as whatever he tossed struck home. He pulled me to my crunchers, and I saw the four guards sagging to the floor, pieces of metal sticking out from their faces, eyes, and necks. Orchid had pulled Vaughn through the closing door. The murderous look she gave me showed that our friendship was long gone.

I went for the door, but Lee pulled me back the way we had come in. "We go! More will come. Bet you a dollar!"

We grabbed the guns from our cases. I stood over Cartwright. He wasn't breathing. The shots had been true to the heart.

Lee picked up the agent's fallen gun. "Now!"

We went through the conference room door, quickly pushing ourselves flush with the opposite wall. Reinforcements entered immediately after us. The guys Orchid had at her disposal acted better trained then the ones we had previously met. Still, we took out two immediately. The others ducked behind corners, popping out to take shots at us. Lee pushed us down a different hallway. We could hear them coming behind. We turned corner after corner before finding a back stairway. The offices of Hank's Foods may not have been on the top floor, but the flights of stairs still went a long way down.

We hopped down several steps at a time, sometimes partially sliding on the rails. We heard the door crash open above us. We had about six floors on them. Below us we heard more footsteps, lots of them. Lee looked over the rail quickly and pulled back as gunshots came from above.

"We have company."

I kicked open a door and discovered a long hallway. Lee on my heels, we passed large windows and could see we had ten stories between us and the ground. I'd have no such luck as a window washer today. I could see the Chicago River, ferries passing close by. I thought if we could just make the river …

We passed businesses and offices, but I doubted anyone could or would be able to help us, not against an armed force. We came across elevators just as they opened to black-garbed men. Lee with blazing speed fired both guns, one in each hand. I was reminded of Vincent and wished I still had my bodyguard here. We took out the soldiers and launched ourselves into the elevator.

I pulled open the panel as soon as the doors closed. "What you doing?"

"Overriding the call button. That way they can't stop us until we reach the garage and our men."

"Think there still help waiting?"

I paused. "What do you mean?"

"How army men get into building unnoticed?"

"Maybe they were already here? Like another hidden lab?"

"Maybe."

I overrode the switch and hit P1.

"If we can just get to the car," I said it more to myself than to Lee.

We hung to the sides as the doors opened. Our limo was not there, giving credence to Lee's theory. We slowly moved out into the garage, checking behind cars as we moved. The roscoe I was using was almost—if not already—out of ammo.

The Technocrat army came, more soldiers than we had slugs.

Lee pushed me behind a car and smashed three little white balls onto the ground. We were instantly covered with smoke. He found a maintenance manhole cover, and together we flipped it open. I went down first. The soldiers fired into the smoke, hoping to hit something. Bullets sank into the cars around us, shattering glass.

"Okay, Wan. Drop down."

The space was over the Eden Expressway, which ran under the city. I could hear the cars zip by underneath. Lee didn't follow me.

"I hold them off. You get help."

"Lee!" I called up, "This is no time for heroics!"

He smiled as he slid the cover back in place. "Perfect time for heroics. Be good. Tell wife I think of her at end. Really, I think of Jayne Mansfield."

I heard two sets of gunshots—Lee's attack and their response.

The shots slowed down until there were no more. "Lee? Lee! *Wan!*"

The soldiers would find the hatch once the smoke cleared. I moved forward, bent at the waist. The tunnel twisted and turned over the expressway. I could see through vents to the cars and trucks below, but I couldn't find a way down. From the smell, I was getting closer to the river. If I made the end of the tunnel, I'd find a way down. I was so focused on my task, I didn't know the soldiers had caught up to me until the bullet hit my leg.

I screamed as hot metal tore through flesh. I fell forward and through the grate in front of me fifteen feet to the pavement below. I tried to stand, to get out of the way, but my leg was useless. An oncoming sedan slammed on his brakes, but not quick enough to avoid hitting me square in the chest. The impact sent me up and over the bridge railing, and I plummeted fifty feet into the cold, unforgiving Chicago River.

Chapter Eighteen

When I hit the chilly autumn waters, the shock brought me to alertness. Everything hurt, my leg and chest especially so. I came up for quick air then dropped back down, hoping no one saw me surface. It'd be better if people thought I had drowned.

I wanted to make sure that didn't actually happen. I stayed under as long as my cracked ribs would let me then came up again. I could see from the trains that I was near the Roosevelt yards, so I dug at the water with one arm, holding my chest with the other. My leg still bled, and if I didn't get out of the water soon, I'd be dead.

Wading ashore near a stairway, I slid across the concrete and propped myself on the bottommost cold, hard steps. A slime coated them, a result of their proximity to the river, and I didn't even care that the chipped edge of one of the steps was digging into my ribs.

With a great deal of pain, I pulled off the suit jacket. Using my pocket knife, I made strips out of the suit material. The bullet had passed through the meat in the back of my left leg. I tied the wound tight, watching the brown tweed turn maroon instantly, so I added a second layer to keep it tight. Using longer strips, I secured my chest as best I could in an attempt to keep my ribs from grinding together. When I was done, I grabbed the rail and started my ascent.

Roosevelt was near Maxwell. Being late afternoon, if I moved quickly, I could make the markets before they closed. I stayed to alleyways and shadows, trying to look like the bums Cartwright had despised.

Lee was dead. He couldn't have survived that many armed men, whatever tricks he had literally up his sleeve. He'd saved my life, one last time. Now he was gone.

The world grew fuzzy, and I wanted to hit the hay. I was going to die here, in my hometown. Irony was a bitch. I could see the Maxwell Street Market ahead. I'd come down this alley with my dad as a child. He'd say, "Let's go hear the Negroes play. You can do your homework later." He never realized I'd do the homework in my head while listening to the music. I'd count the beats, follow the patterns. I equated everything to math and learned to appreciate the math of music until I no longer counted, just listened.

I could hear it. It called to me. The world grew lighter when it should've been getting darker. But the music, the music was lifting me. I found a booth to sit behind while a coke guitar rang through my brain. I counted the rhythm again, my eyes closed. I miscounted and had to start again. *Sweet, sweet music. I am you.* I opened my eyes, and a boy with a face so dark that his eyes looked like headlights stared down at me.

"Mister? You okay?"

I counted the beats again.

"Mister? Hey, pappy! Come back here!" The music stopped and I screamed.

* * *

I awoke to the smell of sweat and wondered if it was mine. The air was moist, and I could hear water running. I was on a gurney and the room was tiled and white. My leg still throbbed but felt different. I got up on my elbows and looked at it. It had been bandaged up professionally, as were my ribs. My shirt had been stripped off and my left pants leg cut around my hip. I had bandages on my face where I hadn't even realized I had been cut.

The boy sat watching me. "You okay, mister?"

"Yeah. I feel better." I tried to swing my legs over the side of the gurney, but the movement sent shots of pain through my body. "Doc said to tells you to not to move. That's why they puts me here."

"Where is here?"

"Doc's gym."

A locker room. Of course! The running water must be showers. "What happened?"

"Yous a strange white man. My pappy said that. He said he'd never seen a white man so need the blues."

"Huh?"

The boy laughed. I finally got my legs around and sat. He came over to my side to help me stand. We had a moment or two where I thought I was going to fall back onto the table, but we got my sea legs under me. "You screamed for him to not stop playing. So he played until you passed out. We thoughts you dead. He didn't wants to be caught with no dead white guy in his booth, so we gots you to Doc's. Doc said you still alive but not for long. Doc wants no dead guy in his place either, so he done fixed you up."

"How long ago?"

"Shit. I done missed dinner watching you. Didn't think you'd ever wake up."

I found a clock on the wall. It was well past ten. "I have to go."

"Uh-uh. You ain't going nowhere till Doc talks to you. He says you that crazy-ass white man everyone is looking for."

I must have looked confused because he continued. "On TV, mister. The news came on and says police got a dragnet for you. Something about some dead G-men."

Using the boy as my crutch, I gimped out of the locker room and into the gym. Punching bags of various sizes and shapes lined the walls. In the center, though, sat a full-size boxing ring. Two men squared off against each other. Both were Negros, though one was much lighter than the other. His size wouldn't rival Vincent's, but he was a brute nevertheless. What struck me was how he used his bulk. He was the predator stalking his darker opponent. The ring was his domain, and the weaker man knew it as they stepped up.

The predator's gloved dukes landed in rapid succession; sound waves echoed from the hits like sonic booms. His opponent took swings, but he moved like a panther and each time the fist reached the spot, the predator had vanished. Jab, duck, jab, jab, duck. They danced like a ballet, only the swan would occasionally punch the prince—hard!

The opponent, who appeared no more than a living punching bag to the predator, dropped twice before a whistle blew. A small gray-haired Negro came into view from the opposite side. He popped himself into the ring with the gladiators and ran down what he saw during their spar.

I suspected who I'd just seen in action, but the cosmic alignment was too much to believe.

"Hey, kid?"

"My name is Cleavon."

"Cleavon, then. Who's the brute?"

"Man, that's Tyrone Sterling. He's going to fight Rocky Graziano next week." There was pride in how the boy said the name, like it carried hope with it.

"Goddamnit!" I said, hoping to keep the curse under my breath, but the acoustics were too good. The three gentlemen in the ring turned in unison to glare at me.

Cleavon whispered, "That's Doc staring at you."

"Thanks."

He giggled. "Yous is a strange whitie, ain't you?"

I mussed his tightly curled hair. "So I've been told."

Doc gave the men some instructions and then squeezed himself between the ropes. He motioned me toward an office.

Cleavon moved in to help me, but I waved him off. "Go get dinner. If there is anything left, bring me a roll or something." I gave him all the loose change I had in my pocket. He saluted as if I had given him an important mission and darted away.

I got to the office and, without grunting too much, plopped into a chair. One side of the small room was lined with trophies from fighters Doc had trained. I recognized a few names. His desk was cluttered with posters, forms, and pictures in frames.

"Thank—" I started, but he cut me off.

"I don't want your thanks, nor even your money, if that's what you're going to offer next. Don't need it. Don't want it." He chastised me with deep-set, bloodshot eyes.

Doc's hair looked like gray cotton, and he had a tattoo poking out from under the sleeve on one arm. It was a pinup I'd seen before—a sexy Red Cross nurse. I think they called her Rose or something.

"Okay."

"Black-eyed Johnson says he finds him a half-dead honky in his booth and says I should fix him up, well, I'm going to fix him up. That's what we do around here, take care of our own."

"I'm from around here."

"No you ain't, Mr. Glass."

I raised an eyebrow.

"Oh, yes. I know who you are. Have a son your age. I read abouts you back when you was all hot shit and whatnot. Thought to myself, 'My son is smart too. He could be just like this white boy.' Know where my boy is now, Mr. Glass?" I shook my head. "He's in the big house doing a dime for selling heroin. See, even though he was smart, maybe smart as you, he saw what laid ahead of him: a world of pain and hurt and missed chances. He used his smarts to become one of the richest drug dealers on the West side.

"Oh, he knows numbers. Knows how much a pound of reefer should cost, how much to pay his pushers and still make a profit. He isn't just street smart. He's a businessman!"

"Why are you telling me this?"

Doc sat back and old eyes took me in from across the expanse of time. He tried to gauge me, like what made me so different from his son. Did he believe that it was just the color of our skin, or was there something different in our make-ups?

"There are men looking for you."

"I heard, the police."

"No, not just them. Other men. Men we don't like having in our business, but there they are. Police we know. Police we can handle. Not these guys. They're spooking my people, Mr. Glass.

Why are they doing that? Who are they?"

"They think they can change the world."

When Doc laughed, it was gravelly, like a smoker's laugh. "Ha! Lots of people think they can change the world. The president of the United States is coming here to tell everyone to change. Ain't nobody going change the world, Mr. Glass. Not you. Not me. Certainly, not them."

"They're going to kill a lot of people to try and make it happen."

He shrugged. "Lot of people died in the big one. Served as an ambulance driver. Learned a lot too. Like fixing people. But there is one thing I didn't learn how to fix. Doctors couldn't fix it either. Know what that is?"

I shook my head again.

"Souls, Mr. Glass. You can't fix souls. They are either bad or good. The bad ones, well, ain't a lot that can change it to good. Maybe the good Lord can, but I wonder at that sometimes." He sighed. "Trumble Park, Mr. Glass. What you white folk is doing down there, just as evil as what them Germans were doing overseas. No, there needs to be new souls before there is going to be a change."

He made sense, in a way. I thought about the Russians and Americans. We were heading into some sort of strange loop where one side would perpetually try to outdo the other until we nuked each other. Maybe the Technocrats were right to wipe society clean and start over. An engineered society would mean Doc's son would've had every chance I had as a kid. Was it wrong for me to stop them?

"Thanks, Doc. For the fix-up and the talk. I've got to go."

He gave me a nod. "Just don't bring any trouble here. When you get, get out the back. Stay low and watch those ribs. The leg I got cleaned before it was infected, but the ribs are going to sting a while."

"Got it."

I slowly got up and left the office. I walked over to the ring. Tyrone was by himself, punching air and dancing. His gloves were off, but his hands were still taped.

"Tyrone!"

He stopped and looked down at me. "What you want?"

"Where's Merlot?"

Having met his sister, I should have pegged Tyrone for a blowtop. I couldn't move away from the ropes fast enough before he was to them and over. He pressed his huge chest against me.

"You stay away from my sister, you hear me, you goddamn piece of shit!"

"Whoa, tiny! Back off. I don't want to hurt her. Just talk."

He stepped back. "She's done with you. Came back here all messed up. Said you had something to do with it." He pressed his hand into my chest repeatedly to accent his point. I think it would have hurt like hell even if I didn't have the cracked ribs. "If it wasn't for the call to sing for the president, she'd still be messed up."

"I need to talk to her about that and to apologize."

He kept pressing. "She don't want no apology. You stay away or I'll kill you."

"Tyrone! Don't you strip your gears before the fight!" Doc called from the doorway to his office. "I just fixed up that honky. Don't you go breaking him again!"

Tyrone stepped away but not before pressing into me one more time. "Stay away!"

"You better get out of here," Doc seconded. "Tyrone is overly protective of his sister. Can't rightly blame him. She's special, that one. Knew her momma. Special girl too. One of a kind."

I nodded, thanked Doc again, and left out the back door. Cleavon sat on a trash can, waiting for me with a ham sandwich. It tasted like heaven on a slice of bread.

"You looking for Miss Margaret?"

"Yeth," I said through a full mouth.

"My pappy's playing with her over at the Mill tonight. Want to go?"

I swallowed hard. "Lead the way, soldier."

* * *

Things had been better for Uptown, Chicago. The mob money was gone, and the neighborhood eroded the way coastlines did under years of abuse by the sea. It was the type of place a guy could get some—whatever "some" he wanted.

In the center of it all sat the Green Mill, like a forty-carat emerald mounted on costume jewelry. McGurn may have planned "The Massacre" right between those same walls, and here I was, trying to stop a different massacre. One last attempt to erect a wall against the sea before I, too, eroded and the waters washed over me for good.

I knew I couldn't go into the Mill the way I looked, so I traded my watch for some clothes and aftershave. Cleavon's connections with the Market were good and despite the late hour, I looked—and smelled—a whole lot better.

The Green Mill was not your standard gargle factory. It was a sanctuary for those who loved jazz. Every so often, they would highlight an up-and-coming blues singer. Those were the busiest nights—band rats hoping to catch a glimpse of the next Bessie or Big Mama. Merlot had come from nowhere, to the unknowing public. Her singing for the president made her the hot ticket on Chicago's Broadway Avenue.

When I stepped past the bouncer, I felt as though I had stepped through time. Ambient lighting hid behind clamshell reliefs. The front felt dark and claustrophobic, but it opened up farther back toward the stage. I squeezed past the jerks and fillies at the bar, a surprising fusion of blacks and whites. All were dressed nicely, though, doing their best to keep racial tensions outside.

I squeezed into a spot at the bar, near the end where private booths and small tables began. A soft, gold light bathed me from a glass chandelier above. Similar lamps hung over dimly lit tables, making sure the patrons couldn't be recognized in the half-light.

There was a jab at my ribs and I winced noticeably. I thought *gun,* but as I looked to see, it was a camera. Its owner was young, maybe late twenties, with dark, curly hair.

Embarrassed, he apologized. "Oh, sorry. I'm trying not to be conspicuous. I hope I didn't stick you too bad." He was genuinely concerned, so I let it be. He didn't want to let things go, though. "Let me buy you a beer."

I hadn't even thought of how to pay when I came in here, so I let him. After we had our first draw, he offered his hand. "Artie. Artie Shay. Pleased to meet you."

I didn't want to give my name, nor come up with an alias, so I made sure to keep him talking. Maybe he'd forget. "What do you do with that thing, Artie?"

"I take pictures for magazines."

A shutter hound. Just what I needed. If he picked up on my identity, I'd have to break from there sooner than I'd like. I kept myself angled away from him, as if I were anxious to see what would come on stage. However, Artie adjusted accordingly until he had a three-quarter view of my face.

"What do you do?"

"I listen to the blues," I told him.

"Like as a critic?"

"Nope, just an alligator."

His brow creased. "Alligator. Don't tell me. That's a music lover who wishes he could play but doesn't or can't."

"Uh-huh."

He beamed. "I've been hanging out in Chicago for ten years, on and off. Haven't heard that one used in a while. You must have lived here a long time."

"All my life, just not always here."

"Moved around, huh? The wars? Yeah, I see a lot of that. See a lot of stuff that others don't see. Like the streets, the crime, stuff like that. I like taking pictures of people no one else will or can." He waited for a reaction that wasn't coming. "You know what else I see?"

I looked directly at him, my first really hard look. I saw a hunger in his eyes. A special type of hunger that comes from knowing your next meal has arrived.

"A guy on the run."

Yeah, I didn't need to be a scientist to put two and two together. Artie had pegged me as soon as I walked in, maybe sooner. He said he was shooting the streets. He could have caught a whiff of me anywhere.

"I can't be a meal ticket tonight, kid. Sorry."

"Noel, I could care less about the money. For nearly two decades, you've got a bunk habit, but in less than two weeks, you've made the front page of every newspaper in the world—twice. The second time was only because of the first. Your disappearance under military watchdogs has spooked all the wrong guys."

"I could care less. I'm just here for the show."

Artie looked behind him to the stage. "Looks like it'll be a few minutes. Why don't you fill me in, at least enough to really earn the beer I bought you? Or I could drop an anonymous tip at the payphone outside."

"Fine, but what I'll tell you, you aren't going to like."

The photographer gave me a *you kidding me?* look. "Buddy, if you only knew the trouble I've seen."

I choked down a laugh with my drink. I heard the shutter click but saw no flash. What did it matter? We'd all be toast by the end of tomorrow anyway. "Kid, you may have seen whores, drug users, crime lords, and whatever. But I've heard the universe, listened to it sell its sweet music, and watched it wipe clean any trace of its presence. When you hold the remains of your lover in your hands and you can't recognize her from all the blood, then you'll know trouble."

The music stopped and the stage lights dimmed. The band came on from stage left. Playing rhythm guitar was Cleavon's dad, Black-eyed Johnson. He was a long-necked player playing a long-necked axe. He wore a mustache the shape of a horseshoe and never smiled. He leaned back as he played, as though relaxing in a wicker chair. I could tell he didn't care about the crowd; he was just playing for himself.

The bass man was a polar opposite. He bobbed his head continuously, as if he were petting a kitten on his lap. He played in trance, so I figured he was probably hopping something. His eyes were shut so tight, you'd swear the man was blind.

Their skins man sat behind them in sunglasses and *was* blind, but that didn't stop him from keeping the beat. A cigarette hung loosely from his mouth, and he wore a surfer bandana, as if he'd just come off of Catalina Island.

The odd duck out was a little Irish sax man, who played his gobble pipe as though he'd been born in Mississippi. They beat it out for ten minutes and gave me the distraction I wanted from Shay and his questions. That lasted until she came out.

Merlot wore a white dress that hugged the curves like James Dean on a race track. It seemed ages ago I ran my hands under the folds of her breasts, felt those thick, red lips on my neck. Damn, she was the last thing I expected to care about. I still didn't trust her, but I couldn't resist her.

My taboo.

"Is that the type of trouble you're talking about?"

Was I drooling?

"She's got nothing to do with me."

"Of course she does. She's the only reason to be here tonight." I knew he'd ignore my telling him anything but. "Noel ... she's playing for the president. It's everywhere. You got something big going on, and you need her help. I can help."

"And how's that?"

"I have to take her picture for *Life* after the set. I can get you backstage. Just give me the details of what you're into after you finish chatting her up."

It did solve a lot of problems. There were guards by the greenroom door.

Merlot leaned against an alabaster statue of some Greek or Roman woman as she sang.

"Who's the stone chick?" I asked.

"Ceres. Goddess of the harvest. Also fertility."

Merlot ran a hand down the statue's face and over her exposed, hard breast. I wondered if anyone wasn't thinking about planting seeds right then.

"Okay, you got a deal."

* * *

The first set finished, and the band slipped back for a smoke break. Keeping a low profile, I followed Artie past the guards, carrying his photo case like a sycophant. I waited outside the dressing room as he set up the shot, took it, and stepped into the narrow hallway.

He winked. "She's all yours."

Her back was to me as I entered, but she could see me in the mirror. She recognized me as quickly as she had the first time back in Chance City. Her mouth made to smile, but then went cold.

"What do you want? I only have two minutes."

I closed the door behind myself. "You look good, sound good up there. I don't think I ever told you that night how much I liked your singing."

Nothing.

"Anyway, I'm sorry about what happened at the apartment. I know you had nothing to do with Jorge's death. Again, I'm sorry."

She looked away from my reflection to the tray of powders. She went back to touching up her bait. "You're in trouble again, I hear."

"Yeah, so are you. Who got you the gig?"

Her head shot up. "What? That has nothing to do with you and your science stuff. Jorge is dead. My ties were cut. This is a legitimate performance. I had to go through background checks and everything. I don't know nothing about whatever shit you have going on."

"Yeah? Who's your agent? Or did the cash and a note just show up on your doorstep one day?"

"You're crazy! I do have an agent, and he got a call from some woman at the mayor's office. Next thing we know, there are all these people at my door. It's all on the up-and-up." Merlot's face grimaced. "You're coming to mess up my chances, ain't you? First, you take away my man, you drive me from Chance City. Now you come to Chicago with more stupid theories!"

I went to her chair and spun it around. "What are you? Naive or just scared?" I pulled her up from the chair by her shoulders. She pushed me back hard, and I stumbled, ribs throbbing. "Why do you think you got this gig, baby? No one knew you a week ago!"

"Ha! Charlie pulled strings for me!"

"Did he tell you that? What type of strings do you think the mob has with the mayor right now? Capone's days are over! Your mom's name can't carry you that far, not anymore."

She slapped me hard. I slapped her back. The look of betrayal made me regret it immediately. "You're not this stupid! Tell me you're not, please? They're going to kill the president, and they want you too. Two-for-one special, gift wrapped in the end of the world!"

She held her cheek. I don't think anyone had ever hit her. By hitting her in such a way, I'd signed a death warrant with her brother, the mob, whatever, but whatever kept her alive.

"Why me? Why would they want to kill me?"

"You're a loose end. They're cleaning them up. Any small bit of information Jorge might have told you could be the end for them. The noose is tightening, they can feel it. They're getting nervous. They're betting everything on one last hand. They're going to collect the world if I don't stop them."

"I don't care." Merlot gritted her teeth. "Even if I went out that way, I'd go out like my momma. I'm doing the one thing I am good at, and if I die while doing it for someone important, then that's how life is. They'll remember me, the same way they remember her. I got nothing else, Glass. Nothing."

"And if there is no one left to remember?"

I couldn't change her mind, so I opened the door to leave. She returned to her chair and applied fresh makeup to the slap mark. I looked at her reflection one last time before closing the door, but not before saying, "You do one other thing good, sweets. You kiss like a goddess."

I stormed down the hallway. I passed Shay, who followed close behind. "I need a snort."

We reached the bar, but before we could order, Tyrone, Merlot's brother, entered the Mill and locked his Edisons on me. He pushed people aside in rage. I turned to run, but found my arm being pulled behind the bar. Artie pointed to a trapdoor in the floor.

"Down here!"

We descended into tunnels carved from stone. I'd heard of Capone's famous escapes from the Green Mill, but I never imagined I'd be following in his footsteps. There was shouting from behind us. Tyrone descended into the tunnel just as Artie and I ascended the stairs to the street. We were blocks away from the Mill.

"Wow!" Artie said. "What was all that about? Never mind. You can shoot me the works later."

I had no intention of telling him anything, but I did owe him my life. "Yeah, let's find us someplace safe, and I'll spill the beans."

We hoofed our way through backyards and alleys until we were back on Broadway.

Artie motioned toward a parking lot. "My car's over there."

A limousine pulled around the corner near Shay's car. It slammed on the brakes, and two men in suits jumped out. Artie didn't have time to blink before he got punched in the gut. Wind knocked out of him, they threw him over the hood of his own vehicle.

The second guy squared off with me, but didn't hit me. I clearly had no fight in me. They secured my arms and held me firm. The back door opened, and Amanda Orchid got out. I wanted to spit in her face. She just smiled.

"Please join us, Noel."

Her hand gestured toward the spacious backseat. I couldn't see the "us" from where I stood, but knew in my gut, I was about to meet the person behind all of this. The Technocrat Master Engineer sat in there. The person that pulled even Orchid's strings.

"Fine. Let's go. I don't have all night."

I slid in, bravado speaking my words. "Your timing couldn't be better. I was about to hail a cab …"

My eyes followed the gams up her body. Dressed all in black, her skin radiated a pale glow as white as the alabaster statue in the Mill. You'd swear she was a black-and-white photo save for the single shock of red hair escaping from where she'd pinned it up under her tilted black hat. A small lace veil hung from the rim, but I could see the green eyes peering at me.

I didn't remember them being so green. There had been a lot I had forgotten, save what I saw in my dreams.

"Tangie."

Chapter Nineteen

A bodyguard sat beside me and placed a chloroform handkerchief over my face. In the darkness of my mind, I didn't dream. The nightmare of reality was enough to shut down my subconscious for the time being.

In the past ten days, I'd been knocked out too many times. It wasn't good for my brain. I had started to see things, like Tangie alive. She looked good, angelic, even fourteen years later.

This couldn't be reality. I must've died in the Chicago River, and this was my first day in hell. That had to be the explanation. Nothing else would do. Heaven was denied me, my sins too great. I would forever play this scenario through my mind: Tangie as my enemy. Tangie as the manipulator. Tangie as my killer.

I woke blindfolded and bound, but my mind was free.

I met Tangie at Walter Rautenstrauch's conference.

She was analytical, the consummate engineer, a great recruit for the Technocrats.

She had unlimited access to the magnetron designs.

The note wasn't in the book because Tangie didn't want the experiment stopped.

Tangie was strong in bed because of the Bogdanov treatments.

Orchid, in her office, had unknowingly deferred to Tangie.

Tangie's voice sounded different over the intercom. Her body, unrecognizable.

Unrecognizable.

Who had I buried? Why was Tangie doing this? Was this why she wanted me dead? Because I'd recognize the great engineer for who she was? She changed tactics midstream, wanted me kept alive. Why? What purpose did I serve her? Where did I fit in her plan?

The blindfold came off. They'd placed me at the end of a large conference table in a boardroom. The room was dark, save for three lights. One illuminated the Technocracy Incorporated logo. Another shone down on me. The final showcased Tangie sitting at the opposite end of the table. Behind her, in full warrior garb, stood the remaining Hero Twin.

Other lights came up, and more people in Janus masks appeared around the table. In front of them were their company logos. It was easy to guess Vaughn sat behind the Hank's Diner logo and Orchid behind NMIT. Tangie herself had a Little Technologies nameplate. The other companies represented were a surprise: Atlantic Brewing, makers of Ancient Stout; DuMar Broadcasting Company, fourth largest television network; KHGO Radio, Chi-town's biggest station; and six other names representing textile, steel, mining, and power.

The power represented here could pull our country out of any catastrophe, the shape of things to come. When the world experienced chaos in the form of World War III, these twelve companies would survive and could immediately rebuild the infrastructure. Food, energy, raw materials, communications, all the things Frederick Taylor had laid down as necessities for a Technate. The Technocrats readied to take over the world.

"It's time," Tangie said. "In less than twenty-four hours, the plan our ancestors put into play will come to fruition. The Technocracy will rise!"

The board echoed her like a congregation at a Baptist church.

"The Technocracy will rise!"

I wasn't feeling the spirit.

"I'm sorry. Ancestors? I know this DNA is big with you guys, but is crazy genetic?" No one had thought to gag me, so eleven masks turned toward me.

Tangie gave me a half smile. Her voice was smooth like fine Irish whiskey. It slipped over my mind, numbing my senses, but burned when I tried to swallow it. "Ah, Noel. It doesn't surprise me you haven't put this oh-so important piece together with all your sleuthing. You were too busy trying to find a killer when you should have been looking for a savior."

She pushed a button, and a light from below illuminated the table. The surface was a map. I was no cartographer, but it looked like the Atlantic Ocean. In the center was a large island I knew didn't actually sit at the coordinates shown. Its name written in Latin, I'd read enough ancient Greek to recognize it—*Atlantis*.

"Our homeland, Noel. Lost physically many millennium ago, but about to be reborn in the new world."

I barked with laughter. "You think you're Atlanteans? Next you'll be trying to tell me there're Martians in the White House!"

Tangie stood, palms down, on the table. She *tsked* me. "This is why I never included you in my plans, Noel. Your vision is too limited. You don't know how to see the bigger picture!"

"Oh, I see the bigger picture. There is no way you're my Tangie. Maybe we loved stories about rocket cars and lost civilizations, but we saw them as inspiration, dreams that could be someday made into reality. We never saw them *as* reality."

"You didn't, but I already knew what was reality and wasn't. This world you hold onto, Noel, that's the fantasy. My grandfather knew this. He knew someday the illusion would come crashing down and it'd take a strong leadership to rebuild society. One based on science, not greed. That's why he wrote all those books, Noel, and proposed Technocracy in the first place. He knew because he had proof it worked once before."

"Wait! You're not telling me …"

She crossed her arms and looked so smug. My mind was torn between the desire to hold her and strangle her. "Yes, it was so painfully obvious you ignored the biggest clue, Noel. My name is Tangie *Taylor* because my grandfather was *Frederick Taylor.*"

It wasn't possible. The government had done background checks on every member of my staff! I'd seen them with my own two eyes.

"No way, toots. You had government clearance. Some pencil pusher would've come across that tidbit if it even was remotely true."

"Come on, Noel. Use that brain of yours. You don't think one of his children couldn't have had an affair? A dalliance? I was illegitimate, but Grandpa Fred knew I was one of his before he died. From my test scores, he also knew what I carried in my blood. That's why he entrusted me with the true future of the Technocrats."

Slaw-jawed, she'd completely lost me.

"Let me take you back and see if that battered brain of yours can follow."

Tangie walked out of her spotlight. I could see the outline of her shape as she moved past the heads of industry and their masks. When she came into my circle of light, she was holding a pointer. That was classic Tangie. She loved the pointer when giving presentations. She got excited being in command, directing.

I knew that intimately.

Tangie pointed at the island continent. "All the histories state Atlantis was well ahead of its time in science, medicine, and technology. They were a Technate, run by the very same principles we Technocrats hold onto today; an engineered society where technology works for the betterment of mankind, not its enslavement. They lived harmoniously with each other and the technology they designed. They were benevolent leaders of the world, molding their uncultured brethren towards an ultimate evolution.

"If the ancient texts hold true, they were at least fifty to one hundred years ahead of where the world is now." She smirked. "Well, at least most of the world."

I smirked back for effect.

"When their scientists predicted Atlantis was to be destroyed, the Great Engineer set in motion two plans. The first was an attempt to try to save their island, but failing that, he created a second plan to save their ideals and designs. The Atlanteans encoded all their collective knowledge into their children.

"Blueprints, designs, and medicines, all stored in the greatest computer ever made—the human mind."

"How'd they do that?" For fantasy, it was an intriguing tale.

"Why, in their DNA, silly. The Atlanteans knew about genetic engineering and knew how to rearrange DNA sequences to pass these designs on from generation to generation."

"Designs, like what? Splitting the atom?"

Tangie snuggled in close to me. I could smell her intoxicating perfume. My head swam with her words. "Yes, and microwaves. And computers, televisions, even cars that run on water, Noel. But not only that, medical breakthroughs like penicillin and the polio vaccine. Even cancer will be cured one day soon. The solutions to all mankind's problems are locked in our very molecules. And with each generation, a great mind unlocks another secret."

She stood up and my head cleared some. As she walked back to her seat, she tapped the pointer on the table in between each person. None moved.

"My grandfather unlocked the secret to a peaceful society."

Tap.

"Each and every one here unlocked some great idea that brought them to this table."

Tap.

"Even you, Noel, even you are a descendant of those children, who were scattered to the four corners of the world while their homeland sank."

Tap. Tap.

"They knew one day their children's children would return the world to the glory of Atlantis!"

The board clapped.

I looked to my closest neighbor and asked, "Do you think you could untie me so I can clap?"

"Damn it, Noel. Can't you take anything seriously? I just told you that you were destined to play a part in the new world order. You are one of us, a scientist of unparalleled intelligence. You've already unlocked such great concepts from our ancestors, you could be part of the rebuilding of a peaceful and technologically advanced world. Doesn't that mean anything to you?"

My nose itched. "If what you say is true, we"—I indicated the group with a nod—"are all related in some way, correct?"

"Yes, but no more so then we are to the children of Adam and Eve."

"Well then, *sister*, let me tell you what you can do with my slice of forbidden fruit."

And I did.

There was a collective gasp behind the masks.

Any sign of concern Tangie had for my well-being disappeared in that moment. She motioned to the Hunter, and he came at me fast, his fist striking my face with unbridled fury. My chair was knocked over, taking me ass over teakettle with it. My nose was broken, but at least it didn't itch anymore.

The iceman sat me back up. I could feel blood pouring over my lip. I tried to clear my nose of blood and snot but only succeeded in getting it all over the image of Atlantis. I looked over to my assailant. "Sorry about that. Got a tissue?"

He struck me again. I couldn't tell, but I think he enjoyed hitting me. He pounded my face and my already aching chest and even stomped his foot on my jelly roll. I asked him to stop, but I don't think he heard me over my screams.

Tangie finally called out, "Enough!"

I'm sure the Twin was relieved; his fists must have hurt something horrible. I was past caring about myself. A switch had flipped in my brain. Not the mythical Atlantean genius switch, but something that turned off my emotions.

Tangie; alive. Instead of elation, disgust. My soul couldn't handle that, so I just turned off.

I coughed blood and my body throbbed with the damage done. "I would like … to apologize for … my appearance in … front of such an illustrious … gathering. If I could … have a moment to … freshen … up?"

"Leave us," Tangie commanded. "You have your jobs to do."

The spotlights turned off, save for hers and mine. The Twin left too.

When it was quiet, she pushed a button, and all the lights came on. I could see maps on the wall, charts of the United States, Russia, and the world. The U.S. one disturbed me the most. There were circles covering a majority of the country, and in the center of each circle was the icon of a radio tower. Many circles intersected each other, leaving less than 35 percent of America free from their influence.

Tangie strode over to me, pity in her expression. "It's been so long, Noel. Why did we have to meet like this?"

I couldn't answer her. I had no answers.

"When I saw you again, you looked so weak. Fourteen years. You were still a mess after *fourteen* years! What sort of man are you now?"

That I had an answer for. "A man who lost the one good thing in his life."

That rattled her cage a little. "But you had science, Noel. And if you had used it, you would have discovered the frame-up back then. You fell apart, and that was one thing I hadn't expected of you. You said nothing would stop you from finding me, nothing! You said you'd kill for me! Die for me! Where was that Noel for fourteen years?

"I saw … I saw your body."

"A double. All the staff were switched when Jorge came over to the power station. Your staff was loyal to me; I had recruited them even before you. Their doubles were street people we paid. They had no idea what they were getting into."

"You belong … in a cackle factory … muffin."

She sat on the edge of the table. "Why? Because I want a better world? One that works right? Society got off track somewhere, Noel. The wrong people are running the world with the wrong goals in mind—profit, waste, power. When we start over, it will be about people, conservation, harmony. Isn't that worth dying for?"

"If you're the one … dying, yes. Not innocent … people."

She snorted. "Oh, come on! Nobody's innocent anymore. Certainly not the lowbrow cretins the surviving Atlanteans had to breed with. That's why I had Jorge refine the exciter drug, so we can weed out anyone that doesn't have the Atlantean gene. It might take a few generations, but we'll get back to a pure strain."

The maps now made sense. A cannon-based MASER could be rigged to a 180-degree broadcast. Tangie could send the signal out from towers, immersing the country—the whole world—in the MASER effect. If they ate food from Hank's or drank beer from Atlantic or a dozen other sources I might not even know about yet, then non-Atlanteans would explode where they stood. Genetic genocide!

"We can be the progenitors of the future, Noel." She leaned toward me. "We'd have strong, pure children, you and I. And thanks to Bogdanov's treatments, I can have babies until I'm eighty and not even break a sweat during childbirth. Our own lineage to run the new world. They'd all be geniuses. Just like us."

"I'm no genius. I'm just a dumb palooka … who fell in love with … an evil bitch."

Tangie didn't hit me. I expected she would. I thought she'd kill me, ending this waking nightmare. Instead, she leaned in farther and bit my ear erotically. She whispered, "The reason Rocky hates you so much is because we screwed behind your back. Like little rabbits. Maybe he'll give me the heir I need."

She stood up and I spit blood at her, but she dodged it. "Tsk, tsk, Noel. You'll have to do better than that. Oh, but then I could always outthink you, couldn't I?" She walked away and opened a door at the opposite end of the room. Tangie looked back at me wryly. "I'd really hate to waste such good genes. Once the old world is gone and we start building the new, maybe you'll let go of your old notions.

"If you don't, I'll just have to take your seed and dispose of you. It works for the black widow, after all.

"I'll send someone in to clean you up and get you to the bunker." I scowled. "Oh, do cheer up, Noel. It's going to be a brave new world out there!"

And she left.

I wanted to cry. I wanted to scream. I would've done anything to free myself just to ring that bitch's neck, but instead I blinked in astonishment.

And then Wan Lee dropped from the ceiling.

"Damn, she never stop talking, huh?"

"Wan?"

He smirked. "You worst gumshoe ever. I take back everything nice I say about you. I sit in crowd at bar, you no see me. I climb on roof of limo, you no see me. I climb up wall and hang from ceiling and you even get knocked on butt, you still no see me. You go back to dick school."

Wan leaped down from the table and cut my bonds. I put my hands to my nose to staunch my nostrils before I passed out from blood loss. "I bet Vincent's here. We should find him."

"We need to shake leg. They come soon."

"He's part of their plan, Lee."

"No time!"

"Lee!"

"*No time!*"

Lee was in all black. His garb had tiny pockets all over. From one he pulled a stick that looked like cinnamon and broke it two. He pulled my hands away and stuck each half up my nostrils. I yelped. "Oh, don't be such big baby. This will stop blood."

"What is it? Some ancient Oriental herb?"

"Nah, cinnamon stick for my tea. Let's go before ugly guy or bitch come back."

"Okay, fine. But I can't leave without this." I ripped the map of America off the wall.

*   *   *

Climbing stairs had been excruciating, but Lee pushed me forward. We were behind the eight ball. There would be no second chances or last-minute miracles. I should've been more surprised to discover the bunker the Technocrats used was under the Atlantic Brewing's Chicago bottling plant.

"Bleh. I tell you I like Wisconsin beer better? I only buy Ancients 'cause they cheap."

I would have laughed if I didn't have a broken rib piercing my lung. The pain robbed me of my ability to breathe normally. I wheezed and it took Herculean efforts to keep from blacking out again. There was a guard on the other side of the door Lee kicked open. The soldier drew down on Lee, but the old man's hands were too fast. Two blades shot from his sleeves, piercing the man's chest and throat. Lee pulled them from the body as we passed.

"These things expensive."

We moved along the edge of a driveway. The alarms went off, and we saw through grease-smeared window panes people running around. Just before we reached the corner, two men with guns came around it. Lee dropped me onto a pile of shipping crate and then charged at the soldiers.

Wan leaped to the left and ran along the wall, parallel to the ground. The soldiers tried to trace his movements, but Lee's squat form made him a difficult target. He spun off the wall and landed behind them. They turned and Lee put a blade in each of their throats. My friend helped me back to my feet before their bodies finished twitching.

More soldiers came. Lee whistled and two similarly dressed men got out of a waiting car and laid down suppressing fire. I was unceremoniously dropped into the backseat. Didn't Wan know I was injured? The driver apparently didn't either as we burned rubber out of there. Lee and the other Asian traded gunfire with the soldiers. We escaped without further incident.

The plant was almost to Rockford, so we had a long drive to Fort Sheridan. Lee did give me a drink that deadened the pain some. I didn't ask what it was this time.

"I thought you were dead."

"I think same of you."

"There seems to be a lot of that going around tonight."

He was silent for a moment then said, "That her, right? Your love? The one you think you kill?"

I nodded. Suddenly, my chest hurt worse than it did before. I couldn't breathe, only rasp.

"What wrong?

"Hospital," was all I could squeeze out.

"Huh? Why?"

"Lung ... collapsed."

* * *

For the first time in recent memory, I went into the black willingly.

I dreamt of her—the better days.

We sat at a picnic table outside the commons area playing chess. Tangie loved the game, yet she never got better at it. Once, I played below my skill, so she'd have a chance. She caught on right away and withheld sex until I promised never to do it again. Tangie never won in all our years together.

"I just don't know how you read my patterns so easily."

She was frustrated again. She had taken to playing Jorge, Yousev, and even Orchid. She had beaten them all, but now I wondered if they lost on purpose, afraid to win against their master.

"I can tell you, if you want. Check and mate, by the way."

"Ugh! I can't believe it. You did it again! How?"

I put pieces back into the wooden box that formed the set. *"Chess, like so many other strategy games, has little to do with luck or skill, but logic. It's a numbers game. Given a piece that can only move so many different ways, which are you most likely to choose? There are a finite number of moves in the game."*

"And you know them all?"

"Hardly, but I have been watching your patterns for years. I know which pieces you favor, which pieces you're not comfortable attacking with."

Tangie raised her eyebrow. *"Am I so predictable? Is there no mystery left to me?"*

I reached over and kissed her. *"Oh, there is still much mystery to you. I just know where you'll move your pieces when we play chess. Nothing more, nothing less."*

* * *

Stitches swelled under bandages, and an oxygen mask covered my face. Needles attached to tubes stuck out of my arm, and a warm fluid ran into my veins. As the anesthesia wore off and I returned from the dream, I could feel every cut and bruise on my body. There were a lot.

I heard a beeping sound. I looked around and saw I was in one of Yousev's computerized beds from the secret lab. A bottle of blood hung above me and ran down into my arm. I sat up and saw that another tube ran from my other arm and emptied into a separate container.

"It is a good thing that you are awake."

"Horatio?" My throat was dry and squeaked with disuse. Horatio slipped off my mask to let me sip from a glass of water. He smiled, his bright, white teeth a welcome sight for me.

"Where am I?"

"Fort Sheridan. You were transferred here from the hospital Mr. Lee took you to. The doctors there were most capable and repaired your damaged lung, but you had lost a lot of blood."

"And we had just finished setting this up here." Fred joined us. "We brought one of these"—he ran his hand over the transfusion machine the way a father runs his hand over his child's head—"from Industry City because it's the easiest and quickest way to get the exciter fluid out of a man and the wave-blocker in."

"It's done? You actually perfected an antidote for the exciter drug?"

"Well, that would not be an entirely true thing Dr. Ligerman has suggested. While we have created a counter, it cannot completely block the microwaves generated by the MASER weapon."

Fred frowned, his thunder taken away. "Yeah, but it will significantly slow down the process."

Light flooded in through the window, and the previous night's activities came with it.

"Guys! Oktoberfest! Beer! Oh my God! The beer! It's laced. Do you have enough blocker to inoculate—" but they stopped me by holding up their hands.

"Lee told Archdeacon everything," Fred explained. "He went with the CIA, FBI, and army as they raided the Atlantic Bottling plant, but the Technocrats had collapsed the stairways leading down to the bunker he described. It'll take a day or two to clear the rubble."

Tangie had vanished again. She could be at any one of the other board members' businesses. Or she could have gone off the charts altogether. She didn't need to be here for the slaughter. She could be anywhere.

Horatio hung his head despondently. "Is it a true thing he said? Is our own Miss Taylor behind all this death and madness?"

Fred, too, waited for an answer. I didn't know what to say. My own emotions were numb. I didn't want to destroy their memories of her, the good ones—the times together at Hank's, the late-night debates, the early-morning doughnut runs. I gave them the only answer I had.

"I don't know. It looked like her, but it wasn't the Tangie I knew. That Tangie died the day of the experiment. I don't know who this was."

They each laid a hand on my arm in a comforting way. I nodded a thanks.

The transfusion finished and I was unhooked from the contraption. I had to admit, I felt better for whatever the guys had done. They had brought bottles of the Project Bogdanov blood with them, selecting key genetic types, such as mine and the president's. There hadn't been a lot of time to test the blood for additives, but since the Technocrats were using it in their own people, chances were that the blood was copasetic.

General Archdeacon came in and explained the precautions being taken for the president's speech at Oktoberfest. The army would act as security, checking each and every citizen for weapons. The FBI would be stationed around the tops of buildings, snipers at the ready to take out the Hero Twin and the Technocrat's MASER. The CIA would filter through the crowd and staff of the festival. Fort Sheridan would be practically bare, so many of the personnel had been brought in to protect Ike and the other dignitaries.

The news reported many civic leaders would be in attendance, as would representatives of the black community. The Klan also made a statement, saying they would be there to protest anything the president might say. In addition to Merlot, the president invited residents of the Trumble Park Apartments, where the recent riots had taken place, to sit up on stage with him.

Everyone was going to be at this shindig. With my transfusion, I knew I'd be there, too.

Despite my renewed health, I was kept under observation for the night. I had a surprise visitor for dinner.

"'Allo? Can I come in?"

A lanky man who entered bore a tray of food. He had on a lab coat and had a serious cowlick in the front. His teeth protruded from his mouth when he smiled. He was the oddest looking thing I'd seen since Mendelssohn.

"Oh, good. You're awake. I was afraid you'd dozed off again. I tried stopping in first thing this morning, but you were still unconscious."

He spoke with a British accent, but he wasn't from there. Behind the words, a native Chicagoan hid waiting to be discovered.

"Do I know you?"

"Only by correspondence, I'm afraid. I'm Jim Watson. I hear you have a DNA problem?"

CHAPTER TWENTY

We're Atlanteans, huh? And here I was thinking we were Tars."

He referenced our high school team mascot, a sort of pirate. While ten years' difference, we had both graduated from the same high school. He ate the last of the pudding as he sat cross-legged in the hospital room chair. I figured I owed him that, at least, for flying back to the States just to see me. He smacked his lips.

"You know, on the other side of the pond, you have to watch out what you order that's named 'pudding.'"

"So is it possible? Could there be some sort of DNA marker in our blood that makes us special?"

He set down the bowl, thought about it a moment, and shrugged. "Damned if I know. Is it possible? Yes. Can we test for it currently? No. We've just started mapping the human genome. It could take a hundred years before we know what each block means." He set the empty bowl back on the tray. "If you want to know whether we are masters of our own destinies or if we've been programmed to be this intelligent, all I can say is, if there was a code inside of certain individuals that made them smarter, how much different is that from two athletic parents producing a child with athletic skills? The child still has the freedom to be an athlete or choose a different path."

He looked over to the empty bowl as if he wanted more. "You and I, Noel, we chose science because we were good at it. Race memory, the type Miss Taylor talked about, it hasn't overridden our dreams, but it might have enhanced them."

Watson got up and paced in front of my bed to distance himself from the lost pudding.

"Since we revealed this information to the world, there must be a hundred different schools of thought on its potential. Universities and private companies by the dozens have launched DNA research projects. It's gotten quite out of hand. New reports come across my desk daily. Can't say I've seen through the lens of a microscope in the last month, at least not before Fred and Horatio called me."

"Thanks for that, by the way." I sat up a bit. The treatment was working through my system, and I was getting bolder by the moment. I wanted to walk around, but erred on the side of caution.

"No trouble at all. I'll say I was a bit disturbed by their findings, though I concurred with them. To think that our DNA discovery could be twisted so. We envisioned saving the human race while someone else was looking to destroy it. It's like Poland all over again."

"You can understand how I felt then when I heard about the MASER."

"Oh, yeah, definitely. It makes you feel dirty."

I couldn't have agreed with him more. "It's worse when you find out you've been used by the ones you kept closest."

Watson thought a moment. "Are you sure it's her?"

"I don't know who else it could be."

He placed a finger to his top teeth and tapped them while thinking. "You know, I could verify that for you, if it's her or not, I mean."

I was stunned. I decided I did need to get up. I swung my legs over and tested them on the hard tile. It was difficult, but they held. "How's that?"

"Well, we know that everyone was their own specific DNA sequence and no two are alike—identical twins being the only ones without discernible differences. So if I could get a large enough sample of Tangie's DNA from before the experiment and one from the woman claiming to be her, I could compare them and see if they match. It would take a while. It's not an exact science yet."

Watson's theory had exponential possibilities. "You understand what you're saying, Jim? We're talking about a whole field of research around DNA investigations. Whose blood was found on the knife or victim? Who was in a house when a murder took place?"

He liked the idea. "Yes, you're right. You could tell if a man raped a woman by just a sample of his hair."

"Or sired a child?" I thought about Tangie's illegitimacy claim.

"Yes, exactly. That's a lot to think about. However, I do believe you have more pressing matters."

I nodded. "So what's to be done?"

Again he shrugged. "Not much right now. Let the government stop these Technocrats. The wave-blocker is in too limited a supply to inoculate an entire burg, let alone the country or world. And even then, there is more than one way to start a world war."

"By Jove, Watson! I do believe you've hit upon something!"

Watson laughed. "Ah, so it would seem that you're Sherlock Holmes, now, what? Well, it stands to reason. Watson was the smarter one."

"Really?"

"Yes, read the books. You'll see. Holmes needed a Watson to feed off of. Watson always knew what to say to help his friend reach the right conclusion."

I raised an eyebrow. "And you think you're smarter?"

"SAT scores?"

"Graduated a year younger."

He grinned, the bottom of his teeth sticking through his lips just a hair. "Touché. I have got to catch a plane. I hope I've helped."

"Yes, some. Thank you." We shook hands. "Tars to the end?"

"Actually, I got picked on by the football team."

Watson grinned wider still. "Yeah, me too."

He was almost to the door when I thought to ask, "Hey, you knew C.J. Reece, huh?"

Watson stopped and turned. "In a capacity, yes. Why? What did you hear?"

There was concern in his voice. I decided to be vague. The man had just helped me, and I wasn't going to accuse him of anything insidious. "He said something about helping you with the DNA research, private funding."

"Ah, yes. What a clever way to put it. Yes, he privately funded some of our research. Why?"

I got to the real question. "Do you think you would have reached the same conclusion without his 'funding'?"

He took a moment to phrase his answer. "Yes. I know we would have. I don't know if we would have been the first, but we would have gotten there. Does that help?"

"Yes, yes it does. Thanks, Jim."

"Any time, Noel."

After he left, I got bold and stood. It felt good, so I moved to the window for some time, thinking about everything Jim had told me.

C.J. Reece had been prompting me for years without my knowledge. Maybe Tangie's mythical Atlanteans had been as well. But in the end, all that really mattered was that I had the final say in what I did or didn't do with the information.

Tangie was wrong. She wasn't smarter than I. That's why she wanted me taken out of their genocide game. She knew if I could look at all her pieces, then I'd know which way she'd move. I knew which pieces she favored: The knights, in the form of the Hero Twins. I'd captured one, leaving one still in play. Mendelssohn, as a bishop. She'd sacrificed him, but kept her other, Orchid, hidden behind a wall of pawns. Reece, another sacrificed piece. He should have been king, but switched and took the place of a rook. That's why Tangie needed me. A new king to her queen only I wouldn't play on her side.

She allowed me to take Hank's and Atlantic Brewing out because they'd already done their job. The exciter drug was out there, already in the bloodstreams of hundreds of thousands of people including soldiers, diplomats and maybe the president. She'd set up MASER towers all over the country in places such as behind every Hank's, and on top the Liberty Tower. Even the Empire State Building. Once Tangie flipped the switch, the Technocrats would face little resistance in rebuilding the country into their own image.

But Russia was a bear of a different color. Tangie's counterparts over there must've spiked the vodka and food rations to drug their populace. How would the president even convince the premier that they faced genocide on their side, as well?

That's why Tangie wanted a war. War levels the playing field. Fewer people on both sides of the Pacific meant fewer people to zap with the MASER. She needed World War III, or she could never succeed.

I could see across Fort Sheridan from my room. The place was a bustle of activity. The trucks I saw yesterday upon arriving were being unloaded. Giant crates moved via conveyor belts into warehouses for storage. I had no idea what they were or why Agent Cartwright had been so nervous when I questioned him about them. The military had a private game going, one I hadn't been invited to play.

That left me with the Technocrats. I didn't know Tangie's endgame yet, but I could see her next move. Tonight, at Oktoberfest, she would try to kill the president and somehow blame it convincingly on the USSR. She'd also try to kill Merlot in the process. I couldn't let that happen.

I found a set of clean clothes and got dressed.

* * *

"Whoa there, Glass! Where do you think you're going?"

I'd met Agent Ream in the hallway outside command central. A war room had been set up for the president. I'd heard about it as I sought out Archdeacon. Being the consummate guard dog, Ream scrunched up his thin face at my appearance in his zone.

"Well, I heard they were serving hot coffee and scones in there and I'm just famished."

He wasn't amused. "The president is in there, and nobody without four stars is welcome, got it? You've done your part. Now go heal somewhere and let us handle our part."

While I was feeling better every minute, I wasn't in any shape for a fight. Luckily, the general stuck his head out. "Glass? I thought I heard your name. Get your ass in here. You've been laying around too much as it is."

I grinned as I passed Ream. "I'll save you a scone. Blueberry, right?"

The U.S. military war room didn't come off much different than the Technocrats' one below the Atlantic brewing company. They had a big map of the world in the center of their table, too, though it was pleasantly missing the mythical island of Atlantis.

Another similarity was the map I'd acquired from that place, now hung nicely on the Fed's wall. Five red Xs marked five towers that'd been taken out.

President Eisenhower smiled broadly. "Glad you could join us, Dr. Glass. How are those ribs?"

"Not killing me anymore, Mr. President, sir. Thank you."

"No, thank you. Your uncovering of Hank's Diner as a Technocrat ally was a huge breakthrough and may have forestalled a greater tragedy." His smile warmed even more and despite silver hair, did not look old. There were wrinkles at the corners of his eyes, but one expected the leader of the free world to have some sleepless nights. I wondered how my own face was doing.

"Your friend Mr. Lee gave General Archdeacon a detailed report of what he overheard in the Technocrats' bunker. Strange little fellow, that one, I am told. Can he be trusted?"

"Before Reece walked into my office a couple days ago, sir, I don't know if I could have answered that question. But since then, Wan Lee has saved my life on several occasions. I trust him explicitly. If he heard what I heard, I can attest to the fact he has as much at stake as every American citizen."

He offered me a seat and locked his fingers together in a steeple in front of him. "And what is at stake, Dr. Glass?"

"Well, to start, the Technocrats wanted to make your assassination look as if it were a Russian plot. This would, in their estimation and mine, start World War III."

"But we know better, and so does the Kremlin." countered Archdeacon. "We've gotten through to their top people and so far, they've been shocked at what information we've been willing to share."

"Maybe, but still, we're talking about super-science and things that defy logic. Plus, the Technocrats control several powerful news organizations. In the ensuing cacophony, it would be easy for all we've learned to be lost on the people left in charge. Has the vice president been informed of the Technocrats movements? Has anyone checked to see if he's somehow involved? I'd be looking down the list to see who is legally in charge if government officials start exploding."

There was a chorus of "Of course," but then these slowed to a whisper as doubt crept in. Ike shook his head. "Someone get Dick on the phone and make sure he's briefed." Three people left the crowded room. "That was an oversight, Dr. Glass. Thank you for catching it."

Richard Nixon running the country, now there was a scary thought.

"The Kremlin should do the same."

"Agreed. What else do you have?"

I hesitated. "Other than trying to get you to call the whole thing off, not much yet." I nodded toward the American map. "You've been busy dismantling MASER towers."

"Yes, Ed is sending teams to take them out. Hoover's men are meeting some resistance. It's been time consuming, but they are making progress. Having a list of those Technocrat board members helped him immeasurably. The Bureau has been able to track and seize holdings for each of those companies."

I was sure that was making Tangie furious. She didn't have enough resources to protect all her chess pieces. The Tangie I knew a lifetime ago might grow desperate when she started losing valuable men.

The president stood up, "Well, gentlemen, it is time I got ready for my speech. I'll expect you to be on top of things, Dr. Glass. This Taylor woman seems intent on doing me harm. I expect you to outsmart her. Is that clear?

"Yes, Mr. President."

His tone turned soft for the moment, almost intimate. "Noel, it is clear to everyone involved that the world has done you a great injustice, branding you a murderer and a traitor. It is my intent, after all this is over, to make sure your record is cleared, and I'd like to invite you to Washington to sit on my cabinet as scientific advisor."

The president offered his hand and I took it. I found my voice, though it cracked a little as I spoke, "I-I'll consider it, Mr. President, when we have the Technocrats in custody. Thank you."

The meeting broke and General Archdeacon walked with me back to my room.

"You're holding something back, Glass. I don't know much about science, but I know a poker face when I see one."

"You got me, but it's hunches only."

"This *is* the president's life, you know. Any intelligence could be vital."

I stopped. "The problem is there is no intelligence behind it. This has turned into a chess game with Tangie, and I'm trying to stay one move ahead of her. If I move too soon, she'll make a different move, one I can't predict. It's better that I just hold my cards close for a bit."

The general shook his head. "Poker, chess, and that Lee friend of yours had a Go board in his possessions. Is all of life just a game to you, Glass?"

"You play war games, Duane, don't you? Lee said people play games as they live life. I've been playing different games because life isn't made up of just one. Every person you meet has their own favorite game with house rules only they know. If you play Go by chess rules, you'll lose. I had been playing the Technocrats' game by the wrong rules, mine. Now that I've learned what they are, I just have to beat them."

"Fine," said the general. "Just know that if we're not prepared for the worst, and you could have prepared us ..." He trailed off, but I'd received his message.

There were worse things in life than being branded a traitor.

We started walking again, and we passed a window. I pointed to the warehouses. "General? What's been going on out there?"

"Sorry, Glass. Can't tell you."

"Oh, now who's keeping stuff back?"

His face was stone expressionless. "This one is too big. Can't say a word."

"Not even a clue?"

"Enough, Glass. I have a duty to uphold and some places I just can't budge."

His wall of silence wound me up like an eight-day clock. "It's that big?"

"It's big. So don't try to find out more. If you even get near those warehouses, neither I nor the president could protect you from the trouble you'd be in."

I let it go, for the time being, but he'd confirmed something I feared.

There was only one secret in America *that* big.

* * *

The sun was low over Lake Michigan. Its orange rays gave my room an eerie glow. Horatio was wiping my puncture wound with an alcohol swab. He stuck a bandage to it. "That should do for the here and now. Even if you've had the DNA sequencer injected into you, this should hold off any body exploding."

Fred had already injected Lee and Ream, my escorts. He brought out a small case from his lab coat. "Here are four more vials. We've already taken care of the president and his guards. The general refused to take it unless there was enough for all his men. Stubborn old coot, that one, but then he always was."

Bravo for Duane.

Agent Ream spun his hand in a hurry-up motion. "The motorcade is getting ready to leave." He was dressed in standard Fed wear.

I asked, "Aren't you supposed to be in *lederhosen?*" and got a growl in return.

I felt more confident I was safe from MASER attack than I had been with the X-ray vest on. The wave-blocker took a half hour to work its way through a person's system. I'd have to work fast to get Merlot—and everyone else—inoculated once we reached the fairgrounds. We exited the building and crossed the parking lot. I could see the warehouses. There were still quite a few soldiers in place, guarding whatever was in there.

Chicagoans lined the streets, waving American flags at the passing motorcade. Most people really did like Ike.

Most.

One group of men in white sheets held signs proclaiming *Niga lover go home!* and *We didn't vote a negro as presadent!*

Ream reassured us. "Don't worry about them. Those guys came up from Ohio. There is no real Klan presence in Chicago anymore. Ran out in the twenties."

"You don't have to be a Klan member to create problems. Isn't that why the president came? Normal, everyday whites making life difficult for normal, everyday blacks in Trumble Park?"

"He'll get things back on track. Eisenhower is a great leader."

I found myself overcome by a sense of surrealism while passing through streets I knew as a child in a presidential town car. The vehicle's glass was supposedly bulletproof, the windows shaded black.

It took me back to the day Reece had picked me up at my office.

My safety net was gone. I no longer had the protection of ignorance, nor the guilt of failure. They, Tangie and the Technocrats, had played me for a damn sap from the beginning. I'd been set up to fail, and I had played my part too well. I was young, cocky. Spending the last fourteen years as a pariah ages a man's soul. I was wiser and ready to turn the tables on those who thought me just a pawn.

We pulled into the fairgrounds. Damn, there were a lot of people. Beer tents were set up in rows, one set for whites, one for blacks, yet the races mingled too close for my, or anyone's, comfort. I wondered who thought packing a couple thousand people into a confined area and getting them fractured on beer was a good idea even on a non-Armageddon day.

We got out of our ride. There were armed soldiers at every gate observing while the Chicago PD performed pat downs. I'd see them occasionally pull something knife or gun-shaped from a citizen's belt and drop it in a box before letting the person come through. Festival goers would then head for a booth and buy tickets. Each ticket was worth one beer.

One guy fisted fifty tickets.

A stage had been set up and cloggers—kittens by the looks of it—were on stage, dancing in wooden shoes. People watched from the fairground's bleachers. I was assaulted with the smells of grilled sausages, sauerkraut, and funnel cakes. My mouth watered for a beer and brat, but a sign reminded me to stay on task:

Chicago's 1953 Oktoberfest
Sponsored by Hank's Diners and the Atlantic Brewing Company

There hadn't been enough time to get new sponsors, plus the damage had already been done.

I scanned the parking lot for a limousine and spotted one sticking out from behind the bandstand. I moved in that direction, but Ream stopped me.

"Where you going, Glass?"

"I'm giving the mayor's special guests the inoculants."

"No can do. We might need that for an emergency." He stared at my through his dark shades. "Plus, we all know you're sweet on that singer."

"It will be an emergency if anything happens to that canary. Merlot draws a lot of water around her, and you don't want to be drinking that tonight."

Ream didn't back down. "She was Mendelssohn's ex. She could be one of them, you know? She might be playing you and all of us for the fool."

"She isn't. See those thugs in the crowd that look like 'made men'?" Ream looked out seeing several thugs who looked as out of place as his own people. "Well, they are. And they're here to make sure nothing happens to Merlot. Things could get ugly if she gets hurt."

"Fine," he relented, "but we do this my way, okay?"

I nodded. Ream called over three men and gave them orders. They, in turn, blended into the crowd around us. Ream took the lead and got us by the limo. I found Merlot's brother guarding the stairs to the greenroom.

"Oh, no! Not him! He don't get back here!"

I was glad to have a government agent along. He flashed a badge. "Listen, sir. We're on presidential business. Step aside."

Tyrone didn't move. "I don't give a rat's ass who you are. That man don't get near her."

"Tyrone," I said, as compassionately as possible, "I'm here to help her. I can save her life. I don't want to hurt her."

"Yeah, like you tried to save her life by hittin' her?"

Ream and Lee both glared at me.

"It was a slap, and she started it."

"Yeah, sure," said the boxer. "You ain't comin' back here."

The CIA agent wasn't the patient type. "I don't have time for this." He tried to push past Tyrone. The large Negro shoved Ream hard. Ream planted a foot to stop his backward momentum and turned his inertia around into a fist. He planted the gut shot right in Tyrone's abdomen. There was a large exhalation of breath, and the contender for the belt, Tyrone Sterling, went down.

"What did you do?"

Lee answered, "He use Tae Kwon Do. He use opponent's force against him. Harder the joe push, the more force behind reverse."

I might have been impressed, but so was Ream.

"Right on the money, Mr. Lee. I learned it over in Korea. First time I've gotten to use it." He looked to me. "Thanks for that opportunity, Glass. Anyone else you want to piss off?"

We mounted the stairs, and Ream cleared us with the Chicago PD detail in front of the greenroom.

As we entered, I saw her.

Merlot. She wore the drape, the steel gray one I'd first seen her in. She was heartbreakingly beautiful. An older black man and woman had her in deep conversation, so she hadn't noticed me. She smiled and laughed at something that had just been said. With our arrival, the couple stopped talking. Merlot followed their eyes to me and the smile disappeared.

"Ah, hell no! Not again!"

The mayor stepped forward. "What is the meaning of this?" His wife stood to the right of him and placed a hand on his arm. Their three guests stood as well. Everyone was focused on me.

"Um, well." I wasn't thinking fast enough. "The president, the president has a cold and we're here to give you all a penicillin shot." Ream gave me an incredulous look but picked up the dialogue after flashing his credentials.

"Yes, Dr. Glass here has an antibiotic shot for you. It'll keep you from getting sick."

All the occupants of the room bought it, save for Merlot. Her street smarts knew baloney when they heard it. Her expression told that and so much more, but playing the good girl, she didn't say anything.

I reached for the case and remembered there were only four vials.

"What wrong?" asked Lee when I paused.

"I only have enough for four." I looked at the five people, realizing I might be dooming one to death. As I stalled, I saw plates of food with Hank's napkins and empty bottles of Ancient beer. I had to choose someone. Merlot started to open her mouth, and a part of me reeled in horror.

No, not you!

Luckily, one of the guests beat her to it.

"I rarely get sick," said the Trumble Park man. "Make sure you give it to the women and his honor. I'll be fine. I've handled much worse than a cold this year." His wife looked at him with adoration. The mayor looked relieved.

Merlot, however, looked scared. Maybe it was my being there with a CIA agent, not in handcuffs, that forced the gravity of the situation on her. Her eyes pleaded with mine to smile, but I was serious in my task. Her rage at me gone, she trembled like a fawn by the time I bared her arm.

I gave the women the inoculations first, and then finished with the mayor. Trumble Park leaned over and kissed his wife's bandage. I cursed the God of probabilities. Why couldn't Fred have given me five vials? Damn!

Merlot pulled me aside as I made to leave. "What's this about, Glass? You aren't pulling something, are you?"

"I wished to hell I was, doll face. There's bad mojo out there. But don't you worry about that. You just show Ike what your mother taught you. You give him, and the world, everything you have. I'll listen to your song, and I'll watch your back. So don't you worry, not one bit."

Her face softened and I thought she might get leaky. I took her chin in my hand. "None of that. You'll ruin your makeup."

Merlot said, "Well, I'm going to need new lipstick regardless," and kissed me, hard.

Ream whistled. Lee groaned and pulled me away … eventually. "Come on, lover boy. Barbecue's gotta set stage on fire and you gotta save world."

CHAPTER TWENTY-ONE

So, Glass. What we do now?"

I didn't know. Wait for the Hero Twin to attack?

Police and armed guards patrolled throughout the festival. There had been a few scuffles between blacks and whites, but nothing had gotten out of hand, as of yet. The crowd waited on the president's speech before they got really hammered.

The hour struck eight, and lights came up on the grandstand. The mayor and his wife and their two guests sat in comfortable looking chairs. There were additional ones for the president and other state dignitaries. I had been assured by Fred and Horatio via radio that they'd all been given anti-MASER shots.

Within moments, most the missing congregation filled in their seats. The mayor stood and shook hands with them before he approached the microphone. Ike would be next.

"Ladies and gentlemen, if I can have your attention."

The army had cordoned off a twenty-foot area in front of the stage, and there were hundreds of people already packing themselves in around the barrier. At the mayor's words, more people left the lines at the booths and joined the assembly. Sardines had more room than these folks.

"Along with the governor of Illinois, it is my great pleasure to welcome to the second largest city in America, the president of the United States, Dwight D. Eisenhower!"

A cheer erupted from the mob. Ike made his way up the stairs and waved to the audience. He had two Secret Service agents on either side of him. They followed him like skin as he went down the line of people on stage. After he had finished the row, he moved back to the center, waved at the crowd again, and took his seat in the center. He would talk after Merlot's bit.

Ream tried to hear his squawking walkie-talkie. "What? Please repeat!" His face went ashen.

"What happened?"

He leaned toward my ear to yell, "We found one of my men dead in a horse stall. The Mayan hunter's mask was found next to him."

I spun around, looking at every point the Hero Twin could aim the MASER from. All the points. All of them were covered! We had redundancy. Agents watched over the police who watched over other agents. Everyone scanned the crowd. There were soldiers at the tops of bleachers, in the press box, the broadcast booth. There wasn't a place not covered in front of the stage! Even in the dressing rooms behind the stage.

Behind the stage.

Microwaves can punch through anything, but lead. The Twin didn't need to be in front of the stage! He could be *anywhere* behind it.

I ran as the mayor quieted the crowd.

"I'd like to introduce you to a wonderful young lady I had the pleasure of meeting backstage just a little while ago. A local prodigy who I'm sure you will come to enjoy as much as I do."

I didn't know if Ream and Lee were behind me anymore. I jumped the rope beside the stage and kept going.

"Chicago, give it up for the lovely Merlot Sterling and 'The Star-Spangled Banner!'"

There was applause behind me but not as loud as there had been for the president. There'd be those in the crowd that wouldn't take the national anthem from a black woman, no matter how she sang or for who.

They were in for a surprise when they heard her voice. Hopefully, that'd be the only surprise they got. Exploding people didn't make an Octoberfest a joyous event.

The buildings behind the grandstand were used for 4-H livestock judging. The CIA would have been over this place before the festival started, but might not have given it much thought later when they focused on the front of the stage.

Merlot's number began.

Oh, say can you see …

I rounded the corner to a building two hundred feet directly behind the stage. Two bodies lay splattered against the side— MASER effect. Ream came up behind me, saw the scene, and called in an alert on his walkie-talkie.

"I've got men down—"

By the dawn's early light …

I cut in. "Look for someone in the crowd with a walkie-talkie who isn't one of your guys. He's probably giving the Twin coordinates."

What so proudly we hailed …

Ream, Lee, and I drew our heaters and entered the large shed. We had to move past stalls layered with hay and cow shit.

At the twilight's last gleaming …

I wouldn't have been able to hear Merlot if not for the speakers that ran through all the buildings. There was another noise—the charging of the MASER. I caught it between stanzas as Merlot took in a breath.

Whose broad stripes and bright stars, through the perilous fight …

The remaining Hero Twin, the Hunter, poised to fire. He'd propped himself over a half-door, the MASER aimed forward toward the stage. A walkie-talkie sat on the floor near him, a female voice directing him from its speaker.

"Thirteen degrees to your left. That should be enough. Fire when ready."

Amanda Orchid.

We moved in silence, positioning ourselves.

O'er the ramparts we watched, were so gallantly streaming?

I got close enough to see the side of his face. Skin peeled from flesh, a result of the flame bath I'd given him back at Liberty Towers. He'd lost the hair on that side of his head, possibly a result from when his mask had been removed. He looked more skeleton than man, death personified. He wielded an electronic scythe and readied to take a whole bunch of people through the pearly gates.

And the rockets' red glare, the bombs bursting in air …

His trigger finger twitched and I shouted, "NOW!"

The MASER's sound ratcheted up. A scream came from the speakers.

The Hunter spun, his finger still on the trigger, but the full charge had not been reached. We dived out of the way of its arc. He sprayed the whole area with its invisible rays, but I felt no effect. Neither did any of our team. We stood up in full line of sight as the Hunter kept his finger on the trigger.

"We're immune." I told him. "It's over. The whole plan is over."

Orchid's voice came through again. "What happened? Loren? One person collapsed, but the president didn't explode. He's moving. You need to hit the stage again."

Ream, myself and Lee pointed our guns at him.

Lee whistled. "Man, you ugly summabitch."

The scarred assassin dropped the MASER's gun and shrugged out of the backpack. He rose his arms slowly, as if to surrender, but then darted to the side, faster than we could fire.

A dissonance of noise echoed between the room's speakers and the Hunter's walkie. Shouts came through garbled, mixed with the gunfire and screams.

We slowly crept into the section where the Twin bolted. As we just crossed the threshold, he opened fire with a Chicago piano.

Lee and I dived to the left, Ream to the right. As the Hunter hosed down the stall, splinters flew around us. Ream made hand gestures, but Lee and I had no idea what he meant. He mouthed instead, *Move up.* Then he made the hand gestures again, and we understood we were to fire and cross into the stall in front of his.

Lee and I fired low, Ream high. The Twin avoided our shots by ducking back into his stall. It gave us the opportunity to move over space forward, before the Hunter returned fire again.

I landed on something hard when I hit the ground. It moaned. I brushed away the straw to find a bound and gagged Vincent. The Russian's eyes were wide with anger. I ungagged him.

"Cut me loose, Glass. Now!"

I pulled a knife and cut his bonds. He got up and Lee finally noticed he was there. "Ack! It's the Ruskie!"

Vincent had looked better. The Technocrats had worked him over even worse than me. Near him, another MASER waited,

"It doesn't work. It was there only to make the CIA think I was the one responsible."

"Huh?"

The Hunter laid down another line of fire. An anxious Ream waited for us to help take out the assassin, making "get on with it" motions.

"Noel, I don't have time to explain, but this is all a trap. They didn't need to kill the president. They just needed to start a riot."

"Vincent. You're not making sense!"

He picked up my gun from where I'd set it down to cut his ties. A sadness crossed his face. He laid a hand on my shoulder and squeezed warmly, brotherly.

"The real target was always Fort Sheridan, Noel. And thank you."

"For what?"

"For being my friend despite who I was."

The Russian sleeper agent hardened then, turned as stone cold as I'd first met him. I saw nothing but murder in those eyes, then.

"Now, I have a score to settle."

Vincent leapt out from the stall before I could stop him, not bothering to dodge. He fired my gun in rapid succession. The Hero Twin took a hit to the shoulder, but never let up with the tommy gun. Hot lead pierced Vincent's legs, but it didn't deter the man-mountain. Vincent kept firing until the gun was empty. He threw it when he was close enough to his prey. The Twin backed up as Vincent launched forward. The machine gun still sang as Vincent eclipsed the Hunter, pulling him to the ground. A terrible crack replaced the sound of gunfire and silence followed. Vincent's hands let go of their prize and the limp form of the remaining Hero twin dropped like so much dead meat.

God sure don't like ugly, I thought.

Vincent spiraled to the floor a moment later, his chest shredded. I knelt next to him, lifting his head.

"You fool! You didn't need to do that! We could have taken him together."

He wheezed, "No way … your government would let … me go."

"Damn you, Vincent, you stinking Red bastard! Don't die on me!"

"Call me … Vadim. And yes … hired to protect you … remember."

"I remember, Vadim. You've done a good job. The old man would be proud."

Vadim Rezvoi smiled. "Good-bye … brother." He closed his eyes and was gone.

Lee placed a hand on my shoulder. "Remember, mourn later?"

"Mourn later. I remember."

Another senseless death. One more to avenge.

Ream talking into the walkie-talkie again. He paused and addressed us. "It's a riot out there."

"What happened?"

"Apparently the Trumble Park man collapsed."

"Is he?"

Ream shook his head. "Paramedics think it was only a mild stroke, but should be okay."

Finally, someone I didn't have to hold Tangie to accounts for.

"The blacks thought the police shot him and immediately turned on anyone in uniform. Lots of veterans in the mix, so it got ugly real quick. The Secret Service got the president out without a problem. He's on his way to Air Force One. He's headed back to D.C. for the time being. Archdeacon and Chicago's bulls have their hands full. The fighting is spilling out of the fairgrounds and into the streets."

"What's he doing?"

"Calling in more reinforcements from Fort Sheridan."

"It already pretty thin, no?"

"He's calling in some of the reservists he left there."

"Wait!" Vincent's words were starting to make sense. "Ream, what are they guarding?"

"I can't—"

"Knock it off, for God's sake! What were they guarding?"

He inhaled and let out the answer with his breath. "Nike missiles."

"So what? Just regular missiles, right?" Lee asked.

Ream shook his head. "These are prototypes They have a nuclear payload. Designation: Hercules. They aren't supposed to roll out for years."

And I finally got it. Tangie's gambit.

She never intended to kill the president. Vincent said as much. Tangie wanted access to the missiles, but to do so, she needed to get enough of the army off base to make the nukes barely guarded. Now the base was vacant enough to take them quickly.

If she got a hold of a load of nukes, she could start World War III anytime she wanted.

"I need a car."

*   *   *

Merlot's limo was the closest one to us. Ream got behind the wheel. As I went to get in, I felt myself lifted off the ground by my collar.

"Where is she?"

Tyrone threw me away from the car and charged. I didn't have time to even ask what he meant before he planted a haymaker. Ream and Lee got over to me before he struck again. Tyrone stopped at the sight of two guns pointed at him. My jaw was sore, but not broken.

"What? Do you mean Merlot? How should I know?"

"You tell me! She's gone! She left with some quail."

Orchid.

I stood up. "Listen, Tyrone. I have nothing to do with this. Well, not directly anyway. They grabbed her to get to me. But I have an idea where she might be."

He stepped forward, fists bunched. "Where?"

"Slow down, champ. I need something from you." I turned to Lee. "You, too."

I told them each what I needed, their jaws hanging limp. It *was* a lot to ask.

I climbed back in the limo with Ream. He couldn't believe my *cojones*.

"What did you just do, Glass?"

"Everyone else has an army at their beck and call. I hopefully just got my own."

*　*　*

Black-garbed soldiers stood in rapt attention on either side of the entrance gate to Fort Sheridan.

They were not U.S. Military.

The place was locked down tight, with armed guards patrolling the perimeter. I believed the power had been cut, due to the lack of lights in the main building. I hoped they had just detained the remaining civilian personnel inside and not killed them. I doubted the army reservists had fared well.

"So what's the plan, Glass? Wait for your cavalry?"

I had no idea how long that would take. "No, if we can get to the armory, we could dismantle their vehicles before they leave."

"If they don't already have the missiles loaded."

"I watched them unload. I saw how slow a process it was."

"Yeah," agreed Ream, "but they only need a couple of warheads and that would be enough."

He was right. Time was definitely a factor. "So what do you think? Water assault?"

"It's the only option available to us."

"Yee-ha."

*　*　*

There was a time—before Europeans settled America—that Lake Michigan was crystal blue, clean as purified water, and tasted divine. As I tried to get the taste of oil from my mouth, I wondered how long ago that actually was. Years of tramp steamers, motorboats, and other assorted mechanicals had left their mark on the lake. I felt sorry for the fish.

Ream and I didn't have to stay under for long, though. We made our way around the edge of the base and quietly swam out past the fence. We dove under and swam until we could walk on our knees. Ream broke the surface just to his eyes and gave me a thumbs-up. We had luck on our side. The silvery glow of a full moon lit our way.

Having no time to rearm before leaving the chaos downtown, we were armed with knives. Not what I wanted to bring to a gunfight.

We crept up on shore, me following the FBI agent's lead. Ream kept to the edge of the fence until we hit the first building. He took out one patrolling guard so quietly, I thought I might still have water in my ears. Peering around the corner, we spied the black army loading the Nike missiles into business vehicles, not military. They had broken open the crates and carefully placed each missile in prepared racks in the beds of Hank's Foods, Atlantic Brewing, and even a DBC news truck. By spreading out the style and logo of transports, the Technocrats upped the mission's success odds once the theft had been discovered.

I estimated about hundred armed men with Amanda Orchid strutting around directing the operation. My revulsion for her was unparalleled. I hoped she would catch a grenade.

Ream tugged on my wet sleeve. *Time to go,* he mouthed.

I looked at the vile woman once more, and then followed Ream to the ammunition bunker.

Two guards secured the back door. Ream wouldn't be able to use his silent touch on them in time to avoid an alarm. What we really needed was a distraction.

I looked at my watch. The agent saw me and whispered, "If they were coming, they'd be here by now, correct?"

"Yeah, probably."

"Then while I deal with them, you get in and get what we need."

"You too? What is it with you self-sacrificing types? Lee pulled that shit, then Vincent, and now you?"

"I don't plan to die."

No one does.

"Besides, Glass, as much as I hate admit it, we've only gotten this far because of you. We all bring something to the table. You have the brains; I like to kill things. We're both doing our best for this country. If I die here today, then I've done my duty."

"Fine, but we're both going in."

I took the gun from the soldier Ream had silenced earlier from my waistband. "On three?"

The agent nodded. "One, two—"

A large explosion went off near the front gates. Immediately after, the sounds of Chicago lightning erupted into the night. Men screamed as they fell, accompanied by shouts and curses in many languages.

Ream and I moved back along the building until we could see the parade grounds. Cars and trucks poured into the base, men hanging off the sides with guns blazing. I heard yelling in Latin, Russian, and Japanese.

The combined might of the Chicago mob had come to save the day.

Lee stood on the trunk of a car, yelling orders. "Stay away from trucks. Big boom! Over there, you wops! Ai-yah! Didn't mama teach you how to fire gun? You! Reds! Block that van. Don't let it leave!"

Ream and I stayed low, dodging shrapnel, until we reached Lee.

"Ack, Glass! This some mess. But happy to be invited! Hold on." He called out to the Asian hoods. "That no way to hold a knife. What you think you are? Samurai?" Lee turned back to us. "Kids! What can you do?"

"How'd you get them all to work together so quickly?"

He reached into his coat and withdrew some papers. "These!"

Ream grabbed them. "These are federal pardons! How'd you get these?"

He grinned from ear to ear. "I like that Ike. He very cooperative man when he in hurry to catch plane."

I shook my head in astonishment. Ream's jaw dropped.

An engine started. Orchid had gotten behind the wheel of the television truck and made for the gate. The front window glass shattered as she drove through the hail of bullets. Lee yelled, "Don't shoot truck! Big boom! I tell you, you be sorry!"

Orchid drove at a good pace, but bodies and cars slowed her progress. I calculated the angle I'd need to intercept. Despite wet clothes and shoes, I ran with a strength I didn't know I had in me. I outpaced Keam and got to the back of the truck just as it cleared the gates. I managed to grab hold of a ladder attached to the outside, feeling my feet go out from under me as she accelerated onto Sheridan Road. I held on and got my feet onto the bumper of the truck.

I opened the back door carefully and slipped in.

There wasn't a lot of room, seeing as the bed was filled with four nuclear missiles. I climbed over them carefully. Orchid didn't have a rearview mirror, and the howling wind covered my forward movement. I drew my gun and stepped into the cab.

"It's over, Amanda."

She jerked the steering wheel hard to the left, causing me to stumble toward her. Orchid elbowed me hard, and the gun flew from my hands and out the window. She jammed the wheel hard to the right, and I launched backward against the passenger seat. Her pegs swung sidesaddle and kicked me hard in the face. With her foot off the gas, the van slowed. She swung her legs back to pour on the coal again, giving me another chance to take her out, but all I got was another elbow, this one to the groin.

Changing tactics, I grabbed the wheel and held it steady. She let go and scratched at my face, her own contorted with rage.

The schoolmarm was gone. Her hair came partially undone from its bun, and the wind flailed it behind her. A modern-day Medusa, her gaze wanted to turn me to stone. Orchid screamed at me as she tried to gouge my eyes. I let go of the wheel and fell back against the other seat. I grabbed her powerful legs when she tried to kick me again. Lights illuminated the street ahead of us, and we saw an army blockade.

I let her legs go, and she applied the brakes to stop us five feet from the roadblock. A lot of pissed-off soldiers had their artillery pointed at us.

I raised my hands and yelled, "She surrenders!" To her I said, "Say you surrender ... *Now!*"

Orchid reluctantly raised her hands.

CHAPTER TWENTY-TWO

How'd you shut down the riot so fast?" I asked General Archdeacon. Lee's impromptu brigade had barely finished mop-up operations when the soldiers of Fort Sheridan returned.

Back at the riot, I'd sent Tyrone to get Doc and as many men as he could. They were supposed to join us in the storming of Fort Sheridan. When I didn't see them among Lee's commandos, I'd assumed Tyrone had failed to get support.

"Your friends Doc and Tyrone. They were amazing," said Archdeacon. "Sterling got up to the microphone with the champ, Rocky Graziano, pleaded for rioters to stop. They called for tolerance, more articulate than I would have given boxers credit for. Hell, they did a better job than I think Ike would've." He held his hand to the side of his mouth. "Keep that between us, okay?"

A shackled Amanda Orchid was being led away when Tyrone arrived and caught sight of her. He busted through the soldiers trying to hold him at bay

"That's her! That's the one that took Merlot!"

I stepped in front of the freight train before he got himself in trouble.

"Don't worry, Tyrone. I'm sure she's back at the base just fine."

"No, she not," came Lee's voice as he joined us with Ream. "We check everything out. No songbird."

Tyrone pushed me aside like a mosquito. He grabbed Orchid right out of the hands of the two soldiers escorting her. "Where is she? Where's Merlot?"

While she should have been afraid for her life, Orchid laughed.

"Isn't it ironic? Noel Glass's old flame with his new one. I'm sure they'll have lots to talk about." She continued to cackle in that insane way people do when they have nothing left to lose.

Tyrone dropped her and turned on me. "New flame? I'm gonna kill you!"

"Hey!" I said. "I didn't want her caught up in this any more than you did." I looked over to the former dean of NMIT. "Amanda, where are they?"

"You're the dick. You figure it out."

I don't think she meant detective.

"I can help," said Lee. He pulled a small vial from another hidden pocket and popped its lid. I could see the trails of green smoke coming from the container as he waved it under Orchid's nose. She went slack, her eyes closed, and her lips curled into a slow smile. She giggled like a schoolgirl and hummed to herself.

"Okay, Glass," said Lee. "Ask her anything."

I knelt down by her. "Where's Tangie and Merlot?"

Orchid giggled again. "Oh, Noel. Noelly, Noelly, Noelly. She's going to do what you couldn't fourteen years ago. Tangie is going to change the world. For really-reals this time."

"You're not making sense."

She opened her glazed-over eyes and looked up. "What a big, pretty moon. Don't you remember, Noelly? The moon? She's going to do it. She's going to put us back in control of this God-awful world."

I followed her gaze to the moon. Fourteen years ago, I was going to create radar so powerful it could track planes anywhere over the United States. I was going to do this by bouncing it off the moon. Tangie was going to do the same thing, to my horror, with her MASER wave. She was going to wipe out everyone who didn't have Atlantean DNA. It was her endgame. Wipe the board clean.

"When!"

"Soon. Because I failed, and I failed because of you. Always you. I wanted to be the one, the one to seduce you, but nooo! It had to be Tangie. You were too important. Too many big bad ideas in that head of yours."

Lee's potion worked too well. This wasn't what I wanted to hear.

I shook her. "Where? Where is this going to happen?" I followed her eyes again. She was looking at the truck, the DBC broadcasting truck.

"Ream?" I asked without turning my head, "What did you come up with on DuMar Broadcasting?"

"They have a broadcast station in Bloomingdale."

"That's forty miles from here. And she's already got a head start."

"If we can get the coordinates, we can send a ballistic missile and destroy the whole complex," Archdeacon suggested.

Both Tyrone and I said, "No!"

Archdeacon remained adamant. "Glass, the fate of the world or one innocent?"

Getting into a command car, I knew he was right.

"I'm going to go for her. Target the place." I did some quick calculations. I looked at a clock. It was twenty after eleven and chances were she'd use the beam at midnight, when the moon was at its zenith.

"If you don't hear from me in forty minutes, do it."

There were protests as I started up the car. Lee jumped in before I pulled away.

"No way you leave me out of this one."

I gave him my best smile. "Glad to have you along, Wan. Wouldn't have it any other way."

* * *

The DuMar Broadcasting Company didn't own their stations; they rented them. Affiliates would take a network feed and choose what shows to broadcast to the viewers. Comedians were the kings of television with serious actors keeping to the silver screen (or on those rare times, visiting variety shows.) Names such as Jackie Gleason, Milton Berle, and Bob Hope were known in every household. I didn't own a TV, but I had Lee, who picked an unusual time to fill me in on who and what was popular.

"When Uncle Miltie wear a dress, he so funny. I think he look like my wife, only taller. Think he will be there?"

"You know this is just a relay station, right? They don't film anything here. It's usually shot in New York or L.A."

"Bozo the Clown in Chicago."

"Yeah." I sighed. "Bozo is in Chicago."

"He be there?"

"No, he won't. His show doesn't come on for six hours."

"Oh." Lee was disappointed.

"What?"

"If I die tonight, I want meet real star first. Then no regrets."

"And you'd be happy with Bozo?"

"Wise man once said, 'beggar cannot be chooser.' I think it important to die with no regrets."

"You met the president! What more do you want?"

"Yeah, but he not on TV 'cept when something bad gonna happen."

I shook my head. "Why does any of this matter right now?"

"When family burn incense at my shrine, they can say, 'He good for nothing, but he knew Bozo personally.'"

"How about we stop my psychotic ex-girlfriend from murdering a couple million people, and then we'll see about meeting Bozo."

Lee beamed and pulled out a black hood from a pocket.

It left room for his eyes but nothing else. "You going to tell me who you are?"

He slipped the hood over his head obscuring all but his eyes. "You introduce me to Bozo, we yap later."

I pulled over about two hundred yards from the entrance. I had no plan.

Stealth wouldn't work as the relay sat in the center of a freshly mowed field. Technocrat soldiers vigilantly patrolled the parameter, as they had back at Fort Sheridan. I had no lake to use for an approach. No plane to drop in from above. I saw very few options.

I began to discuss this with Lee, but found him already gone.

Okay, that's creepy.

"Lee? Lee?"

I looked in the backseat. I poked my head out the window.

Vanished.

Again.

He had pulled another Houdini.

"Oh, sure. 'Don't leave me behind,' he says. I'm going to put a leash on that dog when I find him."

Keeping to the drainage ditch, I considered cutting the power to the building, but Tangie wouldn't be that stupid. She'd already have a backup generator in place.

As I got closer, something spoke to my bones. Maybe it was the fictional Atlantean DNA. I could feel it. I didn't need to sneak in. I was expected. I looked at my watch and estimated how much time I had left. I returned to the car, got in and started it back up. I drove the rest of the way, stopping at the gate. After a flashlight in the eyes, I was waved through.

I pulled up to a small, brick building with a large tower sat behind it. Unlike most broadcast towers, this one had a giant concave dish attached to it. It pointed directly at the moon.

At the front door, two guards patted me down, taking only my gun. My pocketknife seemed no concern to them. There were no guards inside.

I passed through a small reception area and found the room I needed. A glass window allowed me to see inside the broadcast booth. Tangie sat in a chair, fiddling with knobs and dials. The board looked almost identical to the one I had sat behind at NMIT the day of the experiment fourteen years ago.

The day my life changed.

I tried the door, but knew it would be locked. She looked up and her expression showed she was not happy. Maybe it was the fist-shaped bruise on her face.

The girls must have had a talk.

Tangie motioned for me to look to my left. Another door sat propped open. I could hear the hum of the magnetron and reasoned that was the power room. I walked over to the door, stepped through, and found Merlot, bound to a chair.

I went to her, and the door closed behind me. I didn't have to check it to know it'd never open again under my power.

Merlot looked at me as if I was some sort of idiot. Maybe I was.

"Noel, this is a trap. You knew that, right? The bitch wants to kill you."

"Don't they all?" I cut her free of her ropes, and she rubbed circulation back into her wrists. Then she hugged me.

"I like your new girlfriend, Noel. She's got spunk!" I looked for Tangie's voice and found it came through a speaker on the control board. "Oh, don't bother trying the switches. They're all disabled."

"Stop this! We're not playing a game here, Tangie. You're talking about committing mass murder."

"And you just came running in to save them all, did you? No, you came to save her. You couldn't care about the rest of the world."

I placed my palms on the glass separating us. "I do. I do care. About them. About her. *And* about you. This doesn't have to end this way."

She shook her head. "What? With you dying? Or maybe you think we'll all die? No, not you, Noel. You are not the type to lay down your king and commit suicide. You must think there's some way to win." She ran a hand through her long, red hair. "The only one walking away from this is me, Noel. Me and the chosen few. You could have been one of them. We could have been the new Gods!"

The fire in her eyes might have looked like passion to some, but it reeked of insanity to me.

"You were already slated for crashville, baby, long before this started. And I am walking out of here. I'm taking Merlot with me. And if I need to, I'll throw your crazy ass over my shoulders."

She cackled again. I was losing her. "I don't see how. You're unarmed. The army will never get here in time. The MASER is ready to go. All I have to do is turn up the power and flip the broadcast switch. I've made it so your side will flood with microwave radiation and no matter what you've done to slow the effect, it won't be enough to keep you from bursting at the seams like overcooked hot dogs."

"And you?"

Tangie waved above her head. "I had this room lined with lead. C.J. wasn't the only one who could build a vault." She then stepped over to the window and placed her palm against it, mimicking mine. "This is a specially designed Atlantean glass hybrid you're looking through, something we 'brewed' up at the bottling side of Atlantic Brewing. Stronger than metal, really. You'll never break it in time. It's over, Noel. I've finally beaten you!"

Tangie had made one fatal flaw, I suddenly realized. Something she couldn't have accounted for. I had her and I began to smile. Hell, I gloated. Merlot looked at me as if I'd gone as looney as the redhead. I took her hand below line of sight and squeezed, letting her know everything would be all right.

"Oh, Tangie. You still don't know how to play chess, do you? You've had fourteen years to learn, and you're still hung up on the fundamentals."

She cocked an eyebrow. "Oh? Do tell? How did I fail?"

I pulled out a chair and motioned for Merlot to sit. Her expression showed concern, but she acquiesced. I stood behind another chair, my hands gripping the back.

"You use the same pieces. Once I knew who your pieces were, it was easy to take them out, one by one. Let's lay it out.

"Orchid. The missile strategy failed and she's behind bars.

"Your board of Atlanteans? Being rounded up by Federals across the country. A similar thing is happening in Russia. They're turning on you, flipping. We'll have the whole Technocrat organization rounded up by morning.

"Your assassins, the Hero Twins? Dead. You took all the strongest pieces and used them as pawns, to be discarded. I did that. I took them out. Me. And you know how I did it?"

The explosion that rocked the building couldn't have been timed better. Wan Lee hadn't specifically told me he'd brought explosives, but I was just beginning to understand how the guy thought.

Tangie looked around frantically, as if we were in an earthquake.

"That's your tower. No way to send the signal to the moon. No MASER, Tangie. Not anymore. And I did it by playing GO while you were busy playing chess. For every piece I took down of yours, I built a wall of friends and resources. I removed all the places on the board you could play, until all you had was one piece, while I had hundreds."

Lights flickered and Tangie's eyes went wild. She went to turn the dial to fry Merlot and me. Before she could get it to full, I had taken the second chair in our room and, with my Bogdanov-enhanced strength, smashed it through the unbreakable glass window.

Shards flew in Tangie's face, and she raised her hands to protect herself. Stepping back, I jumped through the gap and rolled. Tangie launched at me and I backhanded her. Her strengthened blood must be running low on juice, because she flew back away from me like a ragdoll. I turned off the magnetron before it reached full power.

Seeing that Merlot was safe, I offered her a hand into the control room.

Tangie curled into a ball, arms wrapped around knees, gently rocking. Venom leaked from every pore as she stared us down.

"You bastard. You stupid, fucking bastard!"

I looked down at her with pity.

Tangie Taylor, the woman I loved, had died fourteen years ago. Whatever this wretched creature was, it wasn't her.

"Tangie, you should've sacrificed your queen. You never learned that, did you?"

We left the room. I closed the door to the control room, smashing the lock before hustling Merlot out the front door.

There were bodies of Technocrat soldiers all around our car. Lee sat the backseat, motioning for us to go. He mimed a missile and a big explosion.

We were back on our way to Fort Sheridan by the time the radio station had been obliterated. I only hope that the twisted dreams of a madwoman had been obliterated with it.

The night became orange and thundered with sound of my past mistakes being erased once and for all.

Merlot leaned into me. "You wouldn't have sacrificed me, would you, Noel?"

I recoiled. "You'll hit me if I tell you."

She snuggled in closer. "No, I won't, sugar. I promise."

"Really?"

"Really."

"Yeah, I had already. I was just going to stall until the rockets hit. I wasn't planning for either of us to get out alive."

She hit me.

＊　＊　＊

The cleanup over the next week was rough. The president made his speech for racial tolerance, but he made it from the White House.

The Technocrat Board of Atlantean Trustees had been arrested and new, non-Technocrat leadership took charge of their individual companies. I had been surprised to discover that each of the businesses were primarily oblivious to their CEOs' secret dealings.

Rocky Graziano took down Tyrone Sterling, Merlot's brother, in the seventh round, but at least he paid hard for it. Lee and I watched ringside, and we'd never seen such a balanced fight in our lives.

The Nikes were settled in at Fort Sterling, ready for the next great threat to America. Over all, thirty reservists gave their lives protecting them; not of them had one surrendered.

Lee and I saw Sacha, the Russian doctor and reluctant spy, off to the airport with his wards. Two coffins, draped with Russian flags, rolled on to the Aeroflot jet.

"Now it is time to go home and mourn." He said, resignedly.

I placed a hand on Sacha's shoulder.

"Yeah. Vincent—Vadim—came through for us all, in the end. He was a truly big man, not in size, but in heart."

"*Da.*"

Lee added, "I burn incense for him by picture of Mt. Fuji. He like that."

Sacha grinned. "Thank you, comrade."

We all shook hands, and Sacha made to leave but turned back to me. "I do not know if what I say will be consolation or not, but Alexander Bogdanov did many unethical things, as well as making many scientific breakthroughs."

"I'm sure he did, but what—"

Sacha held up his hand to pause me. "When he was given Lenin's brain, he tried many different ways to bring him back. One such thing was to grow Lenin new body. He was sure he could create new premier from cells of old premier's body. He called it 'cloning.'"

My mouth went dry. "Did it work?"

Sacha shook his head. "Not that we in secret police could find. But that was long time ago." He gave me a compassionate nod of his head, as if he'd said everything he'd come to say. "If that helps."

I think it did. It gave me an idea to focus on that wasn't so depressing.

We shook hands once more, he clasping my elbow in a sign of affection. He exited the boarding area and returned to his fatherland.

Lee and I visited the studios of WGN later that morning. Wan got to meet Bozo the Clown. He also ran into Milton Berle, who was doing an interview at the station. Lee ran up to him and said, "Wow! You look much better than my wife in person."

Uncle Miltie leaned over and with a grin said, "Security?"

Lee and I returned to Industry City triumphantly. Wan with his two signatures and me, free of guilt, for the first time in many years.

EPILOGUE

Summer 1954

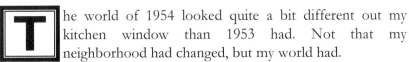he world of 1954 looked quite a bit different out my kitchen window than 1953 had. Not that my neighborhood had changed, but my world had.

Horatio went on to help Dr. Salk with the polio vaccine, ridding the world of yet another evil. Fred took over as dean of NMIT when Rocky was caught buck naked with Shirley the cheerleader in his office. She came out unscathed and, in fact, ended up going on to Cambridge to work with Jim Watson on DNA research. Damn, that girl was smart!

It made me think about what Tangie told me about her and Rocky hauling ashes, and I decided it held no real weight. He was never good at keeping secrets, and he would have tracked me to the ends of the Earth to brag had they really done it.

My phone rang for the twelfth time this morning. Lee stood in my doorway impatiently tapping his foot.

"Glass, get move on it. They waiting!"

"I'm trying, but I'm sure this is Archdeacon again, and I don't want him showing up at the ceremony."

I picked up the receiver, and sure enough, the general's booming voice came through.

"Glass! You can't ignore this anymore! Your president has asked you to serve your country. Are you really going to tell him 'no'? People don't do that. Not on my watch!"

"For the last time, Duane … send my regrets to Ike and Mamie, but the answer is still no. N—O!"

"I don't care if you did have dinner with them, you do not get to call the commander-in-chief 'Ike.' Do you hear me, Glass? Glass?"

I put down the phone.

Lee's wife was in the hallway, scolding him for making us late and warning him what would happen if he missed dinner again. Like a good soldier, he took his thrashing with honor.

He whispered to me as we left, "We used to that abuse from centuries under warlords. Biggest babies around."

Lee had finally confided in me that his family descended from a Japanese clan of assassins. The skills he used were handed down from generation to generation, however, since they no longer served a Daimyo, they just used them for fun these days.

"We scare neighbors from time to time. Take their cats and put them in trees. Turn off lights while they still in room. Stuff like that," he'd told me on the flight home from Chi-town.

But that wasn't all he had revealed. He dropped a bigger bomb on me than the Nike.

"I actually work for company in Japan that want to make cars. Ford came over and taught us many things. Now we want to do what America do, only better. I sent to find you when word leak of *Atlantis* design. We want to buy it and mass-produce. Only, company want it to run on gas like other cars so people don't think we trying to wipe out America again."

My jaw hung loose, and Lee pushed it closed.

I said, "You're kidding. Please tell me you're kidding."

When he showed me a check with more numbers than an Einstein equation, I knew he wasn't kidding. There would be no deal from Little Technologies, the only company that didn't survive the Technocrats' plan. I wasn't sad, though. C.J. Reece *had* taken his love with him in the end.

I let *The Atlantis* designs go to Lee's benefactors. It fit better with my future plans anyway. Flush with funds, I immediately told Inger and Sigarr to fix the Custom 8 back to cherry. It waited for us on the street, gleaming in the June sun. Lee and I hopped in and headed downtown.

Wan worked as my assistant now, doing odds and ends that needed doing, even things such as getting the car from the garage and fending off the duck vendor, who turned out to be a relative of his. But then who here wasn't?

We made good time to the police station. There was a throng in front, but I'd seen worse. Lee and I were escorted to the front steps where Chief Charles Sweet waited.

"You're late, Glass! You'd think of all times you could be early—"

"Can it, boss. Or don't you want me to come over to dinner tonight with a very expensive bottle of wine?"

"French?"

"Only the best."

"Fine. You remember where it is?"

"How can I forget? Your wife like the bay window?"

"Absolutely. Though I heard that someone bought the lot behind us. Damn it all! When I meet the asshole, I plan to give him a piece of my mind."

The irony was all too delicious. I'd tell him the truth over the Bordeaux that I'd bought the land behind his. Then, after he yelled a bit, I'd tell him I had no plans to build … yet.

Sweet and I turned to the mass of reporters, city dignitaries, and scientists gathered to watch us. The chief stepped up to a lectern and addressed them.

"It is my pleasure to be here today. Science, I discovered, is nothing to fear. It can do things instinct can't." He stepped back on his words a bit. "Not that instincts are bad, mind you. But hand-in-hand with science, it can create a new era in criminal detection. That is why it is with great honor that we unveil the brand-new Industry City Forensic Science Department!"

A drape dropped from behind us to reveal the brand-spanking-new wing, with its own entryway. Flashes of photos being snapped came with a round of applause. Sweet gave it a moment before quieting the crowd.

"And here to cut the ribbon is the man whose generous donation made this all possible. The director of the ICFS, Dr. Noel Glass!"

So sure, I was broke again. The place had cost me almost everything Lee's friends had advanced me. But it was worth it. Somewhere along the way, I had created a new species, a scientist detective. I'd never be happy doing only one or the other.

Like Reece, my crazy fairy-godfather, I made the world conform to me.

Once the din quieted again, Sweet made one last introduction. "And as a treat for everyone, to celebrate this momentous day, we have a special guest: Checkerboard Record's newest singing sensation, Merlot Sterling!"

Merlot came from inside the building all aglow. She was a sight in a heat-making gown that left nothing to the imagination. I hoped the police wouldn't arrest her for public indecency when she was done.

Sweet mimed wiping his brow, and I gave him a grin. Lee waggled his eyebrows and said, "Hubba-hubba."

She broke into "Happy Days Are Here Again," slow at first, like a blues number, but then picked up speed as the ICPD Marching Band kicked in. For some reason people felt the need to play this song when things were going well. I think it should be buried, but then no one asked me.

They rarely did.

Instead, I smiled as she looked my way and winked.

What the hell? I figured and we balled the jack all night long.

* * *

Merlot slept soundly, but my restless mind wouldn't let me enter the realm of the content.

I didn't drink to calm my raging brain anymore, so I got up to take notes on things I needed to remember for my first day of work. I stepped into my office, flipped on a light, and sat behind the desk.

There was a pile of mail waiting for me. Whether it was Lee or one of his children who had brought it in, I never asked. I had no secrets from them. They came and went as they pleased. And how could I stop them even if I wanted?

On top was a large envelope with a lot of postage. It was from Cambridge. I swallowed hard.

Between what Watson had told me in the hospital, and what Sacha had suggested at the airport, I wondered if anything Tangie had said about the bodies in the lab back at NMIT was true. The lab assistants? The ones she'd said she'd recruited to the Technocrat cause and replaced with homeless people? None had ever made a blimp on the radar as being found alive, new identities or not. That left me wondering if there was more to the story.

So, I had taken samples of Tangie's hair I'd found in the Babbage book and sent them to Watson with samples of Tangie's hair from the body retrieved from the television station rubble. Jim said he would do a comparison with what rudimentary equipment they had, but true DNA matching was many years away.

The international letter sitting in front of me had to be what results he could find.

I took my letter opener and slid it through the neck of the envelope.

The single page read:

Dear Noel,

    I wish I had better news to tell you …

AFTERWORD ONE

Original Acknowledgements from 2008 Edition

Over the course of the three years writing this tale, I've acquired a great number of people to thank. However, due to three PC crashes and an aging mind, I've forgotten quite a few of them. So if I missed you, you have my eternal thanks and the right to yell at me via e-mail.

Here are the ones I did remember: Andrea Howe, Blue Falcon Editing; The Colorado Blues Society; The Denver Public Library; The Colorado History Museum; The Green Mill, Chicago; The Kingston Mines, Chicago; The Chicago History Museum; The Chicago Public Library; David Smith, Arizona Snowbowl; Max Décharné, author of *Straight from the Fridge, Dad*; David Grazian, author of *Blue Chicago*; Barbara F. Varon, author of "The Japanese Americans: Comparative Occupational Status, 1960 and 1950"; National Fire Protection Association; The Tattoo Archive; the Sidney Bechet Society; The People and the Town of Grand Lake, Colorado (my favorite place to write!); Stella's Coffeehouse, Denver; And … the hard-working men and women who sing the blues!

Special thanks go to: God for blessing me with my imagination and skill and for putting the right people in my life at the right time to get me here; Dylan Boop for putting up with Dad's butt in front of the computer all the time; Peggy Boop for financing the research trip to Chicago and so much more; The

BTC Writer's Group for suffering through this when it was just a concept; Megan Kopetzky for being my first reader; Sarah A. Hoyt for identifying my greatest writing weaknesses; and finally … David Rozansky of Flying Pen Press for pestering me to finish this damn thing. Glad you felt it was worth the wait!

AFTERWORD TWO

Acknowledgments for 2016 Edition

Over the span of seven years, *She Murdered Me with Science* sat dormant as I searched for a new publisher, a new home, for it. It had to be a special place where I could be part of a family that would take my little story, and me, in.

In the interim, a friend and mentor had launched his own house, WordFire Press, to release books of his that the print rights had reverted back to him. Kevin J. Anderson and his wife Rebecca Moesta did such a fine job of re-releasing their early titles that many of their bestselling friends were asking them to do the same with their reacquired titles. Soon, Kevin and Rebecca took a step in a very scary direction. They decided to republish lesser-known authors who showed promise, sometimes acquiring these authors' self-published novels, sometimes publishing all-new, all original material.

She Murdered Me with Science had been out of print since 2010, when in 2014 Kevin asked me if WordFire could republish it. This was like a life preserver to a drowning man. I'd spent the previous five years fighting a losing battle with my mom against cancer, only coming up for air long enough to write short stories and finish my college degree in creative writing. When she passed in 2013, the next year was devastating, and it looked as if SMMS would never see light again unless I self-published. But then there was Kevin. And then there was Peter J. Wacks, who, as WFP's managing editor, worked with me to find Noel's voice again, though it took much longer than anyone expected as he fought through my ever-present depression.

So, thanks Kevin and Rebecca for believing in me despite years of waiting.

And thanks Peter for encouraging me when I was at my lowest.

And to Brittany Baggott for continuity edits, including last minute ones.

And to my fans who have asked time and again, "When is your novel coming out?"

Hopefully, the next novel won't take so long. I think my readers (and Kevin) would strangle me first.

AFTERWORD THREE

Slang is Timeless

For my novel, *She Murdered Me with Science*, I had to study a lot about 1953. One of the most interesting things to research was slang. How much slang we hear in movies was actually used in that era?

I came across a great book: *Straight from the Fridge, Dad*, by Max Décharné. Décharné not only provided his readers the most complete dictionary of the slang terms from the thirties through the sixties, but also gave examples of when the expression was first recorded (for example, a man's feet, as "dogs," can be traced back to Dashiell Hammett's 1929 book, *Red Harvest*).

So, how does this play out in this novel? Slang has no definitive time line. There are expressions from the fifties we still use today. We call a heart a "pump," which was heard in 1941's *Maltese Falcon*. Also, regions have dialects and expressions that might be in use for years before they come to national attention.

This means that many of the characters, Noel and Lee specifically, use a lot of slang from their era and the eras around them. However, I have tried to limit the selection to slang terms they *would* say, not just throwing them in because I can.

Please enjoy my story and forgive any slights I may have made in regard to slang. I wanted to keep the flair of a fifties pulp novel, but you will be the only judge of how close I have gotten.

AFTERWORD FOUR

On Alternative-History Fiction

All historical fiction is alternative-history fiction.

Fiction by its very nature is a brilliant lie. No matter how many facts you use to support your lie, in the end, it is a lie. So taking that as a truth, if you write a fiction about something that happened yesterday, you've altered history.

The term *alternative-history fiction* had been bandied about for decades referring to aliens fighting on the side of the Nazis or questioning the outcome if the South had won the Civil War. However, I propose alternate history starts the second you place anyone who didn't exist in a historic setting, whether it be last Tuesday or ancient Egypt.

The novel you are about to read (or have already read and are now just getting to the notes) takes place in 1953. To make the story work, I have made fictional cities that exist right alongside real ones. I've created fictional characters that interact with real people. And in some cases, these real people are still alive.

It is because of this, I claim my work to be a part of the ambiguous sub-genre alternative history. There are only certain people who could do what I needed to have them do in this story, whether they would or would not have done so in real life. I have taken liberties with people's timetables but, I hope, not with their morals and personalities. Where I could, the real people within were painstakingly researched. Others, where the data was lacking, were filled in using a commonly held practice among writers: I fudged it.

Luckily, I can do this because, as I said earlier, this is all a beautiful lie.

Enjoy!

ABOUT THE AUTHOR

David Boop is a Denver-based speculative fiction author. He's also an award-winning essayist, and screenwriter. Before turning to fiction, David worked as a DJ, film critic, journalist, and actor. As Editor-in-Chief at IntraDenver.net, David's team was on the ground at Columbine making them the first *Internet-only* newspaper to cover such an event. That year, they won an award for excellence from the Colorado Press Association for their design and coverage.

His novel, the sci-fi/noir *She Murdered Me with Science*, returns to print from WordFire Press after a seven-year hiatus. Additionally, Dave is prolific in short fiction with over fifty short stories and two short films sold to date. While known for weird westerns, he's published across several genres including horror, fantasy, and media tie-ins for Predator, The Green Hornet, and Veronica Mars. His RPG work includes *Flash Gordon* , *Rippers Resurrected* and *Deadlands: Noir* for Savage Worlds. David regularly tours the country speaking on writing and publishing at schools, libraries and conventions.

He's a single dad, Summa Cum Laude graduate, part-time temp worker and believer. His hobbies include film noir, anime, the Blues and Mayan history. You can find out more on his fan page, www.facebook.com/dboop.updates or Twitter @david_boop.

IF YOU LIKED …

If you liked *She Murdered Me With Science*, you might also enjoy:

Death Warmed Over
Kevin J. Anderson

Love-Haight Case Files
Jean Rabe & Donald J. Bingle

Enter the Janitor
Josh Vogt